PRAISE FOR *BATTLE FOR HIS SOUL*

"This book will get you thinking about the spiritual battle waging all around us, and your guardian angel that fights for you. I have recognized my guardian angel more in my life since reading *Battle for His Soul*."

~**Lisa Mayer, author of** *The Arrow Bringer*

"Teens, maybe more than the rest of us, focus on the here and now. That's why *Battle for His Soul* is a must read. It'll widen your ideas about temptation, prayer, mercy, and God's call in your life."

~**Carolyn Astfalk, Christian romance writer and author of** *Ornamental Graces* **and** *Stay With Me*

"After encountering this novel, you will never again think of angels as being far away! Another page-turner by an author at the top of her craft."

~**Susan Peek, author of** *St. Magnus, The Last Viking* **and many other saint stories for teens and children**

BATTLE

FOR

HIS SOUL

THERESA LINDEN

SILVER FIRE
PUBLISHING

Lean On Me
Words and Music by Bill Withers
Copyright (c) 1972 INTERIOR MUSIC CORP.
Copyright Renewed
All Rights Controlled and Administered by
SONGS OF UNIVERSAL, INC.
All Rights Reserved   Used by Permission
Reprinted by Permission of Hal Leonard Corporation

http://theresalinden.com
Library of Congress Control Number: 2016911183
First Printing 2016
ISBN-13: 978-0-9976747-0-5
eBook ISBN: 978-0-9976747-1-2
First Edition Silver Fire Publishing, October 2016

Cover: Theresa Linden
Editor: Susan Peek

DEDICATION

This story is dedicated to all those who struggle to overcome great sin. Your cross may at times feel heavier than you can bear, your trials seem unsurmountable, and temptations overwhelming, but God knows you. And He knows that you can claim the victory in Him. Know that your guardian angel is always by your side, hoping that you will listen to his holy inspirations, open your heart to the grace of God, fight the good fight, and through Christ win the battle for your soul.

ACKNOWLEDGMENTS

I wish to express my gratitude to the people who saw me through this book, especially Carolyn Astfalk, Don Mulcare, and Susan Peek, whose encouragement and assistance I find irreplaceable. I also want to thank Lisa Mayer for a last minute proofreading. You are awesome! I hope my beta readers and those who read advanced copies know how much I appreciate their help, too. I also wish to acknowledge the love and support of my husband and three boys, without whose understanding and support this book would not be possible. I am eternally grateful to my own guardian angel for choosing the side of the Lord before time began and for remaining ever by my side through the trials of life. I look forward to the day I will see you in the heavenly kingdom where together we can praise God for all eternity.

CHAPTER ONE

FEEL THE AIR

Ellechial

Seventeen-year-old Jarret West gripped the handlebars of the mountain bike, lifted a foot to the pedal, and shot a half-crazed look down the hill at *the ramp*. A wide, flat rock jutted from the rim of a five-foot cliff, its tilt and smoothness making it an ideal bike ramp. He needed speed to make a jump that avoided the bushes and landed in the clear. After a few tries, he seemed to have figured the distance required to accomplish that. He had even taken the time to rid the path of anything that would impede his ride. A root and a big half-buried rock remained in his way, though he had tried to dig them up too.

Ellechial watched with a light soul. Whatever the boy did, he threw himself into it.

"I wish I could convince you to abandon this reckless pursuit," Ellechial said. "Have you not been out here long enough? There are other things to which you ought to attend. The horses could use your attention. And Roland will be looking for his mountain bike any minute—"

Jarret leaned forward, elbows out, and started down the slope. Now he stood and pedaled furiously, making his approach. He dropped onto the seat, assuming a more controlled posture, and

1

weaved around the root and the half-buried rock. In order to land safely, he needed to hit the ramp dead center.

Pedaling harder, grimacing, he neared the rock.

Closer, closer, and . . . three, two, one . . .

With a jerk of the handlebars, he cleared the ramp and stopped pedaling. His expression softened and froze as he relished the euphoric moment.

Weightlessness.

The wind brushing his face and arms.

The beating of his heart.

He gazed at the sky and the farmer's field before focusing on the ground. Then he shifted his weight, adjusting his angle of flight to ensure a two-wheel landing. In full control, he came down with a thud. A squirrel scampered away. Blackbirds and grackles flew up from the cornfield.

Jarret hooted, long and loud. This was his best jump yet. Losing momentum, he crossed onto the neighbor's land and spun the bike around, his leg brushing the end row of knee-high corn.

Ellechial smiled. He liked seeing the boy enjoy himself, especially after his recent trials and sufferings, but Jarret had a tendency to push everything to the limit.

He had originally come out to the back border of his family's property to get away from his twin brother Keefe, not to teach himself how to jump a mountain bike. But the slope of the land and the discarded board he'd found lent themselves to the idea. He created his first ramp by propping the board on stones. He had increased the angle with larger stones every few goes. Before long, he had learned how to move his body to control the bike. He had come close but—thank you, Lord—he hadn't crashed once.

Jarret pedaled past his first ramp, the board on the stones, hopped off the bike and walked it to the new one. His eyes gleamed with his desire for more. He glanced over his shoulder at the first ramp.

"Not a good idea, Jarret." Ellechial zipped to his side. "Experimenting with steeper and steeper ramps will only lead to trouble." Not to mention, rusty nails—rife with *Clostridium tetani* spores—protruded from the board. "You have had enough for today. Time to go home."

Jarret laid the bike on its side and jogged to the old board. He stooped and reached, about to make contact with a rusty nail.

"A little more caution, my boy." With only a thought, Ellechial coaxed a *Nicrophorus americanus,* an American burying beetle, into action. It flitted at once to Jarret's hand.

Jarret jumped back, cussing and shaking his hand. The black-and-orange creature flew off, soon disappearing from Jarret's view. Jarret scanned the board twice before gripping it this time.

He carried the board to the rock ramp, dragged a log over, and collected a handful of sturdy sticks. He positioned the log near the far edge of the stone ramp and laid one end of the board over it. Then he used the sticks like tent stakes to keep it all in place.

Stepping back, he propped his hands on his hips and looked it over. The new ramp had a steeper angle. He stepped onto it and bounced a few times, the board squeaking under his weight.

"Yeah, that'll do," he said with a grin.

"Jarret, no," Ellechial said. "I know you see it as a way to get more air time, but it is not as sturdy as you believe it to be. Pressure on the board will cause the log to slip. Then, once the bicycle reaches the end, the log will act like a fulcrum and the board will tip. The angle of your ascent will be all wrong."

Jarret turned and stepped off the board.

Ellechial shot to his side and shouted, "Listen to me!"

The hair on the nape of Jarret's neck pricked. He made a sweeping glance into the surrounding woods.

"That's right. I am trying to warn you. Take heed, my child."

Jarret peered into the woods and glanced at the open areas of tall, sunlit grass. He probably thought his younger brother Roland had discovered him with his Iron Horse, or that his father or Keefe were watching with a disapproving glare.

"It is only I . . ." Ellechial sighed. ". . . trying to keep you safe. How I wish you would listen to me."

Jarret shook his head, obviously dismissing the warning, and grabbed the bike. He climbed the hill, moving slower than he had the last few climbs, probably feeling it in his thighs.

"You've been out here for hours." Ellechial kept to Jarret's side. "You should give it a rest."

At the top of the hill, Jarret swung his leg over the bike and pulled the band from his ponytail. He dipped his head and shook out his long black curls. Perhaps he wanted to feel the wind in his hair for this jump. He'd inherited his mother's hair. With her mixed Mexican ancestry—Spanish European and Native American—she'd had long, gorgeous locks. He treasured his hair now because it reminded him of her, and he'd lost her in childhood. Despite the cool façade Jarret put on in front of others, Ellechial knew his grief ran deep, even after all these years.

Jarret ran a hand through his hair and frowned, probably thinking now about Keefe's haircut. Jarret had not understood the changes in his twin brother or the reason for his haircut. Keefe had tried to explain that it symbolized something, reminded him of a promise he had made. For Jarret, it seemed to symbolize the end of his control.

Ellechial sighed. All his life, Jarret had relied upon others and the power he had to manipulate them, especially his twin brother. Now, at age seventeen, it had all ended. Even Keefe no longer agreed with him or went along with him on things. A rift had formed. They had parted ways.

Jarret clenched the handlebars, determination flashing in his brown eyes. Every jump he made seemed to boost his confidence. He may have lost control over most things in his life, but he thought he had control over this.

"This is a mistake, Jarret." Ellechial hovered above him. "I will do what I can to protect you, but you make it difficult, my reckless child."

Jarret lifted his elbows and started down the hill, standing, pedaling hard, his gaze fixed on the path. Nearing the ramp, his heart pounded faster. Elation brightened his face. Almost there . . . in three, two, one . . .

The front wheel of the bike smacked onto the low side of the board, causing the opposite side to pop up a few inches. The tree trunk slid.

Jarret's eyes bugged, and his mouth opened with the realization.

The bike raced to the top of the ramp. The board tipped forward like a seesaw. Jarret headed downward rather than up for the jump.

Catapulting off the faulty ramp, the bike twisted. The pedals spun away from his feet. He released the handlebars, and his body sailed over them.

Ellechial flew into action. "If only he would have worn a—"

Jarret threw his arms out but not soon enough. He landed hard on his face, Ellechial softening the impact to avoid a broken neck. Jarret slid with the bike tangled around his legs, rocks scraping his arms.

". . . a helmet," Ellechial said.

Jarret lay on his belly motionless and not breathing. Still not breathing. Still not . . .

Ellechial leaned over him and spread his wings. "Breathe," he commanded.

Jarret dragged in a breath of air and rolled over, groaning.

"You're okay, my child. Nothing is broken." Ellechial sat beside him. Wanting to be left alone, the boy hadn't even brought his cell phone. No one knew he was back here, half a mile from the house. If Ellechial had permission to travel, he could summon help. But alas . . .

Pain contorted Jarret's face. He hugged his ribs and rolled to his side.

Ellechial perched on a three-foot stone near Jarret and thanked God he had been granted permission to avert total catastrophe. If only Jarret would have listened to him . . . but Jarret had numbed himself to the voice of his guardian angel long ago.

A few minutes later, guardian angel Nadriel breezed onto the scene, glowing with radiant joy. "Greetings. I bring good—" His attention snapped to Jarret who lay curled up in the fetal position.

"Oh, what a shame." Nadriel flashed to Jarret's side. Angels and demons alike knew how to read people by their expressions and physical signs, but Nadriel had a unique gift for it. He assessed a situation quicker than most angels did.

"He'll be fine," Ellechial said. "He would've broken his collarbone, or worse, if I hadn't redirected and softened his landing. But that was all I could do. I am largely powerless to help him."

Nadriel peered at Jarret's face. "I don't like the look in his eyes."

"Nor do I. I believe he is feeling sorry for himself. Though I had worried about his physical safety while he jumped the bike, his self-pitying thoughts had been largely kept at bay."

"Mmm." Nadriel examined the bike with its bent rim and forks. "I tried to get Roland back here to look for his mountain bike, showed him tracks in the damp dirt. I hoped he might help Jarret, maybe curb his reckless behavior."

"Roland would not come? He usually listens to you."

"Yes, well, Roland couldn't imagine who would've taken his bike or why a person would take it back here. He went on without it, which brings me to my good news." Nadriel's wings lifted as he smiled.

"Good news?"

"Yes—"

"Zoe," Jarret mumbled, hugging his ribs and rocking.

Ellechial glanced heavenward. "I do hope he does not attempt to renew their relationship. Jarret has not taken their break-up well. He wavers between resentment and wanting to believe she didn't mean to break up with him after the baby."

"Incidentally, the baby does well." Nadriel beamed.

"I am glad." Ellechial smiled. Every baby born gave him great joy. "You have visited the adoptive family, then." Nadriel was blessed. As an angel supported by prayer, he had much more power to come and go in the world. Ellechial wore the long, restrictive robes of an angel who traveled little.

"I have. The new family does well. They rejoice daily in the child."

"Zoe, I need you," Jarret moaned, still hugging himself. He was most likely remembering Zoe's comforting ways, how she always seemed to know his thoughts and feelings. He hadn't been able to see past the physical, though, or to recognize her spiritual or emotional needs.

"His emotions rule him," Ellechial said, "and could change the direction I envision for him."

"Direction?"

"Yes, I need to keep him from self-pity and from Zoe. Then once his father and Roland go to Arizona, he will have no one but

Keefe. I have hope for him if he begins to listen to Keefe as he once did."

Nadriel's wings lifted. "My news may increase your hope."

A wave of joy coursed through Ellechial. "Oh?"

"Cyabrial has a plan. It begins now." Nadriel rose a foot off the ground as he often did when about to take flight.

"A plan from Caitlyn's angel? It will affect Jarret?"

"Yes." Nadriel disappeared before his thought faded. "Many souls depend upon Jarret."

Ellechial sighed. "That they do." So much depended upon the soul entrusted to his care, yet his wings were tied. "May Cyabrial's plans be blessed—"

A sudden gust of hot wind made Ellechial's wings ripple.

Deth-kye, the demon bent on seeing Jarret in hell, appeared. He crouched and whispered in Jarret's ear. Then he cackled. His evil laughter echoed in the woods. A flock of sparrows spread their wings and took flight.

Ellechial grieved, knowing that Jarret would listen to the demon's lies. He ached to protect.

A long, low moan escaped from the depths of Jarret's soul. He grabbed the hair on the top of his head and curled up. "Leave me alone."

"No one cares about you," Deth-kye whispered, making nearby blades of grass shudder. "You're worthless. You think Zoe wants you. Ha! You used her. She had to make choices she wasn't ready to make. She hates you for that. She hates you," he hissed, "but you need her. Go to her. Go now. You can get her back under your control."

Jarret moaned and tucked his head under his arm.

"Do not listen to him," Ellechial shouted, coming to full stature. "He seeks your ruin. Turn to the Lord who is quick to—"

"Get up!" Deth-kye spat.

Jarret pushed himself up on his elbows, wincing at the pain.

"That's my boy." Deth-kye laughed, acknowledged Ellechial with a glance, and laughed harder, evil resonating through his being.

CHAPTER TWO

SECRET MEETING

Roland

Fifteen-year-old Roland West ran. The ground jiggled and trees flew by to the steady beat of his black Nikes. He pounded down the path behind his friend Peter Brandt's house.

If only he had his mountain bike, he wouldn't need to run. What could've happened to it? Who would've taken it? Now he was going to be late.

Two days ago, he received a letter. He had smiled when he read it, knowing exactly who wrote it, though she hadn't signed her name. He and Caitlyn Summer had recently become friends again, not that they had been enemies, but there had been some tension between them for a few months. He couldn't wait to see her. What could she want?

His lungs and heart begged him to ease up, so he slowed to a fast walk. Sweat trickled down his neck and chest, soaking his gray t-shirt. He was over halfway to his destination, but it was the middle of summer and too hot to be running anywhere.

He'd cool off when he got there. *There.* He shuddered. Why did she want to meet *there*? Why not somewhere else? Roland pulled the note from the back pocket of his jeans and read it again.

You are called to a secret meeting. Tell no one! Thursday, 3:00
PM. Be at the Hiding Place.

As he shoved the note into the pocket of his t-shirt, he
stumbled over a root. What time was it? He checked his cell phone.
3:01. *Shoot.* He picked up his pace, jogging again.

He had seen the Hiding Place for the first time almost a year
ago. Peter had led him deep into the woods behind his house,
down to the river, and to the waterfall. Moving from one rock to
another in the river, Peter had gone right up to the waterfall. Then
he'd stepped through it.

Sure, it was amazing, but Roland had had no desire to follow.
Ever since he was a child, and for reasons he didn't understand, he
hated the feeling of cold water pouring on his head. He hated it
with a passion. Whenever it happened, it sent a shock though his
system and paralyzed him with fear. Would he be able to go
through the waterfall this time? Any chance the *secret meeting*
would be on the riverbank rather than the cave behind the
waterfall? Maybe he should've worn his Twins baseball cap.

No one else had such a stupid fear. Why couldn't he get over
it? Didn't therapists suggest facing your fears? He had faced it,
forcing himself through the waterfall several times last fall, every
time Peter got a crazy idea and wanted to go back there. So why
was the dread hitting him even now? He couldn't even see the
waterfall or the river.

"Chill out," he said aloud. Soon he and Papa would be in
Arizona, and this would be a memory. He could do it. Relax.

Before long, the rumble of the waterfall rose above his labored
breaths and the murmuring of leaves. The trees thinned out, and
the river showed through them more and more. He followed a
rocky path that ran parallel to the river, the rush of the falls
growing louder with each step.

Emerging from the woods, he directed his gaze to the ground and half climbed, half slid down a steep slope to the riverbank. Reluctant even to look at the threatening waterfall, he crossed the sandy, rocky bank to the river's edge. Rocks leading to the cave jutted out of the troubled tea-colored water. He would have to jump from rock to rock to get there.

His heart thumped so hard that he imagined he could hear it over the noise of the waterfall. Taking a deep breath, he jumped to the first stone. As he made it to the next stone, drops of icy water hit his face. He shuddered.

Don't think about it. It'll be so hot in Arizona that I'll look back with longing on this moment. He forced his gaze upward and beheld the white rushing monster before him, sunlight shimmering on its grasping claws. His stomach flipped. *I'll look back with longing? Yeah, right.*

He jumped to the next stone and the next, the spray of the water increasing, his stomach tightening. Tons of roaring water loomed directly before him, icy and seething, waiting to jab its claws into him and consume him with its chill. The idea of stepping through it seemed about as absurd as stepping through a brick wall. Why was he here?

Caitlyn.

With a last breath, he readied himself to become a victim of the foe in order to get to the other side. He squeezed his eyes shut and plunged into the water.

Knives of ice attacked. Cold ripped through him. His mind went numb. Pounding, slicing, slashing . . . He groaned. *Keep moving. Another step. Another step.*

It was over. He stood on the ledge behind the waterfall, soaked, trying to compose himself and waiting for his eyes to adjust to the darkness. A long shudder passed through him.

A group of kids stared at him.

Peter laughed. "Man, you look like you've been running from the devil." He stepped forward, a towel in his hands.

Roland shuffled along the narrow ledge, past the pool of water behind the fall, and to the dry part of the cave. He took the towel from Peter.

Kiara and Phoebe sat on matching logs near a low rock shelf. Peter and his father had dragged the logs and other things into the cave years ago, making the place kind of homey. Dominic sat on the edge of the pool, his legs dangling in the water.

Caitlyn, in a 1940s vintage-style beige dress and white tennis shoes, stood in the back of the fifteen-foot-deep cave, her hands clasped in front of her. Burning candles filled the holes in the wall behind her, the light from their flames bouncing off her long red curls and making her look like an angel.

Dominic got up and slapped Roland on the arm. "*Hola, Vato.*" *Vato* probably meant something like *dude* in Spanish. Dominic said it all the time, that and a lot of other Spanish words nobody knew but him.

Roland gave him and the others a nod as he dried his hair and moved to the back of the cave.

Caitlyn smiled. "I'm glad you made it."

"Yeah, better late than never." Peter smirked at him and then turned to Caitlyn. "So, now maybe you'll tell us what this is about, huh? What's the secret?"

She folded her hands and bounced once on her toes, her gaze flitting over each of them. "Well . . . I have an idea."

"Uh-oh," Dominic said.

Peter laughed.

Caitlyn continued unfazed. "I think we should start an intense, radical prayer group."

"What?" Peter's voice squeaked. "Are you kidding me? We're here for a . . . prayer group?"

"Let's hear her out," Kiara said. "She must have a reason for her idea." She returned her attentive gaze to Caitlyn. "You have the floor."

"Thank you." Caitlyn curtsied to Kiara. "Last year, well almost a year ago, God did something special for us." Her eyes went to Dominic. "For you, in particular, but for all of us, really."

Roland glanced at Dominic to gauge his response.

Dominic rubbed his legs and dipped his head, his black bangs falling in his face. A year ago, Dominic would not have been in this cave. Not easily, anyway. A car accident two years ago had left him confined to a wheelchair, and he had lost hope of ever walking again.

"Peter," Caitlyn said, "when you inherited the relics of Saint Conrad, it was for a reason. Don't you think?"

Peter shrugged and exchanged a glance with Dominic. "Well, sure."

"And when God showed us his love and power by healing Dominic through Saint Conrad's intercession, there was a reason for that. He didn't have to heal Dominic, but he did. And we witnessed it, well, some of us."

Roland remembered it like it had happened yesterday. Kiara and Phoebe hadn't been there, but the news spread through the high school and Saint Michael's Parish. Everyone knew Dominic needed the wheelchair. And then everyone saw him walk. The doctors were astonished. They all gave credit to God and to the prayers of Saint Conrad of Parzham.

"So, I think God is trying to tell us something," Caitlyn said.

Kiara jumped to her feet, beaming. "God wants us to turn to him, to keep asking for things. He wants to answer our prayers."

Caitlyn beamed back, her green eyes glittering in the candlelight. "We saw a miracle. God hears us when we pray, and

He still works miracles." Caitlyn and Kiara came together, wide-eyed and grinning, and locked onto each other's hands.

Phoebe stood. She folded her arms and scowled like a schoolteacher. With her honor-roll status and freaky image—blue-streaked hair, mismatched clothes, and gaudy jewelry—Roland never knew how to take her. "Don't get carried away, girls. Miracles are rare. We don't know why God chose to work a miracle for Dominic. I can't imagine that there'll be more miracles in our little town just because we ask. God doesn't work that way."

"Yeah," Peter said. "Why can't we pray by ourselves? Why a group?"

"There's power in numbers," Kiara said. She almost never got upset with anyone, so it was strange seeing her without the pleasant smile. "Where two or three are gathered in my name..."

The discussion continued, Caitlyn and Kiara insistent on the idea, Peter and Phoebe objecting, each shouting to be heard over the waterfall and the voices of the others.

Nadriel

"This is not going as I had hoped," Cyabrial said to the other angels present.

Guardian angels hovered close to their charges, wings pulsing as their prayers rose to heaven.

"Caitlyn has heeded your suggestion," Nadriel said to Cyabrial. "It is now up to the others. I will encourage Roland." He winged to Roland's side and leaned to whisper. Roland responded with a tilt of his head and a quickening of his heart rate.

Dominic's guardian angel stepped forward, his wings fanning out. "We must keep Doubt and Dissension from having their way!" Spinning to face the demons, he whisked his arm out and pointed.

15

The demons Doubt and Dissension retreated to a dark corner. But they did not leave.

"*Silencio!*" Dominic stepped into the middle of the teens and they all stopped talking. "I, for one, like what Caitlyn is saying here. And I, for one, will join her. Maybe God does not want to perform another miracle, but he still answers prayers. And I know *mucha* people with *muchas* needs. My aunt, for one, she suffers from leukemia. My second cousin, he gets made fun of because of a lisp. My *abeula* in Mexico has been sick for years."

He faced each of them, holding each one's gaze for a second. He stopped at Roland. "And what about you, *amigo*? You stand here in the shadows saying nothing. I want to know: what do you think?"

Roland blushed under the sudden redirection of everyone's attention. "I, uh, I'm not gonna be around. I'll be leaving for Arizona in a couple of days." His gaze turned to Caitlyn.

Nadriel, Roland's guardian angel, exchanged a thought with Cyabrial. Roland and Caitlyn had recently become friends again, so Roland probably had reservations about leaving for the summer.

Caitlyn took a step toward Roland. "You can still pray. You can pray for our group's intentions. We'll be united in spirit."

Cyabrial's wings lifted in his admiration for his charge.

"I'll join you, Caitlyn," Kiara said with a firm nod of her head. "Just tell me when and where."

"Count me in, too," Dominic said, turning to Peter.

Peter squirmed. "All right. I-I guess, when I left those relics with Father Carston, you know, to keep at the church, I sort of left my prayers with them. It won't kill me to start really praying again."

Everyone faced Phoebe now.

16

She sighed, propping her hands on her hips. "I need more. Tell me your idea. Where do we meet? What do we do—exactly? And what are we looking for? Don't tell me we're looking for more miracles. I think it's presumptuous to expect—"

"Okay, okay." Caitlyn put a hand up, silencing her. "We won't ask specifically for miracles. We'll accept whatever way God wants to answer our prayers. But we'll believe that he *does* answer them. Okay?"

"Fine." Phoebe stuck her hand out and Caitlyn shook it.

"There's one more detail," Caitlyn said.

Peter moaned.

"Because I want everyone to feel as called about this as I do, and to make sure this is God's will, I want each of you to ask for a sign."

"Now you're pushing it," Phoebe said, exchanging a glance with Peter.

"A sign?" Peter said. "I mean, I thought we agreed we weren't asking for miracles."

"A sign isn't a miracle," Kiara said. "What's wrong with wanting to know if this is God's will?"

"Right," Caitlyn said. "I don't mean the sun has to spin or fall from the sky or anything. I just think it'd be nice if everyone received something small and personal, a little sign that left each of you as convinced as I am that God really wants this. Saint Therese the Little Flower asked for a sign when she started praying for a criminal's conversion. She got her sign. I can't explain how strongly I feel about this. I believe that God wants this of me. But I don't know what I'm doing." She frowned, her bottom lip sticking out. "And I can't do it alone."

When her gaze landed on Roland again, sympathy showed in his eyes. A frown on her face always made him shift about uncomfortably. "I'll ask for a sign."

Dominic draped his bony arm around Roland's shoulders and flipped the hair from his eyes. "Me too, *amigo*."

While the others added their affirmations, Cyabrial and Nadriel smiled at each other and at the other guardian angels present.

"I guess we have some work to do," Nadriel said.

CHAPTER THREE

ENCOUNTER

Jarret

Jarret walked the damaged mountain bike home, hoping against hope that he wouldn't find Keefe waiting for him. He left the bike behind the stables and snuck inside through the veranda to avoid notice. Unfortunately, there was Keefe, sitting on the couch in the family room. To Jarret's annoyance, Keefe jumped up and followed him through the house.

At the foot of the stairs, Keefe grabbed Jarret's arm. "Are you alright?" He looked Jarret over, his gaze lingering on the biggest dirt smear on Jarret's designer t-shirt.

Jarret yanked his arm free and climbed the steps by twos.

"Hey, we need to talk." Keefe remained at the foot of the steps. "I guess you're going to take a shower, huh?" A pause. "I-I'll wait in the kitchen. Come down when you're done."

Jarret threw his twin a cold glance from the top of the steps. Once upon a time, Keefe would've understood his situation. Keefe would've been on his side, but now he only wanted to talk him out of things. No, they did not need to talk.

Stripping his muddy shirt off over his head, Jarret stepped into the bathroom. If he took long enough cleaning up, maybe Keefe would find something else to do.

He cranked the water temperature to hot and adjusted the shower head to get a full-pressure spray. The pounding water soothed his aches and numbed his mind. Rolling clouds of steam filled the room. He imagined himself as a bird coasting beneath cumulus clouds. Not a care in the world.

He left conditioner in his hair an extra-long time and even shaved the scruff off his chin and upper lip. Once back in his room, he put on his gray Armani shorts, the blue t-shirt with the wild black pattern—Zoe had given it to him—and the cologne she found irresistible. Ready to go, he stuffed his car keys into a pocket.

Sandals in hand, he stepped from his bedroom into the dark hallway. The vacuum cleaner hummed in some distant part of the house, probably the family room. No lights showed at the foot of the stairs. Maybe Keefe had given up waiting on him.

Jarret crept down the steps.

Keefe's bedroom door flew open. "Hey, you got a minute?" he said from the top of the stairs.

Jarret bristled but stopped. "No. I'm going somewhere."

Keefe bounded down the steps, slowing as he neared the bottom. "Where you going?" He gave Jarret the once over, the hint of a smile passing over his lips. "You got a date?"

"No." In the past, Jarret would've told him everything. Part of him wanted to now. But he hated to even look at his twin with his cropped hair, dark-rimmed glasses, and protruding ears. Keefe was a stranger to him.

"So, where, then?" Keefe circled around Jarret, checking him out. "You're wearing cologne or something. A clean shave. You put gel in your hair?" He stretched out one of Jarret's curls.

Shoving Keefe's hand away, Jarret sat on a step to put on his sandals. "Not that it's your business, but I'm going to Zoe's." He cringed. Why had he told him? He had not only lost control of his twin, he'd lost control of himself. He was unpredictable.

"Zoe? I thought she broke up with you. I thought she said—"

"She didn't mean it." Jarret sneered as he fumbled with a sandal strap. "She's been through a lot. I'm gonna talk to her."

"I don't think that's a good idea. You should try to get over her."

"Who asked you?" Glaring, Jarret got up from the step, pushed past Keefe, and stomped down the hall. The hum of the vacuum cleaner grew louder.

Keefe followed. "I want to talk to you for a minute."

Jarret cruised through the great room and into the family room. The suit of armor in the corner and the shield over the fireplace reflected the muted sunlight that streamed in through the tall windows on either side of the entertainment center. Couch cushions leaned against the coffee table and the sides of the couches. Their live-in housekeeper, Nanny, stooped over a stripped couch, vacuum cleaner hose in hand, singing "Barbara Ann" by the Beach Boys as she worked.

"Come on. Just for a minute." Keefe shouted over the noise and tried to walk alongside him as they passed the veranda.

Jarret yanked open the door to the garage and pulled the car keys from his pocket. "About Zoe?"

"Yeah."

"No." He smacked the garage door opener and walked around to the driver's side of his three-year-old cherry-red Chrysler 300. The sunlight creeping beneath the opening garage door made its custom paint job shine. He loved that car. He kept it clean, show room clean.

"We can't talk?" Keefe followed him around the car.

"You got that right. Not since you became a holy roller." He smirked at Keefe, swung open the car door, and dropped into the driver's seat.

Keefe grabbed the door before he could close it. "I know I don't see things the way I used to, but I'm still your brother and I . . ."

Jarret yanked the door but Keefe wouldn't let go.

". . . I still care about you. And I think you're about to make a big mistake."

Jarret shoved the key in the ignition and threw the car in reverse to back out.

Keefe stumbled forward but had to let go.

Once Jarret cleared the four-car garage, he slammed his door, cranked the steering wheel, and shifted into drive.

Keefe jumped in front of the car. "I only want to talk," he shouted.

"I'll talk to you all right." Red flashed before his eyes. He shifted into park, flung the door open, and jumped out.

Keefe stumbled back, his hands up in a gesture of surrender. "Zoe wants to change the direction in her life. She told you that, right?" He backed off the driveway and into the yard. "I've wanted to talk to you about things. You're not seeing things right, and not just about her."

Jarret admired Keefe's uncharacteristic boldness in confronting him like this. Then again—

He drew his hand back and formed a fist. "Oh yeah?" His sneer turned into a grimace. He lunged and swung at Keefe's face.

Keefe jerked to the side, Jarret's fist only skimming his chin. "I'm just saying, I think you need to give her some space." His voice was calm and concern oozed from his eyes, but he continued backing up. "You both need time to think."

"What do you know?" Jarret followed, lunged, and swung again, aiming for his brother's gut.

Keefe twisted, avoiding the full impact of the blow. "Man, what's wrong with you lately? I just want to talk." He latched onto Jarret's arm and yanked.

Jarret stumbled forward. Keefe's shoe cracked against his shin with a jolt of pain. Keefe shoved his chest.

Unable to break the momentum, Jarret toppled to the ground. He landed on his shoulder, and blood rushed to his face. Seething, he shot up and rammed his shoulder into Keefe's chest.

Keefe staggered back but didn't fall. "Jarret, it's me. What are you doing?"

"What I should've done a long time ago." The next move he would get right. He feigned a punch to the face.

As Keefe dodged it, Jarret made his move, shoving him hard with his full body weight, knocking him off balance.

Arms flailing and glasses flying, Keefe landed on his side and rolled to his back.

Fire burning within, Jarret dove onto him.

Ellechial

Ellechial stood by, powerless to defend, powerless to join in the fight. He hadn't the power even to draw near and so watched from a distance.

Monettello's armor gleamed as he fought the two attacking demons, Deth-kye and Hursk. Streaks of sky-blue and golden light followed his every graceful strike. Keefe's faithfulness to prayer and acceptance of his daily cross had made his guardian angel Monettello strong, well-armed, and something to behold. No longer clad in the long robes of an angel without permission to

23

battle, he wore the short tunic of a fighter, a tunic that allowed movements swift and fierce.

Deth-kye, too, possessed weapons, strength, and armor. Armor with thin, razor-sharp plates! Jarret, having given rein to him since his youth, had made him powerful and effective. While clutching a short dagger with one hand, he swung a blackened scythe with the other.

Monettello brought up his shield, gold light flashing upon impact.

Deth-kye stumbled back, laughing hideously. He had flung his dagger into Jarret's back and pierced him to the soul. Curses erupted from Jarret as he pinned his struggling twin to the ground.

The demon Hursk crawled to Keefe's ear. While Keefe had once listened to Hursk's lies, held captive under false compassion, he now recognized the truth. The demon grew weaker daily. His only weapons now were his ability to rile Keefe to *justifiable* anger and a three-inch shiv.

"Be gone!" Monettello commanded.

Hursk thrust the shiv, cracking it against Monettello's plated boot. It had no effect.

Monettello, sparing no glance for the little demon, kicked him and sent him sailing through the air. He hadn't even broken rhythm in his exchanges with Deth-kye's scythe.

With a sudden twist of his body, Keefe flipped over and got up on all fours. Jarret clung to him, one arm around his chest, the other around his neck. The two often fought and wrestled with each other for fun and competition, but it grieved Ellechial to watch them now.

Deth-kye slipped under Monettello's shield and crouched by Jarret's ear. He could incite anger like no other demon. He whispered fragments of Keefe's past offenses and mistakes. As

Jarret's anger intensified and his attack grew rougher, Deth-kye's chill laughter rang out.

Monettello yanked Deth-kye back by his neck and cracked the shield against his head. Deth-kye spun around, poised to stab the angel with his dagger. Monettello met the blade with his own.

The fighting, both human and spirit, lessened as Roland and his guardian Nadriel drew near, though only angels and demons knew of their approach. With wings held high and sword half-drawn, Nadriel swept onto the scene. Roland stopped and gawked, visibly troubled to see his brothers at war.

"What have we here?" Nadriel said to Ellechial.

Hursk, still a good ten feet away, skulked toward Keefe. He stopped when Nadriel spoke. Deth-kye, too, lessened his attack and perked his pointy ears.

Jarret pinned Keefe, holding his arm behind his back and pressing his cheek to the ground.

"Keefe wishes to dissuade Jarret from visiting Zoe," Ellechial said. "We all do."

Nadriel nodded. "That could prove to be a spiritually destructive encounter."

"Stay outta my business," Jarret spat, his face an inch from Keefe's. "I'm gonna do what I'm gonna do, and it ain't no concern a-yours. Got it?" He lessened his grip.

Chest heaving, Keefe stopped struggling and gave a single nod.

Jarret stood and brushed off his shirt. "Look what you did to my clothes." After giving Keefe a scathing glance, he headed to his car.

Keefe stumbled to his feet and searched for his glasses.

Roland came over to him, stooping along the way to pick up Keefe's glasses. "What was that about?" Concern troubled his cool gray eyes.

"That brother of ours needs help." Keefe took his glasses from Roland, put them on, and stared as Jarret dropped into the driver's seat of his Chrysler 300 and slammed the door.

"Help?" Roland watched Jarret too.

"That's your sign," Nadriel whispered to Roland.

Roland's heart fluttered, though his expression showed uncertainty. He hadn't accepted Keefe's words as the sign he'd asked for to know that God wanted him to be part of the prayer group.

Monettello gave Keefe a spiritual nudge. "Point your little brother to God."

"He needs help that we can't give," Keefe said to Roland.

"Okay, Roland?" Nadriel smiled. "You've got your sign."

Keefe faced Roland. "You pray, don't you?"

Roland's eyes opened wide. "Uh, yeah."

Nadriel laughed, sharing the joy of the moment with the other two guardians. Then he raised a wing over Roland. "Got it, my boy? God wants you to help Jarret through your prayers."

"It'll take more than prayer to help him." Roland spoke so low that Keefe hadn't heard him.

Ellechial and Nadriel exchanged a glance. It was strange how Roland sometimes seemed to hear them.

"He is right," Ellechial said. "Prayer will not be enough. It will take many more sacrifices."

"Roland is ready." Nadriel's gaze held deep love, perhaps for Roland, but more than likely from the word *sacrifice*. The attribute of God that gave him the greatest joy was *sacrificial love*. It sent him into ecstasy to ponder it. It occupied his every thought and prayer of praise. He loved to witness Roland, or any human, enter into and embrace sacrificial love. Unable to suffer like a human, an angel could only ponder and praise this mystery.

As Keefe started for the house, Roland caught sight of his mountain bike. It lay on its side, dirt caking its bent rim and fork.

"My Iron Horse!" Roland ran to it and fell to his knees. Anger, frustration, and sorrow showed in his face, his eyes, his posture. "What happened to my bike?" His gaze slid to Jarret, who sat fixing his hair in the rearview mirror of his car.

"Roland is ready, is he?" Ellechial said. True, Roland had grown much in the past few months. But could he be ready? Keefe was ready. Ellechial had seen it in him. Yes, if Jarret remained home with Keefe, he would find help. Unless his visit with Zoe changed things.

Jarret revved his engine, drawing the attention of men and angels. Then he sped off down the driveway. Ellechial moved at once, he and Deth-kye passing with equal speed into the car with Jarret. Deth-kye rode shotgun.

CHAPTER FOUR

THE PAST IS PAST

Jarret

Jarret pressed the pedal to the floor, speeding down Forest Road.

He hated the emptiness inside him. Loneliness gnawed at his soul, deep, painful loneliness. Why did he feel this way? Why the driving need to have certain people in his life? He had unbeatable skills and plenty of things to do. He knew how to have fun. Why wasn't that enough?

Roland was a loner. He had friends now, but he was a loner at heart, perfectly satisfied to be alone for days on end. His happiness didn't depend on anyone else.

He hated that about Roland, almost as much as he hated that Papa favored him.

Then there was Keefe. Keefe didn't seem all that troubled about losing Jarret's friendship or the close relationship they once shared. Sure, he wanted to talk, but only so he could push his new beliefs on him. He didn't miss the bond they'd known growing up.

Jarret sneered. He gripped the steering wheel and pumped the pedal, his gaze fixed on the two-lane road, trees whizzing by on his left, houses on his right. He passed a van, a car, and a tractor. The dude in the car honked and waved a fist.

He hated that he needed others in order to feel secure and in control. Alone, he felt like half a man. Maybe if he hadn't been a twin, connected to someone else from the first moment of his existence, he wouldn't feel this way today. Hardly a day had passed without Keefe by his side.

What would it take to find happiness and peace on his own? What was the secret? He couldn't look at or even think about Keefe without wishing things could go back to the way they were.

Why had Keefe turned into a psycho-Christian convert? Everything held deep spiritual meaning to him now. Every choice had moral considerations. They couldn't just talk and have fun anymore. They couldn't do what they wanted simply because they wanted to do it. Consequences. Keefe considered consequences.

Keefe made him sick. Keefe judged everything he did or suggested and tried to talk him out of —

A siren blared behind him. Blue and red lights flashed in the rearview mirror.

Easing off the gas and tapping the brakes, Jarret slowed and pulled over to let the police car pass.

The cop did not pass. He stopped inches from the Chrysler's rear bumper.

Jarret cussed and smacked the steering wheel. His chest tightened. Nothing went his way anymore. The whole world hated him.

After getting a lecture and his first speeding ticket, he pulled back onto the road. In a couple of minutes, he'd arrive at the McGowan's house. He couldn't wait to see Zoe.

Zoe once filled Keefe's place, not entirely but enough. He liked having her in his life. She understood him, accepted him, and made him happy. He never knew loneliness with her.

Last Thanksgiving, he'd had a revelation. The Brandts had invited Papa for dinner, and so he and Zoe agreed to go too. She'd made him angrier than ever that day, but she also made him realize that he loved her.

The month before, when he'd learned of her pregnancy, he'd told her to take care of it. In the Brandts' driveway, he'd found out she hadn't. He'd blown up, taken it out on the steering wheel and the driver's seat, then told her to walk home. She got out of the car.

Watching her walk away, he'd realized, no matter what, he couldn't let her go. He needed her. That's when he knew he loved her, and he told her so. She'd said she loved him too.

How could she stop loving him?

He had changed his mind about the abortion and stayed by her throughout her pregnancy. After the baby, she'd dumped him. Said she had to figure out her life.

Giving up their baby had hurt him, too, but that was history. Now they both needed to heal. She needed him as much as he needed her. Maybe when she saw him, she'd know it. She'd see it in his eyes. He'd see it in hers. She'd come back to him.

Papa and Roland could go to Arizona. Keefe could . . . do whatever the heck he wanted, so long as he kept his distance. Then he and Zoe could spend the summer together.

He turned down Zoe's street. As he neared her two-story house, he smiled.

Yeah, he and Zoe could spend the summer together. If her father didn't like it, they could sneak. He'd be careful this time and take it slow. In no time, she'd want him as badly as he wanted her.

He pulled into the empty driveway and shut off the engine. Her parents usually parked in the garage. Closed living room curtains, letters peeking out of the mailbox by the front door . . . Maybe no one was home. Maybe she was home alone.

Pressing his lips together, he remembered her kiss. He closed his eyes and breathed deeply. Her scent, fruit trees in the country, came to mind. Her skin, smooth as rose petals . . . Her hair, like a black silk scarf . . . He ached to hold her.

He squared his shoulders and focused on the door as he got out of the car and strutted up the drive. He lifted a fist to knock but then hesitated. Why? She'd be happy to see him. She'd probably been waiting for him.

He knocked and, not wanting to appear desperate, turned away from the door. Sunlight gleamed on the chrome and the sparkling, cherry-red paint of his Chrysler 300. A couple of kids squealed as they chased each other through the front yard of a house across the street. An airplane flew silently in the blue stratosphere.

The door opened and his heart skipped a beat.

"Jarret?"

Zoe's voice drained all tension from his body but set his heart to pounding. He turned around and wanted to pull her into his arms. "Hey."

Beautiful and composed, she leaned on the edge of the half-open door. She wore white jeans and a graphic t-shirt, her shiny black hair falling over one shoulder. She offered no smile, but her dark eyes sparkled as she looked him over. "What're you doing here?"

It took all his strength to keep from touching her. He wished she'd step outside. "I miss you." His face muscles tightened. "Can we talk?"

She glanced over her shoulder, not making eye contact when she turned back. "I don't think so."

He winced. Then his hands nearly shot out— he wanted to hold her so badly—but he stuffed them into the front pockets of his shorts. "I can't stop thinking about you."

Still not stepping outside to talk with him, she rested her head against the edge of the door. Finally, she lifted her thick-lashed eyelids and sunlight danced in her honey-brown eyes.

"Aren't you gonna tell me that you miss me, too?" He hated that he hadn't been able to control his tone, that he sounded hurt.

Her lips tightened and she lowered her gaze. She looked like she might cry.

He stepped into the house and stroked her cheek with his fingertips. "Take a ride with me. I wanna talk to you."

She pressed her cheek to his hand, her chin trembling. "I can't."

He pushed his hand through her hair and touched her neck, moving closer so he could whisper in her ear, wanting to remind her of how they used to make each other feel. He was certain her heart hadn't changed. "Yes, you can. Take a ride with me."

She met his gaze, her eyes turning hard. She pulled back and said in an unwavering voice, "No. I told you what I need right now. I need to figure things out. And I need to do it alone."

Her words cut him to the quick. Scowling, he backed off. "How long do you need? Are you gonna see me after that?" He paused and then spit out, "Or are we through?"

"I don't know. I—"

Footsteps sounded in the kitchen. Then her father stepped into view. "Who's at the door?"

His low, powerful voice made Jarret's skin crawl, but he refused to budge. He was here to see Zoe, and he *would* see her.

Mr. McGowan hadn't taken more than two steps down the hallway when his eyes landed on Jarret, and he stopped cold. "What do you think you're doing here?"

Mr. McGowan's face flushed, his eyes narrowed, and he peered down his nose. The look reminded Jarret of two moments from his past, both equally disturbing. The first moment was when Mr. McGowan had discovered Jarret had gotten Zoe pregnant. He'd slammed Jarret against the wall right here in the hallway.

Pinning Jarret to the wall, the man had shouted threats, sprinkling Jarret's face with spittle.

The second time was on the trip Papa had forced Jarret to take, shortly thereafter, once Papa found out that Jarret had not been "respecting his girlfriend." They'd arrived in California, Jarret clueless as to where, exactly, they were going to spend the next few weeks. Clueless until a tall, dark-eyed monk answered the door to welcome them.

"I want to talk to your daughter." Jarret folded his arms and glared at Mr. McGowan.

Mr. McGowan chuckled, a rather sinister chuckle, and his eyes darkened. "Get out of my house. She doesn't want to see you anymore."

Jarret didn't want to believe him, but when he faced Zoe, she averted her gaze. Then she exchanged a glance with her father, her eyes holding no trace of anger or resentment toward him. None at all.

Shards and gravel tore at Jarret's heart. Cuss words and bad names filled his mind. He shot a black glare at Zoe and another at her father, then he stalked away.

He didn't need her. He'd never needed her. They were over a long time ago. She did nothing but betray his trust ever since she'd gotten pregnant. She wanted to use that as an excuse to end their relationship? Fine. They had no real relationship. She was lucky she'd had him for as long as she did.

Ellechial

Eyes black with wickedness, Deth-kye grinned at Ellechial as he whispered lies in Jarret's ear. "The witch isn't worth your time. She's a liar. You'll find another girl, many more girls. They will

BATTLE FOR HIS SOUL

satisfy you much more than she ever had. It's not her you loved. It's what she gave you."

Frowning, Jarret slid into the driver's seat and peeled out of the driveway. Deth-kye again rode shotgun while Ellechial took a back seat.

"Faster, faster," Deth-kye said. "S-s-speed can numb your mind."

"Enough!" Ellechial longed for the grace he could use if the prayer group ever took root. "You have done enough. You are only angry that this situation did not work to your advantage."

"Is that what you think?" Deth-kye's face twisted, his countenance displaying his malignant joy. "This turned out exactly according to plan. Jarret has listened to my voice, has done what I commanded. Oh yes, this is exactly as I had planned."

Ellechial turned his eyes to heaven. Deth-kye couldn't help but lie. His father, after all, was the Father of Lies. He wanted Jarret and Zoe together so they could resume their sinful, destructive relationship. He lost. Yet, Deth-kye had reason to be satisfied. Jarret had listened to him.

"I suppose you think the boy will run back to Keefe." Deth-kye wrapped his arm around Jarret's shoulders and pretended to groom his hair with affection.

Ellechial refused to answer the demon, though he *had* wanted it, had hoped for it. Keefe could help, if only Jarret would let him back into his life and listen to him, learn from him.

"He will not," Deth-kye spat. "He is appalled by Keefe's intrusive display of his new-found faith." He smirked at Ellechial and continued to speak, lisping his words this time. "These are thoughts I like for him to have. I will keep them locked in his mind."

He rested his chin on Jarret's shoulder and whispered in his ear, "Remember California. Remember the trick your father played. He was wrong to take you there. He only wanted to push his values onto you. But you are wise. You can think for yourself. You don't need someone else telling you what to believe." With his chin on Jarret's shoulder, he tauntingly twisted his face to Ellechial and whispered, "Re-mem-ber."

"That memory should only do him good," Ellechial said. "How can you use it to ruin him?"

Deth-kye roared with laughter, his dark wings quivering. "You shall see. By these memories, I shall soon own him. You will lose him forever. You had hoped, I know, that one day he would take the seat I left vacant in Heaven." He frowned, continuing with deepening harshness. "He will not. That seat will remain forever vacant. God will look upon it with sadness. And I will laugh. Jarret has a seat prepared for him in Hell, and I will see that he takes it."

As Jarret turned down the long gravel road that led home, Ellechial wished he could fly to Monettello and have him prepare Keefe. But his wings were tied and would remain so unless he received power from prayer or permission from God. Monettello would have to encourage Keefe in the moment of the encounter. Perhaps it would be enough. Jarret must choose to stay at home with Keefe.

"Remember your imprisonment. Remember when you first went to the door of that miserable place . . ." Deth-kye reclined, resting on Jarret's shoulder as he whispered memories.

Jarret

So the memories began . . .

It was mid-April and the ride from the Sacramento airport was long and dull, the highway and flat landscape offering nothing of interest. Boredom overwhelmed Jarret. He cursed Papa in his mind for not letting him bring his cell phone, MP3 player, laptop, or any other distraction.

Papa had said something about a vineyard to the cabbie, but he hadn't told Jarret a single detail about the assignment. Jarret hadn't bothered to read any signs along the way, but he should've suspected something when, nearing their destination, they drove past a big white cross.

Their taxi stopped on a quiet road, a small, drab building on one side, rows and rows of bare grapevines on the other. Papa often took the family to help with archaeological digs and occasionally brought them to investigate old mines . . . What assignment could he possibly have at a vineyard?

"Go tell them we're here." Papa pointed to the building, a tan A-frame surrounded by trees.

Glad to get out of the cab, Jarret yawned and stretched his legs. What he wouldn't give to be back home. What was Zoe doing now?

He followed the sidewalk to the A-frame and grabbed the thick metal ring in the middle of the door. No one answered so he turned to watch Papa.

Papa stood by the open trunk, stuffing his wallet into his back pocket and handing something to the cab driver. Lean, tall and composed, Papa came across dignified, never embarrassing, even with his old cowboy hat and boots. The short, husky driver flailed his arms, gesturing at the cab, the road, and then Jarret. Shaking his head, Papa pulled his wallet out again. The cabbie must not have gotten a big enough tip.

The door to the A-frame opened and Jarret turned around.

"God be with you." A tall balding man with dark creases around his mouth peered down his long nose at Jarret. "May I help you?"

Taking the man in from head to toe, Jarret shook his head.

The man wore a long white hooded robe with sleeves that draped down to his knees, hiding his hands. A black garment peeked out from under the robe at the neckline. Was he a monk? Was this a monastery?

"I uh . . ." Jarret staggered back. He glanced to either side to get some further clue as to where they had come: trees, grass, distant

36

buildings, and vast vineyards. "I think we're at the wrong place. This is a mistake. Sorry."

He sprinted down the sidewalk as the taxi pulled out. "Wait!" He waved his arms, desperate to get the cabbie's attention. He skidded to a stop by Papa.

"Did he tell you where our rooms are?" Papa lifted a suitcase.

"What? Rooms? Here?"

Papa smiled. "Yes, here."

"No, no, no. We can't stay here. We're not where you think we are. Where's your assignment? What are you supposed to be doing? And why didn't you tell me anything about it?" Jarret glanced behind him and gestured at the building. "I think we're at a—"

The white-robed, handless monk strolled down the sidewalk toward them.

"Look," Jarret said, "there's a—"

Papa stepped around Jarret and headed for the monk. "Howdy, there." He took off his cowboy hat, set his suitcase down, and stuck out his hand. "I'm Ignatius West."

"What the—" Jarret jogged to them. "Is this a monastery?" Cringing, he looked the monk over again. "We're not staying here. I'm not staying here. I'm not staying at no freakin'—"

Papa turned on Jarret. "Shut your trap, son, and get the rest of the luggage. Our job is here."

Jarret huffed, dumbfounded. When Papa had said they were going to northern California and gave the cabbie the address of a vineyard, Jarret hadn't pictured monks. He hadn't thought monastery.

He grabbed the other suitcases and stumbled along behind Papa and the monk down a long, shady, gravel walkway. They stopped at a low building with several doors and windows all close together. Dinky apartments? The monk unlocked a door and pushed it open. He motioned for Jarret to go in while he remained outside and talked with Papa.

Jarret stepped inside what would be his prison cell for the next few weeks. Gray cement-block walls closed in around two plain couches and a desk. A room with two skinny beds and a nightstand came off the first room. And that was it. No carpet, no computer, no television, and no radio. There wasn't even a door to separate the two rooms for privacy. Papa had said the assignment could take as long as whole month. A whole month here?

Jarret flung his suitcase onto the bed, unzipped it part way, and reached a hand in along the sides. He needed a cigarette and he needed it bad. Once he found the pack, he slipped it into the back pocket of his jeans.

"Jarret?"

He jumped and then turned as Papa stepped into the room. "Yeah? Hey, you know what? I can't stay here." He tried to leave the bedroom, but Papa blocked his way, so he looked him in the eye. "There's got to be a hotel nearby."

"Sorry, Jarret. We're staying here. There's no hotel." Papa went to the window.

Jarret gazed longingly at the doorway.

"Just try to relax, son. Our work is here. And this is a nice place, the trees, the vineyard." He inhaled slowly. "It's peaceful here."

"You could've told me that we were staying at a monastery. Or is this punishment for what happened to Zoe?"

Papa gave him the eye. "Just concentrate on our assignment. Don't get all worked up about staying in a monastery. I'm not gonna leave you here." He smiled, his eyes brightening as if the thought amused him. "Besides, we're not actually in the monastery. These are guest quarters."

Jarret shook his head and turned to go. He'd have a smoke and think over his fate. Maybe he could find a bright side to it. It was a vineyard, after all. Maybe they made wine here.

"Where're you going, Jarret?"

"Taking a walk."

"I'll go with you. I'd like to check out the grounds."

Jarret huffed. This was gonna be hell.

CHAPTER FIVE

NEW DIRECTION

Ellechial

Since the creation of the world, waning midsummer sunlight set Ellechial's soul ablaze with praise for God's majesty. Leaves danced, and the road to the Wests' house shone under golden light. Ellechial turned his mind to the Lord. In an instant, he knelt before the heavenly throne to offer adoration and give glory to the Almighty One, the Majestic King. Traveling at the speed of thought, he returned to his post in Jarret's car.

The West family's castle-like house soon came into view, sunlight most gloriously illuminating the cylindrical turrets and the battlements. While the works of man could never equal the creations of God, they were, in their own way, beautiful. Over the ages, many worldly structures directed his thoughts to the Almighty One—St. Basil's Cathedral in Russia, Basilique de Sacre Coeur in Paris, the Palace of Versailles—reminding him of the power and majesty of God, the attributes of God that he would forever praise and proclaim.

Once Jarret caught sight of his house, he eased off the gas pedal, probably unsure of what to do after Zoe's rejection. He never took rejection well. It made him vulnerable and most susceptible to temptation.

Wings back, Ellechial leaned forward and whispered in Jarret's ear, "Go talk to Keefe." *Please, Lord, let me touch Jarret's heart. Let me point the boy in a good direction.* "Keefe has always helped you, comforted you."

Deth-kye, sitting in the front passenger seat, made a low growl.

Ellechial had been so immersed in prayers of petition and giving glory to God that he could have forgotten the demon was ever near—if such human weakness had belonged to angels. As it was, he never forgot the presence of the evil ones. He awaited with hope for the Great Day, the day that Deth-kye would be chained and Hell swallowed up forever.

Deth-kye gave a crooked grin, a pig-like snort accompanying it and reflecting his warped pleasure. It no doubt pleased him immensely that the twins no longer relied upon one another. He whispered in Jarret's other ear, "Why talk to Keefe? You don't want to see his smug face when he reminds you that he told you so. He *did* tell you not to see Zoe. Maybe he and Zoe have been talking. Maybe he planted ideas in her head."

Ellechial sent a prayer to heaven. *As you have brought about the conversion of his twin brother, so now convert Jarret. Open his heart to Your grace, I pray Thee.*

"What's this?" Deth-kye's attention snapped from Jarret to something outside the car. He leaned forward, his head poking through the front windshield.

In the front yard, two teenage boys crossed swords. Each donned a wire-mesh facemask, a white fencing jacket, and a single white glove. They moved in slow motion, taking deliberate steps and swinging their foils in unison. As Jarret's car neared, the boy with a shock of blond hair glanced at it, but the other kept stepping and swinging.

41

Deth-kye yanked his head back into the car, his expression contorting. "I really hate that kid."

"Who's with Roland?" Jarret muttered, squinting. He drove to the garage and parked outside, his gaze on the fencers. His face muscles twitched, showing he recognized the boy. "Peter?"

"Yeees," Deth-kye hissed, though of course Jarret couldn't hear him. "Don't you just hate him? Remember when he . . ." He whispered past offenses and a few lies.

"I hate that kid," Jarret announced as he swung open the car door and got out. He strode across the front lawn toward Roland and Peter. He had always been easy to read, displaying his emotions and thoughts on his face, in his walk, and in his posture.

Ellechial kept step with Jarret and prayed. "Don't do it. Go inside, talk to Keefe instead." He hoped Jarret would sense his admonition.

Deth-kye leaped and skipped ahead of them. "Just look at the cocky boy." He pointed a crooked finger either at Roland or at Peter. "Doesn't he just beg for a beating?"

Roland and Peter stopped fencing and watched Jarret approach.

"Look at the way he stands." Deth-kye waved his arms dramatically. "Who does he think he is?"

Ellechial appeared between Deth-kye and Jarret. "Let them be. Roland will be gone in a few days. You need not trouble yourself with him or with Peter. You ought to speak with Keefe."

Jarret walked through him.

"Wouldn't it feel good to knock him to the ground?" Deth-kye wrapped his arm around Jarret's shoulders and smirked, his voice a slithery hiss. "He wouldn't be any competition for you, but it would be fun all the same. It would release tension. It would feel good, rewarding. Can't you taste it?"

Deth-kye often directed Jarret to unleash his frustrations on Roland, but Jarret locked his eyes on Peter, revealing his intended target. Peter's guardian angel lifted his wings and swung his shield forward.

Peter pushed up his mask and held his foil awkwardly at his side. "Hey-ya, Jarret."

Jarret gave him the once-over and a subtle smirk. "What's up?"

"I'm showing Peter a few moves," Roland said.

Roland's desire to befriend Jarret always clouded his ability to read Jarret's mood and to foresee his intentions. Keefe had been good at it, almost as good as any angel, though he hadn't always been effective in steering him, being weak himself.

"Allow me." Jarret snatched Roland's sword and gave Peter a nod. "Assume your stance."

Peter threw Roland a wary glance before securing the facemask and assuming the *en garde* position.

Peter's guardian whispered a word of caution to Peter, his wings expanding in his readiness to protect. He gave Deth-kye a warning look.

Deth-kye cackled and backed up. "He's got it from here." He referred to Jarret, who needed no more inciting. Once he got an idea, he typically followed through.

"Monettello, Keefe, where are you?" Ellechial glanced up at the dark bedroom windows.

Jarret raised his foil casually and grinned, his evil intention written on his face. With a jerk of his arm, he swung his sword.

Peter stumbled back with a nervous titter. He swung the foil left and right, awkwardly blocking each fierce attack.

Jarret lunged one way and then another, keeping Peter off balance. Then Jarret spun with dramatic flair and advanced from behind Peter.

43

Regaining balance, Peter made a move to face his opponent, but it was too late.

A smug grin on his face, Jarret put his foot to Peter's hind end and shoved.

Peter's arms flailed as he tumbled to the ground, the foil slipping from his hand.

Jarret chuckled and whacked Peter's backside with his foil. "Touché."

The demon *Revenge* appeared from out of nowhere and shot to Peter's side. Beet red and fuming, Peter jumped up and tore after Jarret. Peter's guardian angel rushed for Revenge, trying to beat him back.

Jarret threw his foil down, braced himself, and formed a fist, unwittingly mimicking the motions of Deth-kye.

At Nadriel's prompting, Roland flung himself at Peter and wrapped his arms around him from behind. "Let it go, man," Roland said. "You don't want to do that."

Glaring at Jarret, Peter wrestled to get free. "Oh yes, I do."

Roland clung to him.

"Oh no, you don't," Jarret said, grinning. He dropped his fist to his side but his eyes held a cocky look, a look that might get an angel riled up against him.

Deth-kye appeared in the midst of them, his vile laughter filling the air. "Don't you *love* a good fight?" he said to Ellechial. "Especially when it's so unbalanced, so unfair. I mean, look at Peter: unskilled, incompetent. He can't touch Jarret, not with Jarret's arrogance and talent. Look at him gloat." He threw his head back, laughing harder. "It's so beautiful."

"The word *love* ought not to come from one like you," Ellechial said.

Deth-kye sneered and vanished, most likely to set another snare.

Jarret swaggered across the yard to the house, a smug look on his face.

Ellechial followed.

As Jarret stepped into the house, his grin faded. He shut the door behind him, and his gaze traveled to the staircase halfway down the main hallway.

"Yes, go talk to him," Ellechial said. "Fighting has never calmed your restless spirit. Keefe has. His message may be foreign to you, but be not afraid."

Jarret's eyelids flickered. His head turned, and his gaze skated down the front hall, to the door of his father's study. After a deep breath, he strutted in that direction.

Had he decided to go with his father, then? Ellechial floated along with him, keeping close to his side and attentive to his mood, praying for the Lord's will and waiting to see it unfold.

His father's voice traveled from the study. "Sure, I'd like that."

"I'll be free next week," a woman said, her playful voice coming from the speakers of a computer.

Jarret slowed as he neared the door. He stopped where he couldn't be seen and leaned against the wall. His gaze flitted, focusing on nothing in particular, the way it did whenever he eavesdropped.

"Nah, next week is too soon," his father said. "I'll be in Arizona. My friend Juan asked me to come out, Juan Zamorano. Remember him?"

The woman laughed. "I think you're putting me off again. Are you afraid of me?"

Jarret's eyes narrowed as he recognized the voice. He peeked into the room.

His father sat sideways at a long oak desk, his boots propped up on one end. He played with an ornate desk globe, spinning it one way, then another. He smiled at a large, flat computer monitor.

The angle of it allowed Jarret to see the image of the blonde woman with whom he spoke. "Yeah, Anna, you know I'm simply a cowboy at heart, comfortable with fields and solitude. You're a real live woman. Of course I'm afraid of you." He chuckled.

Jarret nodded and smirked as if the visual confirmed what he'd already guessed. His father spoke with Miss Anna Meadows. Jarret met the woman this past spring when his father made him go on an archaeological dig in Mississippi. His father had known her in college, years before he'd met their mother. Their friendship resumed several years after their mother's death, but it had yet to progress to a romantic relationship.

"Really now, Ignatius, I'm starting to think that you—"

"No, no," his father said, "it's just that I made these arrangements last—"

Jarret stepped into the room. "Hey, Papa."

His father's boots slammed to the floor. He straightened up and swiveled the monitor, preventing a view from the doorway. "Hey, uh, I'll have to call you later." He spoke low and turned the volume on the speakers down, but not before she said, "Okay, cowboy, but don't make it too much later. I miss you."

"What's up, Jarret?" He shut off the monitor and slid the globe to the back of the desk.

"I'm going with you to Arizona."

His father smiled. "Oh yeah?"

It wasn't spoken in a tone of challenge, but the curl of Jarret's lip showed he took it that way. He huffed. "Well, can't I?"

His father stood and walked around the desk. "Of course, yeah, of course you can. What made you change your mind?"

"That would be me," Deth-kye said and hissed, his voice coming from a dark corner of the room.

CHAPTER SIX
DOUBT & DISSENSION

Roland

Saint Michael's Church felt like a sanctuary, providing cool relief from the hot afternoon sun. Light streamed in through tall, stained-glass windows, painting colorful abstracts on the pews. Candles burned in shrines and over the tabernacle.

Roland took a deep breath. The sweet, woodsy smell of incense lingered in the air. Nothing was more peaceful than sitting in church before the lights went on.

"I can give you fifty reasons not to go." Peter sat next to him with his arms folded across his chest, slumping so that his knees touched the back of the pew in front of them. "Well, a dozen anyway. Maybe fifty if I got creative."

Roland shrugged. He had a few reasons of his own for not wanting to go to Arizona at this particular time.

Caitlyn sat two pews ahead, whispering loudly with Kiara and Phoebe who sat on either side of her. She wore her hair up in a sloppy ponytail, a few red-mahogany curls hanging free. Judging by the tone of her whisper, she felt defensive.

"The weather, for one," Peter said. "An Arizona summer has gotta be hotter than hell."

"Peter!" Kiara whispered harshly. "We're in church."

"I'm not swearing. It's a fact." He lowered his voice and leaned toward Roland. "It'll probably be a hundred and twenty outside. Can your ghost-white skin even take the sun?"

Roland rolled his eyes. Peter liked to mock his pale skin every chance he got. It wasn't Roland's fault he'd inherited his skin pigmentation from the fairest of his relatives.

"Do you doubt me?" Peter said. "Don't you watch The Weather Channel? It's hot down there."

The three girls glanced around the church.

"So where is everyone?" Phoebe made a dramatic gesture at the empty pews, her dozen or so metal bracelets jangling.

Roland and Peter had arrived at Saint Michael's first, twenty minutes early, having bummed a ride from Peter's aunt, who had a tight schedule. Caitlyn, Kiara, and Phoebe showed up at five to three. The prayer group was to begin at three o'clock.

"Yeah," Peter said in his outdoor voice. "I thought you invited the Catholic youth group. They show up for everything, don't they?"

"The Fire Starters," Phoebe and Kiara said together. They were always the first to correct anyone who didn't know the Catholic youth group's new name. It had something to do with Luke 12:49: *I have come to cast a fire upon the earth, and how I wish it were blazing already.*

Phoebe reached past Caitlyn and grabbed Kiara's wrist to check her watch. She let go of Kiara's wrist, huffing.

Caitlyn turned to Peter. "Well, um . . ." She frowned. "Dominic was supposed to tell them. Maybe he forgot. He has a lot going on in his family."

"So nobody's here." Peter started bouncing one leg. "We still gonna do it?"

"Don't say *nobody's here*. There are five of us," Caitlyn said. "All we really need is two." She and Kiara exchanged a nod. "Where two or more are gathered in His name . . . Right?"

"I guess so." Peter looked at Roland. "Where's Keefe? Isn't he coming?"

Roland shrugged. Keefe had been horseback riding since late morning. He seemed distracted lately.

Peter faced Caitlyn again. "So how's this gonna work?"

"I don't know," Caitlyn said. "I thought—"

"You don't know? Shouldn't you have it all planned?" Now both of Peter's legs shook, bouncing to a broken rhythm.

"I thought we should *all* decide how it goes. This is only our first meeting. It doesn't need to be perfect. We can make changes as we go along."

"Where's Father?" Phoebe said. "Are you sure you told him? Isn't he supposed to bring the relic?"

Caitlyn took Kiara's wrist and glanced at her watch. "I don't know where he is. I guess he's late. We can start planning our prayer time, anyways. When he comes we should probably know what we're doing." She picked up a Mass Missal and flipped to the back. "Since he's going to bring out the Blessed Sacrament, I thought we should start with the Divine Praises. It's in the back here. Then maybe we could do a song. Or maybe we should sing first."

"A song?" Peter practically shouted. "I'm not singing. There're five of us. Whose gonna sing?" He turned to Roland. "Are you gonna sing?"

Caitlyn looked at Roland, her green eyes gleaming with hope.

Roland shrugged. He didn't want to disappoint her, but *no*, he wasn't going to sing. He never sang, not even in the shower. Everyone would hear him. Could he even hold a note? This was not the time to find out. He'd find out alone in the woods sometime, maybe, but *no*, not now.

"Well, whoever wants to can sing," Kiara said, flipping through the Missal. "I like to sing. What song?"

"You pick one," Caitlyn said. "We girls can sing."

Phoebe narrowed her eyes. "Then what?"

"Well, how about some spontaneous prayers?" Caitlyn said.

"Spontaneous?" Phoebe's eyes bugged, emphasizing the thick, black eyeliner all around them. "You don't mean like that weird charismatic stuff, do you? . . . everyone raising their hands, shaking their bodies, and making strange noises."

"That's not what I mean. Can't we just say a few prayers out loud, from our hearts?"

"Why can't we say them in the silence of our hearts? We can share our intentions then pray the Rosary or something. I'm not into that charismatic stuff. In fact, I find it kind of disturbing."

"Okay." Caitlyn frowned. "I wasn't going to speak in tongues or anything."

The frustration in Caitlyn's eyes made Roland's insides lurch. "I'll say a prayer out loud."

Caitlyn smiled at him, thankfulness written on her face.

"Yeah, sure." Phoebe glared at him. "Get spontaneous prayer started and then leave. You aren't even going to be around after this first meeting, are you?"

Not wanting to hold Phoebe's fierce gaze, he looked at Peter.

Peter shrugged, but his pouty lips and sulky eyes showed he sided with Phoebe. He scooted closer to Roland and whispered, "Reason number two for not going to Arizona: you'll miss all this." He grinned.

Roland chuckled.

Phoebe checked Kiara's watch again. "What's keeping Father? Do you think he forgot about us?"

Caitlyn peered at the vestibule. "Maybe someone should go check on him."

"I'll go." Phoebe slid to the end of the pew and got up. "You decide what we're going to do. My vote is for the Divine Praises and the Rosary."

"Rosary?" Peter frowned. "No one said to bring a rosary." He looked at Roland. "Did you bring a rosary?"

Roland dug into a leg pocket of his cargo pants and pulled out his black rosary.

"Oh." Peter shifted his position. "I guess I can use my fingers."

"What about the Divine Mercy Chaplet?" Kiara said to Caitlyn. "And I brought my Bible. Maybe one of us . . ."

"But really, man," Peter whispered to Roland. "Reason number three: Why the heck would you want to go anywhere with Jarret? Is he really gonna go with you guys now?"

Roland nodded.

"I mean, he spent the past year tormenting you, thrashing you, locking you up, getting you into trouble at school, and—"

"Why don't you shut up?" Roland snapped.

Caitlyn turned her head.

Roland's face warmed. He slid down in the pew. "People can change," he whispered.

Peter rubbed his hind end where Jarret had kicked him. "Seems like he's changed."

"Well, maybe he hasn't changed yet, but I'm not giving up on him. We can pray for him."

Peter raised his brows. "Are you kidding me? I'm not praying for him." He bounced his brows and grinned. "I've got payback on my mind."

Roland sighed and rolled his eyes. "That's the Christian spirit. Glad you're in our prayer group."

"Want me to leave?" He slapped his hands on the pew in front of him and leaned forward.

Roland tugged him back. "Sit down. Here comes Father."

The doors to the vestibule opened and Keefe strolled in.

"Father, huh?" Peter smirked.

Keefe genuflected and slid into the pew next to Roland, smelling like he had jogged all the way to the church. "Hey." He gave Peter and Roland a nod. "I thought I was late. Where is everyone?"

Cyabrial

With his thoughts close to the Lord hidden in the tabernacle, Cyabrial prayed for Caitlyn. Doubt had flickered in her eyes while her friends argued over what to do and how to pray. He could almost hear her wondering if this was really God's will.

As soon as Keefe and his guardian Monettello had entered the church, Dissension and Doubt withdrew to the shadows. When Monettello gave them no more than a cursory glance, Dissension crawled back to Peter, Doubt to Caitlyn.

Cyabrial, his gaze on Doubt, put a hand to the hilt of his sword. "Be gone." Caitlyn had been tested long enough, as God had willed it, and had clung to faith. She'd even offered a prayer that he had carried to Heaven. *I believe you want this, Lord, so even if it's only me and one other, I will do it. I will watch one hour with you.*

Doubt grimaced. "I am not done here."

"Oh, but you are." Cyabrial stepped toward him, unsheathing his sword.

Doubt cringed and backed up.

Before Doubt could flee, Monettello swung chains around both him and Dissension. "Not so fast," Monettello said. "There is one thing you must do before you go."

A side door of the church creaked open and Father Carston hastened in. He genuflected toward the tabernacle, greeted the five teens, and rushed to the sacristy.

Dissension grunted like a tied pig. Doubt writhed and tugged at his chains.

The church lights flickered on. The priest stepped into the sanctuary, cradling the silver reliquary that contained the relics of Saint Conrad of Parzham. After placing it on the altar, he returned to the sacristy.

Peter's face flushed. Perhaps his thoughts went to his discovery of the relic last fall and the transforming effect it had had on his faith. He blinked a few times and bowed his head. His guardian angel lifted his gaze to Heaven.

A moment later, Father Carston brought out a tall monstrance, set it under a golden beam of sunlight that fell on the altar, and went directly to the tabernacle.

All whispering ceased and the teens fumbled with the kneelers. The angels knelt too, the seven angels around the altar bowing low.

As the tabernacle door opened, Monettello tugged at the chains. "Every knee will bend."

Dropping to their knees, Dissension groaned louder and Doubt whimpered, "Why torture us? Let us go. We will leave the children alone. Don't make us look upon . . . Him."

Father Carston placed the Blessed Sacrament in the monstrance, knelt, and whispered a prayer.

The angels fell prostrate and worshiped the Lord of lords and King of kings, hidden to human eyes but not to them. "Holy, holy, holy is the Lord," they sang with one voice. Glorious prayers of praise and adoration rang out, and grace burst forth.

CHAPTER SEVEN

SCHEMES

Ellechial

Ellechial prayed as he watched his charge.

Jarret moved to the beat of the song that blasted through his computer speakers. He stuffed a pack of cigarettes into an outer pocket of his carry-on bag and strutted to the walk-in closet. He yanked two shirts from hangers and laid them on the bed. With folded arms and narrowed eyes, he appraised the shirts, both of which had cost him a sinful amount of money. Having packed almost everything he wanted to bring, his two suitcases and carry-on bag could hold no more.

With his gaze on the white Diesel polo, he picked up the tan-striped Marc by Marc Jacobs cotton knit. "Roland," he mumbled, staring at the shirt. "I'll wear this and stash that one in Roland's suitcase. Yeah." He grinned.

Ellechial sighed. Tomorrow morning Jarret would be on a plane headed for Arizona. Then he would spend the next few weeks in the home of the Zamoranos where, for him, challenges and temptations would abound. If only Keefe could change his mind and convince him to stay home. Keefe's new openness to God could make him instrumental in leading Jarret's thoughts to the spiritual side of life. He could help him recognize that God had been tugging at his heart.

After a brief prayer, Ellechial passed through the bedroom door and into the hallway.

Roland's voice traveled from his bedroom through the open door. "I'm not afraid of him. And I really want to see where my father grew up. Why should I let him change my mind?"

In the open area of Roland's room, between the bed and the window, Peter held a sword aloft and bounced on his feet like a boxer. Grunting, he lunged toward the wall. "I wouldn't go anywhere with him, even if he were my brother, which, thank God, he's not."

"He's not that bad." Roland set a stack of dark t-shirts in the open suitcase on his bed and turned to the dresser. "Don't worry about it. I think you only want me to stay so you can practice fencing."

"Maybe you're right." Peter chuckled, lowered the foil, and wiped the sweat from his brow. "Finish packing and let's go duel outside somewhere, but not near the house. I don't want Jarret interfering again. And I don't want him to think of me when my plan unfolds."

Ellechial sighed. What was Peter's plan? Jarret had enough temptation.

Roland glanced at Peter through the mirror over his dresser. "You know he's going to blame me."

"Na." Peter plopped onto the bed, knocking over the pile of t-shirts in the suitcase. "Have you ever pulled a prank on him? He'll know it was me. He'll suspect as soon as he gets the note."

"Where'd you put the note?"

"It's on his dresser, right where his car keys were." He glanced at the open bedroom door. "I'm surprised he hasn't gone to the rec room for them already." He stood. "Come on. Let's get outta here. I don't want to be nearby when the confetti falls."

With a few shorts and socks in hand, Roland returned to the suitcase. "What if it doesn't work?"

"It'll work." Peter scooted to the doorway and peeked down the hall. Rock music blared from Jarret's room.

He faced Roland again, folded his arms and leaned against the dresser, a smug grin stretching across his face. "I tied fishing line to the key ring, put the keys on the desk in the rec room, and ran the line around a hook in the back of the desk. The line goes right up to the ceiling. So when he picks up his keys, it'll pull the line and tip the overhead tray. Then colorful glitter will shower down . . ." He wiggled his fingers. ". . . and get stuck in his lovely black curls."

Peter combed his fingers through his blond hair, grinning. "I can't wait. I'd like to see it happen . . . but from a distance. Maybe we can watch from outside, through the windows in the family room."

Peter pushed off the dresser and strolled to the bedroom window. "Think we could? If we can't see inside the rec room from there, at least we'd see him coming out . . . all full of rage, sparkles in his hair."

Roland shook his head. "He'll kill you, you know."

Peter laughed. "He'll try."

"Besides, I thought you were doing something with Limburger cheese."

"I did. Before I set up the confetti, I hid Limburger cheese in his car. He'll find it when he gets back from Arizona." Peter paced, gazing up at the ceiling. "Let's see, you'll be gone a few weeks, right? His car ought to smell like an outhouse by the time he discovers it. I wonder how you get that smell—"

Peter's eyes grew wide at the sound of footfalls, but it was only Keefe stomping up the stairs.

Monettello greeted Ellechial with a nod and then raised a brow at Ellechial's tunic. He had no doubt grown accustomed to seeing Ellechial in the long robes.

Ellechial smoothed his short tunic, happy to be wearing the garb of an angel with permission to travel. "The prayer group. Keefe prayed especially for Jarret. I am thankful."

"Ah." Monettello smiled. "I am happy for you."

"I'd hoped the two of you would arrive soon," Ellechial said. "Has Keefe come to speak with Jarret?"

"He has." Monettello did not stop at Jarret's door but continued down the hall toward the open doorway of Roland's bedroom. "But first, there is something he must hear."

Keefe stopped and stood still as a statue at Jarret's door, his fist poised to knock. A second later, he faced Roland's bedroom doorway.

Roland and Peter's conversation had turned from Jarret to the guests at the Brandt's bed and breakfast. A group of Franciscan brothers was scheduled to arrive soon.

Monettello smiled, watching Keefe. "Well, come on. You know you want to hear more. Come." He made a welcoming motion toward the doorway as if Keefe could see him. "Ask Peter."

Keefe took a step in that direction but then stopped and rubbed his forehead.

"You know, brown robes and bald heads," Peter said to Roland. "Do you think they'll all be bald? You know, with that little strip of hair? What's it called?"

Roland gave no audible answer.

Peter continued talking. "Anyway, there'll be half a dozen of them, I guess. And they're staying free. You can thank Father Carston for that. He must not think it costs money to run a bed and breakfast. But I guess he knows them, the brothers or friars or whatever, and he told them . . ."

The music in Jarret's room ceased.

Keefe's gaze snapped to Jarret's door. He immediately lifted his fist and knocked with his own unique beat that Jarret would undoubtedly recognize.

Monettello closed his eyes and shook his head. "Jarret still has quite a pull on Keefe. I hope Keefe has heard enough, that the seed has been planted."

"Seed?" Ellechial said.

"What d'ya want?" Jarret said through the closed door.

Keefe opened the door and strolled into the room. His gaze fixed on the luggage. "So you're really going, huh?" He sat on the bed. Monettello sat beside him.

Jarret shrugged, not bothering to look up from his laptop.

"Does Keefe want Jarret to stay?" Ellechial said.

Monettello gazed at Keefe before answering. "I believe he does. I believe he sees the same opportunity that you do, should the two of them be alone here for a few weeks. He is anxious to regain Jarret's friendship and trust."

"What made you change your mind about going?" Keefe said.

Jarret glanced. "I need a change of pace."

"Trying to get away from me?"

"Maybe."

Keefe sighed and shook his head. "I was hoping you'd stay. I wish you weren't so mad at me. I never did anything to you. I just see things differently now."

Ellechial nodded, thankful for Keefe's words. But Jarret hadn't even blinked an eye.

"You sure hold a grudge for a long time," Keefe said.

"Grudge? I ain't got no grudge against you." Jarret shut off and closed his laptop with one hand, reaching for the case with the other.

"You don't talk to me anymore. And I think you avoid me. Like you see me coming and you go the other way."

Jarret managed a crooked grin.

"I wish you'd get over it," Keefe said. "And I see what you're up to lately. It's like you've got a death-wish or something. I saw Roland's mountain bike. What'd you do to wreck it like that? Were you hurt?"

Jarret snickered and slung the strap of the computer case over his shoulder. "Just having a little fun."

"I saw your speeding ticket."

Jarret's eyes darkened. His gaze snapped to the ticket lying on the dresser. "You snooping around my room?" He stomped to the dresser and stuffed the ticket into a drawer. Then he reached for the corner of his dresser, where he typically kept his car keys.

A note, not the keys, lay there.

He snatched the note and read it, a scowl twisting his face. He spun around with an accusing glare. "Did you write this?"

Keefe stepped closer and read the note. *Looking for your keys? Try the rec room.* "No, I didn't write that."

Jarret shook his head, distrust in his eyes. "Why are my keys in the rec room?"

"I don't know. But before you go, let's talk."

"Talk? Let me guess, you want me to think like you do. Want me to give up doing what I want. Want me to think about my *soul*. You want me to be you." He laughed coolly. "No thanks. If you want to be friends, come back to my side."

At his words, Deth-kye appeared now as a small, sooty cloud near Jarret's ear. "Controlling. Restrictive," he whispered, "Keefe has become your enemy. Close your ears to him." Hissing filled the air as his form stretched and grew to its regular height and lanky shape.

"Why do we have to be on sides?" Keefe said as Jarret bolted from the room.

Jarret stormed down the steps.

"You need to think about the direction your life is taking," Keefe said, his voice cracking. He followed Jarret, a few steps behind. "Are you the least bit happy?"

Without slowing or even glancing at Keefe, Jarret stuck a hand in the air and flipped Keefe the bird. As he rounded the corner, Deth-kye flew up and alighted on his shoulder.

Ellechial prayed.

"Remember the talks that Papa gave you?" Deth-kye whispered. "Remember the one at the prison-monastery? Restrictive. Controlling. Remember . . ."

Jarret

Papa gave him the talk that first day on the monastery grounds when Jarret had wanted to go for a walk alone. They strolled down the gravel path near the guest quarters. A bell tolled. Jarret turned to locate the bell tower.

"We'll need to get used to that." Papa said, packing his pipe. "The bell tolls seven times a day for prayer. Hopefully, we won't wake at the 3:00 AM toll."

"3:00 AM?" Jarret shook his head and sneered. Could it get any worse?

"Yeah, they pray at all hours." Papa looked at his watch. "They'll be eating soon. But don't worry, we won't eat with them. They keep silence during their meals. We'll eat in the guests' dining room." He nodded toward a building behind a huge black oak tree.

The monks took good care of the grounds, Jarret would give them that. Mowed lawns, flowering bushes, manicured trees, and a little fishpond with sparkling water behind some chapel-like building. Mr.

Digby, their family's groundskeeper, couldn't have done it better himself, not even with his obsessive-compulsive bent.

"Over there . . ." Papa pointed with his pipe to a long, brick building with several garage doors, off in the distance. "That's the winery."

"Winery?" Jarret perked up and gave the building a good long look. He would definitely check it out . . . if Papa ever gave him some space.

"And the monks' cloister line runs on this side of the winery."

"Cloister line?"

"They maintain silence most of the day in the cloister. So if you come across a monk, just nod. Don't ask him anything. If you have any questions, we'll have to ask Brother Mario."

"Brother Mario?"

Papa lit his pipe and carelessly dropped the match. "He's the one we met already."

They strolled toward a dirt road that cut through the vineyards.

"So," Jarret said, "you wanna tell me what we're doing here, exactly?"

"Sure. The monks discovered a room or part of a tunnel behind one of the walls in the winery cellar. They believe there are more tunnels. An older monk remembered some rumors of an underground hiding place where valuables from ransacked churches were once hidden. Those items are blessed, sacred. So, they want us to investigate."

"Sounds like an odd assignment to me." Papa often worked with archaeological excavation teams or did geological surveys and that sort of work, but this? "They're paying you to find this stuff?"

Papa smiled at the orange sun hanging low in the sky. His graying hair and weathered skin made him seem old and tired, but he also had a youthful, ready-for-any-challenge look about him. "No, Jarret, I'm not getting paid for this one."

"What?" The blood rushed to his head. A vein in his forehead throbbed. Papa's generosity irked him sometimes, but to make him a part *of it . . .* "Not getting paid? You don't know these monks. Why are we here? I mean, for real. This is about me, isn't it?"

Papa puffed on his pipe and exhaled a cloud of smoke. They turned down the dirt road. Papa finally spoke. "You're right. I thought the trip would be good for you."

Jarret glared at him, not ready for the talk that he full well expected to get on this trip, but knowing it was about to begin. He wouldn't be on this trip at all if Papa hadn't come up to school unannounced and happened to see Zoe with her seven-month-pregnant belly. A month earlier, Papa had threatened him and his brothers about respecting girls.

"You've made some bad choices lately." He paused, his gaze flicking toward Jarret's waist. "For example, I know you smoke."

Jarret gulped. His hand shot to the back pocket of his jeans. Had Papa seen the pack of cigarettes?

"But that's not what bothers me the most."

When Papa directed his gaze to the sun again, Jarret pulled out his pack. Since Papa already knew, why bother hiding it? After all, Papa was smoking. Maybe they could bond over a smoke.

"Jarret, you're seventeen. You'll be a senior next year and a legal adult in a few months. It's time you start thinking about where your life is headed. Sometimes it helps to get away from things. Without all the distractions . . ." He gestured at the surroundings. ". . . maybe you can think more clearly. Pray. Ask the Lord—" He turned as Jarret lit up.

Jarret took a long drag off the cigarette, calming instantly. He took another step before realizing Papa had stopped walking.

Papa squinted at him and then snatched the cigarette from his hand. "What in the Sam Hill are you thinking, Jarret?" He crushed the cigarette under his boot. "I said I know you smoke. I didn't say I liked it. I didn't say it was okay. Are you trying to get my back up? You need to show some respect. You're not going to smoke right here in front of me." He glared hard for a long moment.

Jarret averted his gaze.

"Now listen. I'm not going to search you or your luggage for cigarettes. I'm going to trust you to get rid of them. Do you understand me? I want you to quit."

Jarret stared at the wasted cigarette on the ground, then he met Papa's gaze. "I'm gonna be eighteen in less than year. And when I'm eighteen, I'm gonna smoke in front of you. I'm gonna smoke with you."

Papa's eyes twitched, but he made no reply.

CHAPTER EIGHT

WELCOME TO ARIZONA

Jarret

The hot morning air slapped Jarret in the face the instant he stepped out of Tucson International Airport. Bald mountains rose up in the distance under a hazy sky. Papa and Roland loaded luggage into the rental car, but Jarret had no interest in helping. He stood gaping at the mountains. He had expected Arizona to have a dry, boring landscape, but the utter lack of greenery came as a shock.

He slid into the back seat of the air-conditioned rental car and slammed the door. "Why did I ever agree to go on this trip?" he muttered. In this heat, he'd be trapped indoors. And how big was their house? Big enough to accommodate him, Roland, and Papa, along with the Zamorano family of six? What if he didn't like them?

He leaned his head back and groaned.

An hour later, they *finally* turned down a residential street. They passed a few rundown ranch houses and a long stretch of nothing but clumps of dry grass before the Zamoranos' house came into view.

His spirits lifted at once.

The Zamoranos did not live in an ordinary house. Their home was more like a mansion: balconies decorated with potted cacti, fancy wrought iron grills on all the lower windows, pale stucco walls, a red-tile roof, and an archway over a front porch flanked with thick columns. Yeah, the Zamoranos' sprawling, two-story Spanish Colonial home even made the barren landscape attractive.

The rental car pulled up the long drive. Jarret jumped out first, ready to explore the place. Roland got out next, mumbling to himself. He turned full circle, still mumbling to himself, saying something about the *great* weather and the pale dirt.

Papa unfolded himself from the car, stretched, yawned, combed a hand through his hair, and adjusted his cowboy hat.

"Let's go," Jarret said with a jerk of his hand. He followed Papa to the carved front door.

A wrinkled Mexican woman, who hadn't the hint of a smile, opened the door to them. She spoke to them in Spanish as she led them through the foyer.

Her words went back and forth in Jarret's mind. Mama used to speak Spanish all the time, years ago. The words began to make sense. "*Señor* Zamorano will be with you shortly," the woman had said.

They entered a spacious, vibrantly colored sitting room. Jarret breathed deeply and grinned.

Large paintings of Mexican scenes—a bullfight, women in colorful dresses, and a fiesta—placed high on the pale walls, gave the room an old-world feel. Light streamed in through tall windows and refracted through the crystal prisms of a chandelier, casting patterns on the leather and dark wooden Western furniture in the middle of the room. Tall vases and spiky plants stood in the corners.

Papa took a seat on a couch, propped a boot on the coffee table, but then slid his boot to the floor. Scuff marks on the edge of the table suggested he wasn't the only one who made himself at home in this room.

"I think I'm gonna like it here," Jarret said to Roland. The two of them stood outside the arrangement of furniture, sizing up the place. Three sets of double doors came off the sitting room: the one that they had come through and two others with colorful, painted doorknobs.

"Yeah?" The half-open door on the far side of the room held Roland's attention. He took off the black Stetson he had bought at the airport and ran his fingers through his hair. "Why's that?" Roland said. "You've been complaining since the jet touched down."

"Are you kidding me? This place is the bomb. Servants, stables, a big pool . . . Yeah, I'm gonna like it here. It's like a deluxe resort. I'm gonna kick back and have myself a good old time."

Roland jerked his head toward the half-open door again.

Jarret looked, too, and glimpsed a girl in a yellow sundress. Roughly their age and with long dark hair, she reminded him of Zoe. "Who's that?"

Roland blushed and glanced at Papa. "How should I know?"

"Well, you were staring—"

The other set of doors opened and *Señor* Juan Zamorano breezed into the room with an attractive forty-something woman on his arm and a little girl behind him. Tall with wide shoulders, tidy black hair, a trim mustache, a strong jaw, and a bolo tie, he was older now but Jarret recognized him at once.

Papa jumped to his feet and met him in the middle of the room. "Juan." Papa spoke with a hint of emotion. He squeezed Juan's hand and pulled him into a bear hug.

"Ignatius, my friend, I am happy to see you." *Señor* Juan's voice boomed. He couldn't have been more than ten years older than Papa, but the composed way he carried himself and his teary eyes made him come across like he was Papa's adoptive father or a mentor or something.

Señor Juan turned to Jarret and Roland. He smiled and shook his head as if in disbelief. *"Bienvenido.* I remember you both as little boys. You, Roland, were still in diapers."

Roland's face flushed. He shoved his hands into the front pockets of his jeans as *Señor* Zamorano reached to shake hands. "Sir, I mean *Señor,"* Roland stammered, jerking his hand from his pocket.

"You probably do not remember me at all, or my wife *Señora* Kemina." He shook hands with Roland and Jarret then gestured to the woman.

Señora Kemina greeted Papa. Then she smiled and gave Papa a hug that made him lose his hat. As pretty as she was now, she must've been totally hot in her younger years. A Mexican beauty, Papa would say.

The little girl stood with her hands behind her back, staring through round brown eyes, watching everybody.

"This is our youngest daughter, Rosa," *Señora* Kemina said, smiling with obvious affection for the girl.

Still with her hands behind her back, Rosa gave a little curtsy.

"Where is Selena?" *Señor* Juan turned toward the doors they came through and looked at the old servant woman as if he'd just realized Selena's absence. The woman shrugged. In Spanish, he asked her to fetch the girl. Muttering, she left the room.

Señor Juan motioned for everyone to sit. He took the chair cattycorner to the couch where Papa sat. "I know it was short notice," he said to Papa, "but I am glad you came. I do not ask for favors often. You do know I appreciate it."

"Favors?" Jarret whispered to Roland as the two of them took a seat on the couch opposite Papa.

Roland shrugged.

"Should've figured." Jarret spoke low so that only Roland would hear. "He's gonna put us to work . . . like he always does when we go places. I should've stayed home. I'm not doing it. Whatever it is, I'm not doing it."

"Maybe *Papa's* doing something for him. He would've told us if he expected us—" Roland's attention snapped to the doors on the far side of the room.

"Would he?" Jarret looked to see what had caused Roland to blush again.

The girl in the yellow sundress came into the room, gaining everyone's attention. She gave a polite nod in Jarret and Roland's direction but bounced right over to Papa. Papa visited the Zamoranos once every two or three years, by himself, so it made sense that she knew him well enough to run to him. But the smile she gave him sure was *fly*.

Papa got up and hugged her. "Selena, how are you?"

"I am good, *Tio* Ignace." Clutching his hand, she sat down beside him and gushed over him.

"Makes you jealous, huh?" Jarret mumbled to Roland. "Sure hope she ain't our cousin." Selena might be just the girl to get his mind off Zoe. Interesting . . . they both had long black hair. He loved long black hair on a girl.

Roland jabbed him with his elbow.

"*Tio* means uncle," Jarret said, thinking Roland needed the explanation. "Which would make her our—"

"I know." He glared as he whispered, "The Zamoranos aren't related to us. Just because Mama was part Mexican and they were friends, doesn't mean—"

"Shut up." Jarret glared. Roland was an idiot. Couldn't he get a joke?

The Zamoranos had been talking with Papa about his work when *Señor* Juan looked at Selena again. "Selena, why do you not show the boys around the house and grounds? They would like to see the stables and the pool, I am sure."

Selena blinked a few times at her father, and then her gaze shifted to Jarret and Roland.

"I uh . . ." Roland leaned forward, his eyes on Papa. "I really want to see your house, the place where you grew up."

Papa's eye twitched. "Oh. No you don't. I mean, not right now. How about another day for that?" He looked to *Señor* Juan. "I'm sure Rufino—"

"Don't be silly. Now is a very good time. Rufino is dying to see you." *Señor* Juan stood. "You don't mind to see a little clutter, I hope."

Papa chuckled. "It's not my house anymore."

The sun beat down with fierce determination and reflected off the stone path that cut through the hard, dry dirt in the front yard. Selena and Papa led the way to the little house down the road. Roland and Jarret followed at a distance so they could talk without being overheard. Roland put on and adjusted his black cowboy hat.

"You gonna wear that every day now?" Jarret said.

"What, the hat? Probably."

"Trying to fit in?" He grinned, knowing his comment would annoy *Roland West, Loner*.

"No." Roland didn't appear the least bit annoyed. "It keeps the sun out of my eyes."

"You mean off your pale skin. I know, you're trying to be the *Pale Rider*."

"The pale rider?"

"Yeah. Clint Eastwood . . . Spaghetti Western . . ."

Roland shook his head and huffed.

"I'm gonna start calling you that. The *Pale Rider*." Jarret grinned. Nothing satisfied him more than riling up certain people, especially Roland. That reminded him of what Peter had done to him. "I still owe you anyway, for that prank. You know how long it took to get that glitter outta my hair?"

Roland smirked and averted his gaze. "I had nothing to do with that."

"Peter's your friend, and he's back home. Not much I can do to get him back. So there's just you."

"But I had nothing to do with it." His voice squeaked. "Besides, you already destroyed my bike. Can't we call it even?"

"Hey!" Papa motioned for them to hurry up. He and Selena had reached a dinky, little house no bigger than a trailer.

"I don't want to go in," Jarret said to Roland. "The place looks like a dump. If Papa grew up there, it's gotta be over forty years old."

"So wait outside." Roland picked up his pace, reaching them as the screen door swung open.

"Hey, *amigo*." A scrawny, shirtless man stood in the doorway, giving them a lazy smile. "You are here already?" About Papa's age but more weathered, he sounded tired and moved like he had molasses running through his veins. "I guess you want to come in." He held the screen with one hand and backed out of the way.

Either the place was very dark or Jarret's eyes wouldn't adjust. The walls seemed to close in on him, and the place smelled funny, so he stayed near the door.

"My air conditioner does not work so good, little *amigo*," Rufino said, nodding for Jarret to move. "Have to keep the door closed."

Jarret stepped aside.

Papa, Roland, and Selena strolled to the kitchen, but Jarret remained near the door, hoping they wouldn't stay long. As his eyes adjusted, he saw why they didn't go to the living room to talk. The couch had clothes and piles of junk on it, and the recliner looked like Rufino probably slept in it every night. And what was the sweet, oily smell that lingered in the air?

"Zamoranos tell you what has been going on over there?" Rufino took a seat at a Formica-topped table-for-two and opened a bottle.

"A little," Papa said with a shifty glance at Jarret and Roland. He shuffled to the sliding glass door off the dinette and gazed out at a flat backyard of dirt.

Rufino took a swig from the bottle. "*Señora* Kemina, she thinks it is somebody close to the family, maybe a friend. There was a party there the first time it—"

"Rufino." Papa threw him a squinty-eyed glare and then turned to Roland. "So this is where I grew up. Nothing to it, huh? I mean my folks owned some land, farmland, you know. Zamoranos own it now but . . ."

"I like it," Roland said. "It's simple. It's all you need."

Jarret huffed. Roland could live in a cardboard box. This place couldn't have more than two bedrooms. There wouldn't be a shred of privacy. The only advantage would be the rich neighbor. Growing up, Papa probably spent all his time—

He caught movement out of the corner of his eye. Something on the coffee table rolled.

The coffee table was a cluttered mess, covered with dirty cups and dishes, junk mail, TV remotes, and science magazines. A paper had probably settled. But wait . . .

Something white and thin—a cigarette?—stuck out from under a magazine. If it was a cigarette, Rufino rolled his own. But the smell in the house . . . Yeah, now that he thought about it, he recognized that sweet smell.

Jarret chuckled. Rufino smoked weed.

Returning his gaze to the kitchen, he found Papa staring at him. Papa glanced at the coffee table, looked back at him, and his eyes narrowed.

A wave of heat washed over Jarret as if he'd been caught doing something wrong. No way had Papa seen the joint from the kitchen. Jarret stuck his thumbs in his belt loops. "Can we get going?"

Papa shook his head and returned to his conversation with Roland, talking about his boring ol' past. The two of them shuffled down the hallway and stood in a doorway, yapping more. Selena and Rufino stayed in the kitchen, Selena with folded arms, Rufino flirting with her. Selena flashed a fake smile at Rufino and turned away from him to face the sliding glass doors. Rufino kept on as if he hadn't noticed her rejection.

When Papa returned from his jaunt down the hall, Jarret got a glimmer of hope that they could leave, but then Rufino started telling a tale about some mountain nearby. Apparently, Rufino had lived in some other dinky house down the street, and he and Papa had played together growing up. They dared each other to climb this mountain at night and bla, bla, bla. Jarret tuned out the rest of the story.

Rufino had another tale, which Papa made him stop telling. It must've been something wild that Papa had done but didn't want to admit to in front of his boys.

"Hey," Jarret shouted so Papa would know he was talking to him, "I'm gonna head back."

"Hold your horses." Papa pushed off the wall and straightened up. "There's something I want you to—"

"No." Jarret looked at Selena now. "You gonna show me the rest of the place?"

Selena opened her mouth and then glanced at Papa. "Um, I suppose—"

"Jarret," Papa said, a hard edge in his tone, "you can wait until—"

"I'm not here to work. This is my vacation. See ya back at the house." Jarret yanked open the door, bolted out alone, and didn't look back.

Squinting against the sunlight, his gaze fixed on the mansion, he strutted along. A moment later, someone came running up behind him. He didn't bother looking to see who.

"Jarret."

At the sound of Selena's voice, he stopped and turned around.

She slowed her pace and lowered her head, watching her steps as she approached. Black hair cascaded over her face and bounced with every step. She stopped a few feet away, tucked her hair behind her ear, and met his gaze. "If you're on vacation, why are you in such a hurry?"

"You gonna give me the tour?"

She stared. Then, instead of heading for the front door, she cut around to the back of the house. He followed.

They reached the backyard, and his attention snapped to a long, curvy swimming pool under the shade of a pergola. The calm aqua blue water called to him. He could almost see himself diving in, feel the cool water refreshing his sweaty skin and giving him goose bumps when he got out.

Selena glanced at the pool and at him but didn't stop. She led him down a stone walkway that wound through a garden of cacti, grasses, and big rocks. The walkway branched off to two stone patios with umbrellas and outdoor furniture, and two sets of glass patio doors.

Jarret set his sights on the glass door, anxious to feel a cold burst of air as he stepped inside, but Selena strolled out into the yard, toward a fenced horse corral.

"Do you see the far fence?" Selena leaned against the wooden fence and flung out her slender arm, pointing.

He squinted. Beyond the horse corral, acres of pale dirt stretched out to a desert landscape spotted with scruffy plants, and purple mesas along the horizon. A little white building with a cross on top sat off to the right. He thought sure that he saw a fence farther back, white against a row of dull green shrubs.

"I see it," he said.

"Our land goes beyond it. I take the horses out there." She smiled but not at him.

"How far out do you ride?"

"We have orange markers to show where our property ends. It could be dangerous to go out too far, to go past our boundaries."

"Dangerous, huh?" He smiled and wanted to give her a flirty glance, but the horizon held her gaze.

"The canyons sneak up on you and there is rough terrain. You can lose your direction or get stuck if you're not careful. And the rattlesnakes. They can spook a horse, you know."

"So you don't go out that far, huh?"

She looked at him, straight-faced, not answering, probably not wanting to lie. His take: she rode out as far as she wanted. She wasn't afraid of anything.

He smiled.

She didn't smile back, but her eyes twinkled as if she were amused. "Why are you so rude to your father?"

"Rude? Me? I'm not rude. He's always trying to put me to work, that's all. We can't go anywhere without it involving work. He flat out told me this was vacation."

A smile stretched across her face, a smile for him, finally. "Are you thirsty? I'll make lemonade." She pushed off the fence and glanced over her shoulder at the house. "If your brother is back, I'll bring him out too. We can sit in the shade." She flashed another smile, one that he couldn't interpret, and then bounced to the house.

He shielded his eyes from the sunlight and gazed at the mesas. Why did Papa always put them to work when they went places? He rarely made them work at home. Papa sure enough made him work at that monastery in California. He did nothing but work there. Nothing but work . . .

"Here, hold these." Papa handed Jarret a small statue of Jesus, then one of Mary.

Jarret backed away and looked for a place to set them.

A few minutes ago, a silent monk had come to their room and led them across the grounds to the winery. The building was longer than Jarret remembered from his first glance. As they descended the stone steps to the cellar, he peered into darkness which seemed to go on forever in either direction.

The monk glided past rows of wooden shelves filled with bottles of wine and directed them to a dark corner. He motioned toward a sheet that hung on the wall over a table, and then he left them to their business.

"These are your crates, right?" Jarret set the statues on one of two wood crates nearby. Papa had said something about shipping his supplies ahead of them.

"Uh, yeah." Papa snatched the statues from the crate and shoved them at Jarret. "Put these someplace else." He waved his hand as if he were swooshing a fly, without indicating any particular place.

Jarret ventured a few feet into the darkness and set them on the first thing he came to, an old, dusty cart. The distant wine shelves rose up like a wall and dim light showed in the direction they had come from, but he could make out nothing else. The few glowing bulbs that hung from the high ceiling did little to drive away the dark. His skin crawled.

He zipped back to Papa. "Why isn't there any light in this cellar?"

"Grab an end." Papa had started without him, moving the wooden table away from the wall, scraping it along the concrete floor.

Jarret lifted one end and helped lug the table to a different wall.

Papa wiped his hands on his jeans and opened one of the crates. A few minutes later, he had a dozen lanterns, safety goggles, gloves, and a sledgehammer laid out on the table. He put the goggles on, picked up the sledgehammer, and yanked the sheet from the wall.

"Turn on one of those lanterns," Papa said. "Let's see what we got here."

A hole about two feet across and chest-high opened to utter darkness. Papa spent a moment peering through the opening, lantern in hand, then stepped back. "That little crack . . ." He pointed to small hole in the bottom of the wall, directly under the larger hole. ". . . and a rat started this whole thing."

"Huh?"

"Brother Maurus, one of the monks who tends the winery, was pestered by a rat, so he followed it. It squeezed right through that crack. Got him curious about what was behind the wall."

Jarret's gaze went to the chest-high hole. He grinned, considering the audacity of the monk. "So he tore apart the wall?"

Papa chuckled. "Curiosity can be a dangerous thing."

"Now that's a monk I'd like to meet."

"Stand back." Papa drew the sledgehammer back and with a batter's swing let go at the wall. It was a good, strong swing, but only a few stones so much as shifted and sighed. Bringing the sledgehammer back, he made ready again.

"Why don't you let me have at it?" Jarret snatched a pair of goggles.

Papa surrendered the sledgehammer with a smirk and stepped out of the way. "It's all yours."

The sledgehammer had some weight to it. It felt good to swing it and slam it into the wall. Stones budged at the impact, smaller pieces sprinkling to the ground behind the wall.

Grunting, Jarret swung again and again, a cool sweat gathering on his chest. The hole widened. Stones caved in and dropped down. His mind went numb to all else, as it did toward the end of his workouts on his weight-set at home, the burning in his muscles giving him a sort of high that made him crave more.

"Jarret. Jarret, that's good."

Papa's voice sounded distant but it snapped him from his trance. He lessened his grip on the sledgehammer and studied his accomplishment. He'd made a jagged opening the size of a door. It opened to pitch-blackness.

"Good job. You saved my back." Papa rubbed Jarret's shoulder and pried the sledgehammer from him, eyeing him strangely. "You all right?"

"Yeah. Why wouldn't I be?" Chest heaving, Jarret took a few deep breaths through his mouth to regulate his breathing. "That's what you wanted, right?"

Papa nodded. "It's perfect." He shoved a lantern at Jarret and nodded toward the new doorway. "After you."

"Huh?" Jarret pushed the lantern away. "You want me to go in there?" His heart pounded from the workout, but it skipped a beat and his skin crawled at the thought of stepping into the darkness, the unknown. "You go on ahead. I'll wait out here and catch my breath."

"I didn't know you were afraid of the dark." Papa's eyes lit up, making him look downright amused.

"I'm not. I'm just not going in there. Who knows what's back there?"

"That's what we're here to find out."

"That's what you're here to find out. I'm here to contemplate my sins, remember?"

Papa chuckled, slapped a lantern into his hand, and shoved him through the hole.

CHAPTER NINE

HACIENDA

Ellechial

Ellechial prayed while tending to his charge.

Jarret rested his forearms on the fence and gazed without focus, his heartbeat and breaths coming slow and steady. His mind most likely wandered in the past.

Ellechial knew that demons often used memories to ensnare one in feelings of guilt or to lure one back into a sinful relationship. Deth-kye, however, seemed to be using them to enflame Jarret to hostility toward authority, religion, and faith. He preferred for Jarret to trust in himself and follow the desires of his heart. Yet, whenever Jarret did so, Deth-kye never failed to accuse Jarret and to remind him of his wickedness. His plan, Ellechial now realized, was to use the memories of Jarret's experience in the monastery to convince him that God had no interest in him. He was too bad for God to forgive, to love, to want. Religion was simply a trap, a way for some people to control others.

The glass door off the back of the house slid open and Selena stepped outside.

Ellechial rejoiced. Selena would snap Jarret from his destructive thoughts.

Jarret turned at the sound of her footfalls as she approached. His heartbeat quickened and his pupils dilated.

"Roland's in the house," she said. "He wants to stay inside. Come on in. You can watch me make a pitcher of lemonade."

Without protest, he walked alongside her to the sliding glass door.

Nadriel and Roland sat at an oval, cherry-wood table in a breakfast nook off the spacious kitchen. Sunlight illuminated tall bay windows behind them, though the high ceilings maintained a comfortable level of shade.

Selena invited Jarret to sit at the table as she bounced around a counter into a kitchen of cobalt blue with lemon yellow and chili-pepper-red accents. She set to work with a juicer and several lemon-halves, a canister of sugar, a pitcher, a container of ice, and three glasses nearby.

Jarret took Nadriel's seat. "Well, *Pale Rider,* I hope you got that outta your system," he mumbled to Roland while he watched Selena work.

Nadriel alighted by Ellechial.

"Got *what* out of my system?" Roland ran his fingers through his sweaty hair. The cowboy hat had left an impression in his wavy hair.

"All that about Papa and his past. What do you care how he grew up? You should be worried about what's going on with him now." Jarret glanced at Roland as he spoke, but his focus remained on Selena.

She had been trying to use tongs to get ice from a container but ended up using her hands.

"What do you mean?" Roland furrowed his brows. "What's going on with Papa?"

Jarret grinned, seeming pleased that he knew something Roland didn't. "He's got something going on with Miss Meadows. Don't you know that?"

"No, but so what? She's nice. I thought he liked her, back when we had to help with that dig in Mississippi, right before you ruined things for them." He shook his head. "I can't believe you did that."

Ellechial sighed. After being a widow for eight years, their father had finally found love again. Jarret, however, told their father that he, Roland, and Keefe didn't like the idea. So their father backed off from the relationship for a time. He shouldn't have. Jarret had only wanted to distract his father and avoid admitting to his impure relationship with Zoe and her resulting pregnancy.

Jarret chuckled. "What did you expect me to do? You guys set me up, telling him that I had something serious to talk about. I had to say something."

"Who Papa sees is none of our business."

"Really?" Jarret folded his arms on the table and leaned toward Roland, an annoyed grin on his face. "You want a step-mother? Somebody else bossing you around? 'Cuz I sure don't."

Selena glided around the counter, glasses of lemonade in her hands. She slid one to each of them, simultaneously. "I hope you like it. I don't use that much sugar."

Jarret took a sip. "Never had better."

She smiled, tucked her hair behind her ear, and sat across from them.

"So how does it feel to live in a mansion straight out of Hollywood?" Jarret said.

"Don't let Papá hear you say that." While she used the same term for her father that the West boys used for theirs, she pronounced it differently, stressing the second syllable. "This is his *hacienda*." She smiled. "Besides, I know you live in a castle."

"Our castle ain't nothing like this," Jarret said. "I mean it's big, and my father's got a thing for antiques, but this place is like a luxury hotel. A *hacienda* he calls it? So where are the *peones*?"

She laughed. "No *peones*. We have *vaqueros*."

"What?" Roland looked from one the other.

"*Vaqueros*. Mounted ranch hands. But Papá is generous. He treats all the hands like family. Everyone is part of the *hacienda* society, so there are no peasants, no *peones*. That is his weakness." She gazed at her glass, twisting it back and forth. "He is too trusting."

Roland brought his glass to his mouth but set it down again. "What did Rufino mean? He wondered if your father had told my father something. Something's going on over here? He said *Señora*, your mother I guess, thinks someone close to the family is, well, I guess responsible for . . . whatever. Do you know what he's talking about?"

Jarret settled back in his chair and rolled his eyes. "Maybe it's none of our business."

Ellechial and Nadriel exchanged a glance. Jarret had never been one to mind his own business. He had only said it, no doubt, to impress Selena.

"It *is* your business," Selena said. "That's why you're here. Your father did not tell you?" She reached for Jarret's empty glass. "Would you like more?"

"More of what?" He gave her a crooked grin.

She narrowed her eyes and took his glass to the counter. "Someone has been taking things from the house and the chapel."

"What?" Roland straightened up. "You mean stealing?"

"Yes, stealing." She returned with a full glass of lemonade and slid it across the table to Jarret.

He nodded his thanks. "What does that have to do with us?"

She shrugged. "Papá always calls on your father when he wants something investigated. Maybe he doesn't know what an archaeologist really does." She giggled. "Maybe he thinks he does investigative work."

Jarret and Roland both smiled at her.

Their affection for her showed in their eyes. Hopefully, it wouldn't lead to uncharitable competition. Ellechial sent a prayer up to heaven.

"So, Papa's supposed to check it out, huh?" Roland looked at Jarret as he spoke.

Jarret shrugged. "Like he told me something?"

"I don't know what he's here to do," Selena said. "I only suppose it has to do with the . . . stealing."

"Maybe we can help." Roland glanced from Jarret to Selena.

"Maybe *you* can help," Jarret said. "I'm on vacation."

"I'd love to help," Selena said, and Jarret's eyes snapped to her.

"I was thinking I'd like to get to know the hands," Roland said, "especially the ones who knew my father when he was young. So now I have two reasons."

"Man, you're *crunk*." Jarret glared at him. "Are you writing a book? What do you need to know about his childhood for? I'm sure he was as boring as you are now." He grinned.

Roland sneered. "I'm sure."

Selena laughed and they both smiled at her, but then Jarret noticed Roland's smile and shot him another glare.

"I had hoped it was not in the Divine Plan for Jarret to come here," Ellechial said to Nadriel. "Temptations for him abound. And I have sensed a great evil somewhere on the grounds."

"As have I. But I do not believe it will touch Jarret." Nadriel floated closer to Roland, his wings flickering as if he were contemplating an imminent battle. "God has allowed Jarret to come here. Here, Jarret must find help."

"Roland?" Ellechial said. "You believe he shall be of help? He has a good heart, but the boy is much too fearful to confront Jarret. Jarret considers him weak and has no respect for his counsel."

A stale odor wafted on the air. Then Deth-kye appeared on the countertop, sitting with his lanky arms and legs sprawled out leisurely. He grinned at the angels as he blew on his fingernails and polished them on his distressed leather vest. "Did you catch what I did? Back at Rufino's?"

"I think Roland is ready." Nadriel made not the slightest acknowledgment of Deth-kye's presence. "True, he lacks Keefe's courage to confront Jarret, but he longs for his brother's friendship and conversion. And, lately, he has been pushing himself beyond his comfort zone. You should have seen him at the waterfall last week."

"Did you notice what I did with the joint?" Deth-kye hopped off the countertop and started circling the table, running his hand along the backs of the teens' chairs. "Rufino had it hidden under a magazine, hidden good. Jarret would've never seen it." His gaze lingered on Jarret.

"At the waterfall?" Ellechial said to Nadriel, wishing Deth-kye would depart.

"You know Roland's deep fear of cold water," Nadriel said.

"Sadly, yes." Ellechial spared Deth-kye a glance, remembering with detail how Roland had developed this fear.

Deth-kye acknowledged the memory with a scornful nod. "So I rolled it out a wee little bit, the joint, that is, and his eyes snapped right to it." He cackled, slapping Jarret on the back. Then he leaned and whispered something in Jarret's ear.

"While Roland stood on a stone in the river," Nadriel said, completely ignoring the demon, "I read his thoughts on his face.

He wanted nothing more than to avoid the waterfall, but Caitlyn had called him there. So he made a conscious decision to force himself through that which he truly feared, making himself a victim in order to get to the other side, to go where he had been called." Nadriel held Roland in his loving gaze. "Yes, Roland is ready. You shall see. He may need to make selfless sacrifices, yet again, in order to follow God's call."

"You would like that," Ellechial said.

"There is nothing more beautiful than sacrificial love." Nadriel's gaze turned heavenward the instant before he vanished.

Deth-kye straightened and sneered at Ellechial. "Roland's goodness will not rub off. You are powerless to protect Jarret. My boy is ripe for the picking. And . . ." He took a step toward Ellechial. ". . . my angel enemy . . ." His charcoal eyes grew wide and round, making his appearance even more hideous. ". . . by Satan's command, it's harvest time."

Ellechial, taking advantage of his permission to travel on earth, left his charge for a moment and appeared in the Summers' home.

A look of pride in his eyes, Cyabrial watched Caitlyn as she paced the floor with the phone to her ear. "Praise be God," Cyabrial said to Ellechial.

"Now and forever," Ellechial said.

"Oh, oh, oh, I'm so glad you called me," Caitlyn said into the phone, the slant of her eyebrows and her higher-than-usual tone giving away her anxiety. "You're so right. This is something we can all help with. We've got to have faith. Call me back when you're done with your phone calls."

Kiara on the other end of the phone said, "Will do," before disconnecting the call.

Caitlyn stopped pacing and called another number.

"I have come to elicit intercessory prayer," Ellechial said. "Grave temptations for my charge lie on the horizon."

Cyabrial smiled and lifted a finger to have Ellechial wait before communicating more.

"Peter?" Caitlyn paced again. "I'm glad you answered. I'm calling you for a *Stop, Drop, and Pray*."

"Huh?" Peter sounded sleepy or annoyed.

"A Stop, Drop and— Well, you know how when there's an emergency, you're taught to stop, drop, and roll?"

"What? No, no, no." Now he definitely sounded annoyed. "That's not for any old emergency. That's for a fire. You know, the smoke. You have to drop below the smoke—"

"Whatever. Kiara told me about an emergency, and we decided that we should all pray about it. It's great that we're meeting at the church on Fridays, but shouldn't we have an emergency prayer line? You know, so we can help each other when—"

"Okay. Did you just say there's an emergency? 'Cuz you're kind of rambling here."

"Oh, yes, um, one of the Finn's children, the four-year-old boy— What's his name? Um, well he's missing."

"Missing? Like ran off and no one can find him?"

"Yes."

"Wow. I mean, you don't live that far from them. Why don't you go help look for him? Don't you think actually looking for him would be more productive than just praying?"

"Well, I can't. I'm watching my little brothers and sisters. And you can't because you live too far away. We aren't always able to do something concrete. But we can always pray." She stopped pacing and propped her hand on her hip, glaring as if he'd see it. "Why are you so against praying?"

"Who said I'm against praying? I'll pray. But hey, guess who's coming to dinner Wednesday?"

"To dinner? I just told you that a little boy is missing, and you want me to guess who's coming to dinner? I've got other prayer warriors to call before I—"

"It's Keefe, Keefe West, evil Jarret's nice twin brother."

Her eyes bugged. "Keefe? At your house? Why?"

"Well, he didn't exactly say. In fact, it was quite a weird conversation. But I think he wants to meet the brothers, or friars, you know, the ones staying here."

"Oh. Can I come over too?"

"Uh, sure. We'll have a big party. Maybe we can even pray with them, huh?"

Ellechial nodded to Cyabrial. It was a good idea, though Peter sounded sarcastic.

"Good," she said. "So I'll be over Wednesday. Can you call Roland? He's still part of our prayer group, even if he is miles away. Tell him about the Finn's boy, okay?"

She no sooner disconnected that call than she started to call someone else.

"Is this your idea?" Ellechial said to Cyabrial.

"The *Stop, Drop, and Pray*?" Cyabrial smiled. "Not entirely. The girls developed it, Kiara and Caitlyn. I may have planted a seed. You know my fondness for prayer, how it stirs my soul to contemplate the desire of God to communicate with men."

"I am glad. Perhaps you could encourage the group to think of Jarret. The boy needs prayer, much more prayer. I feel as though he has entered a den of temptation."

"The Zamoranos? They are a good family."

"No, I do not mean them, exactly. I mean other forces around them."

"Zoe." Caitlyn exhaled. The phone had rung several times before her friend answered. "I was wondering if you—"

Loud voices in the background came over the phone, a man and a woman, both shouting though their words were unclear.

"Caitlyn?" Zoe said. "I can't talk right now."

"Can you go up to your room? I need to ask you—"

"I am in my room. I'll call you later." Zoe ended the call.

"Hmm," Cyabrial said, thoughtfully gazing at the phone.

"Yes, there is much work to be done. Farewell." Ellechial sped back to Jarret's side.

CHAPTER TEN
MAKING PLANS

Jarret

Jarret's heart swelled near to bursting with love for Zoe. He had never felt this way before about anyone. And it scared him to the core.

Zoe smiled. She looked hot in her black dress, her raven hair shining under the chandelier, her amber eyes sparkling as she gazed at him from across the table. He could almost forget the fact that he had to eat Thanksgiving dinner with his archenemy Peter and the rest of the Brandts. And he could almost let go of his anger.

Anger? Why had he been so angry?

His heartbeat quickened as he tried to remember. A few minutes ago, he had been so angry that he'd almost damaged his own Chrysler 300. So angry he saw stars. What was it? What was— Oh, yeah.

His gaze snapped back to Zoe.

She no longer noticed him. She was laughing with Peter. What was so funny? She was keeping a secret from him, but Peter knew. Roland knew. Everyone knew. Lies. Zoe had lied to him. He hadn't wanted her to be pregnant, and she said she'd taken care of it. She lied.

His face burned as he pushed back his chair. He started around the table to confront her, but Toby, Peter's little brother with autism, jumped in his way.

"You eat Thanksgiving dinner with us," Toby slurred, his hands flapping like a bird's wings. "You eat dinner with us?"

"No." Jarret pushed him out of the way, maybe a little too hard.

Peter jumped up from the table, shouting, "Don't you touch my brother!" He lunged, his hands landing hard on Jarret's chest.

Jarret staggered back. Before he could regain his balance, something rained down on him, something silent and shiny. Glitter? What the—

Peter took off.

Jarret wanted to pursue him, but his gaze traveled to the empty table. Zoe. She was gone. Where had she gone?

He dashed outside into the pouring rain. He knew where she had gone. He had to find her, to stop her. She changed her mind to please him. She was going to do it. He had to get to her before she—

"The baby! Don't do it. Don't abort the baby."

Jarret sat bolt upright, his heart pounding, his body drenched in cool sweat. He threw back the sheets.

Shapes, dimly lit and unfamiliar, surrounded him. Where was he? The window was on the wrong side of the room. The window—

A lean figure stood about ten feet away in front of a tall window, a silhouette before a dark, blue-gray sky. Something reached up to the ceiling on either side of the figure, something thin, gray and quivering. Something like . . . wings?

Jarret's heart beat in his throat. "Where am I?" he said aloud, though he hadn't meant to.

The figure moved. "Oh, hey, you're up too?"

He breathed and leaned back on his elbows. It was only Roland. "Yeah, I'm up. What the heck are you doing standing there in the dark? You're such a freak."

Roland huffed. "I'm not a freak. It's morning. So it's a little early."

"Well, turn on the light," Jarret commanded. He would've done it himself, but he couldn't remember if the nightstand was on his left or right. He still couldn't picture the room.

Roland slunk into the shadows and the overhead light came on.

Reality flooded Jarret's mind. He was at the Zamoranos' home, and he and Roland had to share a bedroom. Roland had taken the bed near the back wall, leaving Jarret the one in the middle of the room.

"We're trading beds tonight," Jarret said. "I don't like this one."

"Why? That's my bed. I already slept in it." Roland marched to the bed against the wall and straightened the bedspread.

"Not anymore. That's my bed. I'll have the maid change the sheets."

"Maybe they don't change the sheets every day."

He grinned. "She will when I tell her you wet the bed."

Roland snatched a pillow from the bed and whipped it at Jarret, mumbling something that sounded like a bad name, though it wasn't like Roland to cuss. "I'm getting dressed and going downstairs."

"So you can wake up everyone else?" Jarret whipped the pillow back.

"They're already awake. I saw them outside, the stable-hands anyways."

"Well, hurry up and get outta here so I can get back to sleep." Jarret flopped down and buried his face in a pillow.

When he woke again, muted sunlight filled the room, giving warmth to the yellow-ocher walls and the decorations of blue and orange. Sheer green curtains on either side of the open balcony doors fluttered in a breeze. The warm air carried the scent of dust and motor oil—probably from the creosote bushes. It gave a homey feel.

Jarret took a leisurely shower, dressed in cargo shorts and an off-white Gucci polo shirt, and tied his damp hair back. Then he grabbed his cigarettes and galloped down the stairs. He couldn't wait to lay his eyes on Selena and wash Zoe from his mind.

Voices came from *Señor* Juan's den, so Jarret slowed his pace. Not seeing anyone in either direction, he stopped by the half-open door and listened.

"I know you said this was a vacation," Roland said in the calm, respectful tone he used when trying to pump information from Papa. "But who visits Arizona in the heat of summer?"

Papa chuckled.

"I wish you'd tell me why we're here," Roland said.

"You're here for a vacation," Papa said. "A change of pace. You've been saying that you wanted to see where I grew up, so . . ."

"Fine. You don't want to tell me." Roland sounded offended. "I know about the thefts already."

Papa chuckled again. "All right, Roland. Here it is, but don't blow it out of proportion. Juan asked me to appraise his valuables, the antiques in particular, for insurance purposes. That's it."

"Doesn't an insurance agent do that?"

"Well, I suppose so. But he wants my expertise on the antiques."

"He doesn't want you to find the thief?"

Papa made a loud sigh. "No, Roland. I'm not here to catch a thief."

"Well, why not? Does he suspect who's doing it? I hear it's happened more than once, and *Señora* Kemina thinks it could be someone close to the family."

"Why, Roland, I never took you for one who pays attention to rumors." Papa's tone had a hint of challenge to it.

"I'm-I'm not. It's just, well, I don't like the idea of someone stealing from them. They're nice people. They're like family to you, aren't they?"

"Well, sure they are, but . . . You're not here for that. And you can tell Jarret to relax." He raised his voice. "I'm not trying to put either one of you to work."

Jarret backed farther from the doorway. Had Papa realized he was listening to—

"Are you looking for the dining room?"

Jarret's insides jumped. He spun around. "What?"

Selena stood behind him, arms folded, leaning a shoulder against the wall, grinning. She wore a sleeveless white shirt, faded jeans and boots.

Boots? Why hadn't he heard her come down the hall?

"I said, are you looking for the dining room? Because it's not in there." She nodded toward the half open door of her father's den.

"Yeah, the dining room. Wanna show me the way?" He checked her out again, from head to toe, making sure she knew it.

She pushed off the wall and gestured for him to follow. "You're a late sleeper, huh?"

"Not really." He walked beside her. "I never sleep this late. It's so hot; I couldn't get to sleep. I think Roland had the balcony door open all night."

"Maybe he likes the night sounds. I do too. They're peaceful."

They stepped into the dining room, where a servant woman cleared the long dining room table. She glanced at them but kept working. "Would you like something to eat?" she said in Spanish.

Also in Spanish, Selena gave a big, detailed order, smiling and sauntering about playfully with the servant woman. "She's so sweet," she said, after the woman left the room. "She'll do anything I ask."

"Yeah, I bet." Jarret sat at the head of the table. "Kind of hot for jeans, ain't it?"

"I was out riding." Selena fluttered to one of the dining room windows and gazed outside. "I like to go riding in the early morning before the sun comes out and it gets too hot." She glanced at him over her shoulder. "Or the late evening before it's too dark. But Papá does not like me riding alone at night."

"You could always take me. I'm at home on a horse."

She looked at him a moment before responding. "I'm sure you are. With *Tio* Ignace as your father, I'm sure there is much you can do."

Not sure how to take that comment, he only nodded. "What do you say we go swimming after—"

Selena's gaze shifted to one of the doorways off the dining room.

Dressed in black shorts and a dark t-shirt, cowboy hat in hand, Roland strutted into the room. He gave Selena a slight smile. "Hey, you're up," he said to Jarret as he sat down a chair away from him. "What do you want to do today?"

He had in mind to say, "Nothing with you," but with Selena there, he refrained. "We're gonna go swimming."

"Swimming?" Roland gulped, glanced at Selena, and dropped his gaze to the decorative cactus in the center of the table. "What about . . . I thought we could meet Enyeto. He's one of the stable hands, isn't he?"

Jarret grinned. Roland wasn't gonna listen to Papa. He wanted to catch the thief. "Why do you wanna meet him?"

Selena sat down opposite Roland, her eyes fixed on him, looking anxious to know his answer.

Roland took a deep breath and glanced over his shoulder, back at the doorway he had come through. "Well, I came here because I wanted to learn about Papa's early years, how he grew up."

"But?" Jarret said, still grinning, wanting to hear for himself that Roland was going to disobey Papa.

Roland's gray eyes turned cold. "But nothing. That's why I came. And I hear Enyeto's worked here since Papa was a boy."

"Uh-huh." Jarret made eye contact with Selena, wondering if she, too, had overheard Roland and Papa.

Selena smiled at Roland. "That's nice. I'd like to go with you. I've never thought to ask anyone what my father was like when he was young. Old Enyeto would know. He's the ranch manager now but, you're right, he's been around for years."

Roland nodded, his face turning salmon pink.

Jarret leaned back in the chair and looked away. Roland's uneasiness with girls made it embarrassing to be related to him. How could a girl find him—

Did Selena really choose talking to stable hands with Roland over swimming with him? "So you don't wanna go swimming, huh?" He tried not to look annoyed.

"We can do both. We have all day." She tilted her chin up and gave the hint of a smile. "Or are you going somewhere?"

He acknowledged her challenging tone with a crooked grin. If he wanted something, he would have to go after it.

Strangely, his mind turned to the Monastery in California again. Why did that miserable experience keep coming back to him? He had found something to hold his interest there, too, something forbidden but worth pursuing.

Jarret sat at the table in the guest dining room, leaning his chair back on two legs and watching the activity in the open kitchen. His experience in

the tunnel had left a bad taste in his mind. Now that Brother Mario had stopped by to see them, he knew exactly how to get rid of it.

With the weak light of two lanterns, they had followed the dark, nasty tunnel for a quarter of a mile. Once it split off, Papa decided they should go back for the measuring and mapping equipment rather than go explore and get it over with. Papa thought the tunnels ran from the winery to some of the other old buildings: the chapel on the front of the property, the church toward the back, the refectory, and the monks' cells.

Jarret had wanted out of there. He needed a shower. After walking face-first into fifty-seven, sticky spider webs, every inch of his clammy, filthy body itched. And his mind reeled with a debilitating paranoia.

After a long, hot shower—and a cigarette while Papa cleaned up— he'd started to feel normal again. He and Papa had then strolled to the guests' dining room for dinner.

Papa lifted the lid of one of the covered dishes in the kitchen. "You monks cook a mean meal."

"You have Brother Sylvester to thank. We are all quite pleased with his cooking. Perhaps he is a bit too extravagant for the austerities required of monastic life." The stern-faced monk cracked a smile.

Papa chuckled and said something else, but Jarret ignored it. He gazed without blinking at the bottles of wine the monk had placed on the countertop. Drops of condensation covered the dark green bottles. His mouth watered. A chilled glass of wine would taste great.

The monk said something about them being late for dinner and not getting to taste the wine with the other guests. Jarret's ears perked at Papa's reply. "I'm sure it's good, but we won't be needing that."

Jarret's chair slipped and the front legs slammed down.

The monk gave Jarret a friendly nod and left.

"Hey, Papa." Jarret jumped up. "I'm not really hungry right now." He zipped to the door. "I'm gonna . . . I'm gonna take a walk."

When he opened the door, he saw the monk, Brother Mario, hoofing it toward the cloister line. Not wanting to get caught following him,

95

Jarret waited by the huge oak tree until the monk had gotten a good distance away.

Brother Mario passed the cloister, the winery, and the church before disappearing behind a storage building. With caution, Jarret slunk over and peeked around the storage building. Then he found exactly where Brother Mario and the bottle of wine went: the refectory.

After waiting a few seconds, he jogged to the front door of the refectory. The doorknob turned freely, so he cracked the door open to listen. Hearing nothing, he opened it more. Then he saw them.

Two dozen white-robed monks, most with black scapulars, sat on one side of a long, dark table, hunched over bowls and plates. Brother Mario shuffled to the far end of the table and set the wine bottle next to another bottle. Then he took a seat.

Jarret sighed and closed the door.

CHAPTER ELEVEN

POOLSIDE

Roland

"An Arizona summer has gotta be hotter than hell," Peter once said. After having walked under the high noon sun from the house to the stables and from the stables to the pool, Roland believed him.

Roland sat in a poolside chaise lounge in the shade of the pergola. The Zamoranos' curvy pool of sparkling blue water tempted him. The thought of actually jumping into it and the cold water hitting his head and face made his stomach flip. What if he dove in and totally freaked out—in front of Selena?

Selena, in a fluorescent pink and green swimsuit, swam the length of the half-shaded pool, into and out of the sunlight. Jarret swam, too, deep under the water, probably planning a playful attack. He obviously liked her. Amazing how quickly he could fall in and out of love. Did Zoe even cross his mind anymore?

A warm breeze blew, cooling Roland's sweaty neck. He did want to swim, but he needed to work himself up to it. *Relax.*

Roland laid his head back and closed his eyes.

He had liked seeing Papa's house yesterday. Rufino had added a few of his own decorations, but most of the paintings and wall ornaments once belonged to Papa's family. Sun-faded pictures of Jesus and Mary and the crucifix in each room gave testimony to their faith. In Papa's old bedroom, now a junk room, hung two pictures which had belonged to Papa, both of them in old, dilapidated frames. One was a painting of a forty-niner with a pickaxe on his shoulder, the other a page ripped from a magazine, a picture of a tribe of Native Americans.

The visit brought to life things he'd always sensed about Papa's upbringing, things he admired. Papa showed an interest in archaeology and geology in his childhood. He had humble origins, devout and hardworking parents, and a few close friends. His choice of friends showed no partiality. Rufino had nothing, and Juan had it all.

Water splashed and Selena giggled.

Roland, still with eyes closed, took a deep breath. He wasn't ready to join them in the pool.

It was too bad old Enyeto, the ranch manager, hadn't given them the time of day. It would've been great hearing a few of his stories.

Half an hour ago, they had found him in the cool of the stable's tack room, a clipboard in his hand. A long, coal-black braid hung down his back. He wore jeans and a t-shirt, dressing like the other hands, but he didn't wear cowboy boots. He wore tan work boots instead, the newness of them drawing Roland's eye.

Even with his head down and his back to them, his strong posture and efficient movements gave an air of dignity and strength of character. His age showed only when he turned. The deep creases in his copper skin, his high cheekbones and square jaw made him look Native American, not Mexican like the others. One feature stood out the most to Roland and appeared vividly in his mind even now: Old Enyeto had eyes like an eagle's, sharp and piercing.

When Selena had neared Enyeto, he tugged the rim of his tan Stetson and gave her what might have been a smile. His grim mouth made it hard to tell.

"These are my friends," Selena said. "*Tio* Ignace's boys."

Roland and Jarret stood in the doorway.

Enyeto gave a nod, shifting his eagle eyes to them. He stared for a moment, as if sizing them up. Or maybe the interruption had annoyed him. "Do your friends wish to ride?"

"No, we're going to swim." She glanced at Roland then batted her eyes at Enyeto. "They wanted to meet you since you knew their father when he was a boy. We thought you could tell us a few stories."

Enyeto grunted and turned his attention to the saddles and pads on the wall. "I do not have time for stories today. Maybe some other day."

That ended that.

Jarret had strutted with a bounce in his step all the way to the pool, stripping off his shirt along the way. Without breaking his stride, he stepped out of his sandals and dove into the pool.

Water splashed Roland's legs. He opened his eyes.

Selena clung to the edge of the pool on the end nearest Roland, the deep end. "Aren't you coming in?"

"What? Yeah, I will, in just a—"

"He ain't coming in." Jarret treaded water. "Roland's scared of water." He grinned then submerged.

"Oh, you can't swim?" Selena sounded concerned.

"I can swim." Roland glared at Jarret. "I was just relaxing, just thinking."

"About what?" She folded her arms on the edge of the pool and rested her chin on them.

"Um . . ."

Jarret came up for air, his eyes squinting and lip curling as soon as he saw Selena talking to Roland.

"Enyeto's been here for years and Rufino, too," Roland said. "What about the other hands? Any of them new?"

Selena pulled herself out of the pool and sat on the edge, facing Roland. Water dripped off her glossy black hair and ran in lines down her face and her tan, athletic limbs. "Well . . ."

Jarret shook his head, a sneer distorting his face.

"Most have been here since I was a child," she said. "Alamar's the newest, I guess. He's a stable hand. He's been here two years."

"Why do you need to know?" Jarret climbed out of the pool and strutted toward Roland and Selena. He stopped between them and readied himself to dive.

Not wanting to get into it with Jarret, Roland leaned to peer around him. "Do they all live here? Those are apartments on the back of the stables, aren't they?"

"Enyeto lives there, upstairs. Laszio and Lupeta are in the lower apartment, but the others live nearby. Why?" Her eyes twinkled and a smile played on her lips. "Do you want to check out his house and see if he is our thief?"

Jarret dived into the pool.

"Well, no. I'm not suggesting that Enyeto's the thief." A wave of heat hit him. "If he's been here all these years, I-I'm sure . . . When was the first robbery?"

"A few months ago. I suppose if Enyeto was dishonest, he could've taken something years ago, huh?"

"Maybe it wasn't a stable hand." Jarret climbed out of the pool and walked toward them. "Maybe the maid did it in the conservatory with a wrench." He cocked a brow and dove back in.

Selena laughed. "Maybe it *was* one of the maids, though I can't see why. I can't see why anyone would take anything from us. Papá is so generous to the employees. They often eat dinner with us. They are like family." She paused. "You know what? We had a party two days before anyone noticed things were missing. Maybe it was a party guest."

"What'd the thief take anyway?" Jarret treaded water near Selena.

"The first thing was a jade statue of Saint Francis Xavier. It was in the little chapel." Her eyes popped wide open and she spoke in an excited tone. "We're having another party tomorrow. It's for you guys. But the same guests will be here. Maybe they will try again."

"Jade?" Roland said. "That sounds valuable."

"I'm sure it was," she said.

"What do you think they did with it?" Roland said.

"Sold it, I guess."

"Where would you sell something like that?"

She shrugged. "Online? Or maybe to a collector."

Jarret climbed out of the pool again and sauntered over to Roland. "Maybe it's at a pawn shop. Why don't you stop worrying about it and get in the pool? You said you could swim. Let's see you do it." He stood with a hand on his hip.

Roland bristled, and his jaw twitched. It would be foolish to snap at Jarret in front of Selena. Jarret always got the upper hand. Besides, he couldn't think of anything smart to say. He forced his irritation to take a back seat and said to Jarret, "I wonder if Papa would let me help appraise things. It'd be good to get that done before someone tries to steal something else."

"What do you know about any of that junk?"

"I know a lot. I help him all the time with that kind of stuff. I can look things up. You could too, if you wanted to."

"I got something for you to look up." Jarret grabbed Roland by the arms and yanked him to his feet.

"Don't!" Fearing what Jarret had in mind, Roland struggled like a cat about to be bathed.

Jarret laughed. He whipped Roland around in a semi-circle, from the chaise lounge to the edge of the pool.

"Don't, don't—" Fear gripped him. He couldn't. Not the water. Not like this.

The instant he lost balance, time passed in morbid slow motion. He twisted his head to glimpse his doom. He squeezed his eyes shut, held his breath . . . His stomach lurched as his body slammed down. Icy cold water bit his every nerve ending.

Sinking into coldness. No air. Grasping, reaching, arms and legs flailing . . .

He forgot how to swim.

He opened his eyes in time to see an arm reach around him from behind.

CHAPTER TWELVE

CALLING

Keefe

Keefe stood on the front stoop of the Brandt's house, running his hand over his fresh crew cut, waiting for someone to answer the door. Butterflies flitted in his stomach. He hadn't felt this nervous since his first date. Why now?

He'd made Nanny cut his hair in the morning, despite her protests. She, like Jarret, wanted him to grow out his curls. Then he had spent more time than a guy should picking out the right shirt and pants: a slate-gray polo and blue cargos. He wanted to look clean and simple to make a good impression.

Why? Why did he want to make an impression on the Franciscan friars?

Just hearing about them, when Peter had mentioned them to Roland, stirred up a strange feeling in his soul. Maybe it was simply curiosity.

The front door opened and Peter swung the screen door out. "Hey, there you are." He stepped back, nodding for Keefe to come in. Then he gave Keefe the once-over, a grin spreading on his face. "You're kind of early."

"Am I?" Keefe found himself assuming the meek posture Roland typically took, stuffing his hands in the front pockets of his cargos. He'd never considered himself shy, though he usually played shadow to Jarret.

Cheerful conversation, high activity, and savory smells filled the house. Mrs. Brandt and Peter's aunt worked in the kitchen, one stirring something on the stove, the other arranging dishes on the bar countertop. Peter's little brother Toby paced back and forth from the long dining room table to the countertop, talking to himself and gesturing. A family he'd never seen before, probably guests staying at the bed and breakfast, sat in one of the three booths by the windows. The sliding glass doors that led to the guests' rooms were closed. Men's voices came from down the hall. The friars?

"Uh, we're over here," Peter said.

"What?" Keefe turned.

Peter walked around the couch and crouched by the TV. "I'm trying to keep Toby out here so he doesn't bug the guests." He pressed buttons on a remote until a bowling game showed on the TV screen.

Caitlyn had been sitting on the floor but started to get up when she saw Keefe. "Hi." She put her hands behind her back and dipped her head, her big green eyes peeking through a tangle of red hair.

"Hi, Caitlyn."

"Can I get you something to drink?" She smiled, rocking on the soles of her feet.

"No, thanks. I'll wait. Peter said I'm early."

"Are you here to see the Franciscan friars?" she said.

His cheeks burned. "I'm here . . . um, I don't know." There was no point trying to keep this secret from her. The whole reason he'd stopped seeing her was to listen better to God's voice. For almost a year now, he'd had the impression that God wanted something of him. "Yeah, I guess I am."

Still on the floor by the TV, Peter grinned at him over his shoulder.

Keefe turned away and sat on the couch. When he had called Peter to invite himself over, he'd burned with embarrassment then, too, only no one was around to see it. Their conversation had gone in circles. He should've been straightforward. Instead, he started with, "So uh, we're kind of like friends, aren't we?"

"What? Who? You and me? Uh, sure. What's up?"

"Um, it's kind of lonely around here with my brothers gone and my father . . . gone and . . ."

"Lonely? Or isn't it kind of nice? 'Cuz I think it'd be real nice. Especially with Jarret . . . Uh, never mind. You probably wouldn't . . . feel . . . the same."

"So I was wondering if maybe I could come over one evening, like Wednesday."

"Over? Here? Or did you want to go do something? I'd like to do something. You don't have a car, though, do you? Why does Jarret have a car and you don't?"

"We need a car? I can borrow my father's, I think. But I really wanted to visit. You guys have guests, don't you?"

"Guests? Well, yeah. With the bed and breakfast, you know, we always have guests."

"Yeah. I know."

"Ohhhhh. I get it. You're interested in our guests. Let me guess. You want to see the monks. We don't get monks often."

"They're brothers, aren't they? Friars?"

Peter had laughed. "So what's your interest in the brothers?"

Keefe had cleared his throat. Sweat broke out on his neck. "Nothing. I didn't say I was interested in them. I just said, well, I said it was kind of lonely over here. But if you don't want me to come over—"

"No, no, now don't get your undies all in a bunch. Come on over. That'd be great. The brothers will join us for dinner. At six."

"Six. Okay. Thanks."

So it had been arranged, Peter obviously aware of his curiosity though not aware of his motive. But what was his motive?

The sound of a sliding glass door brought him back to the moment. He craned his head to see.

A couple stepped into the dining room and sat at one of the three booths. The booths could each seat six, and there was one left, but the friars would probably be seated at the long table in the middle of the room. Peter's folks would most likely want to talk with them.

"Toby!" Peter dashed to the dining room, chasing Toby.

"So have you?" Caitlyn said.

Keefe spun to face her. Caitlyn had taken a seat right next to him on the couch. He'd totally missed what she said. "What? Have I *what*?"

"Have you heard from Roland? How does he like Arizona?"

The glass door slid again.

Keefe forced himself not to turn around. He'd see them soon enough. Why was he so anxious? "Oh, I haven't really talked to him. My father said everyone's fine, and the Zamoranos have a swimming pool."

"Oh, that'd be nice. Do you like to swim?"

Peter had Toby by the hand, leading him around the couch. "You love bowling. I got the Wii game all set up. You can go first."

Toby took the remote offered him, while whining something about his mother.

The men's voices grew louder as they came down the hall.

Keefe spun his head to see. Was it them?

Mr. Brandt and Father Carston, the parish priest, came down the hall deep in conversation. They took seats at the long dining room table.

"So how does it feel," Peter said and Keefe turned to face him, "to be without your better, or shall I say *worse*, half?"

"Peter!" Caitlyn said. "You're terrible."

The glass door slid again.

Keefe spun around.

It was them! The room grew silent, all eyes on the friars. Dressed in long brown robes with white cords around their waists and sandals on their feet, they processed into the dining room. Most of them smiled and nodded or gave a simple greeting to whoever looked at them. A few had beards. All wore their hair short. The youngest, maybe in his twenties, had a shaved head.

Mr. Brandt scraped his chair back and stood. "Please, sit with us." He motioned for them to join him at the long table.

Keefe jumped up, glancing at Peter. "Shouldn't we go sit down?"

"Oh." Peter came up behind him. "We're eating out here. Mom said there's not gonna be room in there. We've got way more guests than usual, what with half a dozen friars staying with us."

The six friars took seats as directed, on either side of the long table, Father Carston and Mr. Brandt on one end and a few empty seats on the other. Mrs. Brandt and Peter's aunt would probably join them, but there were two more empty seats.

The glass doors slid open again and another couple strolled through, heading right for the long table.

Keefe sighed.

Father Carston led in prayer, asking God for a special blessing for the friars' work, then everyone formed a line at the buffet counter. Toby ran to his mother. Caitlyn, Peter, and Keefe took up the end of the line. One of the bearded brothers stepped out of line, leaned over the table, then got in line behind Keefe.

Keefe glanced over his shoulder, once, twice, a third time.

"Hello, I'm Brother Lawrence."

"Wow," Keefe said, his mind drawing a blank.

Brother Lawrence smiled. "Who are you?"

"Uh . . ." Keefe glanced at Peter.

Peter scrunched up his face, showing Keefe how stupid he was acting. "He means your name."

"Yeah, um, Keefe, Keefe West." He wiped his sweaty hand on his cargos and shook hands with Brother Lawrence. Then he turned away and forced himself not to look again.

Once they loaded their plates and returned to the couch, Peter sat grinning at him. "So you're *really* interested in those friars, aren't you?"

Cutting meatloaf with a spoon, Keefe shrugged.

"Do you need a knife?" Caitlyn said. "Didn't you grab a fork?"

"No, I can see it," Peter said. "You're, like, unnaturally interested."

"Unnaturally?" Keefe glared.

"Don't be silly," Caitlyn said to Peter. "I think they're cool. Aren't you fascinated by people who give up everything to follow God? I am. If I didn't want to have my own children so badly . . ."

"Oh, give me a break," Peter said. "You're saying you'd consider being a nun."

"Or a sister."

"What's the difference?"

"A nun typically lives in a cloistered monastery . . ." The voice came from behind them. ". . . devoted to the contemplative life for the good of the world, while a sister lives, ministers, and prays within the world, actively engaged in the works of mercy."

"Oh, hey." Peter blushed.

"May I join you?" Brother Lawrence lifted his plate of food. "Somebody took my seat." He nodded to the table.

Peter jumped up. "Oh, that's my little brother. I'll go—"

"No, no." Brother Lawrence put up a hand. "I'm kidding. I gave him my seat. He wanted to sit by his mother."

"Yeah, but—"

"Besides, I'd like to sit out here. My mother never allowed us kids to eat in the living room. I kind of like the idea." He smiled.

Peter got up and went to the recliner. Keefe scooted over on the couch to make room for the brother. They ate in silence for a moment until Brother Lawrence complimented the food.

"Don't you like meatloaf, Keefe?" Peter said, grinning.

"What?" He realized he hadn't been eating. He'd only been staring. "Oh, sure." He took a bite.

"So, tell us what you do," Caitlyn said, leaning past Keefe. "We were just talking about how interesting it is when people give up everything to follow God."

Brother Lawrence nodded, gazing at the ceiling as if considering how to word his response. His golden-brown, thick-lashed eyes had a most angelic quality, as if he saw more than a mortal should. His age was hard to guess. He could've been in his thirties or forties, but he had a youthfulness about him.

"Well," he finally said, "we're a group of friars. We live a common life of prayer and penance. Our particular order has a commitment to live and proclaim the Gospel of Life. We're devoted to serving and defending the most vulnerable of our society: the pre-born child, the severely disabled, the poor, the homeless . . ."

Caitlyn ruled the conversation, asking question after question. Keefe only listened. But every word Brother Lawrence spoke clicked in his mind, fitting perfectly like a giant puzzle coming together. The more he learned of their daily life, their origin, and their unique mission, the more he longed to know.

"How did you know you were called to this way of life?" Caitlyn said.

Keefe's heart skipped a beat.

"Hmm." Brother Lawrence set his plate down. "Well, as a young man I felt this great spiritual longing. I began to pray more intensely, read the Bible more, attend daily Mass. I was going to college to become an engineer, but I felt this tugging at my soul. I had a great unrest, like I say, a longing."

He looked at Keefe who, this time, didn't look away. He couldn't look away. He understood completely what the man meant.

"Nothing worldly could satisfy me," Brother Lawrence said. "I wanted more, to give of myself more. I think, now, it was the Holy Spirit moving me, urging me toward my vocation." He smiled, looking at the others. "I find peace in all I do now, even when things don't work out."

The brother faced Keefe. "Our Lord says, 'If you want to be perfect, go and sell all you have and give the money to the poor, and you will have riches in heaven; then come and follow me.' He invites a few, those who are chosen, to go a step beyond the commandments and to voluntarily embrace the evangelical counsels. When you are called, you find no rest in other pursuits."

Toby bolted into the room and snatched a remote. "Play bowling with me?"

Peter threw his hands in the air. "We're eating. I thought you were eating at the table."

"Toby all done," Toby said, his eyes on Brother Lawrence.

"I take it that you want my seat." Brother Lawrence smiled and stood up.

Keefe watched the brother walk away, part of him wanting to follow, wanting to hear more. But a strange peace had overcome him, so he decided to remain where he was.

Almost a year ago, he'd had a similar feeling of peace. He'd been in Italy on a trip with his father, when they stumbled upon an old church and a Eucharistic miracle. God had spoken to his heart, overwhelmed him with love, and changed the direction of his life. He'd made a promise to listen to God's voice and to obey him, knowing that the Lord would always be with him no matter the challenge.

Could God be calling him to the religious life? Or was this idea merely his own? He was only seventeen, hadn't graduated, and had no idea what his talents were. Maybe the life of the Franciscans appealed to him because it would take him away from his present challenge: helping Jarret.

Ever since Jarret had gotten involved with Zoe and especially since their break-up, he'd seemed troubled, lost. Alone. He needed someone to turn to, someone to help him straighten out his life and get on the right track.

They'd always been close, until Keefe changed. They could become close again.

No. God would not want Keefe to abandon his brother. God wanted people to love Him where they were and help those around them, especially those closest. God had made them brothers, twins, for a reason. It was wrong to consider becoming a Franciscan friar. If he went down that path, Jarret would never speak to him again.

Maybe the brotherhood was in his future. But not now. He wouldn't feel right abandoning someone to please himself.

CHAPTER THIRTEEN

INVITATION ON THE BREEZE

Ellechial

Streaks of blood red colored the evening sky. Flames flickered in tiki torches and in candle decorations on patio tables. A Mariachi band in silver-studded black charro suits and wide-brimmed hats played lively music while couples danced on a flagstone patio. Friends strolled through the cacti gardens. Servants, bearing drinks and snacks on trays, weaved around groups of men in Stetson hats and women in Mexican party dresses. Seventy-eight people mingled in the Zamoranos' backyard. One hundred twenty demons prowled around them.

One hundred and one angels stood guard.

Roland sat on a patio chair near a three-tiered, gurgling fountain, his attention on the couples dancing on the flagstone patio—on one couple in particular: Jarret and Selena. His typically emotionless expression flickered as Jealousy's whispers surrounded him like trails of smoke.

"Rise above the temptation, my friend," Nadriel commanded as he unsheathed his sword.

Jealousy shut his mouth and reached for his own sword.

With a deep breath, Roland turned away from the dancers and scanned the other party guests. His expression softened and Jealousy backed away.

Nadriel sheathed his sword and turned to Ellechial. "Jarret seems pleased tonight."

"Indeed." Ellechial lifted his wings, which, happily, moved freely. He appreciated that he could now travel at will to solicit prayers from others.

Jarret danced with Selena to *Cielito Lindo*. When he'd asked her to dance and she said *yes*, he blinked a few times as if he'd expected rejection. As he led her to the dance floor, he studied the other dancers. He hadn't a clue how to dance to the music of a mariachi band, but he had unbeatable courage and determination. He picked up the Mexican dance style well enough, placing his hands behind his back, marching in place, kicking and turning every now and then.

Selena, in her Mexican party dress, white with red and yellow embroideries, had begun the dance in all seriousness. A few seconds into it, Jarret's kicking made her laugh. Since then the smile hadn't left her face as she swished her skirt and twirled around him.

"I do hope he is soon converted," Nadriel said.

"As do I," Ellechial said. No one but the Lord wanted it more than he did.

"Keefe has received his calling." Nadriel's wings fluttered. "Though he has not yet grasped it."

"Hmm." Ellechial sent prayers up for Keefe. "Then we haven't much time."

"No. The Franciscan friars shall not stay long. I fear Keefe's worry over Jarret may prevent him from discernment of his own vocation."

"Yes. Keefe has great concern for his twin. Jarret has not been forgotten in his prayers." Ellechial lifted his hand and a shiny shield appeared, gold with a blue *M* in honor of the Blessed Virgin Mary.

Nadriel smiled looking it over. "Impressive."

"Thank you." Lowering his hand, the shield vanished, but it would be available to him for some time.

"Have you plans for tonight?" Nadriel said.

"I have. Perhaps you can help."

Nadriel gave a nod and his full attention.

"I should like to get Jarret to the shrine. The artwork there may move his soul. It would also be well for him to see that the girl of his infatuation has a lively faith."

The music stopped, people clapped, and a few couples left the patio. Selena held Jarret's arm as they walked but let go as she neared Roland. Roland got up and met them, and the three of them went to the fountain.

"Now what?" Selena beamed, glancing from Roland to Jarret.

"You would like to see the shrine," Nadriel said to Roland.

Roland didn't appear to have caught the suggestion as he seemed quite taken by Selena's joy. "You looked great out there."

Selena lifted one end of her skirt and bowed. "Why, thank you. Maybe you will ask me for a dance."

Jarret shot Roland a look of warning. "Roland doesn't dance. Do you, Roland?"

He gave the hint of a smile and blushed. "No, I can't dance. I didn't know you could." He looked at Jarret. "Where'd you learn to do that?"

Jarret stood a little taller and shrugged, grinning.

"Well, let's sit down." Selena sat on the edge of the fountain and, eyes on Roland, patted the spot next to her.

"Maybe you ought to get a chair, *Pale Rider*." Jarret sat on Selena's other side. "We don't want Selena to get her pretty dress wet, having to save your hide again."

Roland's mouth twitched. He hid his anger well, but he appeared to be reliving the entire pool incident in his mind. After Jarret had shoved him into the pool yesterday and he'd flailed about in sheer panic, Selena had come to his rescue. Once seated on a chaise lounge, it had taken a good fifteen minutes for him to calm down and breathe easy again, all under the concerned gaze of Selena. Then he seemed to feel it necessary to prove he was okay by joining them in the pool. That time he went in on his own, slowly from the shallow end. Under his breath, he vowed never to swim at the Zamoranos' again.

"What do you want to do now?" Selena played with her skirt, swishing the part that draped from her knee.

"You would like to see the shrine, wouldn't you?" Nadriel whispered in Roland's ear.

"Yeah, I would like to see the . . ." Roland glanced to either side, as if the thought surprised him.

Jarret's gaze trained on a servant with a tray of pink and yellow drinks, each topped with a chunk of fruit. "Let's get some of those drinks and go for a swim." He gave Roland a sideways glance.

"I don't want to swim. The party's for us, you know," Roland said. "And those drinks have alcohol."

"No kidding," Jarret said. "Don't you wanna have some fun? You're so lame."

"There're a lot of people here." Roland changed the subject with admirable calmness. "I noticed some of them wandering off." He gave a nod toward the back of the property, which now glowed pink under the setting sun.

Selena looked.

"Are all of the guests from the last party also here tonight?" Roland said.

"I think so," she said.

"What about the second time something was stolen? Were any of these same people over?"

"Don't tell me you're playing detective again." Jarret sneered. "I'm getting me a drink." He jumped up, but his gaze snapped to his father who stood about twenty feet away with a group of men in Stetson hats.

"We had a dinner party the night Saint George and the Dragon was stolen," Selena said to Roland. "It's a bronze statue. And, yes, some of the guests were the same." Her eyes popped wide open. "I know. I'll go find the guest lists." She jumped up, took a few steps, and spun back around. "I'll get you a drink, Jarret." She smiled and bounced off.

"Don't worry, my boy," Deth-kye's wicked voice sounded somewhere near Jarret an instant before he made himself visible to the angels. "We won't let that little brother of yours ruin a perfectly good party."

Jarret cast a grumpy glance at Roland.

Roland smiled. "We should walk down to the shrine, check it out."

"No, we shouldn't. We should see how many drinks we can snag without Papa finding out."

"No, we shouldn't."

A few minutes later, bouncing to the music, Selena returned with a drink in each hand. She took a sip of one then handed it to Jarret. When she tried to give one to Roland, he shook his head and glanced over his shoulder.

"Let's go put our swimsuits on," Jarret said, leaning close to Selena.

116

She laughed. "I have the guest lists." She pulled folded papers from her waistband and handed them to Roland.

He flipped them open and started comparing them side to side. "Not so many people at the dinner party, huh?"

"Forget about that." Jarret finished his drink and set the empty glass on a table. "I wanna swim."

"The shrine," Nadriel said to Roland. "You want to see the shrine."

Roland looked up from the lists and stared at Selena.

Selena looked up from the lists and met his gaze. "What?"

"Do you think we could see the shrine?"

"Tonight?"

Jarret rolled his eyes and groaned. "Not tonight. Let's do something fun."

Selena faced him with narrowed eyes and a playful grin. "Why can't we do both?"

"No!" Deth-kye lunged at Selena, hands reaching for her throat.

"Get back!" Her guardian thrust his shield, blocking Deth-kye's attack, and drew his sword for battle.

Deth-kye shrunk back, cowering before the angel. He had no permission to attack Selena.

"It won't kill you to go to the shrine," Ellechial said to Jarret, not expecting him to sense it.

Jarret raised his hands, surrender in his eyes. "Lead the way," he said to Selena.

Nadriel and Ellechial exchanged a glance.

"Did he . . ." Nadriel said, ". . . hear you?"

"I don't know," Ellechial said.

With unnatural movements, Deth-kye crawled after Jarret then rose to full height and leaped into the air. Leathery wings shot out from his sides. From his overhead position, he leered down at the angels. "One point for you, my despised enemy. But only one." He sped away, heading for the shrine.

Selena led them to her father first, to get the key. Then they walked three-across between the horse corral and a line of flowering desert willow trees that went all the way back to the shrine. Roland and Selena discussed the guests at the last dinner party, while Jarret flexed his jaw muscles and ground his teeth.

The shrine resembled a little adobe church with a terracotta roof and a wooden cross on top. An angel stood guard at the door, gracefully stepping aside as Selena reached for the knob. When she cracked open the door, a gray mist slithered in along the floor.

Selena flipped the light switch, dipped her finger in the holy water font by the door, and crossed herself. Roland followed her lead.

"Well, go on," Ellechial said to Jarret. "It won't kill you."

With a sigh, Jarret stepped onto consecrated ground and dipped his finger in holy water.

The instant Jarret crossed himself, the gray mist on the floor shot back. It slithered up a wall and into a three-by-four-foot painting.

Roland perused the artwork and statues, taking slow steps. "Wow. This is some shrine."

Candles burned before life-size statues of the Blessed Virgin, Saint Joseph, Saint John of the Cross, and Saint Ignatius of Loyola. Paintings of various saints and religious scenes hung on the walls. Smaller statues, ornate candlesticks, crucifixes, and other religious items filled shelves and niches in the walls.

Selena had gone to a kneeler before the Blessed Virgin and offered a prayer that her guardian took immediately to Heaven.

Jarret took only a few steps into the shrine, but he stopped too close to the picture Deth-kye had entered.

Putrid gray smoke spewed forth from the picture.

Ellechial shot to Jarret's side, shield in hand.

Smoke, which would've shot directly into Jarret's face, rolled off the shield and reformed itself into the shape of a snake. The snake circled in the air around both Ellechial and Jarret, increasing its speed with every turn. Arms and legs grew out of the spiraling snake as it mutated into Deth-kye's ungainly form.

Hot black anger flashed over Deth-kye's countenance. He sprang for Jarret.

In an instant, Ellechial met him in the air. Their spiritual forms collided with a burst of foul gray smoke and a flash of light.

"I command you to leave this place," Ellechial said, wrestling to keep the demon from poisoning Jarret's thoughts.

Jarret's features had softened as he beheld the statues of saints, the paintings, and Selena at prayer. This could be the moment of grace for him. If only —

Deth-kye jerked back, lifting and twisting his hands to flaunt his weapons, a short dagger and a blackened scythe. "Jarret has made me strong. You, I see, still have nothing but a puny shield. You will not tell me to go. I will tell you." Stretching his form to unusual height, he swung the scythe.

Ellechial dodged and flashed back to Jarret's side.

The scythe came at him again, slicing through the air in motions so quick it made a breeze.

Wings held high, Ellechial brought up his shield. The scythe came down and sliced it clean in two. Half of the shield vanished, the other he whipped at the demon.

Deth-kye blocked the projectile with his dagger, then drew near and laughed in Ellechial's face. "The victory is mine." His form disintegrated into a dark cloud, which stretched out and slithered up the wall and back into the painting.

Ellechial turned his thought heavenward. "Why, my Lord?" He remained in prayer, begging God for the grace of Jarret's conversion, for a softening of his heart, for victory. "May God be glorified."

Jarret

Jarret glanced at the door, ready to leave. Something about the little shrine disturbed him. But what? And why?

At first, it had seemed quaint—if that was the word—somewhat old-worldly with all the colorful paintings and statues. It had lifted his spirit in a strange way that made him feel special, or maybe as if something awesome could happen to him. He had even thought about God for a minute there, as if God had wanted to connect with him. Strange thought. Why would God want anything to do with him?

The Zamoranos obviously felt differently, as their little shrine displayed, but he couldn't accept that God would really stoop down and get involved with His creatures. No. People may have found comfort in that thought, but it didn't make it true. People liked to have their little holy pictures or statues or whole shrines devoted to God and the saints, but that didn't mean it moved God. What would He care about this shrine?

Did people think it pleased God to have a shrine built and filled with all sorts of expensive artwork? Silly. They simply clung to their old-world, semi-superstitious beliefs that, whether they wanted to admit it or not, resembled the people in the Old Testament times with their gods of wood and stone. What was the difference?

No. This place was not for him.

Roland turned toward Selena as she rose from the kneeler. "What about motive?" he said, still harping on the thief. "Do you think money alone is the thief's motive? And why only recently? Maybe he has some pressing need."

"Maybe he just discovered that we keep the shrine unlocked." Selena came up to Roland. "I mean we used to." She spun the keychain on her finger, a playful look in her eyes. "Papá even thought about getting a security system. He likes the shrine to be open, though, in case anyone wants to visit. Maybe he will just get cameras and post signs."

"I wish my father would let me help make a detailed list of the antiques." Roland stared at a statue of Our Lady of Guadalupe. Gold candlesticks and flowers in ceramic vases stood on pedestals on either side. "There're so many of them here. I can look things up, help him out a little."

"Have you asked him?" Selena gathered her hair in one hand and released it, letting it cascade down her back.

Liking what he saw, Jarret decided to go to her. Before he took a step, something on the wall moved or came into focus in his peripheral vision. He stopped, looked, and did a double take.

A painting of a saint hung on the wall nearby. The saint—nearly naked, bound to a tree, and with arrows sticking out of his body—resembled *him*. Same curly dark hair. Same eyes and . . . the face . . .

"You look like you've seen a ghost." Selena appeared by his side.

He shut his mouth and wanted to face her, but he couldn't tear his gaze from the curly-haired man in the picture. "He's got an arrow through his neck."

Selena giggled, moving closer. "It's Saint Sebastian. Do you know about him?"

Jarret shook his head and turned away from the painting.

"He was a captain of the Praetorian Guard," she said, "before they discovered he was a Christian. He converted two brothers, twin brothers—"

"Twin brothers?" Shaking his head again, Jarret stepped back.

". . . and then he converted their parents. And also a mute girl named Zoe."

"Zoe?" His eyes popped, nearly bursting. He put a hand up, signaling for her to stop explaining.

"Once Zoe converted, her speech returned. Sebastian converted many others. Then he died during the Roman emperor Diocletian's persecution of the Christians. He didn't actually die from arrows."

"Oh." Jarret glanced about the shrine, looking for something else to talk about.

"He was clubbed to death. Zoe was burned."

"You know what?" Jarret's stomach twisted. "I don't really want to know about Saint Sebastian. I don't see the point in all these people dying, all these martyrs. You think God wants that? Wants them to sacrifice themselves? For what? He gave them brains and strength. Why didn't they fight? Why didn't Sebastian have his own bow and arrows?" He backed up a few steps, hoping he had moved toward the door. "Ain't nobody gonna bring me down without a fight. Let's get back to the party." He turned away from her and raised his voice. "Roland, you've seen enough."

Walking under the row of desert willow trees, brushing into an occasional low-hanging seedpod, Jarret clipped along at a good pace, glad to be shut of the shrine. He couldn't wait to return to the party. The distant sound of the mariachi band, while not his favorite type of music, drew him. It had a certain appeal out here under the dark sky on a hot desert night. And it mellowed his mood.

"Why are you in such a hurry?" Selena jogged to catch up to him.

"There wasn't any alcohol in that drink you gave me, was there?" He hadn't realized it initially, but now he was certain. He didn't feel a thing. He should've at least felt a wee bit fuzzy. As soon as he got back in the mix, he'd take care of that.

She laughed. "I never said there was."

"You're only seventeen." Roland caught up to them and walked on Jarret's other side. "You don't need to drink."

"Need to? No. Want to? Yes." He grinned. "You never do anything fun. Don't knock it till you try it."

Roland rolled his eyes and shook his head, probably wanting Selena to know he disapproved.

Selena dropped her head, giggling, and her hair fell over her face like a black silk curtain. The way she laughed at every little thing, she seemed like a girl who could have some fun.

That's what he needed: a few drinks and some time with her. "What about you?" he said to her.

"Me?" A smile flickered on her face. "What about me?"

"Do you drink?"

"Well, we have wine—"

"Selena!"

They had almost reached the outer row of tables when two stable hands and a middle-aged cowgirl strolled toward them. One of the hands had a cheek full of chew, and he turned to spit. The other, the one who had called, held the woman's hand. Selena ran to them and motioned for Jarret and Roland to join them.

Jarret kept walking, his sights set on a female server with a full tray of colorful drinks. Roland could meet all the stable hands he wanted. He was getting himself a drink.

The server stopped at a table, unloaded two drinks, and picked up two empty glasses. She turned away and Jarret stepped up behind her. As she handed a drink to another guest, Jarret snagged one for himself. He had meant to keep walking, so as not to catch anyone's attention, but it looked so cool and good. He took a sip.

"Is that for me?"

Jarret shuddered at the sound of Papa's voice coming from so close behind him, but he forced himself to appear calm as he glanced over his shoulder. "No, but I'll get you one."

Papa reached around and stole the drink, tipping his hat as he did so. "Don't get any ideas. I've got my eye on you."

"It's a party. Can't I have one little drink?"

Papa gave him a sideways glance as he sipped the drink. "Don't you remember what happened last time you tried that?" He had the hint of a smile and his blue eyes twinkled in the light from the nearest tiki torch.

"What makes you think *that* was the last time?" Jarret gave a smug grin.

Papa waved a brow. "Remember, I got my eye on you." He tipped his hat again and walked away, drink in hand.

"Killjoy," Jarret muttered under his breath as he watched Papa stroll among the other guests and sip on that drink. Papa was right, though. It was the last time he'd had a drink. And he remembered it sure enough. Strangely, whenever his mood sank, he had been able to think of little else but his time at the monastery.

A faint breeze kicked up. It felt good in his hair and on his neck, but it hastened the turn his mind had begun to take. There had been a strong wind then a rainstorm that night, the night he had gone to explore the monastery winery.

Dark clouds rolled in, stealing the last traces of color from the sky. The wind blew strong enough to raise a monk's habit.

Jarret leaned against an outside wall of the guesthouse and stared at the winery. Goose bumps formed on his arms. He stuffed his cigarette between his lips and rolled his sleeves down while his mind took a stroll through the wine cellar, past endless shelves of wine. Jarret had noticed that, after dinnertime, the monks rarely came this way. And Papa had lost himself in the task of creating tunnel sketches. No one would notice if Jarret were to . . .

Did they lock the door to the winery?

Jarret pushed off the wall, took a last puff off the cigarette, and tossed the butt. He skulked across the grounds, glancing behind him as he neared the large, brick building.

The winery had several garage doors on the front, but he went around to the little door on the side. With hope and crossed fingers, he grabbed the knob.

It turned easily.

"Yes!" He glanced in either direction then stepped inside and closed the door behind him.

Darkness blinded him. Windows rattled. The odor of oak and sour grapes overcame him.

He shivered and gagged, breathing through his mouth. His eyes refused to adjust no matter how hard he tried to peer into the inky darkness. Five heartbeats later, he remembered the flashlight he had brought.

He swung an arm back to get it and bumped the corkscrew, which was also stuffed in his back pocket. The corkscrew slipped free. He jerked his hand out, grasping at air, hoping to catch the corkscrew before it—

Corkscrew and flashlight clattered to the floor. They both rolled a good distance and clanked against something hard.

He huffed, disgusted, then squinted at the floor. Unable to see, he peered up, searching for a light fixture, a window, anything.

Gray light seeped in through the cloudy windows high on one wall, but it didn't come close to reaching the floor.

"Just my stinking luck." He dropped onto all fours on the cold stone floor. "Freakin' flashlight . . ." He crawled to where he thought the things had rolled. ". . . probably stuck in a spider's web." He groped in every direction, finding nothing.

Ready to give up, his hand brushed it.

"There you are." He wrapped his fingers around it, found the corkscrew nearby, and tried straightening up. His head banged against a metal desk or cabinet, sending a shockwave through him.

"Son of a . . ." He crawled backward a few feet, stood, and flicked the flashlight on.

The beam fell on two desks, a long table, a low refrigerator, a locker, and then doors on either end of the room. The doors probably led to the wine presses and fermentation tanks that Papa had told him about.

Aiming the beam to the far corner revealed a big, open service elevator with exposed pulleys, gears, and ropes. It looked old and rickety, not that he would risk the noise it would make if he used it. The stairs would do. He swept the beam in the other direction and found them.

As he descended the steps to the cellar, the eerie rattling of the windows faded, but the darkness grew thicker and unsettled his soul.

He shined the light to either side, the beam grazing over something white. He jerked the light back to it, his mind presenting an unreasonable thought. What if he found a silent monk down here?

The light found the white thing again. It was an apron, hanging on the wall.

Despite feelings of foreboding, he crept further into the cellar, heading opposite the hole in the wall that led to the tunnel.

Pallets of sixty-gallon oak barrels lined the farthest wall. Twenty or so rows of wine racks stood before him.

With his eyes on the goal, a smile stretched across his face. It was stupid to think he'd find a monk down here at this hour. He was all alone, just he and the wine.

Feeling fly, he strutted down the rows, shining the flashlight on bottles along the way. He stopped, pulled a bottle from a slot, and brought the light to it. Syrah, the label said. Never heard of it, but yeah, he'd find out for himself how it tasted. Deciding to sample two varieties, he grabbed a bottle from a different row and returned to the steps.

When his foot landed on the first step, a tapping sound came from the room above. Rain pelted the windows. A kink in his plans. He'd wanted to find a spot outside where he could drink without anyone seeing him. Now what?

He turned and found himself heading toward the hole in the wall, toward the tunnel. As much as it freaked him out, it would be the perfect place. Absolutely no one would find him there.

Jarret grabbed as many lanterns as he could carry without dropping the wine bottles. Then he stepped into the tunnel.

Draped in the white sheet that once hung over the hole in the wall, Jarret sat with his back to a cool tunnel wall and his legs stretched out before him. He hugged a near-empty bottle of Syrah. It was good, sweet but not too sweet, and its flavor improved with every swig.

He had left a trail of glowing lanterns, placing them every ten or twenty feet between the hole in the cellar and here, where the tunnel branched off. The light drove the shadows away, enough to comfort him. After half a bottle of wine, the chill in the air left too. His mind floated above him, and his muscles felt like rubber. He had even come up with his own version of a familiar drinking song.

"A hundred bottles of wine on the wall, a hundred bottles of wine. Take one down, pass it round, ninety-nine bottles of wine on the wall . . ."

The full bottle lay by his feet. He leaned forward and, barely reaching, spun it around. It stopped with the cork pointing to the tunnel that branched off to the right. Still singing, Jarret pulled himself up, snatched a lantern and the bottles, and staggered down the designated tunnel.

"Twenny-five bottles of beer on the wine, twenny-five bottles of beer. Take one down, pass it round, twenny-more bottles a beer on the wine . . ."

He brought the near-empty bottle to his mouth, tipped his head back, and drained it. Wine dribbled down his chin. He wiped himself with his arm and flung the bottle. It clanked from the wall to the floor and rolled, but—to his disappointment—didn't break. He had wanted to hear the sound of shattering glass echo in the tunnel.

Staggering down the tunnel, he resumed his song, trying hard not to lose his place. "Twenny-more bottles-a beer on the wine, twenny-more lobbles a beer. Take one down, pass it round, uh, ninety-nine, no . . ." He wiped his numb face and tried to think. "Nineteen, nineteen more bobbles a beer all around."

After staggering along for some time, he reached a stone wall at the end of the tunnel and slid down to rest. He glanced at the full bottle in his hands. What had he done with the corkscrew?

After pondering that for a second, his mind turned to home. What was Zoe doing now? . . . Probably with Caitlyn, talking baby stuff. What about Keefe? Roland? They had probably become friends. Maybe they were out riding horses together, sharing their secrets, not thinking about him at all.

"And here I am!" he shouted, liking the way his voice echoed off the tunnel walls. "All alone. Keefe went to Italy, and I get to go here. A boring old monastery. No one to talk to, nothin' to see, nothin' to do . . . except drink. . . . I'm drunk!" He laughed so hard his eyes watered. "Does anybody care?"

His gaze traveled down the tunnel he had come through, to the blurry light of the distant lanterns. He sighed and leaned against the uneven wall behind him. His head scraped something sharp.

"Ow!" Rubbing his head, he turned to see what he'd bumped.

The wall resembled the one they had broken through in the cellar, stones of different sizes held together with thick, gritty mortar. In the sunken area where the stone wall met the smoother wall of the tunnel, something metallic shone in the lantern's light.

His hand went to it by impulse. The object budged at his touch. He poked, pulled, pried, his fingers numbing in the process, until it finally came free.

"Gotcha." He lifted it and dangled it before his eyes. It was a three-inch, tarnished crucifix on a thick chain.

"Well, whaddya know?" He put the chain over his head and stuffed the unopened bottle into the sunken area between the walls. Wanting to get up, he pressed his back to the wall and pushed with his legs, but then he saw something out of the corner of his eye.

Something in the distance moved.

He slid back down, squinting, trying to make sense of the vision.

A white-robed, hooded figure walked in and out of light from the distant lanterns, drawing near. Even as it got within a few yards, the figure was blurry and tilted. Was it . . .? It was. It was a monk, one he hadn't met.

The monk stopped and hovered over Jarret. At a distance, they'd all looked the same, but this one had a chubby, egg-shaped head, half-moon eyes, and white hair.

"Hello, there, massster monk." Jarret peered up at him.

The monk squatted, his gaze on Jarret's chest. He touched the crucifix, his grim mouth forming a child-like smile.

"This yers?" Jarret wrapped his fingers around it and lifted it over his head.

The monk tugged it back down, keeping Jarret from removing it. He patted Jarret's hand.

"You want me to keep it?" Jarret put a hand to the wall, deciding to stand, and tried to get his feet under himself. His foot slipped, and he slammed down on his rump, the world around him tilting again.

The monk grabbed Jarret's arm.

Jarret pulled away. "I got it." He planted his feet on the cold, stone floor. "Yer rat probably drug it down here."

The monk tilted his head as if he didn't understand.

"Your rat, you know, the one you found in the winery. Papa said you were chasin' a rat, made a big ol' hole in the wall." He chuckled. "That you? You make that hole?"

The monk nodded, smiling sheepishly. Then he grabbed Jarret's arm and yanked him to his feet.

The world tilted. Jarret staggered to one side, bumping into the monk. "How'd ya find me down here?" He draped an arm over the monk's shoulder to maintain balance. "Papa lookin' for me? I told him I was gonna hang out in the library. I didn't think he'd care. I ain't been gone more than half an hour. What time is it? 'Zit still raining?"

The monk wrapped his arm around Jarret and walked him a few yards.

The air had grown colder, now that he stood. Jarret shivered. He stopped, pushed away from the monk, and scanned the ground. "You see a sheet? I had a sheet."

The monk squinted to either side then removed his outer cloak and draped it over Jarret's shoulders.

Made of thick white material, wool maybe, it had some weight to it. Jarret pulled it closed, longing for warmth. "Uh, don't be getting any ideas. I ain't becoming no monk."

The monk laughed, his half-moon eyes waning.

Before long, the monk had helped him back through the lantern-lit tunnel and into the cellar. Soft yellow light greeted them. Not a soul in sight; Jarret was glad. He'd like the drunk feeling to pass before Papa laid eyes on him. How long would that take?

The monk led the way again, his black scapular making him blend in with shadows. Before Jarret realized it, they ended up in the old elevator and the monk was tugging on a rope. As the creaky elevator rose, it tipped to one side.

Jarret's head spun from the motion. His stomach churned. He clung to a wooden rail and groaned. "I think, I think I need to lie down."

When the elevator finally stopped, the monk pried Jarret's hands from the rail and helped him to the door. The wind had died down, but rain fell steadily, its drops pelting Jarret's face with a numbing effect.

Jarret dragged his feet.

"Hurry," the monk said, tugging Jarret's arm. "You'll catch cold."

"Gotcha." Jarret grinned, staggering. "You ain't allowed to talk, are you?"

The monk tugged harder, forcing him to run and leading him through rain and darkness, gravel crunching beneath their feet.

They arrived at the guesthouse all too soon. The monk lifted his fist but hadn't even pounded on the door when it opened to Papa's mean face.

"Where've you been?"

Papa pulled and the monk pushed Jarret inside.

Jarret stumbled and landed on his knees by the couch. A wave of nausea overcame him. He held his gut. Maybe he should've eaten more for dinner. Maybe he shouldn't have downed the wine so quickly.

"Give Brother Maurus his cloak." Papa's hard tone softened when he spoke again. "Thank you. I hope you'll come see me tomorrow when you're free to talk."

Someone removed the cloak from Jarret's shoulders. The door closed, cutting off the soft pattering sound of the rain.

Jarret crawled onto the couch, head spinning. He wanted to lie down and hold his gut. Papa grabbed him by the arm and made him sit.

"Let's get you out of those wet clothes." Papa stooped by Jarret's feet and untied his shoes. "I don't know what you're thinking sometimes. Here we are the guests of—"

The contents of Jarret's stomach lurched. "I'm gonna be sick."

CHAPTER FOURTEEN
BE NOT AFRAID

Monettello

"Awake, my dear boy." Monettello flapped his wings to create a gentle breeze.

Keefe, who had been taking slow, barely-detectable breaths, suddenly inhaled deeply. He squinted into a beam of sunlight then rolled over and hid his face in a pillow on the Brandt's couch.

Monettello leaned and whispered in his ear, "Listen, my child. The friars are awake. Listen."

Bedroom doors on the guests' side of the house opened and closed. The friars processed down the hallway, their sandals padding softly. Once they reached the glass patio door that led to the backyard, Keefe should hear them.

Last night, Monettello had seen to it that Mr. Brandt forgot to check the glass door that separated the family's side of the house from the guest quarters. Toby had been sliding it open and shut for half an hour after the last guest passed through. He had left it open a bit, enough to let sound carry through.

The patio door slid open. Friars began filing out.

Keefe's eyes shifted under closed lids. He inhaled. As the door rolled shut, his eyes snapped open. He bolted upright and jerked his face to either side. Appearing to regain his bearings, he exhaled. Then he yawned and stood, turning toward the kitchen as the last brother passed by the kitchen window.

His eyes popped open wide again.

Monettello laughed. "Well, don't just stand there. Go see what they're up to. It's the reason you stayed the night, isn't it?"

The friars had remained in the company of the Brandts and other guests for an hour and a half after dinner, sharing stories and the goals of the brotherhood. Brother Leo, the eldest, had everyone laughing at one point, teary eyed at another. With his deep voice and way with words, he had a gift for moving hearts. The youngest, Brother James, was asked to share his story and, specifically, how he recognized his calling.

All that he had heard, but especially Brother James's story, had moved Keefe deeply, though he still doubted his own calling.

Drawn as he was to their lifestyle and curious to learn more about them, he couldn't get himself to leave the Brandt's house even after the friars had returned to their rooms for the night. He readily accepted Peter's invitation to shoot pop cans with a pellet gun in the backyard. They had stayed outside for hours, talking about nothing and wandering the trails in the woods behind the house. It was after midnight when they came inside so Mr. Brandt, at the prompting of his guardian angel, offered Keefe the couch.

"Well, go on," Monettello encouraged.

Keefe stumbled around the couch. On his way to the window, his socks slid on the smooth kitchen floor.

The friars were no longer in view.

Keefe dashed to the sliding glass door and yanked it open. He reached the patio door as the last brother disappeared into the woods.

"What could they be . . ." Still in his socks, Keefe dashed after them.

He jogged through dew-laden grass, slowing as he neared the edge of the woods. The songs of the early morning birds drowned out any sound the friars made.

Keefe stepped through a row of lush maples and oaks. Then he saw them.

They stood in a small clearing between thick-trunked trees, a lush canopy of leaves overhead. Books in their hands, eyes to the pages, a few of them spoke in unison. When they stopped, the others replied in unison.

Keefe drew nearer but remained hidden behind trees. His brows lowered and rose; he couldn't make out what they said. To get closer, he'd have to step out where they could see him. He looked up and scanned the branches of the trees.

"Not a good idea, Keefe," Monettello said.

Keefe scurried to a tree with a few low branches and climbed.

Monettello stretched out his wings. "Keefe, please think about this. The branch that extends over the friars may be well hidden, but it is not a good climbing branch. Do not be afraid to approach them. You need not hide. They will welcome you."

Keefe climbed with great dexterity and soon reached the overhead branch. He inched forward.

Though concerned for his safety, Monettello smiled, admiring Keefe's determination. A man discerning his vocation can do crazy things.

The friars continued their back and forth exchange, the words becoming clearer now to Keefe, judging by the joy in his eyes.

O God, you are my God, for you I long, for you my soul is thirsting. My body pines for you like a dry, weary land without water. So I gaze on you in the sanctuary to see your strength and your glory.

Keefe's eyelids flickered, and he mouthed, "For you my soul is thirsting." When he scooted forward for a better view, the branch creaked and dipped. He clung to it, his knuckles turning white, but his legs slipped.

"I've got you." Monettello extended his wings and moved beneath him. He would make certain Keefe sustained no injury.

The friars turned as Keefe's legs swung down. They stopped mid-prayer, gaping as Keefe dropped from the tree and landed on the ground with a grunt. He rolled onto his back.

"Keefe!" Brother Leo, the oldest, darted to his side. "Are you okay?"

Panting to catch his breath, Keefe glanced from one brother to the next, for they had all gathered round now. Red-faced, he nodded and pushed himself up on his elbows. "I'm fine."

Two smiling brothers took him by the arms and helped him to his feet.

"I think Brother Zacchaeus would like to join us," Brother Leo said to the chuckles of the others.

"Zacchaeus? I kind of . . . Well, I can't, really." He glanced at the friars and brushed dirt and leaves off his clothes. "I'm only seventeen. I-I'm not done with high school, and I . . ."

The friars laughed outright, one of them slapping his arm.

"I only meant for Morning Prayer," Brother Leo said, straight-faced now and with a fatherly kindness about him. "If you would like to join us, you can share my book."

"Oh. Morning Prayer." Keefe gave a little laugh, sounding quite relieved. "Yeah, sure, I'd like that."

They returned to their places in the clearing and lifted their prayer books. Keefe stood beside Brother Leo. With wings held high, Monettello joined the other angels in carrying the prayers to the heavenly throne.

On the way back to the house, Keefe walked alongside Brother Lawrence. After a few words on the beauty of the woods in the early morning, Brother Lawrence asked a question.

"Have you ever considered a religious vocation?"

The question threw off the beating of Keefe's heart. "Me? Well I . . ." He paused to take a breath. "I don't know. I think God's been trying to tell me something for the past few months. I've changed a lot of things in my life, and I've been praying, asking, but I haven't received a definite answer. I like the idea of a life dedicated to God. But . . ." He shook his head. "I can't do it now."

A squirrel scampered across their path.

Brother Lawrence's gaze followed the squirrel then drifted back to Keefe. "You are too young?"

"Well, yeah, that's one reason." He stuffed his hands into his pockets.

"Discernment is a process," Brother Lawrence said. "Pray, reflect, listen to the Lord. And perhaps you would like to keep in touch with us. Then once you graduate—"

"No. It'll be longer than that. I have—" He shut his mouth, glanced away, then continued. "I have a twin brother. We're pretty close. Or, well, we used to be before I changed my view of life. He's going down a hard road right now, and I really believe that I've got to help him. Besides . . ."

He smiled, looking Brother Lawrence in the eyes. "I don't think I'm good enough for this way of life. I mean, I don't think I'm worthy." His gaze dropped to the ground. "I've made a lot of mistakes in the past, and I don't have any talents, besides being good at a few sports. But I don't think those skills would—"

"You can't think like that." Brother Lawrence touched Keefe's arm. "If the religious life were only for those who felt worthy, there would be no religious. We are all unworthy. Besides, your skills could come in handy. God surprises us sometimes."

Monettello rejoiced. "Do not be afraid to make a commitment, Keefe. Trust in the Lord."

CHAPTER FIFTEEN

TESTING

Jarret

Thumbs in the belt loops of his denim shorts, Jarret paced the shrine and tried to keep his gaze from landing on anything in particular. The strange feelings he had experienced the night before hit him again the second he'd crossed the threshold and dipped his finger in the holy water font. Why should the place make him feel one way or another?

"It's twelve and a quarter inches tall." Selena stood on tiptoe, measuring the height of a plaque of the Last Supper. Roland had said it was made of cast stone and stained with an antique finish.

"Are you sure?" Roland sat on a kneeler, clicking away on his laptop keyboard. His dark hair fell in his eyes, making him appear childish. Way too young for Selena.

Selena put a hand on her hip. "Of course I'm sure. I know how to use a measuring tape."

Roland glanced at her out of the top of his eyes, his forehead wrinkling. "Oh. I didn't mean—"

She laughed.

He smiled and exhaled. *Idiot.* Did he think he could win Selena by cataloging her father's trinkets?

Jarret rolled his eyes and stepped between them, facing Selena. "I know you go riding in the mornings. Why don't you ever take me?"

"How do you know I ride in the mornings? Are you spying on me?"

He huffed.

"You wanted to go?" She removed the Last Supper plaque from the wall and turned it over, her eyes on it and not him.

"Yeah, I already told you that."

She clicked her tongue, her gaze snapping to him.

He took the plaque from her and handed it to Roland. "Why don't we let Roland do his thing, and you and me can go riding now? I'm dying to go riding. I'm having withdrawals."

Selena laughed. "Withdrawals? From riding?"

"Yeah, I ride every chance I get at home." His conscience gave him the slightest prick. Their groundskeeper, Mr. Digby, ended up grooming and exercising the horses more than anyone else. But Jarret did ride his horse, Desert, more than Keefe or Roland rode theirs.

She smiled, squinting at him as if she couldn't decide whether or not to believe him. "It's so hot right now. We can ride later, in the evening. We can all go." She leaned, looking past him to Roland. "Do you like to ride?"

"Yeah, sure. I love to ride."

"You love it, huh?" Jarret shot a wicked glare at Roland.

"Good, then it's settled." Selena looked from one to the other. "We'll go riding tonight."

Roland snapped a few pictures and placed the plaque in Selena's waiting hands. Selena returned it to the wall.

"Oh, you know who else was at the dinner party?" she said, turning around.

Jarret groaned. Did she have to keep on with the obsessive conversation that Roland had started?

"You mean the night Saint George was stolen?" Roland said. "Who?"

"My mother's friend, Becca. The woman is so annoying." She wrinkled her nose.

"Why is she annoying?" Roland said.

"She and my mother have been friends since high school. I guess they both came from poor families and Becca, unlike Mamá, married a man of modest means. Anyway, now she always makes comments about our family's wealth, like she's jealous and can't get over it."

"What's her husband like?"

"The same. Less vocal. And they have three kids, two boys and a girl. One is my age. The other two are adults now, on their own, but sometimes they still come with her. My mother invites her over several times a year. I don't know why."

"Was she at the last dinner party?"

"Mm-hmm. And so was her oldest son. He shares her attitude about our wealth."

"Did they go out to the shrine?"

Selena shrugged. "I don't know."

"What about shopping?" Jarret said, moving in on Selena. "Where do you shop around here?"

Her serious expression turned into a smile, amusement in her eyes. "What do you need?"

He stopped less than two feet from her and shrugged. "Nothing. But I like to shop. You got a mall around here? Some kind of dinky desert mall?"

"Sure, there's a little mall near here, but if you really like to shop, you want to go to Tucson."

"So take me," he said, meaning to sound suggestive.

139

Roland clicked his tongue and shook his head. When he turned away, his eyes locked onto something on the floor, and his eyebrows twitched.

"I don't have a car," Selena said. "I just turned sixteen."

"You should have a car." He risked touching her hair, finding it as soft as he had imagined it to be, and finding her undisturbed by his action. Did she like him? "Maybe my father will let me borrow his rental. Would you go with me then?"

She glanced at Roland who had set his laptop down and was heading across the room. His gaze was on the floor under the shelf where Saint George had once stood.

Jarret sneered. "What are you looking at *him* for? He's gonna want to do this all day. He's a papa's boy."

"Give it a rest." Roland glared then dropped his gaze and squatted. "If you want to go shopping, go shopping. I'd like to go too but, yeah, I'm gonna finish what I started."

"Why can't we do both?" Selena asked.

Jarret shook his head and walked away from her. "'Why can't we do both?'" he said, attempting to imitate her voice. "Is that your standard answer? Doing *both* means we do what Roland wants first." His gaze slid to her silky hair. He really needed to get her alone, get her mind off Roland. They could have fun.

Selena gave him a strange, narrow-eyed look for two seconds then walked up to him, hands on hips. "Think you can borrow your father's car?"

"Sure."

"Okay. Let's see what we can do here, then we'll go to dinner in Tucson and shopping afterwards. And after we get back . . ." She smiled and her eyes lit up. ". . . we'll take the horses out."

The way she stood so close to Jarret, with her hands on her hips and looking him dead in the eye, made him want to lean down and kiss her. But he let a smile spread across his face instead. "When you say *we . . .*"

She dropped one hand to her side and used the other to stifle a laugh. "I mean all three of us."

"Of course." He sneered at Roland, working up to another sarcastic remark when an idea came to his mind. Maybe Roland wouldn't be able to go.

"What do you think that is?" Roland stood up, pointing to the floor.

While Selena and Roland investigated a small brown splotch on the floor, Jarret worked on a plan.

CHAPTER SIXTEEN
LISTENING TO THE VOICE

Ellechial

Jarret climbed the staircase in the Zamoranos' house. Ellechial glided alongside him, bombarding Heaven with prayers. If he did not perpetually behold the face of God, Jarret's present frame of mind and his devious plan would cause Ellechial deep sorrow. Especially knowing that Jarret never turned away from an idea once it got wedged in his mind.

Jarret stopped at the bedroom door, glanced inside the brown paper bag he carried, and reached for the doorknob.

Roland looked up as Jarret stepped into the room. He sat at a small circular table, his fingers resting on the keypad of his laptop. A yellowish light from a corner lamp shone behind him in the otherwise dark room.

"Greetings and praise be to God," Nadriel said to Ellechial.

"Now and forever." Ellechial sighed. "Be on guard, my friend."

"Always."

"Hey there, little brother." Jarret set the bag on the dresser, between a stack of towels and a statue of an angel, then turned around and stared at Roland for a moment. "What're you up to?" His tone lacked its usual arrogance.

"Organizing my notes." He typed another line but then stopped, probably sensing the change in Jarret's attitude. "What've you been up to?"

Jarret jabbed his thumb in the direction of the bag. "Went with Papa to the drug store."

"What time is it?" Roland checked the time on his laptop even as he asked the question. "You going to shower? Selena wants to leave for Tucson in an hour."

"An hour? So it'll be at least two hours before we eat anything. I need something now." Jarret turned to the bag. With slow deliberate movements, he brought two bottles of juice from the bag, cracked one of them open, and lifted his gaze to the dresser mirror. His pupils dilated, making his eyes appear black as he studied his brother through the mirror.

Roland had resumed typing and rocked slightly, oblivious to Jarret's scrutiny.

"Don't do it," Ellechial said. "You'll regret it. It'll only make you—"

Deth-kye's callous laughter filled the room. He appeared as a charred, lanky figure crouching on the dresser on the side opposite the angel statue. "Why do you bother? He doesn't hear you. Has he ever listened to your advice?"

Ellechial's wings drew back. "He has."

"Not since he was *two*." Deth-kye spit out the last word and grinned. "He's mine. You are unable to touch him, and you know it." Deth-kye leaned his face close to Jarret's and whispered seductively, "You have to do it. How else will you get Selena all to yourself? You see how she likes him as much as, maybe more than she likes you. Get him out of the way. Let Selena get to know you one on one. You can have fun tonight."

Jarret's eyelids flickered and, frowning, he reached into the bag again and drew out a bottle of liquid sleep aid. After taking a long swig of juice, he refilled the bottle with the vanilla-flavored drug, secured its lid, and shook it.

He turned around smiling. "Thirsty?"

Ellechial wept and lifted prayers to Heaven. If only he had permission to fight. He needed grace from prayers and sacrifices.

Roland glanced up from the laptop. "What?"

"I picked up some juice." Jarret strolled over, opened the bottle of tainted juice, and handed it to Roland. "It's a juice cocktail. It's pretty good. I had one earlier."

Roland glanced at the juice then squinted at Jarret, a hint of suspicion in his eyes. "For me?"

"Don't drink it," Ellechial said to Roland, then to Nadriel, "If he doesn't drink it—"

Nadriel shook his head. "God allows it. I am certain it will work around to His greater glory."

"You foresee things, then, that I do not. Jarret's disregard for Roland, I have always feared, may one day lead to great tragedy."

"Today is not that day." Nadriel spread his wings and gazed upon Roland with love.

Ellechial sought refuge in prayer.

Deth-kye hopped off the dresser, cackling. With a taunting gleam in his eyes, he strutted toward the angels. "You might as well go. This is my show now. Or you can stay, watch it unfold. I do like an audience."

He waved his lanky, charred-red arm dramatically as he said, "Act one." He strutted to Jarret and draped his arm around the boy's shoulders. "Jarret pretends to like Roland. The naïve sap believes him instantly."

"You look shocked." Jarret gave a friendly smile, one that Roland had rarely seen directed toward him.

"It's just that—"

"Yeah, I know. I never do anything nice for you." He returned to the bag on the dresser. "I got pretzels too." He ripped open the pretzel bag, tossed a pretzel in the air and caught it in his mouth. Then he sat on the end of Roland's bed, the one in the middle of the room. "Maybe I'm turning over a new leaf."

Deth-kye burst out laughing and flung himself onto the bed. "Turning over a new leaf . . . Isn't that superb?"

He sat up and wiped his face, removing the hideous grin. "Act two . . ." He slunk up behind Roland and peered at him over his shoulder. "Roland drinks of the tainted juice," he said in a stage whisper.

Roland lifted the bottle to his mouth. "Thanks." He took a swig, gulping down almost half the contents. When he lowered the bottle, he squinted at the label. "Tastes strange, sweet, like it's got vanilla in it."

Jarret lifted his own drink. "Yeah, but it's good."

Juice in hand, Roland joined his brother on the bed. He crunched a few pretzels and drained the juice.

After fifteen minutes of small talk, Roland's expression evened out and his focus waned. He stared into space for a moment, blinked a few times, and then asked, "Do you think someone tried to break into the chapel after the locks were installed?"

Jarret's eyelids flickered with a look of annoyance. Then he grinned and downed the last drop of his juice. "Do we have to talk about that? Do you really think you're gonna catch the thief? You know Papa doesn't want you involved. What're you gonna say when he realizes you're all hung up on it? I have half a mind to rat on you."

Roland inhaled and slowly exhaled. "You saw the scrapes on the doorknob. It looked like someone tried to pick the lock, don't you think?"

"Nothing else has gone missing, has it?"

"No, but . . . What do you think of the spot on the floor? Selena thinks the thief left it when he took Saint George."

"Well, it looked like backy juice to me."

"Backy juice?" Roland pulled the pillows out from under the bedspread and propped them against the headboard. He scooted back, yawning, and sank into the pillows.

"Yeah, from chew. You know, chewing tobacco. If you chew, you gotta spit."

Roland blinked in slow motion while making a weak effort to kick off his black athletic shoes. "Who would spit in a chapel?"

Jarret grinned and unlaced Roland's shoes for him. "Same guy who would steal from a chapel. It wasn't a big stain, though. Maybe he drooled without knowing it."

Roland laughed lazily. His eyes closed, and he tried again to kick off his shoes. "I'm kind of tired."

"You've been pushing yourself." Jarret tugged Roland's shoes off as he spoke. "This is supposed to be vacation. You need to relax a little. Why don't you take a nap? We've got time. I'll go shower."

After a long yawn, Roland nodded. "Yeah, I think . . . I . . ." He exhaled long and loud. Every muscle in his body relaxed.

"Atta boy." Jarret dropped Roland's shoes. They fell to the floor with a double thunk.

Deth-kye's face contorted into a vile expression of pleasure. Clasping his hands together, he threw his head back and shot into air. He launched into a somersault, vanished, and reappeared directly before Ellechial. "Act three." He tilted his head to one side and frowned in mock pity. A black chain appeared in his hands, the Chain of Addiction. "Jarret sinks to a new spiritual low." He crept to Jarret, scraping the chain along the floor.

Eyes on the chain, Ellechial prayed. If Deth-kye succeeded in binding Jarret, it would make conversion much more difficult. Jarret's own physical safety would also be in greater jeopardy.

Ellechial whispered to Jarret, "Repent. You know you have sinned. Repent. God is quick to forgive. There is no sin so great—"

"I'm, uh, I'm sorry, little brother." Jarret gazed at Roland a moment, then he shuffled to his own bed, the one against the wall.

Nadriel and Ellechial exchanged a glance.

The chain clanked. Deth-kye crept closer to Jarret, a twisted grin on his face, a lilt in his step.

Ellechial flashed over, wings held high, ready to block the demon. "You cannot have him. He repents of his deed."

"Does he?" Deth-kye spoke with challenge in his tone.

"I'm sorry, but I had to do it like this." Jarret pulled the bedspread off his bed. "You're kinda in my way, you see." He dragged the bedspread to Roland and draped it over his prone body. "I ain't got nothing against you."

Deth-kye crowed, "No, my angelic adversary, he does not repent."

Ellechial spun to face his charge. "Jarret, hear me! You must repent. He is your brother. You don't know what harm you do to yourself in this."

Jarret's eyes shifted. He continued arranging the bedspread. "Things ain't been working out for me lately. I'm losing everything. Lost Keefe first." He glanced at the face of his sleeping brother, his lip curling up on one side. "He crossed over to your side, to the good-boy side. Left me all alone. Then I lost . . ." His voice cracked. ". . . Zoe. And my little baby girl." He blinked back tears, then his eyes narrowed and he gritted his teeth.

"But maybe I've found something better. I think Selena could like me. Don't you?" He reclined beside Roland, all the while staring at his brother's closed eyes. "She seems to like you. But

147

maybe I got that wrong." He paused as if waiting for an answer. "I intend to find out. Can't have you around if I'm gonna find that out. See? It's nothing personal. I ain't got nothing against you."

"Ah, ah, ah. That's no way to think." Waving a finger in mock chastisement, Deth-kye approached Jarret again. "My boy, you have plenty to hold against him." He crouched by the bed and whispered in Jarret's ear.

Jarret sat up, swinging his legs off the bed. Deth-kye jumped out of his way, chortling. "Now that I think about it," Jarret said, "I guess I do have something against you. You, always sticking to the straight and narrow, you don't do much for my image. You're always offering to help Papa with junk. Makes me look bad. He favors you. Always has. I'm the selfish, bad son." He gave Roland a glance over his shoulder. "Why can't you be a regular, trouble-making kid . . . like me?"

"Oh, and what's more . . ." Deth-kye leaned in close and whispered secrets to Jarret, a slithery hissing sound coming to the angels. Then he backed off again and sashayed around the room while Jarret ranted.

"Mama even favored you." Jarret raised his voice, and his eyes hardened. "My memories of her are all tainted with you, little baby Roland, sitting on her lap, toddling after her, crying for her. Yeah, she liked you best." His lip curled again. "So you kind of have this coming. It evens things up. Everyone thinks you're so great . . . but I get the girl."

"You have it wrong, Jarret." Ellechial sat beside him. "God has allowed the suffering in your life for a reason. But you are now adding to it. You resist Him. Jarret, know that you are loved."

Jarret's heart skipped a beat. His hand shot up to his chest. He opened his mouth and began to form a word but stopped.

Deth-kye darted to his other side. "Don't listen to him," he hissed like a snake. "He wants you to feel guilty. Why should you? You haven't killed anyone. Don't let feelings of doubt and guilt own you. You have done nothing wrong, not by your rules. Follow your own rules."

Jarret

Jarret watched Roland sleep. Should he feel guilty? Did he have to follow certain rules to be happy? Why couldn't he follow his own rules?

The priest at the Monastery in California came to mind. He must've been the one to get him thinking in this guilt-ridden way. Papa shouldn't have forced him to talk to the priest.

Arms crossed and slouching, Jarret sat in the dim confessional, facing a priest in a white robe and a black scapular. "Look, I don't wanna waste your time. My father told me to come here, but I'm not ready for confession."

"That's fine, Jarret. Let's just talk." The priest stroked his full white beard.

"Talk about what?"

"What would you like to talk about?"

Jarret snickered, glancing away. "I don't know."

They sat in silence for a moment, the temperature in the little confessional rising with each passing second.

"What?" Jarret straightened up. "You want me to talk about the wine? Yeah, I stole it. 'Thou shalt not steal,' huh? Well, I wasn't exactly thinking about it like that, at the time. I wanted something to do. It's boring around here. I'll pay for it. It's no big deal."

A twitch of whiskers suggested that the priest was smiling under his thick white mustache. He nodded.

"I took two bottles. I only drank the one. The other I stashed in the tunnels."

The priest stretched his legs out and crossed them at the ankles. "Why don't you give it back?" He sounded merely curious.

Jarret leaned forward, locking his eyes on the blue-eyes of the priest. "Because I don't want to. Because I'm saving it for another time." He slouched back again. "Only next time, I think I won't suck it down so fast. Who'd a thought you could get drunk off one bottle-a wine?" He grinned, remembering the song he had made up.

The priest stared.

"Look, I told you, I'm not ready for confession. I'm not sorry about it at all."

"Is there anything else you'd like to talk about? With the seal of confession, you know that everything you say remains here. It's between you and the Lord. No one else will ever know. I stand in the person of Christ. It is He who hears you, and He who helps you."

To break from the priest's unsettling gaze, Jarret scanned the confessional. The wood-paneled walls made the room feel smaller than his bedroom closet. A screen separated the priest from a kneeler. How many of the monks actually used the kneeler? They had to recognize each other's voices. A crucifix, one that actually showed blood, hung on the wall behind the priest.

Jarret touched the crucifix he wore. What would it hurt to talk to the priest? He couldn't tell anyone. It might even feel good to let it out. "Okay. I'm mad at my father for bringing me here. He wants to control my life. He wants to change me. He doesn't like my choices."

"What doesn't he like?"

Jarret eyed the priest, considering what to reveal. "He doesn't like that I smoke. He doesn't like the way I treat my spoiled younger brother. And he doesn't like that I . . . I'm close to my girlfriend, to name a few things. He found out she's pregnant. That's when he made me come here."

"Why do you think he doesn't like those things?"

He sneered and averted his gaze. *"Because I'm not playing by the rules."*

"Whose rules?"

"His rules."

"What about God's rules?"

"God's rules? I haven't killed anyone." Past offenses flashed through Jarret's mind too quickly for him to hold onto any one of them, except for the wine. *"I guess, I know I stole. That's one of 'em, right?"*

The priest had given a lengthy response, but the only comment that lingered in Jarret's mind was, "Jesus waits for you."

What did he mean by that?

A light rapping sounded on the bedroom door.

Selena. Jarret snatched his hair band and left the bathroom, fixing his hair into a ponytail as he strutted across the room. Would she even go out with him without Roland?

Roland lay in exactly the same position as when he first fell asleep. His breathing came deep and regular. He'd probably sleep until morning.

As Jarret reached for the knob, the rapping sounded on the door again. He swung the door wide open.

Selena smiled as soon as she saw him. She wore sandals and a cocoa sundress with an embroidered top. She clutched a little tan purse.

Her perfume reminded him of desert flowers and enticed him to draw nearer, but he didn't. "Hey." He stepped back and motioned for her to come in. She would probably need proof that Roland couldn't come with them.

"It's dark in here." She scanned the room and then looked him over. "Are you guys ready?"

"Looks like it's just you and me." Jarret gave a nod to indicate Roland.

She did a double take. "He's asleep?" She stepped toward the bed. "How can he sleep in the middle of the day?"

Jarret shrugged. "Sleep finally caught up with him, I guess. He's hardly slept since we've been here. He's been up all night, every night."

"Really?"

"Hey, I understand if you wanna change your mind. I get the impression that you don't want to do anything alone with me." He put on the sulky face that had always worked with Zoe.

Roland's eyeballs shifted from side to side under closed lids. He mumbled something.

"I wonder what he said." Selena's eyebrows lifted, making her resemble a girl fawning over a puppy.

"Probably calling his girlfriend's name."

Her little smile faded. "Girlfriend?"

He hadn't meant to insinuate that Roland had a girlfriend, but that's how it sounded, and now that the words were out, he decided to stick with it. "Yeah, Caitlyn. He hasn't said anything to you about her?"

"No." She continued gazing at Roland. "He said he didn't have a girlfriend."

Now, one of them would seem like a liar. He'd better watch it, or it would end up being him. "Well, uh, maybe she's not his girlfriend. They're always together. I don't know. He doesn't talk to me about that kind of stuff. You going with me or not?"

Selena looked at Roland a moment longer then faced Jarret. She smiled and took his hand. "Come on. I'm starved."

CHAPTER SEVENTEEN

QUESTIONS

Roland

Roland woke to a massive headache and a dry mouth. Dying for a drink of water, he tumbled out of bed and staggered to the bathroom. Jarret's toiletries covered the sink-top, as if he had spent a considerable amount of time in front of the mirror and then abandoned everything. Roland found nothing he could use for a cup, except—

His gaze landed on the cap of the mouthwash. He reached but then decided against it. Didn't they have any of those little Dixie cups?

He cranked the cold water on and stuck his face in the sink. After drinking what felt like a gallon of water, he searched through drawers to find something for a headache. Nothing. He staggered back to bed and lay on his side, eyes open.

Sunlight crept around the edges of the curtain. He glanced at the clock on the nightstand and sat bolt upright. Nine o'clock? He never slept in that late. Had he really slept in? What about last night? Weren't they going to—

His eyes popped with the realization. Dinner, shopping, horseback riding. With Selena! How could he have slept through that? The moment she came up with the idea, he had thought of little else. He'd been dying to go out with her, even though it wouldn't be like a date because Jarret—

Jarret's bed was empty and unmade. He had probably gone down for breakfast. Did he go out with her last night?

Roland shook his head to rid his mind of the clouds. How could he have slept through it all? He remembered feeling drowsy, and his feet . . .

His black athletic shoes lay on the floor by his bed. His feet had been unbearably hot. He'd wanted the shoes off, wanted to lie down. He was so tired.

What did Selena think when he hadn't gone with them?

Roland dashed to the bathroom. After a shower, he threw on pale gray shorts and a dark, button-front shirt. He gazed at his reflection in the mirror as he buttoned up. Selena had started teasing him about his dark shirts. *Find something else.*

Unbuttoning the shirt, he returned to the wardrobe. Black, navy, black, slate, dark olive, black . . . He didn't have anything lighter. He'd planned on picking up a light-colored shirt at the mall last night.

He slammed the wardrobe shut and turned around. Could he wear a plain white t-shirt? Wait!

He yanked open the door to the other side of the wardrobe and flipped through Jarret's shirts. Jarret had a nice blue and white plaid t-shirt. He wouldn't mind loaning it, would he? He had almost seemed nice last night, sharing his juice and pretzels.

Did Jarret go to dinner and shopping with Selena? Why didn't they wake him?

Roland stripped off the dark shirt, pulled the plaid t-shirt on, and headed for the door. When he stepped from the bedroom, he squinted.

The guest bedrooms came off the end of a second-floor hallway that was open to the first floor. Sunlight poured in through tall windows on either side of the front door, illuminating the foyer and traveling freely to the upper hallway.

However, light also came from across the hallway, from a room with a half-open door. Whose room was it? Not one of the Zamoranos. Their rooms came off the enclosed hallway. And Papa's room was next to the room with the half-open door.

Roland crept down the hallway. Halfway there, someone in the room moved past the doorway. Roland's heart skipped a beat. Whoever it was probably assumed that everyone had gone downstairs for the day.

Roland stopped at the door and flattened himself against the wall, listening. Soft sounds came from inside the room, like footfalls on carpet and objects sliding on a shelf.

Whoever it was and whatever his or her purpose, Roland had to know. If it was the thief and something got stolen, he'd feel responsible for having done nothing. With a deep breath, Roland stepped into the doorway and pushed the door wide open.

Judging by the burgundy, white, glass and brass, this was a girl's room.

Roland stepped back.

Movement came from the corner of the room. Papa stood by a glass shelving unit. "Roland?"

Roland swallowed hard. He shouldn't have been snooping. "What're you doing?" He tried to sound casual and stepped into the room. "Whose room is this?"

"It's a guest room, but I don't think it gets much use." Papa scanned their surroundings, smiling, then met Roland's gaze. "This was your mother's room."

"Really?" Roland looked the room over with new interest.

The bed reminded him of a princess bed with tall posts, satiny white spread, lacy pillows, and burgundy canopy. Windows flanked the bed. Open burgundy drapes and sheer white curtains let in too much light. Pictures decorated the walls, black-and-white portraits, an airbrushed picture of a castle, and framed pictures of children's artwork. Papa stood by a glass shelving unit loaded with various rocks and minerals. Mama had been a passionate rock hound.

"They've hardly changed anything," Papa said. "Even left her rock collection." He picked up one of the rocks and turned it over in his hand. "I met your mother here at the Zamoranos'. Her family lived in Mexico, still does, but she came here in her teens. I should say, she was *sent* here. Her mother couldn't keep her out of trouble." Papa chuckled, his gaze on the pale turquoise rock he held. "A turquoise mine brought us together."

Roland drew near, and Papa handed him the lump of turquoise. He remembered the story of their meeting, but mostly from Keefe's re-telling of it. He'd always wanted to hear it from Papa, but Papa rarely spoke of Mama since her death.

"Juan, *Señor* Juan, he phoned me one day. I was living in California, working my first job since returning from Florence with a master's in archaeology. He begged me to come for a few weeks and help him with something, but he wouldn't give me many details, as is his way." Papa gazed out the window. "I guess I wouldn't have come if I'd known what he wanted. It had nothing to do with archaeology."

He faced Roland. "Juan was your mother's guardian at that time. And she had an old map and a hunch about an abandoned turquoise mine. So she took her Jeep all over the place, searching for it, narrowing it down. She'd be gone for hours, sometimes days. She was that determined." He sat on the bed and ran a hand through his graying hair. "Juan thought if I helped her, she'd find it that much quicker. And he could stop worrying over her."

Papa looked him in the eyes. "Your mother despised me. She hated the interference, considered me a babysitter."

Roland sat next to him on the bed. Papa had never spoken to him like this about Mama, and he didn't want to break the mood. "Well, somehow she fell in love with you."

"Yeah, that was hard work. She was stubborn. We found the mine, though. And soon after, we married." Papa's eyes held a distant look, his mouth the hint of a smile.

"I'd like to hear how that came about."

Papa blinked and shot Roland a glance that told Roland he wouldn't get that story today. "That mine supplemented our income for quite a while; well, and a diamond mine in Arkansas. I couldn't seem to rope me an archaeologist's job for quite some time." He rubbed Roland's shoulder. "But you're not interested in all that. What's up? Did you want me for something?"

"What? No, I am interested. You never talk about Mama."

Papa nodded and averted his gaze. "Yeah, I guess. I was terribly in love with your mother. Sometimes it still hurts."

A thought occurred to Roland, and he blurted it out. "Is this about Miss Meadows?"

Papa shot a glare. "Come again?" His jaw tensed and an eye twitched.

"Well, I know you love Mama, but she's not here anymore. And we all know you and Miss Meadows got along well. What Jarret told you wasn't true, you know, when he said we didn't like the idea of you two getting together. He only said it to avoid telling you about Zoe, uh, you know, when he got her pregnant." Roland paused, hoping Papa would be open to his advice. "It's really okay for you to fall in love again."

Papa's face muscles had grown increasingly tense as Roland spoke, and now he shook his head with obvious irritation. "You're wrong, Son. My visit here has nothing to do with Miss Meadows."

"Am I? I think you're here to remind yourself of Mama and your love for her. I think you're here because you're afraid of falling in love with someone else."

Head shaking, Papa went to the window. "Not really your business, Son."

"It is my business. Tell me, are you in love with her? With Miss Meadows? With Anna?"

Still facing the window, squinting into the sunlight, Papa sighed. "I don't know. There's not a whole lot I can do about it right now."

"Why?" Roland jumped up from the bed, his blood boiling. "Because of Jarret? Because he doesn't like the idea? It's like the whole world revolves around him."

Papa spun to face him. "Jarret has needs and challenges that I don't understand. But I won't alienate him to please myself."

The hard look in Papa's eyes made Roland stop pressing. He stood down, his gaze flickering to the floor, and the two of them left the room.

CHAPTER EIGHTEEN

WHAT WENT WRONG?

Jarret

Jarret took a sip of lukewarm coffee, settled back in a chair at the dining room table and gazed at Selena. He couldn't take his eyes off her.

She looked hot in a denim skirt and a white tank top, her hair playing around her shoulders whenever she turned her head. And that smile, that flirty smile . . . Why wouldn't she smile at him today? Had he made her mad last night? Was she suspicious about Roland? Is that why their date had ended the way it had?

She probably noticed his attention but made no show of it as she casually followed the grumpy old maid Eremita around the dining room. The two of them spoke to each other in Spanish, probably thinking he didn't understand. They talked about the storm clouds that had been rolling in all morning, about the dirty footprints that one of the stable hands had left in *Señor* Juan's study, and about what the cook was going to make for dinner. When they spoke too fast, he missed what they said. His Spanish was rusty, but he got the gist of their conversation.

After saying something Jarret didn't catch, Selena exploded in a fit of laughter. She threw him a glance, maybe to see if he was still watching her, then whispered to Eremita. Eremita swatted

Selena's arm and continued arranging decorations on the hutch in the back of the room.

Starting to feel a little obsessive, Jarret forced himself to look away. Heavy clouds had raced into the sky, muting the sunlight and giving the landscape a surreal, reddish aura. It had rained on and off in the early morning, though all seemed dry now.

Where had he gone wrong on their date? They'd made small talk on the drive there. Then he let her pick the restaurant. He'd wanted Mexican, but she—having had home-cooked Mexican food every day—wanted something else. So they ate at a family-owned Italian restaurant with red-checkered tablecloths and stained-glass light fixtures, Frank Sinatra songs playing in the background.

At first, conversation came slow and awkward, both of them glancing at everything but each other. But it wasn't like him to be shy, and he knew how to talk to girls. So he made himself relax and started asking her questions about herself.

She had told him she spent much of her time at the stables and knew every one of their fifteen horses. Her favorite was a buckskin quarter horse she called Blaze, short for Trail Blazer. She rode Blaze often and—he'd already guessed it—out past the boundaries of her family's property. "Out to where the wind made the only sounds," she'd said. "Out where the land became unpredictable." She had climbed to the top of mesas and down into lonely canyons, once stumbling across a thin stream and a secluded little pool. She knew the names of snakes and insects, plants and cacti, and how to treat poisonous bites or a sprained ankle.

He soaked in every detail, becoming more and more infatuated. He so wanted to ride with her.

After dinner, they had strolled through two different malls. He tried to buy her things—a turquoise bracelet that she said she loved, a hat that matched her cocoa sundress, a book about Arizona wildlife—but she wouldn't let him. So he got himself a vented, straw cowboy hat that she said matched the color of her buckskin horse.

They had gotten along so well all evening, laughing and finding things in common. When her mood shifted after they returned home, it confused him.

"So what if he can't come riding with us?" Jarret had stood, hands on his hips, glaring at his sleeping brother, despising even the look of his pale, motionless body. Roland hadn't moved an inch, it appeared, since he'd gone down.

"Well, I'm kind of tired anyway. We got home later than I thought we would, later than I told Papá I'd be." She jerked her face to the open bedroom door. "I should tell him I'm home."

He slipped his hand around her arm before she could get away. "Ride with me. I've been dying to go riding. It's dark, and I don't know the land." He paused to let his next words convey his deeper meaning. "I need you."

She twisted her arm free. "Good night, Jarret."

He went after her and grabbed her again, stopping her in the doorway. "Take a little walk with me. It's too early to go to bed."

"It's after ten."

"So?"

Her eyes narrowed and her mouth curled up into something between a smile and a sneer. "I'll see you at breakfast."

He took a chance and leaned to kiss her.

She shrunk back, giggling. "Good night, Jarret," she said in a singsong voice as she walked away.

Forcing himself to the present moment, Jarret took another sip of coffee. Selena was still whispering to Eremita. Eremita was wiping a window with a big rag.

"Why don't we go swimming before the rain comes again?" Jarret's manly voice sounded crude to his ears, unwelcome amidst their feminine Spanish chatter.

Selena and Eremita jerked their faces toward him.

"Aren't we waiting for Roland?" Selena sauntered to the table and sat across from him. "He's been up early every day since he's been here. Is it like him to sleep in so late?"

Jarret shrugged, not looking at her. "Worried about him? I told you that he doesn't sleep well. It all caught up to him. Maybe he'll sleep till noon." He met her gaze. "He can find us out at the pool."

She shook her head, her eyes narrowing the way they had the night before. "Maybe he's not feeling well. Could he be sick?"

Jarret shrugged. "If he is, I'm sure he'll get over it. The rest will do him good."

"Was his forehead hot?"

"What? How should I know?"

She stood up. "Let's go check."

"Are you kidding me?" His jaw tightened. Was she for real? She obviously wasn't going anywhere until Roland showed his ugly pale face. "We're letting him sleep. Ain't you never slept in before?" His tone grew hostile. "He's on vacation. Let him—"

His cell phone rang, and he froze. It was Keefe; he knew it. What could he want? "I'm gonna . . ." he said to Selena as he got up from the table. Eyes on her, fumbling to get his cell phone out, he backed to the doorway of the foyer. "I-I'll be right back."

She cracked a smile and dipped her head forward, her black hair falling in her face.

What did she find so funny? He stepped into the foyer and, without bothering to check the number, brought the phone to his ear. "What's up?"

"Hey, Jarret. How you been?" Keefe spoke fast, sounding nervous.

"Eh. What's up?" He leaned against the wall under the open staircase, out of the line of sight from the dining room.

"I, um, I wanted to talk to you. I-I need your advice."

Jarret huffed. Keefe never asked for his advice. Keefe only gave advice. "Advice about what?"

"Well, this is hard for me to talk about. It's personal, and I really need you to listen. Do you have the time?"

Jarret stepped to where he could peek into the dining room. Selena and Eremita must've moved on, cleaning some other room. Or maybe . . . maybe Selena had told Eremita to stay with her so she wouldn't have to be alone with him.

His stomach tightened and a bad name for Selena came to mind. He leaned against the wall again. "Yeah, I've got time. What's up?"

"Don't judge me before I finish telling you. Hear me out. I don't know who else to talk to about this. I've always had you."

The foundation of a wall formed in his mind, growing higher with every word Keefe spoke. He wasn't going to like what Keefe had to say.

"You know I've changed my views some," Keefe said, "my way of looking at life."

"Yeah." He knew it all right. It's what drove them apart after sixteen years of close friendship, more than friendship. A bond. Something only family, maybe only twins, shared.

"Well, I-I'm coming to believe that God has . . . that he has . . ."

"Has what? Spit it out."

"Plans for me."

"Plans? Really?" He rolled his eyes and let his tone show annoyance.

"Well, what about you? Don't you ever think about what God wants you to do with your life? Your vocation?"

"Do we really need to have this talk? I thought this was gonna be about you."

"It is about me. I only wondered if you ever felt the same. You're my brother, closer to me than anyone and—"

"No. No, I don't. Whatever I decide to do with my life, I'll make that decision alone, and I'll make it when I'm ready, which ain't gonna be anytime soon. What makes you think you know what God wants anyway?" He found himself pacing in the hallway and running his hand through his hair.

"I think He's calling me."

"Calling you?" He snorted. "If you're hearing voices, maybe you ought to think about finding yourself a shrink." That was cruel. He shouldn't have said it. But why was Keefe dumping this drivel on him anyway?

"Don't judge me, Jarret. Hear me out. I met these guys, these Franciscan friars, and when I hear them talk and see how they live and how happy they are—"

"Uh, stop. Are you thinking about becoming a monk?"

"A monk? No. They're brothers. They're Franciscan friars and they . . ."

Jarret huffed. His ears closed and his mind reeled. What possessed Keefe? He was out of his mind.

"You're driving a wedge between us with this new faith of yours. I'd never see you again. What if they send you off to some foreign mission? Or to a monastery out on the edge of nowhere? You gonna devote your life to AIDS patients? Die with them? Don't ask for my support. A monk? A brother? You're way too young to be thinking like this. If you do this . . . I . . . I don't ever want to talk to you again. We're through." He ended the call, spitting out, "Jerk."

Clutching the phone in a trembling hand, he slid down the wall and sat stunned, staring at a muddy footprint on the tile floor.

His gaze fixed to the crosses in the center of the footprint. The rest of the pattern consisted of lines that looked like muddy rays shooting from the crosses.

Keefe, a Franciscan Brother? He was only seventeen. Who made that kind of commitment at that age? He should be out having fun, living life, enjoying himself. Not tying himself down and closing all doors.

Jarret inhaled and leaned his head against the wall. Keefe could ruin his own life if he wanted to. Why should he care?

Voices sounded in the hallway upstairs. He ought to get up before someone came down and saw him sulking on the floor.

"I meant to tell you . . ." It was Papa. "I really appreciate your help. I'll get done with this job in half the time."

"Really?" Roland, sucking up to Papa.

Jarret stood and shoved his cell phone into his belt.

"Yeah, really. So if you want to stay longer, you'd better slow down." Papa chuckled. "I'm just messing with you. We'll be here another few days, regardless. But your work is thorough and saves me a lot of time." His boot landed on the top step. "Hey, I noticed you didn't go with Jarret last night."

Jarret sneered, watching their feet as they descended the steps.

"What? So they went without me?" Roland sounded genuinely shocked. Did he suspect that he'd been drugged?

"They went all right, and Jarret got Selena home late. I need to talk with him about that. Next time you boys want to go somewhere, stick together. I don't want him taking Selena out alone."

Jarret's jaw tensed. As they reached the bottom step, he slid out into the open.

"There you are," Papa said. "What've you been up to?"

"Living a nightmare. I'm trapped in some freaky nightmare that gets worse every day."

"Trapped?" Papa gave him an amused, unsympathetic grin.

Jarret had no reply. He pushed between Papa and Roland to get to the front door. Once outside he fished a cigarette from the pack and lit up, not caring if anyone saw him. It'd been too long since he'd had a smoke.

He hated feeling trapped. He had been physically trapped at the monastery, and he'd hated it. But this was even worse. Nothing went his way anymore. The more things slipped from his control, the more trapped he felt, trapped in a life he despised.

A monk, a brother . . . Was Keefe out of his mind?

Jarret sat leaning against the big oak tree, watching Brother Maurus prepare picnic tables for the Mary Queen of Heaven celebration. Ever since he'd stolen the wine and gotten drunk, Papa had insisted that he help the monks with chores.

Brother Maurus scurried from one side of a table to the other as a breeze lifted the white tablecloth at both ends. He finally got the idea to set a candle on one corner, but the wind blew the candle over before the monk reached the other side of the table.

"Don't you have any tape?" Jarret shouted.

Brother Maurus stopped and gave him his full attention. "Tape? Why, yes. We have tape in the office. Do you need some tape, Brother Jarret?"

"I'm not your brother, Brother Maurus." Jarret couldn't help but smile. He liked the goofy, old monk. He liked talking to him. The monk had even slipped up a few times and spoke during the hours of silence.

"Oh, sorry. It's a habit." Brother Maurus abandoned the flapping tablecloths and waddled to Jarret, his brows wrinkling as he neared. "You shouldn't be doing that."

Jarret exhaled smoke and glanced at the cigarette in his hand. "Are you gonna tell on me?"

The monk pursed his lips but didn't answer.

166

"Don't worry, it's my last. After this one, I'm out. Any of you monks smoke?"

The monk shook his head.

"Didn't think so."

The wind kicked up and blew two tablecloths into the grass.

Jarret snuffed out his cigarette and got to his feet. "Let's get tape."

As they walked, Jarret gazed at the monk's white habit and the black scapular over it. It was like a uniform that every one of them wore, unless one was doing dirty work. They didn't have a choice. They had to wear it. "Do you ever feel trapped here? You all dress the same. Eat the same things. Every day's the same. There's no freedom, no variety, nothing new."

"Trapped? Why, no. I love being here. This is my home. I have my struggles each day, sure, but this is where I belong. God has called me here." His half-moon eyes lit up as he spoke, then his brows lowered and his eyes turned to slits. "Are you feeling trapped, Jarret?"

"Yeah, we've been here too long. I need to get back home. This isn't where I belong." Jarret yanked open the door to the winery and motioned for the monk to go in first. He took a deep breath of fresh air before stepping inside. The sour smell nauseated him, reminding him of how sick he had felt before he'd thrown up.

Brother Maurus stopped at one of the desks and rummaged through the top drawer. "Ah, tape." He held up a roll of transparent tape.

"What about masking tape?" Jarret opened a drawer. "Masking tape holds better. Put some on the corners of the table, under the tablecloth."

"Oh!" Brother Maurus's eyes popped open. His eyebrows rose. "The wine. I forgot to put the wine in the refrigerator. I should've done that already." He hurried from the office. "Come help me."

"Really? You're gonna trust me with wine?"

The monk flew down the steps and began scanning the wooden shelves of wine across from the elevator. "What kind did you drink?"

Jarret followed. "I don't know. I grabbed a couple bottles. It was red. I think it was Syrah."

The monk pulled three bottles from the shelf and handed them to Jarret. He grabbed three more and flew back to the stairs. *"Did you like it?"*

"Yeah." Jarret laughed. *"You sound like you approve."*

"No, no, you are too young to drink so much."

Brother Maurus stopped at a little refrigerator next to a tall metal cabinet. *"Besides, 'We read that monks should not drink wine at all, but since the monks of our day cannot be convinced of this . . .'"* He glanced over his shoulder, smiling at Jarret. *"'. . . let us at least agree to drink moderately, and not to the point of excess, for wine makes even wise men go astray.'"* He took the bottles from Jarret, stuck them in the refrigerator, and straightened up. *"That is from the rule of St. Benedict."*

"Yeah, okay." Jarret grinned.

"When you're older, you come back. You can taste different wines." He led the way to the door.

Jarret laughed, shaking his head. *"Okay, Brother Maurus."* He held the door for the monk.

They crunched down the gravel path back to the picnic tables they had arranged around the old oak tree. Brother Maurus glanced at him a few times before saying, *"You said you do not belong here. Where do you belong?"*

"What? I don't know. I haven't figured that out yet."

"You ask Jesus. He will show you. And don't feel trapped, Brother Jarret." He stooped and retrieved one of the tablecloths from the grass. *"You won't be here much longer. Try to find a way to enjoy yourself, a way to get some benefit from your visit here."*

Jarret's conscience pricked him. He used to say that to Keefe before every trip with Papa. *"While Papa's taking care of business, let's see what we can get for ourselves."* But he knew the monk didn't mean it in the same way.

"*Hey, I never did figure out . . .*" *Jarret scooped up the other tablecloth and spread it on a table.* "*That night of the storm, how'd you know I was down there in the tunnel?*"

"*Hmm.*" *Brother Maurus had been turning the roll of tape in his hand, looking for the end. He stopped and scratched his head.* "*I went to check on something outside because of the rain, and I saw a flicker of light in a winery window. I thought nothing of it at first. It was dim. Maybe my old eyes played tricks on me? But it continued to bother me, so I went to check. I was looking around the cellar when I saw the most amazing thing. It was like an apparition.*"

Jarret grinned and came over to get the tape. "*Oh yeah?*"

"*I saw the figures of the Virgin Mother and of Our Lord surrounded by heavenly light.*" *His half-moon eyes lit up. Then he laughed.* "*Of course, as I approached, I realized it was only the statues we keep in the cellar. They were sitting on a cart, a lantern behind them.*"

Jarret busted up laughing and dropped the tape. "*I put those there.*"

"*Still, I see it as God bringing me to you. Don't you?*"

He stopped laughing and shrugged.

"*Sometimes the Lord whispers. We ought to be open to His inspirations, no matter how small they seem.*" *He whizzed around the table, sticking tape balls on the corners and covering them with the tablecloth, working as if he had always done it that way.* "*I'll miss you when you go, Brother Jarret. I enjoy your company.*"

"*Stop calling me that.*"

CHAPTER NINETEEN

BATTLE & PRAYER

Monettello

Teenagers shuffled into Saint Michael's church by twos and threes and fours, their loud talk and laughter turning to whispers and straight faces as they stepped through the vestibule. The majority of them belonged to the parish youth group, the Fire Starters.

Monettello and Cyabrial waited near the vestibule, greeting guardian angels.

"Blessed be God," Monettello said, bowing his head to Peter's guardian.

"Blessed be God forever." Peter's guardian had his sword drawn and only sheathed it once well within the church.

Dominic strode through the doors next, a Bible tucked under his arm. His guardian had been whispering intently to him but stopped to exchange a greeting. "Praised be Jesus Christ."

"Now and forevermore," Monettello and Cyabrial said together.

Monettello turned his gaze to Keefe. Keefe knelt in the third row, his head bowed with the intensity of his prayer, hopefully discerning his vocation.

"Has he received his calling, then?" Cyabrial said.

"He has. But he has yet to accept it. Worry over his twin keeps him from responding to the call. He wants to do the right thing.

Either Jarret converts and supports Keefe's calling, or Keefe must come to realize that answering God's call will do more good for everyone. Yes, I am concerned for him. Many have let the affairs of the world keep them from their vocation. I do not want to see this happen to Keefe."

Monettello and Cyabrial neared their charges, who sat on either side of Peter.

"I'm so excited the Franciscans agreed to join us," Caitlyn whispered to Peter as she made a sweeping scan of the church. "When will they get here? Why didn't they come with you?"

"Six friars? In our little car?" Peter said, forehead wrinkling. "They have to wait for a ride. Do you know they don't even own a car? They have a car they use back in Minnesota, but 'they're traveling on the generosity of others.'" He used air quotes as he repeated something his father had said. "Can you imagine that?"

"Sure. We're supposed to trust the Lord in all things."

"People were made to work, take care of themselves." Phoebe dropped into the pew behind Caitlyn, Keefe, and Peter. She slumped back and folded her arms. The blue streaks in her hair appeared green under the yellow light streaming in through a stained glass window. "I don't believe in relying on others for your daily needs. Emergencies, sure. What else can you do? But not your daily things."

Keefe rose from his knees and glanced at Phoebe as he sat back.

Caitlyn faced her. "Well, it gives them the opportunity to actively trust in God's providence, and it gives others the opportunity for charity. So everyone gets the chance to glorify God."

Phoebe smirked. "God made us to work. It's right there in the Bible. Don't ask me where."

"They do work." Caitlyn sounded defensive. "They do God's work. How can they go around preaching the Good News and helping people if they have nine-to-five jobs, too?"

Kiara slid into the pew with Phoebe. "What're you guys talking about?"

"The monks," Peter said.

"They're brothers," Phoebe and Caitlyn said together.

"Oh yeah, cool," Kiara said, her voice soft and eyes round. "I can't wait to meet them. Can you imagine giving up everything to serve God? It sounds adventurous."

Caitlyn nodded in agreement. Peter rolled his eyes. Then they both turned to face the altar.

Keefe had heard her too, judging by the flicker of his gaze, but he made no other show of it. Perhaps the very idea tumbled around his mind at that moment: giving up all to serve God.

"I could never give up my freedom," Phoebe whispered to Kiara, ". . . give up having a husband."

"You don't even have a boyfriend," Kiara whispered back.

"So. I will when I'm ready. The way I see it, why should I shop when I'm not ready to buy?"

"Don't you want to get some experience?" Kiara asked. "Then you have a better idea what kind of guy you want to marry."

"Oh, I already know that. I don't need to date to figure that out. Don't you know what you want?"

"Well, I . . . I . . . sort of."

"I think you should have that in mind, at least, before you jump into dating. It's flattering, having a guy like you and all. But a girl might be tempted to compromise on what she really wants. Not me. I don't play that game." Phoebe slumped down farther in the pew and turned her face to the altar, but she had the unfocused gaze of one deep in personal thought.

Caitlyn leaned back and, looking over Keefe's bowed head, caught Peter's eye. "Have you heard from Roland?" she whispered.

Keefe glanced without making eye contact.

"Nah." Peter whispered, too, but his voice carried. "He called once when they first got there. Jarret's probably got him tied up in some secret room. Did you know they were staying in a mansion out there?"

"Really? I wonder if it's bigger than their castle," she said. "And I wonder what they do every day."

"Probably the same things they do here. Roland slinks through the shadows, if he can find any in Arizona, and Jarret finds ways to hurt and humiliate him."

Caitlyn glared. "You're terrible."

In an instant, Hursk came from out of nowhere and leapt onto Keefe's shoulder. He had become somewhat bat-like in appearance. His wings had grown thin and bony, his teeth sharp like spears, and his nose smashed-looking.

Monettello took a stern posture and flicked him away, but not before Hursk had whispered poison to Keefe.

Keefe nudged Peter with his knee. "Isn't Roland your friend?"

Hursk peered at Monettello through beady black eyes then laughed behind a clawed hand. Though he had weakened since Keefe's conversion, he still managed to rile Keefe with *justifiable* anger.

Peter faced Keefe and grinned when he saw the hard look in his eyes. "Well, sure, he's my friend. But Jarret's not. And they're about as different as day and night, black and white, fire and ice, peanut butter and—no, that one won't work, because those go together."

"Roland cares about Jarret."

"So? *I* don't have to like him. He's . . . evil."

Armed with a three-inch shiv, Hursk swooped to Keefe.

Monettello lifted his wings and stepped toward the demon.

Hursk perched, digging claws into Keefe's shoulder. He bared his spiky teeth and hissed at Monettello.

Monettello lifted a hand to flick him away again, but then—

Grudge, a stocky greenish demon, appeared and gimped up to Peter, a dozen demons in his wake. The demons, small but lightning-quick, raced to and fro, whispering lies and tempting the teens to boredom, apathy, vanity, presumption, despair . . . They had a habit of showing up when a great good was about to be accomplished.

Monettello and the other guardian angels drew swords.

Chaos ensued. Angels beat back demons only to find them leaping up again, pouncing on a victim, and turning quickly for the fight.

Keefe's jaw tensed. "Jarret is not evil. He's . . . Well, he needs help, some direction, prayers. Haven't you heard of loving your enemies?"

Unbeknownst to them, a sword clashed over their heads.

"Mmm." Peter rubbed his chin. "I have a hard time with that one. What exactly does it mean? Love your enemies? Besides, there's nothing *I* can do to help him. You're his brother. Maybe that's your job."

Grudge had managed to plant a seed in Peter, which, at present, his guardian could do nothing to uproot, due to Peter's stubbornness.

"You can still pray for him and not bad-mouth him," Keefe said, his voice rising, "especially not in front of me."

Peter leaned toward Keefe, a sneer on his face. "Oh, I'll pray for him alright. But haven't you heard, some demons only come out of a person with prayer and fasting?"

A demon gasped. A few jerked their faces to Peter, slowing in battle.

How did he know?

Did he believe it?

Don't tell the others.

No. They didn't like people to know about that method, seeing as how it had always been quite effective.

Keefe shot a wicked glare. "He's not possessed."

"You sure about that?"

"You guys!" Caitlyn reached past Keefe and smacked Peter's arm. "We're here to pray. You can argue later." She shouted the last two words as the others in the church grew silent. Her face reddened, but no one paid her any attention.

The Franciscan friars had finally arrived. Sandals shuffling softly, they processed down the main aisle. One by one, they genuflected and filed into an empty pew near the front. They knelt at once to pray.

A demon shrieked, "He comes!"

The battle paused. A few demons fled without waiting for confirmation. Others lost their edge in fighting, and every one of those that remained came under the control of an angel.

The teens knelt. Angels fell prostrate. As Father Carston stepped into the sanctuary, demons begged for freedom, making promises they would never keep in strangled voices too hideous for a human to endure. "Please, please, let me go. I will never torment another soul. Only do not make me look upon . . . Him." A few demons gained permission to flee but others were forced to remain, to kneel, to watch, to confess, "Jesus Christ is Lord."

With great reverence, Father Carston brought out the Blessed Sacrament for adoration.

175

CHAPTER TWENTY

PLAN B

Jarret

Wearing only a towel, Jarret stood in front of the bathroom mirror and looked himself over. He had a lean, muscular body and a strong, angular face. Why would any girl choose wimpy Roland over him? After flexing his biceps, he decided that he needed to get back home to his weights. He ran his hand over his chin. Maybe he should shave the stubble, just sport the hint of a mustache. And he could always leave his hair down. Selena might like—

Forget Selena!

He had spent the whole day walking through the neighborhood in the heat, trying to clear his mind of Roland, Keefe, Papa, and her. By the time he felt his skin cracking under the relentless sun, his head had cleared, so he'd directed his steps back to the Zamoranos' house.

When the mansion came into view, Rufino's screen door swung open. So Jarret had stopped and talked with him awhile. He was tempted to ask Rufino for a joint but decided against it. He'd never smoked pot before and, besides, Rufino would probably nark him out. But he did ask to borrow his car, the old green clunker in the dirt driveway. After parting with a few bucks, the keys were his so he returned to the Zamoranos' to get cleaned up. Maybe he'd try his luck at a bar.

Jarret fixed his hair back, decided against shaving, and stepped out of the bathroom.

There, at the little table in the corner of the bedroom, sat Roland. Strangely, he wore a light-colored shirt. Eyes on Jarret, he closed his laptop. "Hey, Jarret. I was wondering what happened to you."

Jarret opened a dresser drawer. "Oh yeah, why's that?"

"I don't know. You've been gone all day. Papa and Juan wanted to take everyone to some kind of museum and dinner. Desert Museum or something."

"Why aren't you with them?" Jarret grabbed tan cargo shorts and started dressing.

"Me? I don't know. I wanted to go, but— Where've you been?" Was that worry or suspicion in his tone?

"Walking." He opened his side of the wardrobe for a shirt when it occurred to him— "Hey, are you wearing my shirt?"

Roland's hand shot to his chest. "I didn't think you'd mind. So you were out walking in this heat?"

"Yeah, I mind." He yanked a red t-shirt from the wardrobe. "You could ask first. And you know I'd say *no*."

"Well, I was going to pick one up last night. But I— Why didn't you wake me?"

Jarret looked him over. Did he suspect? "I tried. I guess you were exhausted. That's what you get for waking up at four every morning."

"I don't get up that early." His bottom lip stuck out in a pouty way, making him look five years younger.

"Whatever. Don't blame me for your little nap." If Roland suspected, what would he say? What would he do? Would he tell Selena? Coward. He wouldn't do anything. He probably wouldn't even bring it up.

Roland stared. "It's too bad we didn't get more of that rain, huh? I watched it fall over the mesas way out on the horizon."

Jarret breathed easy. "So, what're you gonna do now with everybody gone?" He snatched his cell phone, wallet, and the keys to Rufino's car. Then an idea came to mind, a way to have fun and maybe get Roland in a little trouble.

"I don't know. What're you going to do?"

Jarret grinned. "Let's go catch a thief."

"What?" Roland's steel-gray eyes flashed with a gleam of distrust.

Jarret strutted to the table and leaned his palms on it, moving into Roland's personal space. "I know you want to find the thief. You've wanted to ever since you heard things were stolen."

His forehead wrinkled. "Well, I—"

"Well, nothing. Come on." He gave a nod in the direction of the door to the hallway. "I got Rufino's car."

"What about Papa? Shouldn't we tell him—"

"I'll call." He tapped his cell phone. "I'll tell him we're going shopping." He smiled, amused at Roland's incessant worry over doing the right thing. "Bring your smartphone. We'll need it." He strutted to the bedroom door, expecting Roland to follow.

"What are your plans, exactly?" Roland came up behind him, stuffing his phone into a shirt pocket.

Jarret yanked open the door. "I'll tell you my plans in the car."

Ellechial

Ellechial and Nadriel followed their charges down the staircase.

"What do you suppose he has in mind?" Nadriel said.

"I know not." Ellechial had tried to learn Jarret's plan. After all, every movement of a person's mind has an effect on his body. And angels and demons alike can perceive even hidden bodily changes and discover a person's dispositions with great facility. The deviousness of Jarret's intention had been easy to detect, not only from the glint in his eyes and his tone of voice, but also from the change in his heartbeat when the idea had occurred to him. Sadly, bad ideas excited the boy. The details of the plan, however, were known to Jarret and God alone.

"Jarret never seemed interested in discovering the thief's identity," Nadriel said.

"Nay, he never even realized that he had seen a clue the other day. But I see that his plan for tonight is not good. Be on guard. I am thankful for the prayers of his twin and the others in the prayer group. Should the need arise . . ."

Nadriel smiled. "Ah, I will be glad to have you fight by my side."

Rufino's dusty green Chevy Malibu sat in the circular driveway. Jarret walked straight for it, jangling the keys.

Roland took a few steps but stopped. He glanced to either side before his gaze settled on the Malibu. "We're going in that?"

Jarret chuckled as he swung open the driver's door. "Scared?"

"No." Roland tensed, but he went around the car and got in.

Jarret cranked the engine to life and sat gripping the key, squinting and holding his breath while the engine spluttered and rattled.

"Shouldn't we call Papa before we head out . . ." Roland said.

Jarret tapped the gas pedal, revving the engine and gaining a more even tone. He breathed.

". . . and make sure it's okay with him first?" Roland continued.

Without so much as a glance in his brother's direction, Jarret turned the air conditioner on high and blasted the radio. His eyes narrowed as he searched stations.

"Shouldn't we leave a note or something, maybe tell one of the maids?" Roland glanced from Jarret to the radio. "Maybe Rufino would want to know where we're taking his car or when we'll be back." Bits of songs and voices drowned his other *shouldn't we* questions.

A song with a big, lurching beat and rapped vocals came into tune. A grin stretched across Jarret's face, and he moved his head to the beat. He gave Roland a satisfied grin and shifted the car into drive.

Roland shook his head and gazed out the passenger-side window. "You don't listen to me."

"It's almost an hour to Tucson, plenty of time to talk."

They rode without speaking for nearly half an hour, Jarret switching the station whenever a dull song came on. He started to switch from "Lean on Me" when Roland threw him a sideways glance.

"Like that one, huh?" Jarret actually left it on.

Roland bounced to the music.

Jarret condescended to glance, and amusement flickered in his eyes. His self-involved attitude had too often prevented him from appreciating joy in another—especially in Roland. His mouth opened to a crooked grin, a look that said he expected Roland to stop now that he'd been caught moving to the music.

Roland only smiled and exaggerated his movements.

Jarret's grin grew as he broke into song: "We all have pain, we all have sorrow . . ."

Together they sang, "But, if we are wise, we know that there's always tomorrrr-ow."

Jarret leaned toward Roland singing, "Lean on me, when you're not strong . . ."

A happy glow in his eyes, Roland leaned too, bumping Jarret's shoulder. "And I'll be your friend. I'll help you carry on . . ."

"For, it won't be long 'til I'm gonna need . . ." Jarret glanced at Roland and blinked a few times. His eyes grew moist and he swallowed hard. It appeared as though it took effort to continue singing, but sing he did. "You just call on me, brother, when you need a hand . . ."

Had it occurred to him that this was the person he had beaten up, lied to, tricked, and manipulated over and over through the years? Still, Roland never showed a hint of bitterness. Roland wanted his friendship.

Jarret's heart was moved!

Ellechial flashed to the throne of God, offered praise and thanksgiving, then begged for more grace for his charge. Perhaps tonight his repentance and conversion would begin.

When he returned to the car, Deth-kye was there, wearing a sneer so deep it contorted his face. "It won't last. Roland is Jarret's scapegoat, his dupe. That will never change. His plan for tonight, do you know what it is?" He looked at Ellechial.

Ellechial did not return the look, nor had he any intention of answering.

"Well, I do," Deth-kye spat. "He's so delightfully envious of his little brother. He plans to get the boy into trouble. And I'll see to it he does. Or worse. If I have my way—"

"You won't," Ellechial said.

A round, quivering, fist-sized shadow appeared above Deth-kye. A pointy-chinned, blood-red, grimacing face sprang from the shadow, hooking Deth-kye's attention. The demons whispered to each other, then Deth-kye vanished. The red-faced demon, still only visible to the angels as a shadow and a face, turned its ugly gaze on them. "We shall s-s-see you s-s-soon," he slurred and disappeared.

Ellechial turned his thoughts to God, pleading for Jarret's safety and conversion. The prayers of the teens had gained him permission to defend, to a point. Jarret's choices would determine the extent of the help he could give.

Jarret and Roland continued to sing. When "Lean on Me" ended, another familiar song began, and Roland belted it out. Jarret chuckled, his eyes still moist with emotion, then he joined Roland. They sang and sang until they ran out of familiar songs. Then they sat grinning for a while until Roland finally spoke.

"So you really think that you know who the thief is?"

"What?" Jarret's smile faded.

"You said we're going to catch the thief, right?"

"Oh, yeah." Jarret's eyes shifted, showing his discomfort over the topic. "No, I don't know who it is. I just figure you already checked sellers on the internet. And Selena called antique shops, right? And he probably doesn't know any collectors. But I'd bet you my Chrysler 300 he frequents a pawn shop."

"You'll bet your car?"

Jarret glared. "Well, no, but . . . there're only so many pawn shops. Why don't we check out a few? The nearest ones. Maybe we'll see some of the stolen goods there, or maybe one of the dealers will know something. We can ask questions."

"Questions? What if we make someone suspicious? I mean, if one of the dealers receives stolen goods—"

"Don't be a dweeb. We're not gonna say *Hey, you got any hot stuff lately?* We'll act casual. We'll say Papa's name is George, and it's his birthday."

"Huh?"

"He collects antiques, and we're looking for an old Saint George statue or something."

"What about the other stuff?"

Jarret gave a disgusted huff and shook his head. "Okay, so if they ain't got Saint George maybe they'll suggest some other religious stuff, other antiques. If they've got anything of Juan's, they'll want to get it off their hands. We'll tell them we've got money." He grinned, looking pleased.

"I don't know."

Jarret's grin faded, and he threw a sulky glance. "You don't want to?"

Roland opened his mouth but closed it without saying anything.

All the muscles in Jarret's face twitched. He took a deep breath, as if resigning himself, a most uncommon response for him. "Well, if you really don't want to . . ."

Ellechial rejoiced. Jarret was actually considering what Roland wanted. Perhaps Roland could talk him into doing something else, something less dangerous, something Deth-kye wouldn't expect.

"I don't know. Think Papa would care? Think there's any danger? I mean . . ." Roland gulped back the rest of the sentence as he studied his sulking brother. "Well, I guess there's no harm in looking. We're just shopping, right? Nothing dangerous about that."

Jarret smiled. "Right."

Nadriel set about praying for Roland and whispering counsel. Roland had responded as Keefe would have in the past, giving in to Jarret's reckless ideas.

Before long, Roland had their route planned. He located Tucson pawnshops with his smartphone and mapped out the nearest ones. They both went inside the first shop, a crowded but not-too-sleazy place, and spent a few minutes looking around. Jarret did the talking, asking for a Saint George statue, among other things. The helpful but hard-of-hearing owner showed them a few antiques but nothing of Juan's. They stopped at four other shops, asking similar questions, getting similar answers. Roland created a checklist. Jarret called in a pizza order and picked it up between pawnshops.

Ellechial and Nadriel prayed and kept watch.

As the last traces of sunlight faded from the sky, they drove down a street shrouded in shadows in search of the next pawnshop on the list. Streetlights came farther apart, the buildings lower and older. Sirens sounded in the distance. They passed few people but many demons. Evil lingered in the air.

"You know," Roland said, "we don't seem to be having much luck. And this neighborhood doesn't look too safe. Maybe we should call it a night. What time did you tell Papa—"

"Don't start freaking out just because the sun's gone down. What, are you afraid of the dark too?" Jarret slowed the car, squinting at a street sign. "Besides, we're already here. Might as well check it out."

Roland sighed. "Well, let's head back after this one."

As Jarret cranked the steering wheel and turned the corner, Nadriel pointed and said, "Over there."

In an alley near the pawnshop, shadows convulsed with the presence of demons. How many? Was their presence Deth-kye's doing?

Five young, tattooed men also occupied the alley, three of them shirtless and with jeans riding lower than their underwear, two leaning against the wall, one smoking. They all turned as Jarret parked the car on the opposite side of the street. Jarret gave them a glance but redirected his gaze to the *A to Z Pawn Shop*, a plain building with a false front, barred windows, and a half-lit sign. They would have to pass the alley to get to it.

Jarret turned to Roland. "Wait here. I'll check it out real quick."

"Why should I wait here?" Roland nodded in the direction of the men. "Shouldn't we stick together?"

Jarret smirked. "No. You stay here. They look like gangsters. You look like a victim." He reached for the door handle.

"What does that mean? I don't look any more like a victim than you do."

"Yeah, right." Jarret flashed a fake grin and swung open his door. "Just stay in the car."

"No." Roland grabbed his door handle.

Jarret shot a hand out and yanked Roland back with a tight grip on his arm. "You do what I say. If something happens to you, Papa'll have my hide."

"What if something happens to you? He'll have *my* hide."

"Right. You really think that?" Jarret paused, sneering. "If something goes wrong, I'm gonna get the blame. Not you. Not Papa's pet." He released Roland's arm.

"I'm not his pet."

Jarret got out. "Stay." He slammed the door and strutted across the street, his gaze on the pawnshop lights.

With wings spread wide and shield in hand, Ellechial affixed himself to Jarret.

Jarret hadn't given the men so much as a glance as he neared, but as soon as he stepped onto the sidewalk, three of them approached. Five demons came with them, two tall and emaciated, three low to the ground and resembling mangy dogs.

The guardian angels of the men came, too, but they wore the long tunics of those who could do little on their charge's behalf. They were unarmed. Ellechial understood their plight all too well. This battle would be his alone.

As the three men surrounded Jarret, he stopped. "What's up?" He gave each of them a hard stare. "You got a problem?"

The one in his path folded his arms across his bare chest and rubbed his tattooed chin. "What is up with you, *Pocho*?"

"My business ain't with you." Jarret kept a level tone and made a move to step around, but the man shifted his stance and blocked the way.

185

The tall demons swooped down and whispered first to one, then to another of the three men. The men spoke to each other in Spanish, talking quickly. Judging by the flicker of Jarret's eyes, he caught none of it.

The one blocking him finally spoke in English. "Who is your business with then, *Pocho*? This is our street."

Jarret gave the man the once-over, probably sizing him up and wondering if he could take him. Then he glanced at the men on either side. "I'm going to the pawnshop."

"Maybe I am the owner of the pawnshop," the man with the tattooed goatee said, stepping so close that Jarret flinched at the odor of his stale breath.

The other two men moved in, taking slow steps. A low growl came from one of the dog-like demons. The other one inched toward Ellechial's heels.

Ellechial raised his shield. God willing, he would keep Jarret from harm.

Jarret's body tensed. He took a deep breath then reached for the arm of the man with the goatee, as if to push him out of the way. But he never got the chance.

One of the men came up behind Jarret, grabbed his arms and locked them behind his back.

The dog-demons leapt. The towering devils shrieked and reached for Jarret with claw-like hands.

Ellechial swung his shield and spiraled around his charge, light sparking as demons made contact with his shield.

Demons recoiled. Demons lunged. Grasping, cursing, shrieking . . .

For the glory of God and the salvation of his charge, with only a shield to use, Ellechial beat back the attack. But then one demon slipped by.

The man with the tattooed goatee put a hand on Jarret's shoulder. "So sorry, *Pocho*. You cannot go yet." With a fierce scowl on his face, egged on by the tallest of the demons, he raised his fists and took two shots, slugging Jarret in the gut and then on the chin.

Jarret moaned and slumped forward, though his captor did not release him.

Hideous but familiar laughter erupted nearby. Then Deth-kye appeared, grinning and pleased with himself.

CHAPTER TWENTY-ONE

LONG RIDE HOME

Jarret

The punch to his gut knocked the wind out of him, making Jarret lurch forward. It took a full two seconds for him to recover enough to move. Retaliation drove him. The man behind him still clutched his arms, so he decided to make the most of it. He leaned his weight onto the man and thrust his boot into Goatee's chest.

Goatee stumbled back. Was he going down?

No. He steadied himself, screwed his face into a prune-like sneer, and drew back his fist.

Jarret twisted his body and jerked his arms, hoping to break his captor's hold. But the man's hands clamped down like a steel vise.

Goatee shot forward, fists ready.

Jarret tightened his abs, but Goatee delivered one shot after another. Bolts of white hot pain seared through him.

"Hey!" someone called from a distance. Footfalls sounded in the street, drawing near.

His captor's grip lessened. One of the thugs muttered something to the others.

This could be his chance to break free. But his breath wouldn't come, and his abdomen cramped. His stomach lurched. He doubled over. Partially-digested pizza rushed up into his throat and out.

One of the dudes shouted something in Spanish, a word Jarret didn't know, and all hands released him.

Jarret collapsed, his cheek hitting the cool pavement.

"Leave him alone." The voice resembled Roland's, only lower.

Jarret opened his eyes to see, but there on the pavement before him lay a pile of upchucked pizza . . . way too close. The sour stench hit him, making his stomach lurch again.

"Who is this guy? Not police," one dude said in Spanish. The other two mumbled replies.

"Beat it," Roland said, if it *was* Roland. The voice was definitely lower than Roland's. He sounded tough, hardened.

The gang took him seriously. Their boots pounded down the alley. Why would anyone run away from Roland?

With his ribs begging him not to move, Jarret tried to push himself up. A hand clamped his upper arm. Jarret's head spun at the thought of taking another punch, but the person only yanked him to his feet.

"Come on."

Head pounding, Jarret squinted at the shadowy figure. "Roland?"

"Yeah, come on. They might come back." Roland scooted a few steps away, glanced around, then motioned for Jarret to run.

Hugging his ribs and unable to keep from groaning, Jarret ran. Each step made him want to lie down and die. He must've broken a rib or something. Maybe his liver took a hit.

They reached the car and Roland yanked open the passenger-side door. He started to get in.

"You'll have to drive." Jarret pushed past Roland and dropped onto the passenger-side seat, heart beating wildly in his throat and chest heaving as he tried to catch his breath.

Roland stood gawking at him for a long second. Then he shoved something into the glove compartment and ran around to the driver's side. "I can't drive," he said, sliding behind the steering wheel. "I don't even have my temps."

"You have to."

Roland shoved the key into the ignition and adjusted the rear view mirror. "What if I get pulled over?"

"Start the car!" Jarret slumped down in the seat. "Those guys could come back any second." The pain behind his eyes kept him from checking to see.

With a heavy sigh, Roland cranked the key and shifted into drive. Though the street had zero traffic, he looked over his shoulder three times before creeping forward.

"You're gonna have to drive faster than that." It hurt to talk, and his voice came out strained. He gingerly touched his ribs. Could one be broken?

"What's the speed limit here? I don't see any signs, do you? Are you hurt bad? Should I find the hospital?" Roland must've repeated the questions twenty times before they got to the highway.

"Just drive," was Jarret's only answer.

Ten minutes later, Jarret's heart rate and breathing had returned to normal, but his throat burned and he had a sour taste in his mouth. He straightened up as best he could and turned his attention to the glove compartment. "What'd you put in there?"

"Oh. Don't open that." Roland spared a glance. He had a white-knuckled, ten-o'clock-three-o'clock grip on the steering wheel and eyes glued to the road.

Jarret pushed past the pain to reach for the glove compartment. He opened it to a mess of papers, napkins, a tire gauge, and a black semi-automatic pistol. "What the—"

Despite his agony, Jarret reached for the gun. "So that's how you got them to run off, huh?" He examined the pistol, checking the magazine for ammunition. "It's not even loaded."

Roland shrugged. "I wasn't going to shoot anyone."

"Did you know if it was loaded or not?"

"No."

Jarret looked his little brother over with a hint of admiration. "You actually threatened those guys with a gun in your hand?"

"No. Well, yes." He glanced again. "I wasn't going to shoot anyone."

Jarret chuckled, though it hurt to do it. His hands jerked to his aching ribs, causing the pistol to slip from his grasp. It landed somewhere on the floor near his feet. He'd have to get it later. He couldn't imagine the pain he'd feel leaning over. Taking a breath, he looked at Roland. "Here I thought you were spineless."

Eyes on the road, Roland huffed.

While a ride home usually seemed shorter than a ride to some place, this ride felt endless. Eventually, Roland pulled into the circular driveway and fumbled with the automatic shifter until he figured out how to park.

"We gotta get this back to Rufino," Jarret said over the clicks and sighs of the tired engine. "He told me not to park it here at the Zamoranos'."

Roland flung open his door. "I'll move it after I get you inside."

"I can walk." Jarret grabbed the door handle and tugged, but his ribs screamed.

Roland swung open the door and touched Jarret's arm.

"Back off." Determined not to show his pain, though grimacing uncontrollably, Jarret swung his legs out and pulled himself up using the car door. "Why don't you go in and make sure Papa's not around? I don't want to talk to him tonight."

Roland obeyed, jogging up the sidewalk and stepping inside. He left the front door wide open.

With a great deal of concentration, Jarret moved as naturally as possible up the sidewalk and into the house.

The foyer and hall lights were on. Voices came from down the hall, from either the kitchen or Juan's den. Jarret only had eyes for the staircase. He pushed the front door closed with the shoulder that didn't hurt and headed for the stairs.

Roland appeared in the dark doorway of the sitting room. "Papa's with Juan." He gave a nod in the direction of the den as he went to the front door. "I'll go return the car."

"Good. I'm going to bed."

The instant Roland yanked open the front door, Papa called out from the den, "Jarret? Roland?"

Roland stopped and turned around, but Jarret climbed the steps and moved out of view.

"Where've you two been?" Papa's boots scuffed down the hall. "I need to talk to you."

"We went to Tucson," Roland said.

Jarret stepped into their dark bedroom and listened from the doorway.

"Where's Jarret?" Papa said.

"Upstairs. He's not feeling well."

"He's not feeling well?" Papa sounded skeptical. "What's the matter with him?"

"I don't know. We had pizza. He sort of threw it all back up."

Jarret smiled and silently closed the bedroom door. *Good answer, little brother.*

❖

"Get out of bed, cowboy." It sounded like Papa forced the words out through clenched teeth, but the use of the word *cowboy* was enough to convey his anger. Papa always switched to cowboy talk when his temper rose.

"Go away." Jarret refused to open his eyes or move his aching body. A moment ago, he awoke to Papa's loud voice and a rude burst of sunlight as Papa scraped open the drapes. The pain woke up too, but maybe it would subside if he could rest more. Sleep hadn't come easy last night. Unable to find a single comfortable position, he had lain on his back for hours, wishing he felt like getting up so he could take the sleep aid he'd used on Roland.

"I said get up!" Papa yanked the sheet from the bed.

"Why can't I sleep in? It's vacation." Jarret shifted his body a bit. He wanted to turn away from Papa, but his left side ached more than the right.

Hands latched onto his upper arms.

"No!" Jarret tensed in anticipation of pain. He hugged his ribs and snapped open his eyes.

With fire in his eyes, Papa yanked him up and forced him to sit on the edge of the bed.

A groan escaped Jarret. He fought back tears of pain while his arms moved by impulse to protect his ribs.

"What's the matter with you?" Papa peered over his shoulder. "You eat the same pizza?"

"Uh, yeah." Roland stood in the bathroom doorway, arms folded, frowning.

Papa faced Jarret again. "You're not sick. Strip off your shirt, and let me see what's wrong with you."

"No. I'm fine."

"Way you're acting, I'm beginning to doubt that. What were you out doing last night? Didn't bother telling me you were going out, borrowing Rufino's car, not coming back till late. You out kicking up a row?" After waiting a second and getting no answer, he turned his head again. "You lie to me, Roland?"

"No."

"You better not have. That wouldn't be like you. You start hanging out with Jarret and picking up his ways—"

"I didn't lie. I just didn't tell you everything." Roland unfolded and refolded his arms.

"Picking up my ways?" Jarret sneered. What *had* Roland told him?

He leaned to the side, wanting to lie back down, but Papa got him by the wrist. "Easy now. Off with the shirt."

"No."

Papa grabbed the back of Jarret's shirt collar and tugged.

Jarret latched onto the hem as it rose to his navel, wanting to fight for his privacy, but the effort sent a rush of pain. Moaning, he let Papa strip off his shirt.

Papa swore as he laid eyes on the scrapes and bruises on Jarret's abdomen. "Got yourself knocked galley-west, I see." He looked at Roland. "What about you?"

Jarret forced himself to stand. If he could get to the bathroom, maybe Papa would leave him alone.

Papa guided him back down and touched his sides, running his fingers along ribs. "Nothing feels broken. Just got 'em bruised real bad. So, give me your story."

"Ain't got no story. We were minding our own business. Some guy punched me in the gut. That's all." Papa hit a particularly sensitive spot, and Jarret jerked back with a moan.

"Some guy punched you. That's all, huh? Where were you? Out drinking?" He glanced over his shoulder.

Roland came over, peering at Jarret's bruised body. "We weren't drinking. I told you we were shopping. I'm not lying."

"What aren't you telling me?"

Jarret hurt too much to give Roland a warning look. Besides, he no longer cared. Let Papa think what he wanted. Jarret only wanted to ease the pain. Maybe he could take some of that liquid sleep aid and get some rest.

"It's my fault, really," Roland said. "I couldn't stop thinking about the thief and the stolen things, so we went to a few pawn shops to see if we could find anything of *Señor* Juan's. Jarret didn't do anything wrong. This happened at the last pawnshop. Some guys were hanging around outside and, well, I don't know why they beat him up."

Papa faced Jarret again. "They get your wallet?"

"No." Jarret slapped his back pocket and found it empty. He glanced at the dresser. No wallet. He cussed. He had a wad of dough in that thing, and his credit cards, driver's license . . .

"Roland," Papa said, "go fetch *Señora* Eremita. Have her bring bandages, an icepack, and some aspirin."

The instant Roland fled the room, Papa turned hard eyes to Jarret. "You only care about yourself and what you want to do. You never think about consequences. You don't know this area. You don't know Tucson. There are some rough neighborhoods. I could-a told you that. I grew up around here."

"Lay off. Roland told you it was his idea."

"Roland also thought you called me. Did you tell him that?"

Jarret averted his gaze. What else had Roland told him? Forget trying to sleep. What he needed was an escape. He needed to get high. Maybe that would ease the pain. Rufino. He'd find Rufino and bum a joint or two.

"You should've called me, asked me. I'd have told you *no*. Juan's thief is not your concern. You put yourself and your brother in danger—"

"Ha! I put your pet Roland in danger, huh? I'm the one with the bruises." Jarret jabbed a thumb at himself then pointed a finger at Papa. "And you only care that Roland might've been hurt."

"Neither of you would've been hurt if you hadn't been out there. Why do you have to be such a hard case? You're seventeen, somewhere between hay and grass, but I'm still your father. You need to follow my rules. Especially when you've got someone else with you."

Papa's eyes blazed. "Next time you're fixing to go out on the shoot, don't bring Selena, don't bring Keefe, and don't bring Roland. Do it alone." He stormed from the room and slammed the door behind him.

Jarret jumped then took a breath and lay back down. He'd rest for a minute before paying Rufino a—

The door flew open. Old Eremita stood glaring from the doorway, a roll of Ace bandages in her hand.

Roland

When Roland had stepped into the kitchen to fetch Eremita, he'd found Selena with her, both of them working at the counter making salsa or something. He hadn't liked asking Eremita for bandages and whatnot in front of Selena.

"¿Cómo?" Eremita had said, forehead winkling. She stepped to the sink and ran the water.

Selena didn't look up from the big chef's knife in her hand or the onion she diced, but she smiled, probably wondering why he needed bandages.

Roland followed Eremita to the sink and spoke in a low voice, hoping to keep the conversation private. "Bandages, you know, like Ace bandages. You use them to wrap a sprain." He spun a hand around his forearm to demonstrate.

Eremita squinted at his arm. "There is something wrong with your arm?"

"My— No, I'm fine. I just need— Well, Papa said . . ." He glanced at Selena's back. She continued dicing, a pepper now. "Don't you have any bandages?"

"You need for a cut?" Eremita looked him up and down as she dried her hands on a towel.

"No, it's not for me. Papa sent me . . . I need aspirin, an icepack, and Ace bandages, the kind you wrap around a . . . whatever."

Eremita's eyes flickered with a look he couldn't interpret. Irritation? Uncertainty? She spoke English well enough. Why did she seem so confused?

"Do you have a first aid kit?" Roland said, watching her cross the room.

"I will get." She walked with purpose through the far doorway.

"Can you bring it upstairs?" he called after her, backing up. He needed to get upstairs and make sure Papa didn't throw all the blame on Jarret.

Ready to bolt before Selena questioned him, Roland turned. But there she was, standing right in his way.

"Wanna taste it?" Smiling flirtatiously, Selena lifted a spoonful of salsa to his mouth.

"Um, no." Roland tried to step past her, but she stepped with him. "I have to get back upstairs. Papa, um, I need to, um . . ."

"What happened to Jarret?" she said, again offering the spoonful of salsa.

Aware of how close she stood and her desire to spoon feed him, heat rode up his neck. He shook his head to reject the salsa. "Maybe later."

"Where's he hurt?" Selena stuffed the spoon into her mouth and brought it out clean. "Where'd you two go last night?" She wiped the corner of her mouth and stepped closer, her brown eyes gleaming with curiosity. "How'd he get hurt?"

"He'll be all right." Inhaling the flowery scent of her shampoo, more heat rose to his face. There were six inches between her and the kitchen doorway. Should he gently push her out of the way?

She leaned against the doorframe and tucked her silky black hair behind her ear. "You might as well tell me. I've already heard the rumors."

Roland stood staring, dumbfounded. Rumors? It wasn't but a quarter after eleven in the morning.

Uncomfortable with the idea of shoving her out of the way or of answering her questions, Roland spent the next five minutes or so trying to change the subject. He didn't want to betray Jarret. They had never gotten along as well as they had last night. Maybe things would be different between them now. Maybe they could be friends. So Roland asked Selena what she'd been up to lately, what the Desert Museum was like, and what plans she had for the day.

But Selena wasn't having it. She kept steering the conversation back to Jarret, so he finally said, "Why don't you ask Jarret when he comes down? I'm sure he'll be happy to tell you."

Then, steeling his resolve, he took a breath and put a hand to her shoulder. "I've got to get going," he said as he gently pushed her aside.

Halfway through the foyer, footsteps sounded on the staircase. Then a groan. Jarret came into view, walking slower than usual and without the typical bounce in his step. His hair hung loose over his shoulders in matted curls, as if he hadn't taken a comb or even his fingers to it. He wore his new cowboy hat and a different shirt, but the tan cargo shorts were the ones he'd worn yesterday, which wasn't like him at all. Maybe his body ached too much for him to change.

"Hey," Roland said as Jarret reached the bottom step. "So how do you feel?"

"Hey there, Judas." Jarret walked around him, avoiding eye contact.

Roland followed Jarret down the hall. "Judas? Why? Because I told Papa we were at pawn shops? What's wrong with that? I told him it was my idea. I didn't mean for you to get the blame."

"Yeah, well, you're his pet. You'll never get the blame."

"I'm not his pet. It's just that you always—"

Jarret stopped dead, turned, and met his gaze, challenging Roland with his eyes.

Roland shut his mouth and swallowed hard, unable to finish his sentence. It would have come across as judgmental.

Jarret gave a smug grin and pushed past him, bumping shoulders. He shuffled down the long hallway to the sliding glass door at the end.

"Where're you going?"

"None of your business."

"Can I come?"

With a sarcastic grin and a shake of his head, Jarret stepped outside and slid the door shut behind him. He walked off in the direction of the stables.

A few seconds later, Roland stopped staring and turned around. Maybe Jarret needed time to recover from the pain. In the meantime, Roland could get some work done for Papa.

He climbed the stairs and returned to the bedroom. His gaze skated over the tangle of wires and electronic devices on the little table, and he recoiled. Shopping bags and toiletries covered the polished cherry wood dresser. Towels and clothes lay in piles on the floor. The vibrant colors of the decor had never appealed to him, but the mess made it hard to bear. He would never have let his own bedroom get like this.

He closed his eyes and imagined himself standing in his tidy room back home. Silence. A slight chill in the air. The muted light of an overcast day streaming in between half-drawn drapes. A single white pillow on a gray comforter. A dull shine on the clean surface of a black dresser.

With a sigh, he went to the balcony window and squinted against the sunlight. Two stable hands stood by the fence of the corral. A figure moved in the dark doorway of the stables. Jarret had headed that way. He wouldn't try to ride, not in this heat and not with his aching ribs. Would he? No, he probably snuck off to some out-of-the-way corner to smoke a cigarette.

If only Jarret hadn't taken a beating last night, it would've been perfect. They'd shared a moment, actually had fun together singing.

Roland chuckled. He actually sang . . . out loud . . . in front of Jarret, of all people. And it hadn't sounded too bad.

His eyes misted. Jarret had seemed to like him. They were like friends. Until the morning. Then Jarret returned to his old attitude, although . . . something seemed different.

He hadn't been himself lately. Sure, he still had his confidence and charm, but they didn't get him everything he wanted like they had in the past. And he'd never handled failure or rejection well, but lately he'd been pushing people away, starting with Keefe. Was he now avoiding Selena? Had he given up on her? Maybe he regretted even coming on this trip.

Something was going on inside of Jarret, a battle maybe. Whatever it was, he needed help.

Keefe said Jarret needed help they couldn't give. He was right.

Roland turned from the window, blinking away green afterimages, and went to the wardrobe. He squatted, unzipped his duffel bag, and reached inside. Somewhere, he had packed his . . .

He pulled out a silver chain with a Miraculous Medal and dangled it so that he could rest his eyes on the image of the Blessed Mother. Mama had given it to him when he was little, the same year she died. Sometimes he wore it under his shirt, but mostly he kept it by his bed. It reminded him of her. Why was it called *miraculous*?

Straightening, he realized what he needed to do. Jarret needed a miracle. Roland went to Jarret's bed, intending to hang the chain over the bedpost, but something made him stop. It might be better to put it . . . He crossed over to the dresser, opened a drawer, and stuffed the medal into a pocket of Jarret's jeans. Then he closed his eyes and prayed, *Mama, don't forget your boys.* He had meant to pray to Mama, but his heart turned to the Blessed Mother, so he repeated the prayer to her. Then he pulled out his phone.

Peter answered on the fourth ring. "Hey, man, what's up? Haven't heard from you in a good long time. You getting roasted out there?"

His loud, cheerful voice made Roland picture his grinning face. He missed Peter. "Yeah, it's pretty hot. I stay inside during the day, mostly."

"You still ghostly white or have you gotten yourself a good tan, or more like a burn?"

Roland laughed but he checked his arm. Pale as ever. "I don't know. Hey, I wanted to ask you a favor."

"Sure. Shoot."

"Jarret needs some help."

"Uh-oh. What'd he do?"

"Nothing. It's just . . . Well, I thought maybe you could ask the group to pray for him . . . by name. He needs some help. I'm worried about him."

"Yeah, I don't know. I still got revenge on my mind."

"Come on. Forgive already. He needs help."

"Maybe. So tell me what you've been up to."

CHAPTER TWENTY-TWO

CRUSHED LIKE GRAPES

Ellechial

Jarret strolled to the stables, limping a bit and clutching his side.

Ellechial attended him, alternating between prayers for grace and whispers of counsel. "Hear me, Jarret. Don't do this. The Lord has allowed your suffering for a reason. Turn to Him. Let Him comfort you."

"You're a loser." Deth-kye hovered close to Jarret's ear, and his words shot forth like flaming darts. "You're a selfish, wicked brother. Your father is right. You could've gotten your brother hurt, killed. What if one of those men had had a gun? They would've shot him down in cold blood. Roland would be dead."

Deth-kye shifted his evil glare to Ellechial and his voice mellowed. "That was my plan. One of them *did* have a gun. I'm not sure what went wrong."

Ellechial smiled, recalling the boy with the gun. His guardian angel had helped him to avoid mortal sin. Ellechial lifted his wings and praised God.

"Roland was meant to die last night." Deth-kye's face twitched. "If we cannot turn his soul from God, we can at least hurt him or shorten his life. How I hate that boy. How I hate them all." His black eyes shifted back to Jarret. "You worthless, miserable . . ." He lifted off the ground, vomiting curses.

Ellechial brought up his shield, using grace to stave off the fiery darts of Deth-kye's present fury. If only he had a sword. He needed more grace from prayer and sacrifices.

Jarret reached the stables and stepped into their cool shade, wrinkling his nose at the strong odor of hay and manure.

One of the stable hands, Laszio, was mucking out the nearest stall with a rake and a bucket. Two demons flew back and forth above him. One swooped down whispering lies, but the guardian angel swatted him away, preventing him from perching on Laszio's shoulders. The demon resumed its aerial attack.

When Laszio looked up, Jarret gave him a nod and said, "Hey, man, you seen Rufino?"

Laszio simply shook his head, his thoughts obviously elsewhere.

At the far end of the stable, Enyeto stepped out of a stall, a medical bag in hand. He saw Jarret and his eyes narrowed, but he kept walking and disappeared into the tack room.

At Deth-kye's prompting, Jarret cursed Enyeto under his breath as he headed for the tack room. Deth-kye laughed with evil delight, as he often did when Jarret took his suggestions.

Jarret stopped in the doorway of the tack room. "Uh, excuse me."

Enyeto leaned over a saddle and scrubbed it with circular motions, water dripping off the workbench and onto his tan work boots. He kept his back to the door and made no sign of having heard Jarret.

Jarret stepped into the room. "Your name's Enyeto, right?"

Enyeto turned his head. "What is it you want? You cannot take the horses out in this heat."

"Well, I hadn't planned on it." Jarret grimaced. "But why not?"

"It is too hot. Horses heat up much faster than humans."

"Oh yeah?" Jarret smiled, but it looked terribly insincere.

"You may come back in the evening. The horses are used to early morning and evening rides in the summer."

Jarret shook his head, one eye twitching. "I ain't here to ride a horse. I'm looking for Rufino. You know where he is?"

Enyeto turned away and continued scrubbing the saddle with circular motions.

Jarret huffed and stepped back, about to leave.

"I have not seen him. Perhaps you will find him at home," Enyeto said, facing his work. "He will not come to the stables until later today."

After a long silence, Jarret said, "Thanks."

On the walk to Rufino's, Jarret passed two stable hands, Alamar and Vincinte, who were mending a fence. They made eye contact with him, whispered to each other . . . then laughed.

Indignation flashed in Jarret's eyes.

"Leave it," Ellechial said, but it was too late.

Jarret strode over to them, taking long steps and wincing at the pain they caused his ribs. He stopped a few feet away and assumed a wide-legged stance. "You got something to say to me?"

They exchanged a glance and sniggered. Two small demons peeked out from behind them.

"Let it go," Ellechial said as Jarret lunged forward.

The stable hands jumped back, but the two demons sprang up for Jarret.

Ellechial brought out his shield, kicked one demon back and cracked the other in the head, keeping them at bay.

"Easy there, *amigo*." Alamar lifted his hands and smiled. "Nobody is laughing at you. We are only talking about the fence."

"*Si*," Vincinte said, nodding. "We have a green horse making work for us, destroying all the fences."

Jarret gave a squinty-eyed look at the fence and then at the men before walking on.

Deth-kye rolled on the ground with laughter.

Ellechial put away his shield. That skirmish was an easy victory, but a sword would help. He needed prayer and sacrifices . . . or Jarret's openness to grace.

Since trouble had temporarily passed, Ellechial took advantage of his ability to travel and made a visit to Monettello. After requesting prayers, he returned to Jarret's side.

Jarret reached Rufino's backyard and stood gazing out into the distance.

Ellechial gazed with him. The smooth lines of distant mesas and their color, red against the clear blue sky, proclaimed the simplicity of love and the beauty of God. The dry and barren land, thirsty for rainfall to bring forth life, reminded Ellechial of a soul in sin, thirsty for the grace of God.

"Beautiful, is it not?" Ellechial knew that Jarret would not sense him or his thought, but he also knew that Jarret appreciated this beautiful view of God's creation. God's gift of creation gave joy and moved the hearts of believer and non-believer alike. The Lord found pleasure in giving this joy to all.

With a deep breath, Jarret turned and set his gaze on Rufino's house, on the sliding glass door off the back.

Rufino slid open the door. Shirtless and with heavy-lidded eyes, he glanced in the direction of the Zamoranos' property. "Hey, *amigo*. Is there a problem?"

"No, no problem," Jarret said. "Can I come in?"

Rufino glanced over his shoulder. "Maybe now is not a good time. I will come out."

Jarret smiled. "Why? Have you got a *muchacha* in there?"

Rufino made a slow, stuttering laugh. "No, man. It's just I . . ." He rubbed his bare chest and glanced over his shoulder again. The smell of marijuana traveled out the door.

"Is that pot I smell?" Jarret gave a crooked grin.

"Uh . . ." Rufino peered toward the Zamoranos' house.

Jarret stepped up and pushed past Rufino to get inside. "That's kind of why I'm here. I was hoping you might, uh, share?"

Rufino's mouth hung open. He watched as Jarret scanned the kitchen counters and Formica-topped table. A smile spread across his face, revealing tobacco-stained teeth, but then he frowned and shook his head. "No, *amigo*. If your papa found out—"

"He ain't gonna find out. Unless you're gonna tell him." He maneuvered past Rufino to get to the living room. A half-spent joint lay in an ashtray on the coffee table. He picked it up and got out his lighter but paused before lighting up. "Whaddya say, *amigo*?"

Rufino plopped down in the recliner and reached for a bag on the cluttered end table. "I guess so. Looks like you are going to anyways. I do not want your papa finding—"

"I told you, I ain't gonna tell him. You think I'm nuts? This'll be our little secret."

Before long, they were laughing and gossiping about the stable hands. Deth-kye sat at Jarret's feet, toying with a thick chain. Another demon leaned back against the sofa, a bored expression on his gnarled face. He had restrained Rufino with the Chain of Addiction long ago.

Ellechial prayed. He knew, as only an angel could, that once a person crossed a moral boundary, it was easier for a demon to rein him in. What started out as a thread could become bigger and bigger until Hell was dragging that soul with a huge chain. *Please, God, don't allow this to happen to Jarret.*

"You're all cooped up in your little house. You the only one around here who smokes?" Jarret indicated the joint then passed it to Rufino.

Rufino took a hit before answering. "No, *amigo*. Sometimes Alamar and even Laszio. Do you know who I mean?"

Jarret shook his head. "I don't know their names. Never paid attention. I know two of those dudes don't like me. And I know that old dude's name is Enyeto."

"*Si*, Enyeto." Rufino leaned and passed the joint. "He is the manager. He is in charge of everything and everyone. Keeps us all straight." He chuckled.

Jarret chuckled, imitating Rufino's strange laugh. "I don't like him. He seems sneaky."

"No, he is a good man. He is of the old world. He is Navajo."

"I still think he's sneaky. Maybe he's even the thief." He took a drag off the joint. "He's Native American? Don't they smoke weed? I thought they smoked those peace pipes. What do they put in those?"

Rufino laughed. "No, he is against any kind of illegal drugs, but he will drink. He likes his firewater, you know, whiskey. Now, though, even Laszio will not smoke. He does not like to spend the *dinero* except on his sick wife. Pot cost money, you know."

Jarret reached for his back pocket as if he wanted to offer some money, but he didn't have his wallet. "His wife's sick, huh? Was she at the party?"

Rufino nodded. "I'm sure you saw her. She was up then. Sometimes, though, she is sick in bed, has some kind of cancer, only a few years to live. Laszio, he sent her to many doctors but it is always the same outcome, the same diagnosis." Rufino dropped his gaze and shook his head. "He does not take this well. Then he learns about a woman who says she can help. She does not use traditional methods."

"You mean she uses herbs and stuff?"

Rufino exhaled a stream of smoke. "No, that is not exactly what I mean, little *amigo*. I mean she is more like a shaman."

Jarret laughed. "Yeah, okay. You mean a witch doctor."

"No, like a medicine woman."

"Yeah. Witch doctor."

"No, but *Señor* Juan, he does not like for her to be on his property. He thinks she is evil. He is a Catholic, you know. When he first found out about her, he had a fit and threw her out. But Laszio, he still has her come. He thinks she will help."

"So, she uses the dark arts, huh?" Jarret took a long drag off the joint and held the smoke until it made him cough.

"She says she can bridge the natural and the spiritual worlds. That is how she can help people. She casts out the evil spirits that cause problems, you know?"

Jarret stifled a laugh. "Yeah, okay. I'm sure she can. Does she dress up in bizarre costumes and mix strange concoctions . . . dance around, chanting?"

Rufino's expression remained placid. "I have seen her do it. Do not doubt things because you do not understand."

"Yes-s-s, do not doubt, my little boy. Do not worry. Do not think." Deth-kye closed his eyes and pretended to inhale, mimicking Jarret as he took a long drag off the joint. "Oh, the sweet victory." Deth-kye wound the Chain of Addiction around Jarret's ankle. "Breathe deep, my child. You are mine."

Ellechial had permission to do nothing. So he watched Jarret. And he wept.

Jarret

Jarret stayed at Rufino's for over two hours before strolling back to the mansion, still high. By chance, he crossed paths with no one who wanted to talk to him and no one who wanted to know where he'd been or what he'd been doing. He'd even had the opportunity to snag a bag of tortilla chips from the pantry. Once he made it to the bedroom, he opened the glass balcony door in hopes of catching a warm, creosote-scented breeze. After eating half the bag of chips, he stretched out on the bed for a nap.

As he gazed at the warm colors of the décor in the room, the yellow ocher, the fire orange, and the sage green, profound thoughts filled his mind. People in the southwest used vibrant colors to make up for the dullness of the desert landscape. On the other hand, they had more sky here than in other parts of the country, so they appreciated the colors of the sunrise and the sunset.

He smiled. How long would the buzz last? The way his brain seemed to work under the influence, he could probably discover the deeper meaning of anything he set his mind to. Yeah, he would be able to make sense of anything, be able to find connections between little things, connections he previously hadn't noticed.

Brother Maurus always spoke with phrases that seemed to hold meanings beyond his grasp. He would get them now. What was it he used to say? Something about grapes.

Jarret dipped a scrub brush into a bucket of dark, sudsy water and stretched up as far as he could to clean the last of the white junk off the interior steel walls of the cylindrical fermentation tank. The eight-foot-high, five-foot in diameter enclosure amplified the sound of every drip. Soapy water ran down his plastic gloves and his arm to his pink-speckled, white muscle shirt. He'd never felt so drippy and disgusting in all his life.

"Tank's clean! Am I done?" he hollered, his voice echoing. "I'm starting to feel claustrophobic." He squatted, ready to stick his head through the knee-high, circular manhole when Brother Maurus poked his smiling, egg-shaped head inside.

The monk looked up and around the cylindrical tank. "It looks good, Brother Jarret. Let me get the hose. Here, I'll take that." He reached for the bucket of sudsy water.

"I can get it. It's kind of heavy." Jarret snatched the handle away from him.

"Oh, no. You don't get out until it's done." Brother Maurus placed a hand on each side of the bucket.

"You're a slave driver. Who cleans these things when I'm not here?" Jarret helped scoot the bucket closer to the little manhole.

"Be thankful. All the tanks will need cleaning in late summer, and you will not be here."

Finding no consolation in that thought, Jarret huffed. "So, did you finish reading my paper?" His English teacher had had the bright idea of making him write about his experiences whenever Papa took him out of school for a trip. Keefe used to write the papers for him, before he got all self-righteous. This was the second one that Jarret had had to write on his own. Surprisingly, it wasn't half bad.

The monk lifted the bucket with two hands and disappeared as he spoke. "I'm almost done reading it. It is very good." A hose appeared through the manhole, followed by Brother Maurus's head. "I'll turn the water on. You might get wet."

Jarret chuckled. "I might, huh? There're two feet between me and the walls of the tank. And you think I might get wet?"

Water blasted from the hose. Jarret jumped back and aimed the stream at the top of the wall. Stray sprinkles burned his face. "Man, the water's boiling hot."

"It has to be."

The manhole door closed a little, dimming the light inside the tank.

Jarret did a double take at the door then kicked it back open. "Don't be closing me in here. I feel trapped enough at this place."

"Sorry, Brother Jarret. I shall leave it open."

The claustrophobic feeling passed at the sight of Brother Maurus's black and white habit outside the manhole. All this time in the tank only magnified his agitation at having to live at the monastery. He'd already decided that he wouldn't tell anyone about it when he returned to school. He'd make something else up instead.

"I'm sorry you still feel trapped here. I'd hoped you had begun to enjoy yourself. You won't be here that long now."

"Enjoy myself? You put me to work every day."

"Work is good, Jarret. You know, the thing that really traps us and makes us prisoners is sin. One can be locked in the darkest dungeon and still be free, or one can have all the freedom of the world and still be in bondage."

"Yeah, yeah." Those words meant nothing to him, just some gibberish that certain people spouted, people like monks . . . and Keefe. Would Keefe ever see straight again? "So, how far did you get on my paper?"

"I am near the end. I appreciate that you included the history of our Monastery and the work we do making wine. Very descriptive. You even wrote a little about our daily life and prayers. It's a nice paper. I'm sure your teacher will like it. How did you get all that information?"

"Talking to you." He lowered the hose and watched the water swirl around the drainage hole. "Okay, I went over the walls three times. Am I done?"

Brother Maurus shut off the water.

Stooping, Jarret eyed the manhole while considering his exit strategy. He'd struggled climbing in. The access was about three feet above the ground and too small for him to put one leg in and then his head. He'd tried that. Then he'd tried going head first but couldn't figure out how the rest of his body could follow without him looking ridiculous. So he ended up holding onto a ladder and shoving both legs in first. Maybe getting out would be a breeze.

Jarret stuck his head out. Bright light from the open garage door opposite the tanks made him squint. The ladder was gone and there was nothing else he could hold onto, but the cement floor wasn't too far down.

He twisted his shoulders through and then wriggled his arms free. His palms hit the cement floor, which felt cold even through the gloves. Probably not the best way to go, now that he thought about it. He still had no room to bend his legs, and he was starting to feel pretty stupid with half his body in the tank and the blood rushing to his head.

"You'll have to drop down from there." Brother Maurus appeared nearby.

Unwilling to drop down and unable to bend even one leg, Jarret cussed up a storm.

"Just drop down. You can do it."

"I hate being here!" He walked forward with his hands, the rim of the manhole scraping his thighs. "You guys are all crazy. I'm not gonna change. I wish you'd all leave me alone. I want out of here!"

"Just drop down."

Jarret dragged his feet over the rim and abandoned himself to gravity. He fell to the hard cement floor and cussed a few more times at the fleeting pain.

"Very good. You did fine." Brother Maurus hovered over him, grinning and reaching for his arms. "Now to the vineyard." He yanked Jarret up and turned away.

"What? Why don't we rest?" He should've saved his breath. Brother Maurus had already left the winery through the open garage door.

Jarret stripped off the gloves and the rubber boots and washed his arms in a concrete sink. He shook the water from his arms as he dashed through the open garage door. The sun made him squint, but the mid-seventy-degree temperature brought goose bumps to his wet arms.

Brother Maurus passed under a shady tree, heading for the dirt road to the vineyard.

Jarret jogged to catch up.

Brother Maurus walked with his head down, but as Jarret approached, he looked up. He carried Jarret's report. "Your information is good. You must listen very well. I wasn't aware I told you all this."

"Thanks. But I don't have to listen well, you repeat yourself." He grinned, waiting for the monk's reaction. None came so he tried again. "And you talk a lot."

"What?" The monk looked up again, his forehead wrinkling. "I don't talk a lot. Do I?"

"Yeah." Jarret grinned, satisfied with the reaction. "You even talk during your silent times."

"Oh, my, I guess I'll have to work on that." He picked up his pace. "We'll take a little stroll through the vines. I want to check on them."

"They barely have leaves. What's to check on?" He followed the monk, wishing his time at the monastery were over, wishing he were home with his life under his own control. Everything about this place made him think of imprisonment, even the vineyard. The vines, all brown and twisted, made him think of prisoners too weary to stand tall, bodies sagging, arms outstretched along the wire.

"These vines have been here many years." Brother Maurus's half-moon eyes lit up as he gazed at them. "The new ones won't bear fruit yet. It takes careful pruning, thinning, positioning the shoots, removing leaves. But then, God willing, they bear much fruit."

"Are these grapes good to eat; I mean when they're ready?"

"No, you would not want to eat these. They are bitter. When they are ripe, they are plucked from the vine and drained of all juice. They are crushed."

At the word "crushed," Jarret shivered. Maybe he'd gotten a chill from wearing damp clothes, but he sensed that the monk's words applied to him as well as to the fruit.

"Then they sit for a while in the dark, where secret things go on, a secret transformation, and . . ." He paused, making eye contact before he said, "Then you have something wonderful."

214

CHAPTER TWENTY-THREE

SEEDS OF A PLAN

Jarret

Since before he could walk, before he could talk, he'd had command. Of himself. Of his goals. Of others. Everything he wanted he could get. He had merely to desire something and, with little effort, it came to be. So this nadir of powerlessness and influence that had become his life should've caused him a bit of stress. But actually, it felt kind of good.

Every muscle in his body relaxed, even the sore ones, as he sat with aloof coolness in a recliner in the Zamoranos' entertainment room. He had a Coke, a plate of tortilla chips, and homemade salsa at his fingertips, a comfortable breeze from an overhead fan, and a wall-sized TV before him.

Most importantly, he hadn't a single goal for the day. Getting high with Rufino a few days ago had changed his perspective on life. It was like time stopped, or at least slowed way down, and he could think, really think. He'd had a moment of clarity. Now, things that had been so important to him, he could face with indifference. He no longer cared what Keefe did with his life. His need for him had waned. Thus, his need to keep his cell phone within easy reach had gone too. Where had he left the thing anyway?

Selena flitted into view. She wore a white skirt and a flouncy shirt that was all lavender and purple with strips of lace on the chest. It made him want to stare but only for as long as she blocked his view of the television.

Now that he didn't give a rap whether she liked him or not, he didn't have to waste time in the bathroom trying to look good. He hadn't shaved in two days. He hadn't even bothered to change out of the gray cotton shorts and tank top he'd worn to bed.

Roland seemed to have had a transformation of sorts over the days too. Jarret had to do a double take every time he got a glimpse of him. He wore faded denim shorts and a stark white t-shirt, not his typical Goth colors.

About an hour ago, Papa had come into the room, called Roland aside, and mumbled something to him, didn't even say hey to Jarret. So Papa liked Roland best, thought he was responsible and helpful. Who gave a continental hoot?

"Do you want a *bolillo*?" Selena slinked up beside him, a tray of warm *bolillos* in hand.

Jarret took one, stuffed it halfway into his mouth, and set two more on the end table, next to his plate of tortilla chips. He took the *bolillo* from his mouth to say, "Is this lunch?"

Selena smiled and flipped the hair from her face in that flirtatious way of hers. "Are you feeling better today?"

He gave her a strange look. "What?"

She touched her abdomen. "Are you still wearing the Ace bandage? Does it still hurt?"

Jarret twisted around to glare at Roland. "Thanks."

Roland sat on one side of a brown leather couch, eyes round with his attempt to look innocent. "I didn't say anything . . . to her . . . exactly. It wasn't my fault she was standing right there when Papa sent me to fetch Eremita." He shook his head. "I didn't say anything."

216

Selena laughed, looking from Roland to Jarret. "He didn't say anything. *Señora* Eremita told me you were all bruised up. Did you get in a fight?" Her brown eyes sparkled as if she found some demented delight in his misery.

He shoved the rest of the *bolillo* into his mouth. He'd sooner eat live rattlesnakes for lunch than admit to her how three guys beat him up and Roland had to save him.

"Can I see?" she said.

"What?" he said with his mouth full. Was she for real?

"Your bruises, are they really bad?" She dropped her gaze and stuck her bottom lip out.

He swallowed and took a swig of Coke. "You really wanna see?" He couldn't help but grin. Maybe she liked him after all.

She nodded.

Jarret kicked the footrest down and jumped up, stripping off his shirt so quickly that it made all the sore spots scream. Eremita had been taking care of him for the past couple of days. She'd placed strips of adhesive tape around the worst areas and then wrapped him with the Ace bandage. Slightly worried about renewing the pain, he reached for the end of the wrap.

Selena's smile turned into a giggle. Her head dipped forward, hair cascading over her face, and she laughed.

"You're nothing but a tease." He'd meant to keep the thought to himself. But then again, what did he care how she took it?

As he snatched up his shirt, she touched his arm. "No, I'm not laughing at you. It's just that . . . I don't know. I'm sorry you got hurt."

She looked sincere enough, the way she held his gaze. But still. "So, what's so funny?"

"Nothing. I mean, I guess it shocked me the way you ripped your shirt off."

"How else you gonna see the bruises?"

217

She smiled. She was gonna laugh again.

He pulled his shirt on and eased himself back into the recliner. "Why don't you sit down and watch the movie? You put it on, said it was your favorite."

She started strolling along the perimeter of the entertainment room. "I'm kind of sad. Tonight is your farewell dinner. I can't believe you guys are leaving in two days." She stopped at the outer boundary of his peripheral vision. "I'm going to miss you."

No sooner was her sad declaration out of her mouth than she bounced on her toes and scooted over to the couch. "Guess who's coming to the dinner party?"

Roland didn't reply. He probably shrugged.

"We invited the same guests that came over the night of the first robbery."

"Wow. Really? Why?" Roland said.

"It was my doing." She sounded proud. "I thought it would be nice for you to meet them all." She resumed flitting around the room while she talked. "It's too bad we couldn't figure out who did it." She stopped at the edge of Jarret's peripheral vision again and glanced over her shoulder toward the hallway before continuing. "Something else was stolen."

Roland dropped a dish or something, and it clanked on the coffee table. "What? Really?"

Jarret kicked the footrest down and cranked his head around to see.

Roland scraped tortilla chips from the coffee table back into his bowl.

Selena was nodding in an exaggerated way. "Right from my father's den."

Roland stood up with the bowl of chips but then set it down and walked around the coffee table to her. "What was taken? When? Last night?"

She covered her mouth with one hand and giggled, lighting a fire in Jarret. Then she dropped her hand to her belly and laughed, fanning the fire. Composing herself she said, "Could've been days ago, but Papá only noticed it this morning."

"Do you notice how she laughs at us?" Jarret got to his feet and put a hand on his hip. "She doesn't take us seriously."

Selena laughed again. "You are too serious about yourselves, you West boys." She came up to Jarret with that blasted flirty look in her eyes. "But if you want me to be serious, I will do it." She folded her arms across her chest and stared at him, plain-faced, almost pouty.

Was she flirting with him? He took her by the arm and dropped back into the recliner, trying to get her onto his lap. His bruised abdomen screamed.

She twisted away, laughing.

"Look," he said, holding his ribs. "All I wanted was to ride with you. I like it out here. I want to see the land. But you have a hundred excuses. Can you even ride a horse? Or was that a lie?"

More laughter. Turning away. Trying to control it. "We can go out, the three of us. But don't you still hurt too much to ride?"

He shook his head, more to show his annoyance than to say no. "I'll go out for a ride. Before we leave. And I'll go alone."

"Can I go with you?" Roland sounded like a little kid. "I'd like to go riding."

Jarret decided not to answer. He took a swig of Coke instead.

"Hey!" Roland's eyes popped. "Hey, what about those footprints?"

Selena threw her head back, laughing.

Roland edged to the hallway, looked both ways, and came back. "Remember those dirty footprints Eremita was complaining about the other day? Did you see them?"

"Sure," she said. "They were big cowboy-boot prints. Every man on the property, from Papá to Rufino, wears cowboy boots. But the hired hands *only* come into the dining room. They don't usually enter Papá's den or the rest of the house. That's what makes it suspicious."

"Except Enyeto," Jarret said, the image of Enyeto cleaning a saddle fresh in his mind. Jarret would've never let dirty water drip all over his own shoes. "Enyeto doesn't wear cowboy boots. He wears work boots. And every work boot has a distinctive tread on the sole. Real cowboy boots don't have tread."

Selena's eyes grew wide and round. "That's true. They're designed for sliding into stirrups." She dashed to the hallway, glanced both ways, and came back. "I remember. The muddy prints had lines through them, lines like on tennis shoes or . . ."

"Work boots." Roland went to her, and their eyes locked in a gaze of mutual revelation. "Do you remember the print, the pattern?"

"No, and what if I did?" She stifled a giggle. "Do you want to check the bottom of Enyeto's boots?"

Jarret slid from the recliner to his feet and folded his arms across his chest. He could play this game. "I remember what the footprints looked like. I saw one in the foyer." He saw it when he was on the phone with Keefe, when he had slid down the wall and sat on the floor under the staircase. He'd stared at it for a long time, the muddy footprint with the crosses and lines. "I know exactly what the pattern looks like. I'll go check out the pattern from Enyeto's boots. He's probably got footprints all over the stables."

"I don't know," Selena said. "He keeps the place clean, very clean. I am surprised he would even have mud on the bottom of his boots."

"It did rain," Roland said.

"I don't remember boot prints in the chapel," Selena said.

"What about the tobacco juice in the chapel?" Jarret said. "Does Enyeto chew?"

Selena shook her head. Then she and Jarret said together, "Laszio chews."

Selena turned away and peered out the window. "I can't believe our thief is one of the stable hands. We treat them like family. I still think it's one of the party guests, someone from outside." She faced them.

"Let's set a trap." Roland's steel-gray eyes held a calculating look.

She smiled and gave a nod.

"I know exactly what to do." Roland gave them a crooked smile, a look that Jarret had *never* seen on his face before.

"I'm in," Jarret said.

"Me, too," Selena said, and this time she wasn't laughing.

CHAPTER TWENTY-FOUR
TO CATCH A THIEF

Jarret

Millions of celestial lights shone overhead in the blue abyss of space. The flat desert landscape, with its distant mesas and scattering of plants, underscored the night sky, drawing little attention to itself. He hadn't given much thought to the stars before. Too many trees back home. But, now that he really studied it, he saw that some of them shone blue, orange, and red, and not just white.

Jarret leaned back against the stables, took a long drag off a joint, and let his gaze sweep across the sky from one horizon to the other. He rather liked being alone outside at night. And he didn't mind so much that he had to take the first watch while Roland finished implementing his plan, setting the bait for the trap.

Jarret snickered.

Roland's idea for a trap: hide a heavy box of—

What was in the box anyway? Nobody had said.

Anyway, hide it in the bushes on the stable-side of the house. Then join the dinner party inside and whisper about the box and where it's hidden. Whisper loud enough so that everyone can hear. Act like the box contains valuable antiques. Act like Juan knows nothing about it, which he doesn't, because he'd probably wig out if he did. Then pretend we plan to get it to a storage unit for safety, but later, so the thief would have a chance to snag it. One of us has to keep watch from the shadows—my job, at the moment.

No. He didn't mind. Gave him time to think. And with every hit off the joint, he could almost feel his mind opening and his thoughts gaining clarity.

He began to understand Roland. The kid had a devious side that no one saw or suspected. He wasn't shy. He was calculating. Roland had always pretended he wanted to be Jarret's friend, but that didn't square. After all the mean things he'd done to Roland—No. Roland hated him. He had to. A person could only forgive so much.

Roland had himself a goal. And this act of friendship was only so he could get what he wanted: Selena. Seeing as how they'd be leaving soon, he was probably arranging some long-term correspondence with her right now. She'd probably come outside with him on his turn to keep watch.

Then there was Roland's perpetual effort to get Papa to like him best. Why else would he spend his vacation cataloging *Señor* Zamorano's antiques? Maybe he wanted Juan to like him, too. That would explain his obsession over finding the thief. If his little plan worked, he could take all the credit. If anything went wrong, Jarret would get the blame and stay on Papa's you-know-what list, maybe get on everyone's list. If Roland wanted revenge badly enough—

A sound came from the far end of the stable, a door opening.

Jarret straightened and slid into the dark corner where the apartments connected to the stables.

A figure in a Stetson hat approached, scuffing along at a leisurely pace, keeping close to the stable.

Jarret pinched the joint out and pressed his back to the wall. The dark corner wouldn't draw attention. The man shouldn't see him unless he really looked.

A stone's-throw away, the figure walked into the light from one of the stable's floodlights. *Enyeto.* His hard eyes stared straight ahead. As he passed Jarret, he neither slowed nor turned his stern, dark face. He went around to the front of the apartment units. A moment later, a light came on in one of the windows and reflected on the ground. Minutes later, the window darkened, but Enyeto did not come out.

Shouldn't he have been heading over for the dinner party? Maybe he knew about the box. No. He'd been in the stables so he wouldn't have heard Selena and Roland talking about it. But he could be working with someone. Someone could've heard the rumor and called him.

Jarret re-lit the joint and slid back to his spot on the stable wall.

Another dark figure in a Stetson hat appeared at the back of the house.

Jarret made a move for cover but stopped.

The slim figure had a self-conscious, awkward sort of gait. Had to be Roland.

Jarret took a drag off the joint and admired the stars again while Roland strode over to him.

"Hey," Roland said, his face shrouded in shadows.

Jarret gave a nod, exhaling smoke.

Roland sniffed the air. "What're you smoking?"

With a grin, Jarret dropped the joint and crushed it out with his boot. It was nearly spent anyway so he didn't feel too bad about it. He had a good buzz going, and nothing Roland could say or do would kill it.

"So did you see anyone?" Roland peered into the darkness around them.

Jarret huffed. "Did you guys set the bait?"

Roland shrugged. "Yeah."

"Did everyone catch your story?"

"I think so. We talked about it twice, near two different groups of suspects."

He smirked. "Suspects, huh? Isn't everybody a suspect?"

Roland shrugged. "Well, not the family. Not Papa. We didn't want them to hear. So be careful when you start talking. Don't talk in front of them."

Jarret smirked. Roland was such a dweeb. "Whatever. So there's only one guy who hasn't heard about the box of *valuable antiques*. Enyeto." He gave a nod in the direction of the apartments.

"Enyeto? Oh yeah. I guess he wasn't there."

"You guess? Shouldn't you know?" He pushed off the wall and stood with jutted jaw, peering down at Roland. "He's in his apartment. But don't worry. I'll make sure he knows about the box when he finally joins the party."

"Okay."

"If anyone takes the bait, they'll probably come now, while you're here." Jarret smirked and started walking backwards, toward the house. "And what're you going to do about it? You gonna get Rufino's gun?"

Roland shook his head and turned away. "I shouldn't have done that. It was stupid." He looked at Jarret. "I don't know what I'll do. Guess I'll confront him. I have my cell phone. I'll call you if I see anyone. We can surround him or something."

Jarret nodded, slowly, loving the airy feeling in his head. "Where's Selena in her hot little geisha dress?"

"In the house. I think it's time to eat."

"Good. I'm hungry."

❖

Selena leaned against the kitchen countertop and laughed with stone-faced Eremita. Her silky, oriental-style dress, red with a gold and green floral print, drew attention to her slim waistline and shiny black hair, making it hard for Jarret to look at anything else.

Turning as Eremita walked off with a tray, Selena caught sight of him. "There you are."

"Yeah, here I am." He tore his gaze from her dress.

She took his hand and whispered in his ear, "Help me spread more rumors. We have to do it before my mother comes back down. She's putting Rosa to bed."

"Anything you want." He let her lead him to the dining room.

A few guests, men in bolo ties and women in vests and denim skirts, had taken their seats at the long table. Their voices and laughter rose above the contemporary Mexican and classical guitar background music. The table setting looked like a page out of a home decorating magazine: royal blue wine goblets stuffed with gold napkins, blue and orange patterned plates, and candles as centerpieces. Four stable hands stood gossiping in the hallway. A middle-aged couple strolled into the room, both of them dressed in dark jeans and boots.

Selena leaned close and whispered, "That is my mother's friend Becca and her husband Taine. Her son Rick is in the other room."

"So, is this everyone?" Jarret nodded to include the stable hands in the hall.

"No, a few are still in the great room." She stopped by the buffet, examined the *hors d'oeuvres*, and snatched a stuffed *piquillo* pepper.

Jarret leaned over her shoulder. "Did you guys have drinks in the great room?"

She laughed. "Drinks? You mean alcohol? Are you an alcoholic? At your age?" She bit into the stuffed pepper.

He huffed. "I don't have the chance to be one. Don't you ever want to sneak a drink?"

She shrugged and said, "I have wine with dinner sometimes," then she stuffed the rest of the pepper into her mouth.

"A whole bottle?"

Wiping her mouth with her fingers, Selena studied his face. "Are you feeling all right?"

"Yeah, I'm feeling great. Why?"

"You don't look yourself. Your eyes—"

"Don't I?" He couldn't help himself. He leaned in for a kiss.

She put a firm hand on his shoulder, holding him back. "So you will drive me, then?" She whispered rather loudly.

"What?"

Selena glanced as stable hands straggled into the room and seated themselves at the table. "I have a storage unit I want to put something in. Can you take me there after dinner?"

What was she talking about? She said he didn't look himself. Then she wanted a ride to a—

She kicked his shin and widened her eyes as if he should know what she was talking about.

"That hurt," he said, rubbing his shin.

She made him straighten up then whispered in his ear, "Can't you play along? Just say *okay*."

"Okay." Now he remembered. Roland's plan.

She took his arm and led him into the hallway. They both leaned against the wall. "Roland is a much better actor than you." She glanced to either side. "We should probably keep an eye on everyone. If someone wants to sneak out—"

Laszio came into the hallway, a cell phone to his ear. "I will be there. I will come right now." He shoved his cell phone into a pocket of his jeans and adjusted his cowboy hat, nearly walking into Selena.

"Watch it." Jarret straightened up and glared. "What's your hurry?"

227

"*Con permiso.*" He tipped his hat to Selena but only glanced at her. "My wife, she needs me. I must go." He glanced again, worry in his eyes, then went to the door saying, "Tell your Papá I must go. Lupeta is not feeling well."

As the door squeezed shut, Jarret grinned. "Think he's our thief?"

Selena smacked his arm. "Don't be silly. His wife has cancer. She's often sick. I thought she might be sick when I didn't see her here tonight. I didn't want to ask. He doesn't handle it well."

"What do you mean?"

She gazed at him as if studying his eyes.

He pressed his lips together, dying to kiss her. The foyer chandelier cast geometric patterns of light on her silky red dress, playing with her figure.

"I mean he's emotional for a guy," she finally said.

For some reason, her comment hit a nerve. He snapped from his lustful thoughts and watched as two more stable hands clomped into the hall on their way to the dining room.

"Not that I don't understand," Selena said. "It'd be hard knowing that your spouse was going to suffer and die. I think I'd—"

"Do you like Roland more than me?"

She stared. Then she cracked up.

A bad name came to mind, but he stopped it from crossing his lips. He shook his head and turned away as Rufino and Papa strolled into the hallway.

"Hey, *amigo*," Rufino said.

Papa only nodded.

When the hall cleared, Selena had a straight face. "Why can't I like you both? Why must I like one over—"

His cell phone rang. *Roland?* He whipped his phone out and answered it.

"He's here!" Roland whispered, urgency in his tone. "He's going for the box."

"Who?" Jarret gave Selena a nod to answer the question in her eyes.

"I don't know. One of the stable hands, I think. Come out the front, and we'll surround him."

Jarret ended the call and stuffed his phone away. "I'm going out front. You stay here."

"Stay here? Why?"

"'Cuz I don't want you getting hurt."

Her eyes narrowed to slits. She folded her arms across her chest. "You mean because I'm a girl?"

Jarret bolted through the front doorway and plunged into the night. He jogged through the landscaping, weaving to avoid colliding with artistically placed cacti, decorative pebbles slipping beneath his boots.

At the corner, he stopped. Not a soul stirred from here to the stables. The windows of Enyeto's upstairs apartment were even dark. So where was the thief? Where was Roland?

Jarret's jaw tightened. If Roland was playing a trick on him, he'd pay.

He headed for the stables, clinging to the shadow of the house, alternating between walking and jogging. As he neared, something in the shadow of the stables moved. Roland?

Jarret darted to the house and flattened himself against the wall.

A man in a cowboy hat—too tall to be Roland—stepped into the moonlight, cradling the box in his arms. He took a long look behind and to either side but didn't appear to see Jarret.

Jarret dashed into the moonlight and closed the distance between them.

229

The man jerked his face toward Jarret and retreated into the shadow he'd come from.

"I know what you got." Jarret skidded to a stop about ten feet away, his gaze directed to where he assumed the man stood. "Where do you think you're going with that?"

The man stepped from the shadows, without the box. He held something small that flashed, reflecting moonlight. A knife?

Feeling the urge to retreat, Jarret forced himself forward. Then he stood strong, feet shoulder width apart. "I ain't afraid of you, with or without a knife, or whatever you got in your hand, so who are you?"

"Go back inside." The low voice came from the front end of the apartments. A floodlight had illuminated the area earlier, but now it was dark.

Jarret and the thief both snapped their faces toward the voice. It sounded like . . . Enyeto?

The thief stepped back.

Jarret shook his head. "I'm not going anywhere. Why don't you come out of the shadows?"

All of this had seemed to unfold rather slowly, so whatever either one of the shadowy dudes decided to do, Jarret thought he'd have plenty of time to respond. He assumed a fighting stance, legs bent and fists at chin level. If he had to, he could take them both.

The first man lunged toward him, and the second man zipped from the shadows. The knife flashed in the moonlight as it neared Jarret's neck. Arms wrapped around his chest from behind. His feet flew out from under him. Someone had yanked him back and held him.

Wishing for a surge of adrenaline but getting none, Jarret grappled for the attacker's arms and struggled to get his balance. His attacker flung him. He landed hard on his side in a bush along the house.

"You go." Enyeto stood over him, one arm outstretched, pointing to the back of the house, his dark face grim and wrinkled, looking like a Native American of legend.

"I told you, I ain't going nowhere." Clutching his sore ribs, Jarret struggled to get back on his feet. He wasn't backing down no matter what.

"You are in no condition to defend yourself," Enyeto said, "even against him. I will take care of this."

Did Enyeto know he was high? Maybe. Maybe he saw him smoking the joint or heard him bum one off Rufino. "I can take care of myself. You two working on this together? You been stealing from the people who take care of you? I knew you were scum."

"Let me go on," the first man said to Enyeto. Wait . . . was that Laszio's voice?

Jarret squinted at the shadowy figure, trying to make him out. It was Laszio.

And now he was taking backward steps, moving toward the shadows of the stables. "Do not tell anyone about this. I must do this. It is only his word against mine. Nobody will believe him."

Jarret got to his feet and lunged, ready to sprint for Laszio.

Enyeto wrapped his arms around Jarret's torso again. "No, Laszio," Enyeto shouted over Jarret's shoulder.

Jarret twisted and tried to pry himself free, but Enyeto's firm grasp didn't lessen.

"This is wrong," Enyeto said. "You will put the box down, and you will go home. We will talk later."

"I will not." Laszio darted for the shadow where he had set the box.

Enyeto flung Jarret to the side and bolted after Laszio.

Although determined to keep his balance, Jarret tripped on his own feet, landed on his knees, and fell onto his side. By the time he sat upright, the thieves had entered the stables. Enyeto almost sounded like he wanted to stop Laszio, but, no, they must have been in it together.

As Jarret climbed to his feet, people came from around the back of the house: Papa, Juan, and Selena, with Roland in the lead. Nobody looked his way. They marched toward the wide-open doorway of the stable, walking in the light streaming from it and on the moving shadows of the men, who were now fighting. Someone inside shouted something that Jarret couldn't make out.

Jarret jogged to where everyone had gathered, just inside the doorway. He squeezed in between Selena and Roland. All eyes were fixed on the fighting men, Enyeto and Laszio.

Arms entwined, boots scraping the floor, each man struggled to dominate the other. Laszio, the younger and heavier of them, slammed Enyeto's back against a stable door without breaking their bear hug. He freed an arm and, eyes bulging, drew back his fist.

Enyeto, his face as placid as the desert horizon, blocked the blow with an open hand, capturing Laszio's fist in his palm. With a step and a turn, he twisted Laszio's arm behind his back and turned him to face the onlookers. Then he released his grasp and set a boot to Laszio's rear end.

Laszio landed on his face in a pile of hay.

Roland gave Jarret a glance then did a double take, his gaze dropping to Jarret's shirt. "Are you okay?"

"Why wouldn't I be?" When Roland turned away, Jarret brushed the dirt off his white Diesel polo. This shirt had cost him more than—

There came a sound like breaking glass near Laszio.

"Oh, my palomino!" Selena said with emotion, a hand on each cheek.

Laszio lay prone a few feet from the box. The box was on its side, a bit caved in but still taped shut.

"Do not get up again," Enyeto said. "We will talk."

Señor Juan stepped forward. "What is the problem here?" With a voice calm and controlled, he came across gentle rather than angry, his gaze shifting from one man to the other. He must have had no idea that Laszio was his thief. What had Roland told him to get him outside?

"Hey." Jarret bumped Roland's arm. "What happened to 'we'll surround him'?"

"Oh." Roland glanced at his feet. "I made a split-second decision, thought maybe *Señor* Juan should see this for himself."

"Thanks for telling me." His comfortable buzz kept his temper down, but that would've ordinarily hacked him off.

"I'm sorry," Roland said. "I thought—"

"Do you want to tell him yourself?" Enyeto said to the man on the ground.

Laszio eased himself up to his knees. He gave Juan a sad, hound-dog face, then folded over and started bawling.

"I believe you have found your thief," Enyeto said, his eagle eyes turning from the pathetic man on the ground to Roland.

Papa and Juan both glanced at Roland, but then Juan stooped by Laszio. "Is what he says true?"

Hands to his face, Laszio nodded and confessed everything.

"What does this have to do with the two of you?" Papa had squinting, accusing eyes for both Jarret and Roland.

"Why don't you ask him?" Jarret gave a nod to indicate Roland.

Papa's gaze shifted to Roland; he blinked as if he couldn't believe it. "Roland?"

A chuckle rose up inside Jarret, wanting out. He wiped his mouth and lowered his head to control it.

"Oh. Um . . ." Roland took a breath. "I guess, well, it was my idea. I thought it was important to find out who was stealing things before we left. So I . . ." He shut his mouth and turned to the grown men whispering to each other on the stable floor.

"Jarret?" Papa said.

"It's what he said. It was his idea." Typically, now, he would've taken offense at Papa's insinuating glare, but this was all Roland's idea. And Roland didn't have a snowball's chance in southern Arizona of getting away without the blame. Papa would have to turn his accusing eyes right back to the *Pale Rider*.

The corners of Jarret's mouth trembled, laughter threatening to erupt.

"I don't see anything humorous about the situation. This isn't a game. I told you both not to worry about it. Someone could've gotten hurt." Papa's eyes turned to the ground. "Whose knife is that in the straw?"

Jarret didn't bother looking. "Ain't mine. Better ask your other son. But I don't think it's his either. A gun's more his style."

Roland's head spun around, fire in his eyes.

The combination of his fearful-angry expression and Papa's questioning-angry scowl struck a funny chord deep inside. Jarret turned away, trying not to laugh aloud. Maybe he ought to step outside and—

Papa gripped Jarret's upper arm then leaned close and whispered through clenched teeth, "Have you been drinking?"

Now that shouldn't have been funny, 'cuz Papa was obviously on to him. So why couldn't he get control of himself? Why couldn't he keep the chuckle from rising up? "Drink . . . ing?" He said, trying not to laugh. "No, I ain't been . . . drinking."

Of course, Rufino had to arrive at that moment, shuffling into the stream of light that stole through the stable doorway. Judging by his tight lips and wide eyes, he'd heard the question. When

Papa turned his steely blues on him, he took a step back. He might as well have confessed right then. No point in lying now. Papa ain't nobody's fool.

"You been giving dope to my son?"

"Dope?" Rufino shoved his hands into the pockets of his jeans. "*Espera.* Now you wait a minute there, Ignatius. Do not be accusing me—"

Papa's face flinched. He released Jarret's arm.

Rufino's hands shot up, and his eyes opened wider. He stepped back, looking like he might bolt. "No, *amigo,* it's just pot, just marijuana."

"Just pot?" Seething, Papa stepped outside the barn.

Jarret tossed in bed. He'd taken more heat over the pot than Roland had taken for his disobedience. The rest of the night, everyone had droned on and on about "Roland the Detective," praising him for catching the thief, as if he'd done it alone, as if Jarret and Selena hadn't helped. As if Jarret couldn't solve a mystery too. If he wanted to, he could. He had proven that at the Monastery. You'd think Papa would remember that day and give him some credit.

Papa had stood about fifty feet from the winery, peering into a transit level on a tripod. He glanced up from under his cowboy hat and motioned for Jarret to move to the right.

Jarret rolled his eyes, exhaled through his mouth, and stepped to the side. "Here?" he shouted, hands on hips. He stood about a hundred feet from Papa on the dirt road that ran through the monastery grounds. They'd been at it all morning, verifying distances with Papa's new maps of the tunnels. As it turned out, a whole network of tunnels ran underground connecting one place to another, each of them blocked off from the building above it, but none of them having any secret walls or storage areas.

"Yeah, that's good," Papa shouted back.

Jarret rammed a stake into the ground then drilled a finger into his temple. The constant glare of sunlight had given him a headache. Maybe he should've accepted the hat Papa had offered before they'd gotten started. Why couldn't they call it quits already? Maybe the monks were wrong. Maybe there was no hidden stash of valuables, and this was a big waste of time.

Papa crouched next to the tripod and wrote something on the tunnel diagram that lay on his brief case. Papa needed some technology. He always wanted to do things by hand. If he had brought a laptop, he could be using the mapping program he'd recently ordered online. They'd be done by now.

Jarret's head throbbed. He strolled to Papa, rubbing his right temple. "Are we done yet? I'm tired of this. We checked everything there is to check. There's nothing to find. Can't we go home?"

Papa grunted. "Something doesn't square."

Jarret squatted down next to him and peered at the diagram.

"These two check out." Papa pointed with his pencil. "The tunnel from the winery to the chapel and the tunnel from the winery to the monks' cells. But the tunnel from the winery to the refectory is off. I messed up either the angle or the distance. And this tunnel from the monks' cells to the refectory ain't right either."

Jarret straightened up and turned around. The storage building, refectory, church, and chapter room were all clustered in the same general area. "Maybe we're wrong, and it's not going to the refectory."

Still crouching, Papa squinted toward the cluster of buildings. "But that's the only one with a cellar or basement."

"Is it? I'm betting you didn't mess up any angles or distances. You don't mess up like that."

"Sure, Jarret, I make mistakes all the time, but let's say you're right. Where do these angles take us?" He stood.

"Let's find out," Jarret said.

Papa picked up the tripod. "You take the measuring wheel from here. Go straight on toward the stake and keep going till you reach the first building over there."

Jarret turned around slowly, taking it all in. "Looks like the storage building or maybe the church is at that angle."

"Get me the measurements to both. I'll go to the monks' cells to get the angles." Papa strode off, tripod in hand and the diagram under his arm.

Jarret pushed the measuring wheel over the sandy ground and patchy lawn, into and out of shade from a few walnut trees.

After getting the distances, he met up with Papa for the angles and studied the diagram spread out on the ground. It took him a second to figure it out. He looked up, grinning. "It's the church."

"But the church is newer."

"Maybe they built it over something older."

Papa lowered a brow and came up beside him. He studied the diagram for all of one second. "Well, let's go check it out."

They abandoned their equipment and jogged, racing each other for the church. Half way to it, the bell tolled.

"Dash!" Papa skidded to a stop, his boots kicking up dirt. "That's the monks' call to prayer. We'll have to check the church later."

"'Dash'?" Jarret grinned. "Never heard you use that one."

"We're on holy ground. Best to mind your language, don't you think?" Papa cracked a smile.

Jarret chuckled. "Now what?"

Papa turned away from the church. "Want to run up to the store, scare up some supplies?"

"Can I get a pack of cigarettes?"

CHAPTER TWENTY-FIVE
DO SOMETHING

Roland

"Come. On." Selena spit out the words. She stood with her hands on her hips and head tilted, peering down at Roland who lounged on the couch. "Let's *do* something already. It's your last day."

"I know. I'd like to do something." Roland sighed and returned his gaze to Jarret's arm.

Jarret lay stretched out in the recliner, one arm dangling over the side, his fingers resting on a plate of rhubarb and strawberry pastry things that Selena called *empanadas*. He had woken shortly before noon—unlike him—and put on shorts but didn't bother changing the t-shirt he had worn to bed—sooo unlike him. When he'd breezed past the dining room, where Roland and Selena had been waiting for him, he glanced but didn't give them so much as a nod. Not even Selena. He made a beeline for the entertainment room and swiped the remote from little Rosa, who had been watching some animated show. Now, that was like him.

No, this vacation hadn't turned out as Roland had hoped. And now it was over. Sure, he learned more about Papa—and he wouldn't trade that—but he couldn't help wanting more from Jarret. Why couldn't they be friends? Weren't vacations supposed to renew a person's mind and spirit, give a new perspective on life?

The ride out to Tucson had been something good, hadn't it? Singing, laughing, a bit of brotherly bonding. And nothing draws people closer than sharing a crisis. Too bad Jarret never knew when to quit and go home.

Roland shook his head and sighed. He shouldn't have touched that gun. What else could he have done? He couldn't let those guys beat up Jarret.

Selena flopped down beside him on the couch. She folded her arms and propped her bare feet on the coffee table. The strings of her swimsuit hung out of her shirt. She must've asked him five times to go swimming. "I'm glad we found our thief," she said.

"Yeah, me too." Catching the thief had been a highpoint of the trip. He hadn't wanted to keep worrying over it, especially once Papa told him not to, but he sure couldn't get it out of his mind. It had felt like quite the accomplishment, catching Laszio last night. Maybe he'd go into investigative work when he got older.

Jarret huffed and muttered something.

"What'd you say?" Roland leaned forward, the better to hear. Jarret hadn't been himself lately. Something was bugging him.

"Nothing." Jarret turned and glared then snatched an *empanada*.

"You seem like you're mad about something this morning," Roland said.

Selena clicked her tongue. "It's not morning. It's after noon. We've wasted half the day. It's your last day. Let's do something."

"Are we going swimming?" Rosa turned away from the wall-sized TV and the spaghetti western Jarret had selected.

"I seem mad about something, huh?" Jarret peered over his shoulder at Roland. "Nothing about last night, the way Juan handled that, bothered you?"

Roland shrugged. "Why should it? We found the thief and *Señor* Juan had a talk with him."

"What did you want him to do?" Selena said, sounding defensive. "Call the police? I told you, everyone he hires becomes like part of the family. He gives everyone a chance. Don't you ever give anyone a second chance?"

Jarret slammed the footrest down and got up, wiping his fingers on his shorts. "A chance to do what? Steal again? Is your father even gonna get his stuff back?"

"My father has it under control. He is more concerned about Laszio than about things." She turned to Roland, her expression softening. "Laszio has been putting his trust in a shaman over God, and he is a Catholic too."

"I assumed he needed money for medical bills," Roland said.

Selena shrugged. "Perhaps. But when a shaman provides spiritual services, gifts are expected."

"Hm." Roland looked thoughtful. "So what'd you have in the box we used for bait? I heard something break last night when Laszio fell on it."

Selena bowed her head, giggling. "Only some things I made out of clay when I was a little girl: a palomino horse, a wolf, and a cactus. I never cared much about the cactus and the wolf. They didn't turn out right. But I really liked my palomino."

Roland smiled. "I wish I had seen it."

Jarret strutted to the coffee table and stopped across from Roland. "And of course *you're* happy. You got all the praise." He whipped a half-eaten *empanada* at Roland's chest. "I knew you would. You knew you would. All I got was a lecture from Papa about safety. 'You're the older brother. You need to watch out for him.'" He swiped Roland's Coke and took a swig. "Give me a break."

Roland stood up. "You only got lectured because you were high." The words flew out. Maybe he shouldn't have said it in front of everyone.

Jarret grinned as if he admired the boldness. "That ain't the only reason. In Papa's eyes, you don't do nothing wrong. He told you not to worry about the thief. So why aren't you in trouble?"

"I got talked to."

Jarret stepped around the coffee table, staring him down with cold, dark eyes. "I got grounded. I'm seventeen, and he's taking the keys to my car."

"Not for helping to find the thief. You're grounded for—"

Jarret shoved him.

Roland fell backward onto the couch. He jumped up, wanting to shove back, tired of getting pushed around by Jarret, tired of trying to be a friend to him. Jarret didn't want anything to do with him. Why should he waste his time?

A grin of challenge stretched across Jarret's face, daring Roland to push back.

Selena got up from the couch. "Okay, children, stop fighting and let's go do something. Who wants to swim?"

"I do." Rosa jumped to her feet.

"Let's do it," Roland said, holding Jarret's gaze. Jarret probably expected him to decline the offer.

Jarret picked up Roland's Coke again and returned to the recliner. "You guys go. I'm staying put."

Keefe

Standing in front of the open refrigerator, Keefe pulled back the tab on a can of Coke and took a swig. Bubbles tickled his upper lip. The cool, sweet drink burned all the way down his throat. He hated Coke. Jarret loved it.

It did cool him off though. And he'd worked up a sweat working on Roland's mountain bike. He'd straightened the bent rims and fork and put it all back together. It looked good but he'd try it out later and make sure it worked like new. Roland would be happy to see it all fixed when he got back.

Taking another sip, Keefe stared at the calendar that hung on the wall next to the refrigerator. Nanny's handwriting filled just about every square. Keefe had jotted down a few notes of his own, and his gaze rested on them now. He'd written the same symbol on several dates, a letter "F" with a circle around it, "F" for Franciscans. The last "F" fell on today's date.

Keefe's heart sank but seemed to beat harder, slamming with a sickening feeling against his ribs. Was he passing up an opportunity? Was he ignoring his calling?

"Isn't the air-conditioning enough for you?"

Snapping from his trance, Keefe released the refrigerator door and turned around. "Huh?"

Nanny puffed into the kitchen with an armful of folded dishtowels, her curly gray hair all frizzy and sweat dripping down one side of her face. "You boys hold that refrigerator door open like you're fixing to cool the entire house."

"Sorry, Nanny." Keefe took the towels from her and set them on a countertop. "But you do keep the house kind of warm for summer." Nanny had never been one to waste anything, including the electricity, no matter how many times Papa told her not to worry.

"Warm? You think so?" Nanny brows slanted.

Keefe smiled. If he hadn't just come to a decision, he would've offered to help with chores. "Want the rest of my Coke?" He pushed the ice-cold can into her hand. "I've gotta run." He flashed another smile and took off for the kitchen doorway.

"Where are you going?" she hollered after him.

"I gotta do something. Gotta say goodbye to some friends."

❖

Roland's mountain bike humming beneath him, Keefe pedaled like mad down the dirt trail that ran parallel the long, gravel driveway. Would the Franciscans still be at the Brandt's house? Maybe they'd gotten an early start on their journey and he'd miss them anyway. No, Father had canceled the prayer group so he could see them off today. So Keefe's timing was good.

When had he seen the brothers last? Not in days, not since the prayer group had met at church. He hadn't spoken to any of them since that morning he'd fallen out of the tree and got caught spying.

Keefe pedaled harder, a breeze cooling his scalp and sweat making rivulets down his neck and back. If he did get there in time, what would he say to them? He could at least get their contact information. Maybe they could keep in touch, send emails back and forth, until he felt free to join up with them. Did they even have email?

He smiled inside, his heart spinning like the bike spokes. Was this his calling? Would he be wearing that blessed brown robe one day? Living by faith and going wherever God sent him?

Forest Road came into view and a few cars zipped by. Keefe slowed and peered across the road to the Forest Gateway Bed & Breakfast. The neon vacancy sign flashed to the beat of Keefe's heart. A blue twelve-seater van sat next to Mr. Brandt's pickup in the two-car driveway on the left side of the house. Keefe had seen the van at church before. It belonged to one of the larger families, the Finns. Mr. Finn had probably offered to drive the brothers at least partway to their destination.

Keefe glanced for traffic and raced across the road.

The front screen door screeched open.

Keefe's heart skipped a beat. He rode up the driveway and out of view, keeping the long van between him and whoever had stepped out onto the porch. Heart racing now, he walked the bike forward and listened.

The door continued to squeak, more and more people probably coming out onto the porch.

"Oh yeah, we're looking forward to it," a man said in reply to some mumbled words Keefe hadn't made out.

"You never know what doors God will open up," another said.

"Mr. Finn's van door is going to open up in a minute." Peter had said that, his voice louder than the others.

"You are one rude, dude, *vato*." The Spanish accent gave that one away: Dominic.

Several people laughed.

At the end of the van, Keefe stopped. He wiped the sweat from his forehead, his eyes on the four-foot gap between the end of the van and the corner of the garage. Should he step out of hiding? He could always speed forward, hoping no one saw him, and get out of view again beside the garage. Then he could take off down the trails behind Peter's house. Why would he do that? Weren't the Franciscan friars the whole reason he came over? He wanted to say "goodbye" and see if they could stay in touch. Did it matter one way or another? Had any of the brothers even asked about him? Was he wrong to think God was calling him to the religious life?

"Well, we enjoyed getting to know every one of you," Mrs. Brandt said, her cheerful, feminine voice very recognizable. The door squeaked again. Shuffling sounds and footfalls increased. "It won't be the same around here without you."

Several brothers replied at once, mumbling things Keefe couldn't make out.

Keys jangled. "Well, I'll get the van open." Mr. Finn's voice.

Keefe put a foot to the pedal and stepped on it. He zoomed past the open area, glimpsing figures out of the corner of his eye.

They didn't stop talking and no one called after him, so most likely no one had seen him. Keefe didn't look back. He pedaled harder than ever, making a trail through green grass and soon concealing himself in the cover of woods.

Deeper and deeper into the woods he rode, turning down one path and then another, tears blurring his vision. God had spoken to his heart so clearly in Italy, had moved him so deeply. He'd wanted to make a return for that. "I will listen to Your voice," he'd promised the Lord, and he had even cut his hair as a reminder. Then for months he'd felt the Lord nudging him, calling him to something more, something that he couldn't understand at the time. But now . . . It all seemed so clear and muddled at the same time.

The handlebars jerked to one side as the front tire twisted around a root. He tightened his grip to control the bike. Roots and rocks kept getting in his way. He was probably tearing up the tires and inner tubes of Roland's bike. Roland . . . always trying to do the right thing.

Keefe released his grip on the handlebars to drag one arm across his eyes. Salty tears made them sting. He was a failure, a mess, no good at discerning God's will, useless in helping Jarret, and not even capable of making a respectful "goodbye." He'd made a promise to listen to God's voice and to obey. What was the matter with him?

Back there at the Brandt's house, Dominic and Peter had probably seen Keefe. Every Franciscan on the porch had probably seen him, too. What had they thought as he'd zoomed by? Was he eight years old? Confused and afraid? What was he afraid of anyway?

The sound of rushing water broke through his self-loathing thoughts. Without slowing down, he focused on his surroundings. Somehow he'd come to the waterfall.

On impulse, he turned toward the steep slope that ran along the riverbank. He fixed his gaze on the waterfall and pumped the pedals. As he neared the slope, he pushed his weight down on the bike, then punched it, lifting the front wheel off the ground and standing. The back wheel cruised over the lip of the slope, making Keefe airborne, making time stop for a moment and giving him a strange rush that he almost liked.

Reluctant to tear his eyes from the view, he lowered the handlebars and the bike landed on both tires simultaneously. But he was headed directly for the river.

Adrenaline surging through him, he dropped a foot to the ground, released one side of the handlebars and jumped off the bike. The bike swerved around him, landing with a bounce on its side. Keefe's heart raced, pounding in his throat. He righted the bike and rolled it closer to the slope. Then he turned to the waterfall.

The loud roar and white tumbling water mesmerized him for a moment. He moved toward it, staggering through rocks on the sandy bank, teetering on rocks in the agitated water. The spray of the waterfall reached him, cool droplets on his sweaty, tear-streaked face. Then he plunged into it where the brunt of it poured down. And he stood there, gasping for air and struggling to keep his balance as the waterfall washed away his failure, struggling to hold it together as the blinding water reminded him to trust. He was not alone.

The promises he'd made moved to the front of his mind, drowning out all other thoughts.

I will listen to Your voice. I will live knowing that You are with me and that You love me . . . I will not forget, no matter what. No matter what!

The thoughts forced their way out. "I will listen to Your voice!" Keefe shouted and then spluttered. "I'll do what you want! I will live—"

Someone grabbed him, latching onto his arm and tugging, saying something. The rushing water muffled the voice, but it sounded like a girl.

Water flooded his eyes as he turned toward the person. Not wanting to fall, he yielded to her insistent redirection. A few steps later, he found secure footing on the ledge behind the waterfall and he trudged along with the girl, his cold wet jeans encumbering him. He wiped his eyes with his free hand. Then he opened them to see who she was.

Caitlyn held his arm. Shadows hid her face, but he still caught the worry in her expression.

"Wow, Keefe, what do you think you're doing?" Phoebe shouted. "You're drenched." She sat on one of the two log seats at the back of the dim cave, glittery bracelets or maybe rosaries dangling from her wrist. A few candles glowed behind and on either side of her.

"How did you know we were back here?" Kiara said, her soft voice competing with the roar of the waterfall. She stood by the other log seat. "We wanted to include you, but no one answered the phone when we called."

Shuffling to the dry part of the cave, Keefe squinted from one to the other, not sure what to make of the situation. They must've seen him as soon as he'd stepped into the waterfall. Could they have heard him over the noise? "What are you doing back here?" The cool air of the cave hit his wet skin and soaked shirt and made him shiver.

"Sorry we don't have any towels," Caitlyn said.

"We're here because we couldn't pray at the church today," Kiara said, her pleasant smile returning. "But we still wanted—"

"Woo hoo!" someone behind Keefe shouted.

Keefe looked back just as Peter burst through the waterfall. Dominic came in behind him, hooting even louder. Wiping wet hair from their faces, they scuttled along the ledge and joined the girls.

"So what's with you?" Peter came up to Keefe, a big grin on his face. "Just came to spy and run?"

"Spy?" Another shiver ran through Keefe, making him wish for a towel.

"Yeah, *vato.*" Dominic stepped over, combing his dark hair with his fingers and lugging a backpack. "We saw you at Peter's house. That was you on the bike, no? We took off after you but had a hard time keeping up."

Phoebe got up off the log seat and they all formed a circle, all eyes on Keefe.

"Uh . . ."

"Why didn't you come and say 'hey,' at least to the brothers?" Peter was still smirking, looking like he knew something but wanted Keefe to say it himself. "You've been making yourself scarce these days, ever since our last prayer meeting. Something wrong?"

"Well, I . . ." Keefe wanted to step back, but he felt the cave wall behind him closing in.

"I know what the reason is," Caitlyn said, her green eyes glistening in the candlelight and piercing holes through him.

"You do?" Shivering and feeling exposed, Keefe glanced from face to face. Did everyone know?

"You miss praying before the Blessed Sacrament, don't you?" Caitlyn smiled, a look that would disarm anyone.

Keefe exhaled. If she did understand more, she wasn't going to say anything.

"I do, too," she said.

"But since we can't be there, we're here," Kiara said, and she dangled a pink crystal rosary in the middle of the group.

Phoebe crossed her arms and tilted her head, her blue-streaked hair and dark eyes giving her a threatening look. "Wait! The only reason Father canceled was to see the Franciscans off. Why don't we see if he'll open the church for us later?"

"Great idea!"

"Let's do it!"

"Yes!"

"I don't know," Peter whined. "I'm sure he's busy."

"No harm in trying," Dominic said, lifting and unzipping his backpack. "But since we're all here now . . ." He removed a towel, handed it to Keefe, and brought out a black book. "I brought my Bible. I say we open to a random verse for inspiration and say a prayer or two before we take off."

Keefe toweled off his hair and wrapped the towel around his shoulders.

"Yeah, and let's give our prayer intentions first." Caitlyn clasped her hands. Eyes closed, she rattled off a list that went from the pope and government leaders to the forgotten man on the street, souls with no one to pray for them, and the tiny, unborn babies.

Kiara spoke next. Then Phoebe and Dominic. When it came to Peter's turn, he bowed his head, cleared his throat and said in the most serious voice Keefe had ever heard from him, "I offer our prayers for Roland over there in Arizona." His eyelids fluttered up and he glanced at Keefe. "And for his brother, Jarret, who needs our help."

Keefe wanted to nod to show his appreciation, especially after the cruel things Peter had said last time, but emotion overwhelmed him. So he bowed his head.

After a moment of silence, Dominic must've gotten the hint that Keefe wouldn't be adding his intentions aloud. He ran his hand up the Bible and took a breath. "Okay, *amigos*, so I'm going to open the Bible up somewhere . . ." He flipped through the pages. ". . . here where I think is the New Testament. 'Cuz some of those Old Testament verses are, like, you know, kind of kooky. Like some of those things in Leviticus, like skinning and chopping up animals or whatever."

Caitlyn and Kiara giggled. Phoebe clicked her tongue and probably rolled her eyes but Keefe had only lifted his gaze to Dominic.

Dominic opened the Bible to a page, squeezed his eyes shut, and ran his finger down the page. "Okay, I got it. This is from, uh, Matthew, chapter nineteen. *Then Jesus said to his disciples, 'In truth I tell you, it is hard for someone rich to enter the kingdom of Heaven . . .'*"

Heat rose up Keefe's neck and to his cheeks. He'd developed a habit of applying everything Scriptural to himself. Ever since kids at school discovered that his family lived in a castle-like house, they'd called them the rich boys. This verse referred to him.

Heart pounding and physically rattling him, Keefe struggled to hide his emotion. He blinked back tears and dropped his head into his hands. He knew the rest of the verse. He knew what the Lord wanted of him. It might cost more than he wanted to give, but this was the Lord's will and the Lord would make a way.

Dominic continued to read.

"And everyone who has left houses, brothers, sisters, father, mother, children or land for the sake of my name will receive a hundred times as much, and also inherit eternal life."

Roland

Selena and Rosa swam and splashed in the pool for almost an hour before Roland finally joined them. He hated that he had to force himself into the water. What was the matter with him anyway? Where did phobias come from? Why couldn't he get over it?

After swimming, they had a late lunch and then hung out in the stables. Selena told stories about the horses and the places she had taken them, her eyes sparkling as she spoke, as if her re-telling had transported her back to past adventures. Wanting to experience an adventure with her, he blurted out an invitation. "Come stay with us next summer. You can ride our horses."

A long moment later, she answered, "I'd like that."

Later, they joined the family and a few stable hands for dinner, Laszio among them, Jarret absent. As the dinner plates were cleared, *Señor* Juan announced, "We will have prayers at your house, Laszio, for your wife. We will entrust her health to Our Lord and Our Lady."

Eyes down, Laszio gave a slow nod. "You know I am very sorry for what I have done, *Señor* Juan."

"As I told you last night, I forgive you. Trust and surrender, Laszio," Juan said, clasping Laszio's hand. "God is good to us."

With relatively good cheer, everyone filed through the sliding glass doors off the back of the house, making for Laszio's apartment.

"Where's Jarret?" Papa said as they stepped out onto the back patio and into the heat.

"I don't know." Roland donned his black Stetson. "I haven't seen him since morning." A part of him couldn't care less. Jarret could do what he wanted. He obviously wanted nothing to do with any of them. He was selfish, rude, and unchangeable.

"Not morning. Noon," Selena corrected. "It was after noon. We left him in the entertainment room."

Papa gazed in the direction of Rufino's house, but Rufino leaned against the stables with another stable hand. As he turned back, he said, "Did he say what he—"

Jarret came from around the side of the house, strolling in the opposite direction of everyone else, heading for the back end of the stables. He gave a nod of greeting and let a cigarette fall from his hand without breaking his stride. At some point he'd gotten dressed and now wore jeans and his new cowboy hat.

"Jarret," Papa called, increasing the length of his gait.

Jarret stopped. "Yeah, what?"

Papa had a way of ignoring Jarret's rude replies. He even had the hint of a smile on his face as he mumbled to Jarret now. Jarret shook his head, giving Papa a dirty look.

"Do you think he will come pray with us?" Selena said, watching them.

"No." Roland turned away and resumed walking. He would've made an excuse of sorts for Jarret's behavior, and one came to mind, but not this time. People could think what they wanted about him.

He cast a last glance over his shoulder as he headed for Laszio's apartment.

Papa stood staring as Jarret walked away from him. Jarret headed for the big stable door.

Was he going out for a ride? Alone?

CHAPTER TWENTY-SIX

PRAYER WARRIORS

Monettello

Kneeling in the first row of Saint Michael's church, slumped over as if utterly exhausted, Keefe prayed. Every now and then, he sighed heavily and turned his gaze heavenward, his look one of annoyance.

Monettello prayed by his side and carried Keefe's prayers to Heaven.

Cyabrial entered the church with Caitlyn. As Caitlyn slipped into a pew a few rows from the front, he came up to Monettello. "Glory to God in the highest," Cyabrial said.

"And on earth peace to men of good will," Monettello responded.

Cyabrial watched Keefe for a moment. "Keefe seems troubled."

"Yes, he wrestles with his calling," Monettello said. "It is more clear to him now than ever."

"Has he decided to keep in contact with the Franciscan friars?"

"No." Monettello smiled sadly. "He stopped speaking with them after telling Jarret about his calling. And he raced to the cave rather than see them off."

Peter and Dominic arrived together, parting to sit with friends. Peter slid into the pew with Caitlyn. Caitlyn didn't give him a glance, so he turned to see what held her attention.

"So what's the matter with him?" Peter indicated Keefe with a nod.

"I don't know." Caitlyn's eyes held a sympathetic look. "That verse Dominic read in the cave had really seemed to move him, don't you think?"

Peter sneered, his gaze still on Keefe. "I'm guessing it's Jarret."

"What do you mean?"

"Keefe's problem. It probably has to do with Jarret."

"No, maybe he misses the Franciscan friars." She gave Peter a curious glance. "Or do you know something I don't?"

"Maybe. Roland called me a few days ago, wanting prayers. For Jarret. He's worried about him. Sounded like something was really wrong. But you know Roland, not much on the details."

"Oh." Caitlyn's eyebrows slanted. "You should've called me. We could've all done a *Stop, Drop, and Pray.*"

Peter shrugged. "I thought about it. But I started fasting instead."

Caitlyn had turned away to watch Keefe but jerked her face back to him. "You're doing what?"

Peter gave her a smug grin, leaned back, and clasped his hands behind his head. "Yeah, you heard me."

Peter's guardian beamed. He stood with his legs shoulder-width apart, arms folded across his chest, and a thick chain dangling from his hand.

At his feet squatted the green and gnarled demon Grudge, bound by the chain. "This chain was meant for Peter! Not me." Grudge sneered at the angels then set about grunting and gnawing on the links.

"Nice work," Cyabrial said.

"Yes," Monettello said. "Prayer and fasting for one's enemy is a most powerful means of obtaining grace."

"Both for the one praying and the one being prayed for," Peter's angel said.

"Yes." Monettello smiled. "Ellechial will be pleased."

"You're fasting for Jarret?" Caitlyn's eyes bugged. "I thought you hated him."

Peter shrugged again. "Eh, what's the point in hating someone? But let me tell you, my fasting and prayers better be doing some good. It better be worth my effort."

Caitlyn jabbed his side with her elbow.

"Ow!" Peter hunched over and rubbed his side. "What? I'm hungry."

She smiled. "How long are you going to fast?"

"I don't know. I'm gonna call Roland and find out how the trouble-maker's doing, I guess."

"Well, you have my admiration. I wish I could fast."

Peter nodded, glancing around the church. "Lot a kids here tonight. And with hardly any notice."

"Yeah." She looked around, too, smiling. "I'm glad Father let us come at this late hour. It feels special, doesn't it? Like maybe something pivotal is happening."

"Can I sit here?"

Caitlyn and Peter both turned as Zoe stepped into the pew.

"Yeah, sure." Caitlyn straightened up, her full attention on Zoe. "Wow, what are you doing— I mean, I'm glad you're here."

Zoe sat beside her and tucked her hair behind her ear. "Thanks." She glanced to either side and behind her. "I know a lot of these kids from school."

"Yeah." Caitlyn kept staring.

Zoe glanced. "Should I not be here? Is it only for Catholics? Because I'm not—"

"Oh no. You should be here. I'm really glad you are. We've been praying for you. Not by name, of course. I've been asking for prayers for a friend whose parents are going through some troubles."

"They're getting a divorce."

Caitlyn gasped. "Oh, I'm sorry. I have been praying, really."

Zoe smiled and put down the kneeler. "I believe you. I've been praying too. And the funny thing, even though my parents' marriage is falling apart, I feel like God's been there with me. I trust Him. Even if things don't work out the way I want, I know He's with me."

Caitlyn's eyes watered as she watched Zoe kneel and bow her head. "Wow," she whispered.

CHAPTER TWENTY-SEVEN
BACK IN THE SADDLE

Jarret

It felt great to sit in a saddle, finally. It was a good, deep-seated Western saddle, and it fit as if it had been made for him. Enyeto had selected it.

Enyeto was a bossy old Indian. *You should not ride alone. Take a friend. Bring water. Make sure you have your cell phone.*

He said the boundaries of the Zamoranos' property were marked with fluorescent fiberglass posts and for Jarret to look out for them. He said Jarret would be able to have a nice ride before sunset and for him to stay within the boundaries. Red Storm, the chestnut Spanish Mustang he'd saddled for Jarret, knew the exercise trail and would follow it without guidance.

Screw that. He meant to explore without boundaries. Water? No, he brought a Coke. His cell phone? He hadn't paid attention to that thing since the call from Keefe. Whom would he need to call out here in the desert?

Red Storm trotted through the open gate of the white fence at the back of the Zamoranos' pasture, heading for a clear path that turned east. The mansion appeared small from here, its curvy design and natural tones putting it in harmony with the desert surroundings.

A thin, less-defined trail branched off to the right. It was probably a desert wash or an arroyo formed by flash floods and not a trail the Zamoranos used.

Jarret clicked his tongue and tugged the reins, directing Storm down to the wash. Once there, he got her going at a trot. "We're taking a new route today, girl."

Sunbeams blinded him from the right, confirming his southerly direction, their angle telling him that he had a good two hours to explore. He never wore a watch, but he was a good judge of time.

He adjusted his hat to shade his face and soaked in his surroundings.

A hawk flew overhead in the clear blue sky. Clusters of prickly pear, cholla cacti, and dry desert scrub dotted the sandy, rocky land, bits of pale green against a washed-out purple and red backdrop of craggy mountains and mesas. Everything nearby had a crisp clarity, the sharp lines of thorny plants and the cracks between rocks. But the farthest horizon shimmered in the heat, and he had to squint to look at it.

He breathed deeply, enjoying the scent of the arid air and the baked earth, and he sat loose in the saddle, relaxed, glad to be alone in the desert. The only sounds came from the squeak of the saddle and the clomping of the horse's hooves. Even the horse seemed relaxed, her muscular body moving with loose and fluid motions.

Before long, they passed a four-foot fluorescent-orange marker. The boundaries. He chuckled and looked back the way they'd come.

The path he rode on had twisted and curved as it ran deeper into the valley between hills and mesas. Red broken land and a scattering of green and thorny plants blocked the view of the Zamoranos' house.

He continued on, heading south or as south as the twisting trail would allow.

After a while, a jagged, crumbly-sided mesa loomed ahead, casting an inviting purple shadow on the sloped ground beneath it. Tall columns formed the mesa's sides, resembling the rugged teeth of a giant. A section of the mesa's top was flat and wide enough for a good lookout. A trail wound up the slope and up one side of the mesa. Maybe it went all the way to the top.

Whether from signals he inadvertently gave or from Red Storm's desire, they headed for the mesa, picking a trail around rocks, yellow-flowered bushes, and cacti.

"What do you think, Storm? Wouldn't it be cool to reach the top? Maybe we could even see your stables from up there." He pressed his thighs to the horse's sides. Sensitive to the slightest signal, she picked up her pace.

Soon they reached the shade of the mesa. It did little to relieve the heat, but it felt better than the sun's relentless rays. A trickle of sweat ran down Jarret's neck. With the reins loose in one hand and the horse proceeding at her own pace, Jarret removed his hat and combed his fingers through his flattened, sweaty curls.

Storm clomped directly to the mesa trail as if she had been here before. Maybe Selena had taken her out here. This might even be one of the mesas she'd told him about on their "date."

The trail narrowed as they climbed, and it turned so that they now rode toward the setting sun. Then the trail descended and leveled out at about twenty-five or thirty feet above ground. The vertical cracks in the steep sides of the mesa had grown darker and wider the higher they climbed. Ahead, a smooth wall jutted from the mesa, appearing to cut off the trail. If the trail ended, turning around would prove a challenge.

Storm continued on, trotting at a comfortable gait that gave Jarret confidence. Nearing the wall, Jarret saw two things. The trail did not end but wound around the wall, and daylight stole through one of the vertical cracks in the side of the mesa.

"Wait here," he said to Storm, dismounting. He found a stone that took two hands to carry and placed it on the reins, in case Storm should get the urge to wander off. Then he started up the slope that led to the lighted crack.

The slope was no higher than a slide on a playground, but rocks kept falling loose under his feet. His heart raced. Sweat dripped down his neck. Feet tingling, he slid back down three feet. He pictured himself losing control, sliding all the way down, skimming across the trail, and tumbling over the side of the mesa. But he didn't slip again.

At the top, he found a level spot and straightened up. The depth of the crack prevented him from seeing what lay on the other side, so he held onto one wall and leaned forward to see.

The view made his head spin. He reeled back and pressed his body to the rock wall.

A canyon lay below, hidden in the middle of the mesa.

Once the vertigo passed, he slid down to a sitting position and dangled his feet over the edge. A rope lay beside him, one end tied to a nearby boulder, the other dangling somewhere below in the canyon. The canyon wall opposite him rose up about thirty feet from the ground, but his side went up higher, towering some twenty or so feet above him.

He touched the rope. It was old and weathered, but it was a good, thick rope. He leaned to see how far down it hung. It went all the way down, forming a coil on the canyon floor.

Someone must have used it to climb down into the canyon, exploring or maybe— Maybe someone had hidden something in the canyon. Papa used to tell stories of gold prospectors. One of their relatives, Jarret's great-great grandpa, used to hunt for gold. A hidden canyon would be a great place to hide something.

Without further thought, Jarret gripped the rope and swung his body over the edge.

Roland

Roland rode the blue roan they called Diamond because of its shiny silver coat. Once outside the Zamoranos' horse yard, he jumped down to close the white fence. The riding trail, a wide path covered with horseshoe prints and edged with stones, went off in two directions.

Which way would Jarret have gone? Enyeto said the trail wound all through their property and eventually out to the street, and it could take an hour to cover.

As he slipped his foot into the stirrup, a thought struck him. Jarret was the first to take a horse out this evening, Enyeto had said. Maybe Roland could tell which direction he'd taken by inspecting the tracks.

Roland dropped his foot to the ground and led the horse to where the trail split off. Sure enough, the horseshoe prints in the sandy dirt were fresher on the path that turned east.

A smile came to his face as he swung up into the saddle. Maybe he would be an investigator or a detective one day. That would be a fun profession. He could develop his observational skills, learn how to track animals, people . . .

A short distance later, Roland reined in his wandering imagination and peered down at the trail. He had lost the fresh tracks.

He twisted in the saddle to examine the trail behind him and the landscape on either side. No new tracks. Had Jarret turned off somewhere? He could've easily made his own path through the sparse desert plants.

Roland turned Diamond around and, giving more attention to his surroundings, retraced the horse's steps until he found the tracks most likely made by Jarret's horse. The tracks veered off the trail at a dry wash.

"Come on, boy." Roland urged the horse onto the thin trail of the wash.

The slant of the evening sunlight made searching the landscape off to his right difficult, even with his hat pulled down on that side. But the tracks still followed the dry wash, so he probably wouldn't miss Jarret.

Why had Jarret ridden out alone? Why wouldn't he join everyone else in praying for Laszio's sick wife and then ride out? Selena had said she wanted to ride tonight.

Roland sighed. Why did he care? He regretted getting up from his knees and bolting for the door in the middle of the Rosary. Jarret would be fine. He could take care of himself.

A few yards from the trail stood one of the fluorescent-orange boundary makers that Enyeto had described to him.

Roland pulled the reins.

Diamond whinnied and lifted a front hoof. Then he stopped.

"Jarret wouldn't go out past the Zamoranos' land, would he?" He stroked Diamond's neck.

Diamond snorted and bobbed his head.

"Yeah, you're right. The tracks do go on, don't they?" Roland loosened the reins. "Come on. Let's go find him."

Roland rode the horse at a gallop, squinting against the sun on his right, straining to keep sight of the horseshoe tracks that kept disappearing behind clusters of desert plants and rocky terrain. Low hills stretched out and mesas rose up on either side, with more hills and mesas on the horizon. A high and rugged mesa soon showed itself to be his destination.

They crossed into the long shadow of the mesa, and Roland brought the horse to a stop. He rested in the saddle and gazed up at the looming sight. His stomach turned.

"Don't tell me he went up there." He cupped a hand to his mouth and shouted, "Jarret! Hey, Jarret!"

Diamond snorted and turned his head as if to get a look at Roland.

"Well, it was worth a try," Roland said, stroking the horse.

Getting no reply, he loosened the reins and shifted in the saddle. "Come on. We'll have to take the trail up the mesa. I hope Jarret's not trying to climb to the top." The top reminded him of a big currycomb with rows of teeth, like the ones he used to groom their horses back home.

He tapped the horse with his leg. "Let's get to it."

Diamond walked to the trail and began the climb.

The trail inclined gradually, but Roland soon found himself hesitant to glance out over the edge. He didn't have a problem with heights. The horse seemed relaxed. No reason to feel queasy at the sight of the ledge and the landscape below, right?

A rock at Diamond's hoof broke free and skidded down the side of the mesa. Roland squeezed his eyes shut as it clattered to its resting place far below.

They rounded the side of the mesa and Roland gazed out without squinting. The sun had turned the sky pink at the horizon and no longer blinded him. The trail, however, had narrowed considerably, so turning around would be awkward, even dangerous. Maybe they would come across a wider spot ahead. He would hate to have to climb all the way to the top. From the ground, he'd thought he'd seen a flat area in the middle of the mesa's top. But looks can be deceiving from a distance.

God willing, Jarret had done whatever he set out to do, had turned around, and was now headed back to—

The chestnut horse Jarret had taken out, Red Storm, stood a short distance away, where a wall of the mesa jutted out.

Roland's hope deflated. Where was Jarret?

He dismounted and walked Diamond to Storm. Then he secured the reins with a stone as Jarret had done.

The trail wound around the protruding rock wall. Maybe Jarret had thought it unsafe to ride the horse around it. Or maybe he—

Roland's gaze landed on a scraped-up, steeply inclined part of the mesa that separated the trail from sheer rock walls. A few desert scrub plants grew in the loose, rocky dirt of the incline. Footprints went all the way up but they were short, probably from him using the toe of his boots to climb. The scrape marks were about three feet long, as if Jarret had gotten halfway up and slid back down.

Jarret had climbed the incline. But why? There wasn't anything at the top, no place to go from there.

Roland moved closer, examining his surroundings. Maybe Jarret saw something, went to get it, and came back down. Where would he have gone then? Maybe he was still nearby.

He lifted a hand to his mouth and shouted, "Jarret! Hey, Jarret!"

One of the horses whinnied. A warm breeze blew. No other reply came.

Roland stepped up on the slope. The dirt gave way under his shoes, bringing him back to where he started. He studied the slope and the footprints again. If Jarret did it, he could do it. He took two steps back, leaned over and readied himself. Then he sprang up the slope using the toes of his shoes. He got to the top on his first try. Then he saw it.

He stood before a high and narrow gap between rock walls of the mesa. The gap opened to a canyon below. A thick but weathered old rope hung down into the canyon. Would Jarret have climbed down? He did have a reckless side.

Roland sat down, swung his legs over the edge, and shouted as loud as he could, "Jarret, where are you?" His voice echoed in the canyon.

As he waited for a reply, he scanned the canyon, what he could see of it. Rock walls jutted out on either side, blocking the overall view. Beneath him, about thirty feet down, were a few desert shrubs, rocks, a dry creek, and the end of the rope.

Roland called again and waited.

Minutes passed with no reply. His stomach tensed. Something must've happened to Jarret. Of course, the canyon could come out somewhere else. Jarret could be taking a different route back to his horse.

Or he could be hurt and unable to reply.

The sunlight would soon fade. He ought to look for him. No, he *had* to look for him. He had to do it now.

With a prayer to God, he grabbed the rope. He wrapped the rope around one hand and gave it a good tug. It seemed secure enough. Gripping the edge with one hand and the rope with the other, he turned his back to the opening and lowered himself down. His stomach leapt. Not wanting to look down, he locked his gaze to the rope. Then with knees and toes pressed to the canyon wall, the rough rope ripping at the skin on his fingers and palms, he started down. After climbing a short distance, his foot lost contact with the canyon wall. What happened to it?

He reached as far as he could with his foot. Still nothing. He must've been on the side of a ledge, the canyon wall setting back farther. He'd have to rely only upon the rope and the strength of his arms to go the rest of the way.

He glanced down and his stomach flipped.

It still seemed like a thirty-foot drop to the rocky canyon floor. If he fell, he'd land on a big round boulder or on the smaller, sharper rocks next to it.

"You're not going to fall," he whispered, closing his eyes in preparation to move on.

Using his knees, he climbed the last few inches down the side of the ledge. Then he squeezed his eyes shut and let his legs hang free.

His body slammed the wall.

He tried to turn so that his shoulder would hit, but the knuckles of his left hand cracked against hard rock. At the impact, he grunted, then he held his breath while the pain passed.

A moment later, trembling now, Roland breathed. "Thanks, Lord," he whispered, glad that he hadn't fallen.

He forced himself to go on. A few inches at a time, he lowered himself, the rope swinging him as he went.

Then the rope jerked.

And vibrated.

Roland clung to the swinging rope and peered back up. Something thin stuck out from the rope above him, near the edge of the ledge. A fray?

CHAPTER TWENTY-EIGHT
ADVANCING IN BATTLE

Monettello

Atop the altar of St. Michael's Church, amidst a cloud of incense, stood a monstrance of gold, displaying what appeared to human eyes as a small white wafer. Angels and men of faith saw not bread but the Lord Jesus Christ in the Most Blessed Sacrament, the Lamb of God, the Bread of Angels.

Face to the floor, Monettello adored the Lord of lords, the King of kings, with words no mortal could comprehend. Angelic songs and praise went up around him, filling the air with a sacred melody. Angels worshipped around the altar. Saints joined in the prayers: Saint Conrad of Parzham, Saint Peter, Saint Paul, Saint Dominic, Saint Anthony, Saint Therese and Saint Clare . . .

The teens knelt, rosary beads dangling from their hands, eyes closed, praying for the mercy of God. Their prayers, taken by the angels, rose like incense to the Throne of God.

God heard them.

With every heart-felt word they uttered, grace poured forth from the Crucified One, from his hands, his side, his feet. Like blinding beams of light, grace poured forth to the woman who knelt beneath the cross, the Virgin Mary.

Despite the sorrow, trust and surrender showed in her eyes. Her Immaculate Heart burned with pure love, attracting to itself the Divine Love . . . and all grace with it. The Blessed Virgin at once opened her hands and a pale blue light glowed in her palms. The light increased in intensity until rays burst forth. Rays of grace fell upon each of the teens, upon the priest, and upon all others present. Those same rays pierced through the windows of the church, shooting in all directions according to the prayer requests of the group.

The song of the angels continued, their glorious prayers mixing with the feeble prayers of the teens. More angels appeared and flew to the feet of the Queen of Angels to receive armor and orders.

Ellechial arrived last. Joy radiated from his countenance. He knew his time had come. He approached the Blessed Virgin with reverence and dropped down on one knee before her. With great humility, he bowed his head as if he were being knighted by a queen. And so he was.

She opened her hands and warm blue light streamed from her palms. The light surrounded Ellechial, intensifying and turning pure white. The two remained rapt in prayer until the light subsided. Then Ellechial stood, arrayed in shining silver armor.

A murmur of praise and awe rose up from every angel present. His armor—both beautiful and terrifying to behold—gleamed with the grace won through Christ by the prayers and sacrifices of others, the good deeds the Lord had prepared for them. The demons, forced to look upon him, shuddered and bemoaned.

A hand to his breastplate, Ellechial smiled at the Blessed Virgin. "I thank you, My Queen, O Full of Grace."

The Virgin returned the smile. "The flaming sword and a bow will be yours in battle. Go and fight well."

Ellechial bowed and stepped back. He turned to depart, his wings lifting and spreading for flight.

"God be with you," Monettello said, as both a sendoff and a prayer.

"And with you." Ellechial vanished as he spoke.

Monettello lifted his mind to God, thanking Him for his brother angel. Ellechial had always worn the golden sash of faithfulness, as do all angels who made the choice to serve God. But it made an angel rejoice to see him fully armored and off to wage war against the spiritual forces of evil.

Monettello knew that Ellechial had prayed in earnest every moment of every day for his charge, willing to fight all the forces of evil at the very gates of Hell to save him. And when Jarret's last day comes, should he not be ready to behold the face of God, Ellechial would be pleased to conduct him to Purgatory. Then he would bring to Jarret what help and consolation he could, for as many years or hundreds of years as it would take for his purification, longing for the day he could lead him into Heaven, where together they could praise the Holy One for all eternity.

Should the forces of evil prevail, however— *No.* Monettello would not think about that.

Jarret

The splinter wouldn't come out. Stupid how one tiny thing in his palm could agitate his whole body.

Jarret slammed his hand against the canyon wall and spit out a cuss word. Then he squatted by the opening to a little cave.

All and all, the canyon had disappointed him. A dry creek ran the length of the canyon, a tall and flat rock wall at its head and this little cave at its foot. He'd hoped to find something cool. If not something of value, at least something interesting. The old rope proved someone had been in the canyon before. If someone had hidden something, the little cave would be the perfect spot.

He assessed the size of the opening. A bit more than knee high at its highest point and about four feet wide, it probably didn't lead to much of a cave. Not that he could see far into it. No matter how hard he strained, he could only steal from the darkness a few patches of light on an inner wall.

He'd have to do an army crawl if he wanted to get inside and check it out . . . picking up whatever creepy things clung to the entrance and meeting face to face with whatever lived inside. At least the opening was too small for a bear to get through. But this was southern Arizona. He wouldn't find a bear inside. He'd find a coyote or a fox or a venomous snake.

But, still, someone could've hidden something in there.

Jarret heard Roland call again, his voice echoing in the canyon.

He rolled his eyes. Why had the pest followed him? How had he found him? The mesa wasn't near any real trail. Of course, once Roland had started up the mesa, he would've seen the horse. He could've figured it out from there. Why couldn't Roland just mind his own business?

Jarret dropped down flat, the way he did for push-ups, and poked his head into the cave. The cool air refreshed him, but it held an earthy, moldy odor. If only he could see. *Wait—* His lighter!

Twisting to one side, he swung a hand to the front pocket of his jeans and stuffed it deep inside. His finger bumped the lighter and something else. Huh? Was that a chain? How the—

He drew both items out into the shade of the cave: his white lighter and a medal on a silver chain. How did that get there? The lighter slipped from his grip as he lifted the chain for a better look at the medal. The Virgin Mary. Rays coming from her hands. Words circling around her. A sensation of *deja vu* overwhelmed him. Mama had worn one like it—

His attention snapped from sight to sound, and he froze.

270

A grunt and a moan of sheer agony resounded in the canyon.

Jarret scrambled from the cave and stuffed the lighter back into his pocket. He pulled the chain over his head and dropped the medal down the front of his shirt as he jumped to his feet.

Jagged canyon walls prevented him from seeing the point where he'd climbed down. The sunlight had faded, and long shadows filled the canyon. His surroundings appeared strange and unfamiliar, though he had explored every inch of the place, except for the cave.

Had Roland tried to come down?

Jarret took a step and slipped. He threw his arms out to keep his balance. The flat, sturdy rocks he had used as footholds now hid themselves. He headed back to the rope, his feet slipping with every step.

The groaning came again but more subdued. He still couldn't see Roland. A smooth-faced wall stuck out, separating them.

Jarret's stomach sank. Stones slipped under his feet. He called out, "Roland?"

"I . . ." Roland's voice sounded strained. He said nothing more.

A sudden burst of energy coursed through Jarret, thrusting him forward. He ran. Rocks slid under his feet. Pounding, sliding, pounding, his sore ribs taking a beating. Sliding too far. He lost his balance and cracked down on one knee.

His hand shot out to a nearby boulder. Back on his feet. Slipping on stones. Moving too slowly.

Then he caught sight of Roland and staggered to a stop. The blood drained from his head and neck.

Ten feet away, Roland lay on the ground, twisted to one side and clutching his left thigh. Blood streaked his shin. He gave a tortured glance, pain disfiguring his face. "I think it's . . ." He curled over his thigh.

Jarret inched closer, staring at the leg, at the strange twist of his calf and the dark bulge on his shin. Was the leg broken? "Wh-what happened?"

Roland glanced at the canyon wall and strained out the words, "Rope. Broke."

A few feet of rope, badly frayed at the end, hung from the upper edge of the wall. The rest of the rope lay on the ground near Roland and draped over a knee-high rock. A blood-streaked rock.

This couldn't be happening. This wasn't real. It had to be a dream. He'd had dreams like this before. Any minute now, he'd wake up glad it was over, glad it was only a dream.

Jarret took a deep breath and averted his gaze from the mangled leg of his younger brother.

The sky had darkened to a haunting shade of blue. A few stars shown. The moon hovered above the farthest canyon wall between rocks dyed yellow by the waning sunlight.

Roland moaned.

Jarret breathed again and faced him. "What're you doing here?"

"You . . . rode out alone."

"So?" Anger flickered inside him. Roland should not have followed. "I can take care of myself. But you . . ." He sneered, his gaze traveling from his brother's deathly-white face to his contorted leg. The flicker of anger welled up, quickening his heartbeat. He didn't want to give in to the anger, especially not now. Roland needed help. But the words came out anyway. Harsh, ugly . . . "You shouldn't have touched that rope. That was my only way out."

Jarret had gone from one end of the canyon to the other exploring. It twisted and turned, making it impossible to gauge its actual length, but it was small and entirely enclosed. Sheer rock walls with no footholds rose up about thirty feet on one side, higher on the other. Crumbled rocks and boulders covered the canyon floor. A trail down the middle showed where a creek or a stream flowed in the rainy season, coming from the higher end of the canyon and leaving through the little cave, the dark crack where two rock walls came together. As for signs of life . . . near the far end of the dry creek stood a couple of dead trees, maybe mesquite. No, there was no other way out.

Roland, still clutching his leg, turned his head with short jerky movements until he faced Jarret. "You . . ." He winced. ". . . didn't answer. I thought you might be . . ."

"Hurt?" Jarret snapped. Thanks to pain-in-the-neck Roland, his bruised rib cage was hurting again. He kicked a stone, sending it sailing into the canyon wall and bouncing back a few feet. "That was the only way out! We're trapped down here now."

Roland stared at him, his eyes flinching.

Jarret paced. His heart beat in his throat and angry thoughts fought one another in his head. He needed to resist the temptation and focus on getting them out of the canyon. If only Roland hadn't— "You shouldn't have followed me. You're not my pal. We don't do things together." He stopped and looked at Roland to gauge the reaction of his next words. "Don't you know I can't stand you?"

Roland's eyelids flickered. He turned away. "I thought you were hurt down here. Someone will come looking for us. Or maybe we can call . . ." With awkward movements, he reached into a pocket of his shorts. He brought an empty hand out.

"A phone? You brought your cell phone?" White points of light flashed in Jarret's vision. He dashed to Roland's side and shoved his hand into one pocket then another. "Where'd you put it? Where's your phone?"

Roland moaned and grabbed Jarret's wrists as if to stop him. "Don't. It hurts."

273

"Where's your freaking cell phone?" Jarret tried the last pocket and found nothing. He gave Roland a shove before standing up.

Whimpering and with glazed eyes, Roland twisted over and clutched his thigh. His side lifted a bit off the ground and something under him became visible, something small and black.

Was it? Jarret squatted and snatched it up. It was the cell phone all right, but it fell apart in his hands. He picked up the pieces and, cussing, whipped them against the canyon wall.

"Someone . . . will . . . come," Roland whispered.

"Oh yeah?" Jarret kicked a stone. "They're all over at Laszio's praying for his sick wife. Who knows when they'll get back to the house? Are they even gonna miss us till tomorrow? It's not like Papa tucks us in at night. It's not like—"

An animal howled in the distance.

They both froze. A coyote? Selena had said she'd seen coyotes out here, hadn't she? A coyote wouldn't come into the canyon though. It couldn't. There wasn't a good way in or out. Nothing but steep rock walls. A coyote couldn't scale a wall.

Jarret gripped the hair on the top of his head and tugged until it hurt. He paced again, anger clouding his thoughts. Why was this hatred welling up inside? Why couldn't he stop it? Words flew from his mouth. "You're forever acting like you wanna be my friend, but I know it's not true. You're as bad as me. You're calculating. You want things, and you think you can manipulate me to get them."

"Want things? That's not true. What . . . do I want?"

Jarret grinned. "Selena, for one. And to get back at me." He fought the impulse to shove Roland. The loser was already down and out.

CHAPTER TWENTY-NINE

FUELING FIRE

Ellechial

Deth-kye stood behind Jarret, so close they appeared as one. "Kick him, kick him," he shouted. "Today he dies." A stream of curses spewed from his mouth. Then he looked at Roland sprawled out on the ground and laughed.

"Be gone." The power in Ellechial's voice drove Deth-kye back several yards. "Even should he die, he will live."

Ellechial flew closer to his charge. "Jarret, compassion. Your brother is hurt. Have no doubt of his love for you. He has no ulterior motives."

Jarret's face didn't flinch, his hard heart repelling the good counsel.

Deth-kye's eyes gleamed with hate and fire as he drew a double-edged sword from its sheath—a sleek sword, not the clumsy, blackened scythe he had wielded in the past. "This is my hour. Behold the power of Hell!" Wild-eyed and grimacing, he sprinted forward. The sword burst into red flame.

Ellechial lunged, placing himself between Jarret and the demon, and drew his own sword. The swords clanged together with a steely clash. Flames of red and white flashed, reaching into the air and shooting to the ground like long fingers.

Deth-kye fell back. Instantly, he rolled up on all fours, growling like a beast of prey. He prowled around the brothers and Ellechial. Then, with all the fury of Hell, he pounced.

Ellechial shot to the defense. His breastplate cracked against the demon's head.

The blackened scythe appeared in Deth-kye's left hand and the sword in his right. He wielded them skillfully and without hesitation.

Using shield and sword, plated boot and breastplate, Ellechial kept the demon from victory. For now.

Meanwhile, Nadriel hovered over Roland, his armor gleaming, and a thick, curved sword in each hand. He whirled the swords to the left and right, front and back, with graceful, artistic moves, as he fought off three demons at once: Self-Pity, Fear, and Resentment.

The demons retreated.

Nadriel lifted the visor of his helmet and a gold chalice appeared in his hands. He dropped to Roland's side, admiration in his eyes. "Have no fear. The Lord has called you to make this sacrifice. Offer up your pain. Unite it to the sacrifice of the Lord Jesus. Offer it for your brother. Harbor no anger in your heart. Trust in the Savior . . ." As he whispered words of guidance, he brought the cup to Roland's mouth.

Roland closed his eyes. His lips parted.

"Stop him!" Deth-kye shouted to the three demons now cowering in the darkness.

The demons sprang forward. One tore at Nadriel's arm. Another went after Roland. Nadriel swung his sword, warding off the demon intent on hurting Roland. But the teeth of the third demon sank deep into his arm. The chalice slipped.

Ellechial flew, catching it before it hit the ground. He set it on a ledge away from the fight before resuming his duel with Deth-kye.

Deth-kye moved to Jarret's side and whispered in his ear, taking advantage of the moment. Jarret's eyes narrowed as the demon spoke.

"Be gone!" Ellechial shouted, grabbing his bow. He loosed a flaming arrow.

A black metal shield appeared in Deth-kye's hand. He blocked the arrow and withdrew, glowering. "This is the final battle for his soul. Tonight, Jarret will be mine. Tonight, they both die."

"No!" Ellechial lunged.

A dozen demons descended the canyon walls. Hisses and curses echoed in the canyon as the malicious creatures advanced. Hate and fury, black as Hell, surrounded them.

Nadriel spared a glance without breaking measure. Swords swirled above Roland, the swords of the three demons against Nadriel's two. Despite their vicious attack, Self-Pity, Fear and Resentment could gain no edge. Their beady eyes showed cowardice. Soon Nadriel had them wounded and scurrying to the far side of the canyon, but then other demons approached.

"The victory will be mine!" Deth-kye shouted, making a determined lunge for Jarret.

Ellechial spread his wings to protect, but clawed hands latched onto his arms and legs from behind. Demons grabbed Nadriel too, but they hadn't managed to pull him from Roland's side.

With arms folded and a smug grin, Deth-kye hovered above Jarret. "Look at him. Behold your miserable little brother." He shot his arm out, pointing at Roland. "This is all his fault. You know he hates you." Deth-kye floated around Jarret, stopping when he got behind him. He spoke over Jarret's shoulder, his mouth to his ear.

"He hates you as much as you hate him. You know he does. How could he forgive you, after all you've done to him? It is not possible." Deth-kye grinned, stroking Jarret's chin. "See how he looks at you with hate, with disgust. Tell him what you did to him. Tell him."

"Go ahead and tell him." Nadriel twisted to free himself from the demons. "Roland is strong in the Lord. There is nothing you can say to change that." Nadriel vanished, reappearing free of the demons and with the gold chalice again in hand. He dropped onto one knee before Roland. "Drink, my child. For you are closest to the Lord when you make your sacrifice with love."

Deth-kye shrieked. He vanished and reappeared at Roland's side. He swung his fist, knocking the chalice from Nadriel's hands. Demons swarmed upon the angel. The cup clanked against stones, settling somewhere in the darkness.

"Anger! Jealousy! Come hither," Deth-kye shouted.

Like bolts of lightning, the summoned demons appeared. They crouched around Roland, touching their claws to his forehead and heart.

Roland moaned.

Jarret

Jarret gazed at his miserable little brother sprawled out on the ground all weak and helpless. God, he shouldn't feel this way. He shouldn't say these things, but he couldn't stop himself. In fact, something about giving into the temptation felt good. "I bet you figured out what I did to you."

"I don't," Roland strained, "know what you mean."

"Don't you? The reason *little Roland* got so sleepy the other night, had to take a nap? The reason you slept through my date with Selena?" He paced, eyeing Roland. "I tricked you into drinking sleeping meds."

Roland shot a glance, moaned, and went back to clutching his leg.

"That's right. Did you really think I bought you that juice just to be nice?" He chuckled, still pacing, kicking rocks out of his way. "I've been screwing with you since you were born."

A cool breeze blew for an instant then died. Jarret glanced up but focused on nothing. He should stop with his tirade. He should see if there was something he could do, some way out that he'd missed. Did Roland need a splint? Was that a bone sticking out? Why did he have to come down here? *He ruins everything.*

"I'm the reason you're afraid of water." He stopped to see Roland's reaction. "Do you know that?"

Roland squinted at him, then looked away. He propped himself up on his elbows, groaning, and scooted over an inch, as if he wanted to get to the big rock near him, the rock streaked with his blood. Then he grabbed his leg again.

Jarret sauntered over and squatted right by him. He peered into his glazed eyes. "When you were little, still toddling around, I did something to you. You know how bored I always got when we had to go on those digs or to mines for Papa's work?"

Roland's eyebrows lowered over gray eyes that showed pain deeper than anything physical.

"Well, I found me a way to entertain myself." Jarret grinned remembering how freaked out Roland had gotten. "One day, Mama told me to get a bucket of water from the river, and on the way back, I saw you. You were playing with your little four-wheeler truck all by yourself. Keefe wasn't around to talk me out of it. So I snuck up on you and dumped the whole bucket of ice-cold water right on your head." Jarret laughed and fell back on his hind end.

Roland's eyes flickered and his jaw twitched.

"You screamed your little head off, running in circles, until Mama came to save you." Jarret frowned. "She wanted to blame me, but I told her you tried to take the bucket, that it was your own fault. And she believed me." He got up and sauntered away, kicking rocks as he went. "I don't how many times I did that to you, over the years. I even got Keefe helping me. I'm surprised you don't remember. You only seem to remember that you hate water." He laughed and stooped for a rock. "You know the only reason I took you to Tucson was to get you in trouble with Papa. That kind of backfired on me. He whipped the rock at the ground by Roland's feet, not to hit him, just to bother him.

Roland snapped his face to Jarret, worry in his eyes.

Jarret picked up another rock.

As darkness filled the sky, he whipped rocks at the ground near Roland and recounted incidents from the past, one after another, as they came to mind. "Remember when I . . ."

The moon rose high and stars filled the black abyss. The cool breeze and the coyote's cries came more often. Roland had inched his way to the big rock and now sat slumped over, holding his leg. He'd stopped moaning, but he breathed funny.

Jarret's mind had grown numb. It felt good having confessed all that. Not that he was sorry. It just felt good getting it out in the open. He stopped pacing, let the stone in his hand fall to the ground and looked at Roland. "You hate me, don't you?"

It took a moment for Roland to make eye contact.

Ellechial

"That's my boy, Jarret. Let the hate own you." Deth-kye's accursed laughter filled the air. Many of the surrounding minor demons sniggered with him.

As much as he despised the touch of the demons, Ellechial let them hold him for a moment more. They had no clue what was about to happen.

Once again, Nadriel held the golden chalice. Angels dressed for battle had appeared and taken control of several demons, all without Deth-kye's knowledge. He'd been too busy coaching Jarret.

Deth-kye patted Jarret's face and grinned. "You could kill him yourself, couldn't you?"

Jarret, with eyes like coal, turned a fist-sized rock over in his hand.

"You have made this easy for me, over the years," Deth-kye said. "I ought to thank you for your cooperation. Only we demons, we don't believe in that. We seduce and tempt, we rule and control, we manipulate and destroy. We don't thank." He slapped Jarret's cheek then strolled a few steps away with his hands behind his back and his gaze on Ellechial. "Oh, the sweet victory. I can taste it."

Jarret gripped the rock and sucked in a breath of air.

"Do it," Deth-kye whispered in a voice harsh and cold as death.

Behind Deth-kye, Nadriel brought the cup to Roland's lips. Eyes closed, Roland mouthed a prayer that Nadriel carried at once to Heaven.

Roland breathed and opened his eyes, training his gaze on Jarret. "No." His voice held strength. "I don't hate you."

Deth-kye reeled around, eyes wide and fury written on his face. "Who let that blasted angel past?"

"He was too strong for us," Self-Pity said, cowering in the shadows with several minor demons.

Deth-kye streaked through the air to the cowering demons and began thrashing and shrieking, cursing and slashing. Demons fell back, clutching their wounded limbs. Some scaled the sides of the canyon. Others spread their scrawny wings and shot into the air.

Within seconds, a bow materialized in Deth-kye's hands and he drew back a flaming dart, with Roland as his target.

Nadriel lifted his shield with a casual motion as if he sensed no real danger. The other angels simply watched.

Perhaps aware of the futility of letting a dart fly, Deth-kye lowered his bow and spun to face Jarret. "Hate! Hate!"

Jarret's face contorted with anger.

In a flash, Deth-kye raised his bow and shot. The flaming dart sailed through the air toward Roland. At the same moment, Jarret lunged and kicked Roland in the side.

The flaming dart met with Nadriel's shield, but Roland grunted and clamped an elbow to his side. "Why are you . . ." He groaned.

"You *have* to hate me!" Jarret seethed, lifting the stone. "I've done so much against you for so long. You can't forgive all that. Forgive and forget. No, you want revenge. Some things are . . . unforgiveable."

Deth-kye made ready to nock another dart.

Ellechial cracked him in the ribs and ripped the bow from his hand.

A mocking grin stretched across Deth-kye's face. He vanished but then reappeared as a small, bat-like creature near Jarret.

Ellechial swung his sword.

Deth-kye shrunk back and circled around to Jarret's other side.

Ellechial swung again.

The demon shot up and back down, avoiding the brunt of the blade. Then he affixed himself to Jarret's head, digging his claws in deep. He used this method to retrieve certain memories or to bring up the sins of Jarret's past: sensuality, lies, manipulation, thieving, drunkenness . . . Lately, he focused on Jarret's attempts to get Zoe to abort their baby.

"Who could forgive that?" Deth-kye spewed. "God gives life and you wanted to kill it. How could God ever forgive that? How could God forgive all that you have done? Impossible."

"Jarret, no." Roland straightened up, his face flinching but his gaze locking hard onto Jarret. "I do forgive you. You're my brother and I love you." His lips trembled. "I don't care what you do to me. I don't care if you, if you . . . kill me. I still love you."

Deth-kye shrieked and shot from Jarret's side as if thrown by some force.

Jarret reeled back, the stone falling from his hand. Rocks slid under his feet as he continued backing up. He spun away from Roland and cracked down onto his knees, dropping his head into his hands.

Ellechial alighted by his side and spread his wings for protection. All the memories Deth-kye had brought to Jarret's mind in order to deceive him, would now be set straight.

"Remember," Ellechial whispered.

Jarret

"What's with all the snacks?" Papa made a squinty-eyed glance at Jarret's armful of junk food as they walked together to the winery.

"You bought 'em." Jarret used his teeth to rip open a package of beef jerky.

"I thought they were for both of us, to eat a little at a time." He opened the door and motioned for Jarret to go through first.

They descended the steps to the wine cellar.

Jarret chuckled. "There's more. I didn't take it all. Besides, you wouldn't let me get cigarettes so —"

"All right, all right." Papa switched on the practically useless overhead lights.

Jarret glanced at the racks of wine bottles before following Papa to the back corner of the cellar. The inky darkness visible through the door-sized hole in the wall made him shiver.

Papa opened one of the crates and dug through the supplies inside.

Jarret set his armful of snacks on the other crate, took a bite of jerky, and leaned back.

"Here," Papa said.

Jarret glanced up in time to see a pair of safety glasses sailing at him.

Papa picked up the sledgehammer and gave Jarret a sly smile. "Ready to tear down a wall?"

"Yeah!" Jarret grabbed the snacks.

They followed the tunnel to where it split off, took the branch to the right, and kept going until they reached the wall under the church.

"You really think there's a stash back there?" Jarret cracked open a can of Spanish peanuts.

"Well, the monks don't believe there's anything under the church. If there is, someone had it sealed up for a reason." Papa took the can of peanuts from Jarret and offered the sledgehammer as a trade. "I say, it's here or nowhere."

Jarret set the rest of the snacks against the wall, donned the safety goggles, gripped the sledgehammer, and stepped up to the wall. "Hey, you know, I found a crucifix down here. Right back there." He pointed to the crack between the tunnel wall and the wall of stone.

"Oh yeah? Maybe that was a sign." Papa tossed a handful of peanuts into his mouth.

"A sign? Yeah, right." He didn't think God worked that way. Sometimes he wondered if God really existed. Atheists had a few good theories, the Big Bang and evolution and all. Anyway, if God was real, it didn't mean he talked to people or gave them signs.

"Have at it." Papa had stepped back and made himself comfortable leaning against the tunnel wall and munching on peanuts.

"I'll have at it, all right." Jarret drew the sledgehammer back, loving the feel of the weight, and anticipating the first swing and the jarring impact. He could see it all play out in his mind even as he swung forward: swinging, slamming, cracking, going at it again and again . . .

He hadn't been at it long when Papa broke his concentration. Unsure of what Papa had said, Jarret turned to look at him. "What?"

Papa chuckled. "I said, let me know if you want me to take a turn."

"Oh. No, I got this." He took a deep breath, turned his face to the wall, and let fly.

Before long, cracks appeared and stones shifted. The wall sank in and a hole formed. Stones and granules of mortar slid to the ground. A cloud of dust rose up.

Breathing through his mouth, re-gripping the sledgehammer, pulling back, swinging, and dragging it back . . . he fell into a sort of rhythm. His mind grew calm. All anxiety left him. The hole had grown in size so that he had to reach high to clear more, but the feeling of euphoria wouldn't let him stop. His body wanted more.

He drew the sledgehammer back again, ready to swing, when something stopped it and a hand landed on his shoulder.

"Didn't you hear me when I said to stop?" Papa gave him a hard stare then snatched the sledgehammer from him. "The hole's plenty big. Nice job."

Papa set the sledgehammer down and picked up a lantern. "You okay?"

"Why wouldn't I be?" His sweaty chest rose and fell with every breath, and his heart thumped like crazy.

"Let's see what's back there."

Papa stepped over the debris, his boots crunching on stones, his lantern driving away the darkness and revealing walls that had been

hidden for decades. Light bounced off shapes and colors. There was
something inside, all right.

Jarret hesitated to follow. He felt like both sides of a magnet,
simultaneously drawn to and repelled by what he would discover.

He forced himself forward.

No sooner did he get a boot over the pile of debris than he froze at
what he saw. His heart twanged with feelings of longing, of familiarity, of
discomfort. He wanted to flee.

Papa mumbled something as he moved around the room. The room
resembled a little underground chapel with an altar on the far wall and
religious items everywhere else: crucifixes, paintings, statues on
pedestals, dust-covered sacred vessels, and candlesticks of all sizes.

All this Jarret noticed as a backdrop, none of it able to compete for his
attention. His every thought was riveted to the life-size statue before him.
The figure appeared to look directly at him—into his soul—with eyes so
realistic they glistened in the light, with a gaze so penetrating it rendered
him immobile, helpless, exposed.

Jesus stood there with his arms outstretched and fire burning in his
heart. The words of the priest in the confessional rang in Jarret's mind.
"Jesus waits for you."

Jarret stumbled back. Why would Jesus care about him after all he'd
done? He wasn't worthy of such love.

⁂

Doubled over on his knees, Jarret writhed with spiritual agony.
Roland had forgiven him? Just like that? No conditions, no
payback? Could it be that easy?

No. Not possible. Roland had a reason for saying it. He
wanted help getting out of the canyon. That's what he wanted.

No, that wasn't right either. Roland had said that he didn't
care what happened to him. He didn't care if Jarret . . . if Jarret . . .
killed him. Kill him? He would never do that, could never do that.
He could never kill anybody. Could he? Sometimes his emotions

got so hot, so out of control, seemed to rule him. Maybe no bad deed was beyond him.

"Oh, God," he whispered, "I don't want that."

A crack formed in the protective wall he'd built around his heart. Weak and trembling, Jarret uncurled himself but remained on his knees. As he lifted his head—

Light flashed. A single blinding burst less than four yards away.

Jarret flung his arm over his eyes, but the light had already ceased. Had it happened at all? An image hovered in his mind. At the center of the flash of light, had stood a woman in a long gown. And the light had seemed to come from her hands.

Jarret's hand lifted to his chest, to where the medal hung under his shirt. Then he heard a voice.

Come to me.

The voice, strong as thunder and gentle as a stream, spoke to Jarret's soul, giving him certainty that he knew who spoke. Yet, who was it?

Jarret looked around him. Roland was some distance away. Had someone else come into the canyon?

A figure in a long white robe stood in the distance, too far to make out, though his voice had sounded near. The man lifted his hands in a welcoming way. *Do not be afraid.*

Afraid? He wasn't afraid of anyone, of anything. Jarret broke out in a cool sweat and his body trembled. "Wh-what do you want from me?"

Everything. Hold nothing back. The figure drew nearer, taking slow steps, navigating with ease over the broken ground.

"Who are you? What do you want?"

It is you I want. It is for you that I came into the world. Do not be afraid. Do you not know me?

No, he didn't know him. And yet . . . Jarret strained to see more clearly, struggled to sift through his mind. He did know him. How did he know him? From where did he know him?

Once the figure had come near enough to make out, Jarret gasped.

Bruises and blood marred the face. One eye was purple and swollen. Yet no distress showed in the man's expression, only compassion.

Unable to hold his gaze, Jarret slumped over and hid his face in his hands. "Who are you?" He knew the answer even as he asked: Jesus.

Jarret struggled to rise above feelings of worthlessness, guilt, and fear. With furtive glances, he made himself ask, "What happened to you?"

Sin did this to me. He turned his hands palms up, revealing wounds of deep red. *Love allowed it.*

The Lord sat on the ground near Jarret and rested his arms on his raised knees. *I have waited long for you. Do not make me wait any longer. Do not let your sins and weakness stand in the way. Can't you see that I love you?*

Jarret's heart wrenched. "How can you love me? I've lived a life of . . . of pleasing myself, of doing whatever it took to get what I wanted. I . . . I've sinned."

He paused and forced himself to behold the man. "I did that to you." He indicated the Lord's hands with a glance. "I don't think about you, about what I've done to you or what I do to you."

The Lord smiled. *I know everything about you, Jarret. I know the number of hairs on your head. I know your every sin. I know your fear of surrendering control, your longing for love, for intimacy. I know the loneliness you feel inside, how you feel like half a man. I have been with you through it all.*

"No." The words struck him, convicting him like flaming darts that burned but did not consume. Jarret hid his face again.

You have closed your heart to me, but I stand at the door and knock. Open to me. Only I can fill the void in your heart.

"You can't possibly want me after all I've done. I'm not worthy of your love." As he spoke the words, he began to realize that love was possible. Roland had shown him this. If Roland could still love him after all he had done . . .

Jesus put a hand to his chest. A golden, flickering light showed through the fabric. Pulling back the robe, he revealed His Sacred Heart.

Jarret threw his arms up to shield his eyes from the brightness. The light reached him anyway, but it caused no pain. He lowered his arms and gazed upon the flames burning in His heart. Unable, now, to tear his gaze away, his own heart ached with a feeling both new and familiar. He longed to immerse himself in the flames.

The Lord closed his robe. *It is for sinners that I have come. Your misery attracts my mercy. Your sins, many though they are, are as a drop of water compared to the immense furnace of my merciful love. Give them to me, and let me be your Savior.* He held out his hands, palms up. *Open to me the door of your heart.*

Sorrow for his sins welled up within him. Jarret flung himself into the arms of the Lord and wept.

CHAPTER THIRTY

SALVATION

Jarret

Jarret had never bawled so hard in all his life. The feeling of the presence of the Lord had diminished somewhat, enough that he could move. Utterly drained and body trembling, he pushed himself up from where he had collapsed.

Moonlight created patterns on the canyon floor, lighting up rocks and the far wall. Roland sat in darkness. His breaths came steady but short.

Jarret grabbed onto a boulder and pulled himself up. As he stood straight, the blood seemed to drain from his head and glowing gnats filled his vision. Afraid of passing out, he dropped to his knees and crawled to Roland. "Hey." His voice came out as a whisper. He had so much that he needed to say, he didn't know where to start. He wanted to apologize and ask for forgiveness. But first, he had to find a way to help Roland.

"You awake?" Jarret said.

"Yeah. You okay?" Roland's voice trembled.

"Me?" Roland must've heard him sniveling or something, probably thought he was losing his mind. "I'm gonna find a way to get you outta here." He stood and steadied himself, then took two steps and stopped. "Are you cold?"

"Yeah, I'm freezing."

"I think I can make a fire." He had a lighter and he'd seen a couple of dead trees at the other end of the canyon. Yeah, he could make a fire and maybe a splint for Roland's leg. "I'll be back."

Stepping on moonlit stones, Jarret stumbled toward the far side of the canyon. How had he let this happen? He deserved the broken leg. Not Roland. What if he couldn't find a way out of the canyon? What if he couldn't get Roland out? Would Roland die down here?

Jarret's heart pounded violently with his remorse.

Do not despair. Jesus's merciful love washed through him, strengthening him to move onward and giving him hope. He could do this. He would get them out. He would get Roland to safety. Somehow.

Dry branches lay on the ground all around the dead mesquite trees. Jarret gathered the ones in his path as he made his way to one of the dead trees. He would get an armful and head back.

A rustling sounded above him. Probably the wind in a bush.

He picked up a good-sized, sturdy stick. He could use it for the splint, but he'd need another similar-sized one. He went to the tree and snapped off two branches.

The rustling came again. It didn't sound like wind rustling a bush this time. It sounded like a creature moving through dry brush.

Jarret peered at the canyon's rim. There had to be an animal up there. It didn't have to be a coyote or a fox. What else lived in the desert? Besides, it was up there and they were down here. There wasn't a good way down. Was there? Could he have missed something?

Determined to make a thorough check of the canyon walls after he built a fire, he carried his armload of sticks back to Roland. He slowed as he neared the shadows, trying to make out shapes and sounds.

"Roland?"

"I'm here."

He followed Roland's voice, slowing as he stepped from the moonlight to the shadows. His eyes adjusted, and he made out Roland's form.

"Did you happen to hear anything?" Jarret dropped the sticks and started arranging them.

"Hear anything?"

"I thought I heard something up on the rim. What do you think's out here?"

"Our horses."

"They'd be up there." Jarret pointed to the rim of the wall behind Roland. "I was at the far end of the canyon."

It took a good minute for the thinner branches to catch, but the flames soon grew strong. He set aside a few sturdy branches for the splint and crawled to where he could get a good look at Roland's leg.

"What're you going to do?" Roland whispered, his gaze distant, his eyes glassy in the firelight.

"I'm gonna get you outta here. I think you need a splint on your leg before we move you." Jarret pulled his t-shirt off over his head and ripped it. The cool air on his chest invigorated him. He could do this. He had to do this.

"I don't know, I don't know." Roland leaned his head back on the boulder. "I think that's gonna hurt."

"Don't be a baby." Jarret smiled, but Roland wasn't looking.

"Okay, doc." Roland turned toward him and actually smiled back.

Jarret swallowed hard. How could Roland smile with the pain he must've felt?

With trembling hands and careful movements, Jarret positioned Roland's leg and made a rough splint, tying branches

292

on either side. He prayed he was doing it right, the way Papa had taught him. Roland kept his eyes shut and breathed funny, but he only groaned once.

With the splint complete and a fire burning, Jarret set his mind to the next task: searching the canyon walls. Light from the flames reflected off the nearest walls, dying a few feet up, leaving the rest in darkness. He saw no hand or footholds for climbing.

He stepped from one rock to another and peered into the darkness around him. How would he see anything without light? He tried to remember his impressions when he had seen it all in the sunlight. The walls were mostly steep sheer rock, jutting out in several places that had made it impossible to see from one end of the canyon to the other. He had noticed a few cracks where one wall met another. And of course, there was the cave at the end of the dry creek.

Jarret stumbled to the far end of the canyon and stood gazing at the dark opening of the cave. Any chance it came out somewhere? What if something lived in it? It was so dark that—

Roland. Roland was lying there helpless, cold, and in agony.

Jarret snatched a dry branch, dropped down, and did an army-crawl into the cave. Once inside, he sat up and lit one end of the branch.

The flame illuminated the reddish rock of the cave and made shadows shift in eerie shapes on a curved ceiling, high enough for him to stand, and on curvy walls with dark cracks of unknown depths, too narrow to squeeze through. A beam of moonlight made a two-foot, almond-shaped patch on the back wall.

Jarret moved into the moonlight and peered up.

The starlit sky looked down upon him through a narrow crack between the wall with the patch of moonlight and another wall. The walls rose up about twenty or so feet, but a person could probably climb them. Yeah, if he put his back to one wall and used his arms and legs —

He tried it. With a bare back flattened to the cool rock wall, he brought his legs up one at a time and pressed his knees against the opposite wall. He repositioned himself to get a foot on either wall and climbed up a couple of feet. He stopped and caught his breath.

Yes! He could do it. But what about Roland?

Jarret dropped down and crawled out of the cave. They would have to hang onto each other. What else could they do? It was the only way. They had to try.

He returned to Roland and found the fire nearly burnt out. The extra branches lay too far for Roland to reach, but they wouldn't need the fire now.

"Find anything?" Roland said, teeth chattering.

"Yeah, but it ain't gonna be fun." Jarret stooped by Roland's good side and slipped his arm around him. "You're gonna have to get up."

Roland nodded. Clinging to Jarret and straining, he got up on his right leg. "Lead the way."

The walk down the dry creek was long and awkward. Jarret had taken it slow and used extra caution so Roland wouldn't fall. When they reached the cave, he helped Roland down onto his back and dragged him by the shoulders through the low opening. After hoisting him up onto his good foot, they rested under the moonlit crack.

"We're . . . going up there?" Roland said between breaths.

Jarret nodded. "You're gonna have to hold onto me. Put your arms around my neck."

Roland shook his head, gazing at the opening above them. "No way. There's no way."

"Yes, there is. I'm getting you out."

"How's that going to work?"

"I tried it already. The walls are close enough to climb. With my back to one wall and my knees—"

"By yourself, sure, but with me? I can't do it, and I'm too heavy for you to carry."

Jarret swallowed hard. His thoughts flashed back to the drive to Tucson and to them singing together. "You ain't heavy. You're my brother."

Roland smiled and made a weak chuckle. "I'll try." He wrapped his arms around Jarret's neck.

Jarret pressed his back to the wall, but the extra weight kept him from getting a knee up high enough to reach the other wall. So they tried it a different way. Jarret jumped up into position, with his back and knees holding him in place, then he hoisted Roland up with him. It had taken every bit of his strength to do it, but he got Roland up and wedged between the walls with his arms and one good leg supporting him.

"I can't," Roland said, wincing. He let out a long groan and slipped a few inches.

Jarret dropped down, grabbed Roland around the waist, and eased him to the ground.

"I can't do it. I can't climb," Roland said. "Just go. Get help."

"No." Jarret squatted by Roland's side and helped him to a comfortable position. "What if a coyote or something comes down here? What about snakes?"

"What're you going to do if a snake bites me?" He laughed, but it turned into a whimper. He clutched his thigh. "Just go. I'll be right here."

"I can't leave you."

"You have to."

"I . . ." Remorse flooded Jarret's thoughts. "Roland, I'm really . . . I'm sorry, this is all my fault."

"No." Roland put a hand up to silence him, then rested his hand on Jarret's arm.

"I ain't been the best brother to you. All those things I told you I did—"

"Hey. Don't. I don't hold anything against you. We all make mistakes."

"But I—"

Something fell onto Jarret's shoulder.

He jerked back, gasping in a high, sissy tone. "What was that?"

"Snake!" Roland scooted away from the thin dark snake sliding down the crack.

It moved quickly, keeping its body unnaturally straight.

"What kind of a—" Jarret leaned in for closer inspection. He exhaled. "It's a rope."

"Hello, down there." An unfamiliar voice came from above and echoed in the cave.

"Hey!" Jarret jumped to his feet. "Can you help us outta here? My brother's leg is broken."

"One leg?" Now the voice sounded familiar, but all they could see of him was his shadow high on the wall.

"Yeah, just one leg."

"Is he strong? Strong enough to hold a rope?" The voice sounded like . . . Enyeto?

"I don't know."

Roland sat slumped against a wall of the cave. He nodded. "I can hold on."

Jarret shouted to the man, "Yeah. He says he can."

"Good. Make a loop at the end of the rope. He will stand in it with his good leg. I will pull him up."

Jarret set to work on the loop, making a strong double eight knot. Then helped Roland up and into it. Roland ascended from the cave. Jarret let out great sigh, and tension drained from his body as he watched.

Once Roland reached the top, the rope returned, falling like a snake to the ground. Jarret climbed the rope, hand over hand. At the top, his arm muscles trembled and threatened to give out. He struggled to get a good grip on the cold rim of the rock wall and struggled to pull himself up. With a grunt and a final effort, he made it. He pivoted on one knee and plopped down onto his hind end, ready to collapse.

As he caught his breath, he assessed his surroundings.

He sat near a three-foot-high boulder, his feet dangling into darkness. More boulders rose up around him, forming a jagged pattern against the black horizon. To his left, the ground sloped down to a wide, level area. Was this the lookout on the mesa top? He had noticed it when approaching the mesa. He'd wanted to reach the top. And here he was.

A horse whinnied.

Behind him and to his right, three horses stood on the level ground of the lookout, Red Storm one of them. Moonlight reflected on the shimmery coat of Diamond, the blue roan. And there was that old Indian, Enyeto, stooping by Selena's buckskin, Trail Blazer. Enyeto had made himself into a mounting block so Roland could climb onto Trail Blazer's saddle.

Roland mumbled a protest.

"Just force your leg up there," Enyeto said.

Jarret scooted off the boulder and went to help.

Enyeto straightened up and locked eyes with Jarret. "You make a good knot. Your father, he made good knots."

"Oh yeah?"

"I taught him."

Seeing this different side of the old man, Jarret smiled. "He taught me."

Enyeto gestured toward the other two horses. "I found them before I found you. I will take them back. You are light. Trail Blazer is strong. You will ride with your brother. Keep him in the saddle."

Jarret nodded and did as he was told.

Enyeto rode Storm and led Diamond along a trail that zigzagged down the side of the mesa. He sat straight and proud in the saddle, a stately figure under the moonlight, riding between black shadowy mountains under a deep-purple sky. He kept the pace slow, probably for Roland's sake.

Roland sat slumped over the saddle horn, hugging Trail Blazer's neck, groaning whenever they rounded a bend. His leg had to be killing him. Jarret remembered the trip back from Phoenix with his bruised ribs. Return trips usually felt shorter than trips out, but this one would feel endless to Roland.

If anyone knew the shortest path, it would be Enyeto. He rode with confidence, not scanning the surroundings to get his bearings. Whenever he did gaze off in the distance, he seemed to be appreciating something, maybe the beauty of the night.

Jarret's thighs ached from rubbing the back edge of the saddle. With Roland in the saddle, he had seated himself behind it and had to lean forward to keep balance. He wouldn't complain, though. It was nothing compared to Roland's pain, nothing compared to what he deserved. He had a lot to make up for . . . to Roland, to God.

After a time, Enyeto dropped back and rode alongside Blaze.

Thinking Enyeto had something to say, Jarret remained quiet. Minutes passed. Enyeto said nothing so Jarret decided to speak. "How'd you know we were down there?"

Enyeto took a moment before answering. "Many years ago, I rescued your father from that same canyon."

"What? You're kidding?"

"He was a boy of eleven. Always he is searching for artifacts, arrowheads, rock engravings, pottery shards. Anything he can find. It is like a drug to him, and he cannot keep himself from danger."

"My father?" Jarret smiled to himself. This was news. Papa seemed so completely the master of himself.

"He makes a good knot, climbs down safely. Perhaps you found his rope today."

"What?" Amazed at the possibility he'd found the very rope his father had used, Jarret opened his mouth to comment, but Enyeto continued talking.

"Yes, the rope is secure. But when he is done exploring, he cannot climb up. He has no muscles. I find him in the same place I find you, trying to climb the walls like a spider."

"Yeah. I was doing that. I couldn't help Roland, though. Not with his leg."

Roland, still hunched over the saddle horn, moaned softly. He probably wanted the nightmare to end.

"So did my father get out on his own?" Jarret asked.

"No, halfway up, the walls grow too much apart. There he got stuck. I pull him up with my rope."

Jarret laughed.

Enyeto smiled. "Your father, he is not much different from you. We all have our weaknesses."

He tried imagining Papa as a reckless boy. He was probably still reckless as a young man. Jarret wished Enyeto would say more, but as the silent minutes passed, Jarret's mind returned to the Monastery.

❖

Jarret stood unnoticed in the doorway of the refectory, scanning the long table of silent, dining monks. What was he doing here?

One monk stood and read from a book. ". . . whether I come and see you myself or hear about your behavior from a distance, it will be clear that you are standing firm in unity of spirit and exerting yourselves with one accord for the faith of the Gospel. . . ."

Since most of the monks were clean-shaven, he easily found the priest that he'd spoken to in the confessional, the one with the full, white beard. Just his luck that the priest sat at the far end of the table.

Jarret's insides bristled. Why was he doing this? With a deep breath, he forced himself into the room. He had been walking with the stolen bottle of wine at his side, where the monks wouldn't notice it, but now he brought it up and intentionally carried it in front of him.

A few monks glanced up from their soup bowls. Jarret eyed each one who dared to look at him as he strolled to the priest.

The reader kept on. "Do not be intimidated by your opponents in any situation. Their opposition foreshadows downfall for them . . ."

Jarret stopped at the end of the table and stared until the bearded priest met his gaze. Then he planted the bottle on the table and turned to go.

A chair scraped the floor.

Jarret glanced over his shoulder.

The priest stepped around the table and grabbed Jarret's arm. His blue eyes locked onto Jarret's eyes, his gaze piercing right into Jarret's soul as if he could actually see it. The priest smiled and pulled him into a hug.

Trembling with an unfamiliar feeling, and unsure as to why he had done this, he strode from the room to the words of the reader.

". . . but salvation for you. All this is as God intends, for it is your special privilege to take Christ's part—not only to believe in him but also to suffer for him."

CHAPTER THIRTY-ONE

GOODBYE & HOMECOMING

Ellechial

"Why don't you give it to Roland as a token of your new friendship," Ellechial said, curious as to whether Jarret would sense his advice.

Jarret stuffed his blue and white plaid t-shirt into Roland's suitcase and yanked the zipper. He set Roland's suitcase next to his by the open bedroom door.

Ellechial beamed with love.

His job complete, Jarret paused and looked the room over, taking it in slowly as if it brought past events to mind. The beds and furniture glowed with a heavenly hue under the light of the setting sun. His gaze lingered on the beds. Perhaps his thoughts returned to when he'd forced Roland to switch beds with him, or maybe he reflected upon the night he drugged Roland. Whatever the memory, it put a hint of sadness in his eyes.

He reached for the suitcases but then stopped. His gaze fixed onto the angel statue on the dresser. "I don't remember seeing you before," he said aloud, crossing the room to it. He lifted the statue and examined it. His heart turned toward Ellechial in a wordless prayer.

Ellechial brightened and drew nearer his charge. "I'm always by your side, Jarret."

Ellechial lifted up another prayer of thanksgiving. All of Heaven had rejoiced at Jarret's conversion in the canyon and again as he'd knelt before a priest in the confessional, unburdening his soul and receiving sacramental absolution. Jarret had even listened to Ellechial's voice and had apologized to Roland the other day, though it wasn't the smoothest apology.

"Hey, I'm real sorry about what happened, getting you in danger and all. Of course, I don't know why you followed me in the first place. You know I can take care of myself. It's you who—" He shut his mouth and took a breath. *"I mean, it's not just this incident. I guess I've been rotten to you for years, kind of used you to amuse myself or as a punching bag. Maybe if you weren't such a mama's boy when she was alive, and now with Papa . . . You know he favors you. You're his . . ."* He pressed his lips together and gave his head a little shake. *"What I'm trying to say is—"*

"I know what you're trying to say," Roland had said. *"Don't worry about it. I accept your apology. We don't have to talk about it anymore. You don't have to feel guilty. Let's start over."*

"Start over?"

"Yeah, start over. We'll pretend nothing bad has ever happened between us."

Jarret stood with his mouth open for a second. Then he exhaled and a smiled flickered on his face. "Uh, okay."

Jarret set the angel statue down. With a slow and contemplative expression, he grabbed the suitcases, left the room, and headed for the stairs.

Roland had been sleeping in the recliner in the entertainment room ever since he'd gotten the cast on his leg. Though he sometimes sat in the dining room, he spent most of his time in the recliner with his cast elevated. Jarret found him there, now, talking with their father. They both looked up as he entered the room.

302

"I've got all our things packed, except toothbrushes and stuff." Jarret sat down beside his father on the couch.

His father nodded. "We'll leave before the sun comes up tomorrow. Anything else you want to do before we go?"

"Like what? We've been here a week longer than you planned already." Jarret gave Roland a glance, a bit of guilt in his eyes. "I'm ready to get back home, back to green grass and trees. I'm getting tired of the sun, sand, and all those wild, prickly shrubs."

"I guess I am too," his father said as his cell phone rang. He glanced at his phone, checking the caller, then got up and left the room.

"You ready for another game of poker?" Jarret said to Roland.

Roland smiled but, before he could answer, Selena bounced into the room.

"What are my two favorite West boys up to?" She sat on the coffee table and glanced playfully from one to the other. "I can't believe it's your last night here. It went so fast."

"Are you going to visit us next summer?" Roland said.

"I hope so. But I would like to go riding before you go." She turned to Jarret. "Do you want to go?"

"He's not riding no horse like that." Jarret glanced at Roland.

Selena laughed. "I didn't mean him. How many times did you ask me to ride with you? We haven't done it yet."

"Just you and me?" He gave her a crooked grin.

"That's right, just you and me."

Before Jarret decided upon an answer, a shadow slipped out from under the couch. The shadow sprang up and transformed into Deth-kye's foul shape, taking a position close to Jarret. Deth-kye opened his mouth to speak.

"Be gone," Ellechial said in a tone that was firm but not loud. He had gained such strength through the prayers of others and

Jarret's own cooperation, that he had merely to turn his gaze on the demon to make him leave.

Deth-kye threw Ellechial a parting scowl but he obeyed, vanishing at once. He had lost the freedom to tempt or torment Jarret for a time, though he still tried on occasion.

Jarret turned his gaze from Selena to Roland and his big, white cast. His grin faded. He'd been serving Roland and keeping him company for days. "Well, I ain't gonna leave him."

"I'll be fine." Roland reached for the TV remote.

"See? He'll be fine," she said. "Besides, your father's been hanging out with you guys all week. I'm sure he can take care of things. And if not, I can ask Eremita to stay with him."

"Yeah, right. Is she gonna help him in the bathroom? I don't think so."

"She could." Selena giggled.

"Are you guys really talking about me going to the bathroom?" Roland's brows wrinkled.

"Eh, I don't feel like riding right now." Jarret got up, snatched the remote from Roland, and shut off the TV.

Nadriel's wings lifted.

"Don't we have a poker game to get to?" Jarret said to Roland. "I'll go get some Ritz crackers or—" He turned to Selena. "Did I see dinner mints in the kitchen? Wanna play for dinner mints?"

Roland chuckled. "Sure."

"I'll get them," Selena said. "I think we have miniature candy bars too."

Nadriel flew up to Ellechial, his countenance somewhat shocked. "Was that . . .? Did he . . .? Rather than go with Selena, he chose to remain with Roland. That was an act of sacrificial love!"

Ellechial laughed. "Praised be God. Miracles abound."

"Amen," Nadriel said, admiring Jarret.

As Selena went to get the mints, the boys' father returned and sat on the couch.

Jarret joined him on the couch, an accusing grin on his face. "So was that Miss Meadows?"

"What?" Their father's face flushed, a physical response entirely uncharacteristic of him.

"The phone call. We all know you're sneaking around with her. I don't know why you got to hide it."

"Sneaking around? I'm an adult. I don't sneak around with anybody. What I do is my own—"

Jarret raised his hands. "Chill. It's okay. I'm just saying, why don't you bring her around? We all like her. I know I kind-a told you something different before but . . . she's cool."

Roland and their father both gave him a strange look then exchanged a glance.

"What's gotten into him?" their father said to Roland.

Roland shrugged. "He's kind of weird lately."

Jarret glared but then all three of them laughed.

The entire Zamorano family and most of the stable hands woke early to see them off. Selena gave each of them a kiss and a big hug. After a two-hour flight and an hour-long drive, they finally reached home.

Jarret helped Roland from the car and, with an arm around his waist, walked him up the porch steps. Their father followed with the crutches, stepping past them to open the door.

"Welcome home!" came a chorus of voices.

Friends crowded the foyer and both hallways. Keefe, Nanny, and her husband stood in front. Peter, Caitlyn, Kiara, Phoebe, Dominic, and more prayer warriors were there, plus a few of Jarret's friends.

Ellechial greeted the other guardian angels, his sympathy going out to the guardians of Jarret's friends. Without exception, they wore the long robes of angels who had no permission to do battle. Ellechial prayed their day would come.

Peter took the crutches from Mr. West and handed them to Roland while the others cleared a path. "Hey, buddy, I'm glad you're back. It seemed like you were gone forever."

"It went fast for me, except for this past week." Roland indicated his broken leg with a glance.

Peter's eyes narrowed. "Yeah, about that . . . You never really explained what happened. I'd like to know." He gave Jarret an accusing glare.

Jarret glared back.

"Let it go," Ellechial whispered to Jarret.

His mouth twitched, but he resumed talking to his friends. *A victory!* In the past, he would've called Peter a name, at the least.

Keefe gave Roland a hug, greeted his father, and then stood apart from the others, his eyes on Jarret. As the crowd moved down the long hallway and into the family room, Jarret noticed him.

"Hey, Keefe," Jarret said.

"Hey." Hands in the front pockets of his jeans, Keefe approached. "I'm glad you're back. Missed you." One of his arms twitched as if it were all he could do to keep from hugging his brother. After their last conversation, he probably doubted the gesture would be welcome.

Jarret gave a crooked grin. "Did ya really?"

"Of course."

Jarret pulled him into a hug and rubbed his crew cut. "Guess I missed you too."

They started down the hallway.

"I didn't know if you'd be here or not when we got back," Jarret said.

"Why wouldn't I be?"

"I don't know. Ain't you meeting up with those friars?"

"The Franciscans? Well, no, I'm not. School starts in a couple weeks. It's our senior year. Besides, I'm too young to be thinking about that kind of vocation."

"Are you?"

"Well, yeah. You said so yourself."

Jarret stopped. He took Keefe by the arm and turned him to face him. "Yeah, but . . . if God told you that's what he wants, you sure better do it."

Keefe's eyes blinked rapidly. He gulped and then breathed out his mouth. "You mean . . . you won't be mad? You'll still talk to me?"

"I don't know. You gonna be allowed to talk to anybody when you're in there?"

"Sure. Why wouldn't I be? They don't live in a cloister."

"I guess I'll talk to you then." He grinned and tapped Keefe's shoulder with his fist. "They gonna let you have a cell phone?"

Just then, Nanny came bounding down the hall, the phone in her hand. "Oh dear, oh dear."

Jarret chuckled. "Let's go see what's wrong."

They followed her into the family room. Roland sat in the recliner, footrest up and cast elevated. The others stood in groups or sat on the couches, talking and laughing. Jarret's friends had gone to play pool in the recreation room off the family room, and their voices carried.

"They won't be able to deliver the pizza for an hour and a half," Nanny said, hand covering the receiver of the phone, worry in her eyes.

"It's okay," Roland said.

BATTLE FOR HIS SOUL

"No, that's too long," Jarret said. "Roland will be out by then. He's tired. I'll go get it. Tell them I'll pick it up. That is . . ." He looked at his father. "If I'm allowed to drive."

His father grinned. "This time, but remember—"

"Yeah, I know, I'm grounded." To Keefe he said, "You with me?"

Keefe nodded, smiling.

As they started from the room, Peter's mouth fell open. "Oh no," he said to Roland. "His car. The Limburger cheese."

Roland's eyes popped wide open. He jerked the footrest down. "Oh no."

Ellechial flooded heaven with prayers. *Please, Lord, help Jarret to keep his temper.*

###

Did you enjoy this book? If so, help others enjoy it, too! Please recommend it to friends and leave a review when possible. Thank you!

Every month I send out a newsletter so that you can keep up with my newest releases and enjoy updates, contests, and more. Visit my website www.theresalinden.com to sign up. And while you're there, check out my book trailers and extras!

Facebook: https://www.facebook.com/theresalindenauthor/
Twitter: https://twitter.com/LindenTheresa

About the Author

Theresa Linden, an avid reader and writer since grade school, grew up in a military family. Moving every few years left her with the impression that life is an adventure. Her Catholic faith inspires the belief that there is no greater adventure than the reality we can't see, the spiritual side of life. She hopes that the richness,  depth, and mystery of the Catholic faith will arouse her readers' imaginations to the invisible realities and the power of faith and grace. A member of the Catholic Writers Guild, Theresa lives in northeast Ohio with her husband, three boys, and one dog. Her other published books include the *Chasing Liberty* dystopian trilogy, *Roland West, Loner* and *Life-Changing Love*, the first two books in this series of Catholic teen fiction. *Roland West, Loner* has both the Catholic Writers Guild "Seal of Approval" and a second-place award from the Catholic Press Association.

CPSIA information can be obtained
at www.ICGtesting.com
Printed in the USA
LVOW13s2102280917

550415LV00012B/895/P